Renegade Ruin

HAYDEN LOCKE

Renegade Ruin
Cover Designers:
Discreet / Model: Silver @ Bitter Sage Designs
Model: Andrew Biernat
Photographer: Wander Aguiar
Illustrated: Lindsey Staton — @honeyy.fae on Instagram
Editor: Rachel Mitchell
Formatting: Hayden Locke

For everyone out there doing it with a broken heart.

Before You Read

Renegade Ruin is a continuation of a spicy prequel novella called Midnight Renegade. While you can totally read this book without reading the prequel, you'll be missing a bit of character development and throwbacks to Bishop and Willow's beginnings.

If you're not going to read the prequel, (or you just need a refresher), here's what happened:

- A year before the draft (nine months before the crash) Willow hosted a New Years gala for her philanthropy Renegade Hearts. After finding out her boyfriend cheated on her she gets locked out on a balcony with Bishop and has a panic attack in his arms. He dares her to forget being the woman her ex wanted and be herself.

- Bishop is enamored with Willow, but his best friend, Jackson, tells him since he's in the middle of a divorce, he shouldn't be getting involved with the owners daughter. Jackson challenges him to stay single for one year. Bishop agrees, but decides he still wants one night with Willow.

- They share one passionate night filled with lots of great sex.

- In the morning, Willow leaves Bishop without waking him up.

Thank you so much for taking a chance on Renegade Ruin! Here's a few things you might want to know before reading.

TROPES

Baseball Romance, Team Owner x Player, Fancy Peen, Secret Relationship, Fuck the Grief Away, All the Healing, Second Chance, Vibes, Toys as Teammates, Angst for Days, Found Family

TAGS

MF, spring training, grief, mental health representation, let me help you, situationship agreement, finding yourself, where do I belong, facing grief together, team bonding

CONTENT WARNING

This book contains some themes that might be distressing to readers including: character death (not a main character), mental health surrounding grief and loss, assault, alcohol consumption.

If you have questions or feel the need to protect your boundaries please don't hesitate to reach out and ask for clarification on these warnings. While for some it is healing and helpful, it is ok if for you it is not. It is ok to close the book, breathe, and step away. Knowing your mental health and what you need to do IS A STRONG THING.

CHAPTER ONE
Bishop

It's over.

I don't bother looking back, exiting the courtroom with my head held high like I've just been released from prison and not my divorce proceedings.

"Bishop." My ex's shrill voice echoes off the tall ceilings of the otherwise silent courthouse lobby, but I don't turn around. That tone would have once sent me running to her, but now it's nothing but a reminder of all the lies and manipulation she spews.

Corrine put me through hell over the last year.

Scratch that.

The last year plus the three we were married.

I would have done anything for her to make this work. Something I've been told is my fatal flaw. I believe in love and desperately will hold onto it despite any and all red flags. And she threw it all away because—I don't actually know why. I never got a straight answer as to why she decided to cheat on me with not one, but two men. Or why she falsely accused me of fathering her child after I left, leading to a very public scandal and paternity test. I'll never understand why she sought to make me the bad guy in the press. Or why she went out of her way to postpone this court date until the Renegades were three wins away from the playoffs resulting in me missing a key game. I should be with them in St. Louis.

But it doesn't matter now.

It's over and I'm free.

The sun hits my face as I step through the courthouse doors onto the stark white steps. On any other day the hustle and bustle of Manhattan would overwhelm me, but today it only adds to the contentment reverberating in my chest. This city may never sleep but it's downright magical in the morning. Everyone is starting their day. New adventures. Which is exactly what I need.

Fuck, I sound like I'm in one of those fairytales Phoebe always makes me read her. Where everything is magic and rainbows and nothing can bring the main character down. Which means something inevitably will. But not for me. Not today. Today is a win and the beginning of a new chapter.

Tugging out my phone I scroll, ignoring the numerous missed calls and messages, until I find Jackson's number. He should just be waking up and getting ready to head to the field for batting practice before the afternoon game in St. Louis.

It rings and rings before heading to voicemail.

I double-check the time, accounting for the hour time difference. He knew I had court this morning and told me to call him as soon as it was done. Next, I try his wife, Norah. She may have started as my best friend's wife, but over time she has become just as important. Hell, it was her idea to make me Phoebe's godfather and they took me in after the divorce, so I'd say I'm practically family at this point.

Just like with Jackson, it rings until it ultimately goes to voicemail.

I try them both again with the same results.

When I call Tommy, my closest friend on the team outside Jackson, and get the same result that irritation begins to settle in my chest.

It's not unlike Jackson not to answer, especially if he's getting in the zone before the game, but Norah is attached to her phone. Especially when she's away from Phoebe. It doesn't matter this was supposed to be a nice getaway for her and Jackson—a last-minute trip added because she had vacation time to use and there was room on the team plane for a handful of spouses. She wouldn't *not* answer.

Making my way down the steps to hail a cab, I ignore the way my irritation tries to morph into worry. I know they'll call me back when they can, and then we can celebrate together.

"Bishop."

My heart seizes in my chest, and I freeze.

I know that voice.

The melodic sound has teased me in my dreams since I last heard it on New Year's, calling out my name as I pistoned my cock in her tight pussy with the hope to someday make it mine. Then again, a few months later, when we serendipitously met at a party during spring training. We promised each other it was just one night.

We were good at those.

Slowly I turn around, wondering the whole time if it's some act of fate that she's here on the day of my divorce. Because Willow York is the kind of woman I would absolutely like to make my end game, and if it wasn't for that stupid promise I made to Jackson to stay single for a year I absolutely would have already.

The year isn't up yet, but I'm not sure I can say goodbye again.

The sight of her nearly knocks the air from my chest. She's a vision standing in the rays of the fall sun, blonde curls wild and cascading down over the flowy white blouse tucked into a formfitting skirt that should be a goddamn sin with the way it accentuates the curves any man would worship. She's wearing heels I'd bet money she hates, but I love because they define her calves in a way that should be illegal. But my favorite— okay, close second favorite—part of the woman standing in front of me is her eyes. Bluer than the bluest sky, they are the window to her soul, never quite able to hide what she feels.

And right now, they're filled with tears.

Fuck.

Willow crosses the space between us, her heels clicking like a ticking time bomb. When she reaches me there is zero hesitation. She hurls herself against my chest and wraps her arms around my waist.

"Whoa there, Kitten. I'm happy to see you too. Surprised, but happy."

She tenses and pulls back. Her glistening stare meets mine openly scrutinizing what she sees, searching for something that isn't there.

"Shit," she whispers, and I can't help but chuckle because I know for a fact this woman was raised to be a proper member of society and therefore rarely curses. "You don't know."

My brow furrows. "Know what?"

She tries to step back, but I interlace my fingers at the base of her spine and hold her in place. I've waited far too long to have her in my arms again to let her go now.

"I'm so sorry," Willow says, her eyes falling to my chest, fresh tears brimming against her lower lashes.

"Sorry?"

What could she possibly have to be sorry for?

"Shit, I thought—Adrian was supposed to call you."

My agent? I think back to the plethora of missed calls.

"Whatever it is he very well might have. I've had my phone on Do Not Disturb since last night. I wanted to be in the right frame of mind for court this morning. I just got out."

"Fuck," she breathes.

"What's going on? You're starting to scare me."

"I don't—shit I don't know how to tell you this. I figured you already knew and wouldn't want to be alone. Okay, that's not true, I was worried you were on the plane, and then when I found out you weren't I figured you wouldn't want to be alone." Tears flow openly down her cheeks and each one only serves to up my anxiety.

I reach up and wipe them away, "Whoa, whoa, whoa, take a breath."

"I'm sorry. You know I ramble when I'm nervous."

I do.

She takes a steadying breath and continues as I wrap my arms back around her. "I didn't want to be alone. And you're the only one who would get it. Then Adrian said you were in court, so I came here."

"I'm here. But what happened?"

"There's been an accident with the plane."

Time slows and my field of vision narrows until there's no one else but me and Willow, standing there on the steps of the courthouse.

"The—I don't have all the details yet but—" She chokes on a sob. "They're dead, Bishop. The team. My father. They're all gone."

If I thought time slowed before, it comes to a standstill as I try to process what she just said. I heard her words, but my mind refuses to believe them. It doesn't matter that it adds up. They didn't answer when I called. I try to reason that it wasn't because they're dead. They're just busy. They'll call back.

They have to call back.

"No," I mutter.

My arms drop as if she burned me, and I take a step back needing the space to think.

"Bishop, I—"

"No." I vaguely feel my head shaking, but it's like I've been plunged into the deep end of a pool—everything distorted and disorienting. "It's not possib—they—no."

There isn't a world in which this is real. Planes are supposed to be safer than cars. I feel like I read that somewhere. And this wasn't just any plane. It was the best Richard York could buy. He insisted. Nothing but the best for his team.

"No." This time my protest is nothing more than a whisper. I would've known. I would have seen the news this morning. Someone would have called.

Then I remember I put my phone on Do Not Disturb. All those missed calls and messages. The notifications I ignored.

Fuck.

I yank my phone from my pocket, and through my blurred vision, somehow manage to pull up the news app.

A strangled sob rips through the air, and it takes me a moment to realize it didn't come from Willow. It's mine.

Tragic Plane Crash Takes the Lives of New York Renegades

Tommy.

Jackson.

Norah.

Fuck.

Phoebe.

"I—I have to go," I mutter, stumbling toward the curb. There's only one thought on my mind. One thing spurring me forward and that's my goddaughter.

"Bishop"—Willow steps in front of me, her eyes a watery mix of pity and profound agony—"please let me help. I've got a driver. We can take you."

This woman. I don't deserve her. Through the haze of agonizing pain, it occurs to me she lost her father, her only remaining parent, and her first thought was to come here and make sure I was okay. She came to me so neither of us was alone.

"I need to—shit." I nod and take a step to follow her, only barely keeping my knees from crumbling. "I need to get to Phoebe. Her parents—"

Fuck I can't say it out loud. That makes it real. And I'm not ready for that. Yet I know it is.

Willow nods and wraps her hand around my bicep, leading the way. Which I'm grateful for considering I'm seconds away from my knees buckling and losing it right here on the steps of the courthouse.

Today was supposed to be a happy day.

We're six feet from the black sedan when a short man with horn-rimmed glasses comes out of nowhere, blocks our path, and shoves a small handheld microphone between us.

"Do you have any comment on the future of the Renegades?"

My gaze darts down to the lanyard around his neck that reads news something or other.

How the fuck?

I clench my fists at my side, and if it wasn't for Willow's steady grip, I have no doubt one of them would have already connected with his face.

"We don't know anything. I'll refer you to the Renegade's press office."

Glancing over at Willow, I nearly stumble back at the sight of the mask that envelopes Willow's face.

Despite her tearstained cheeks, she remains calm and collected in the face of this asshole reporter. I hate it and everything it represents. It's a stark reminder of exactly who she was raised to be and who she never wanted to become.

"But as the new owner—"

"The what?" I interject, confusion furrowing my brow.

The gangly reporter looks between us, realization dawning on his features.

"You didn't know?" he asks, his lips twitching into a small grin like he's just happened upon the golden ticket for his story. "*The Foul Line* just reported Ms. York has been named the owner of the Renegades in accordance with instructions left by her father with the commissioner."

My head whips to Willow, whose mouth hangs open, clearly hearing this news for the first time.

Her hand drops from my arm, taking with it the warmth of her presence. It's a line in the sand she doesn't even know she's drawing. The shift is subtle, but it doesn't go unnoticed. Willow steps in front of me, embracing the role thrust upon her in the last sixty seconds like she's born to do it.

Willow is the new owner of the Renegades.

It's at that moment the final piece of my heart shatters.

She's my boss.

Autopilot takes over and I turn, lifting my hand to hail a cab. God must take pity on me because one appears instantly and I slide in, ignoring the way she calls my name.

I can't look back, but I don't especially feel like looking forward either.

This was supposed to be a new chapter, not a nightmare.

The cab pulls away from the curb, and I only just get out Norah and Jackson's address before I'm reduced to heaving sobs.

This was supposed to be our time.

Jackson and Norah, trying for a second child.

Tommy's first pennant run.

Willow.

CHAPTER TWO
Willow

Four Months Later

My eyes dart to the door for the tenth time, an uneasy flutter taking flight in my gut. He's supposed to be here already.

I search the room one more time for an unkept mop of brown hair and matching eyes. Every flit of gray gives me pause that maybe it's his favorite gray suit and I just missed his entrance, but once again I come up empty.

Panic starts to buzz at the base of my spine, and I glance unceremoniously at my Uncle Graham, who is fidgeting with his tie on the other side of the stage. With a slight nod, I signal him over, hoping none of the press takes notice.

The last thing I need are these vultures coming up with yet another story based on unsubstantiated facts. As it is, they've had a field day with the addition of Graham to our coaching staff. They're calling it nepotism, when really there isn't anyone more qualified for the job.

Graham isn't my uncle, but as my father's college best friend, he took his godfatherly duties seriously and earned the title. He never forgot a birthday or Christmas, even when baseball took him to Texas and then on to rebuild the team at Seattle State. He was there for me when my mother died because, initially, my father couldn't deal with the grief. Their friendship fell apart when he was exiled from major league baseball for getting caught up in a cheating scandal. It didn't matter that he was cleared of all the charges, his friendship with my father was never the same. But he never left me.

Which is why, even though I caught a lot of flack for it, he was my choice for the open manager position. It was one of my two demands as the acting owner of the team. The other was keeping Bishop Lawson—aka the current shitstorm I'm dealing with.

My uncle slides up beside me, and I pull my clipboard up to whisper. "Where is he?"

"Hell if I know, Wills. I got a text when he arrived at the stadium, but from the moment I left my office, I've been fielding asinine questions from the press."

I pinch the bridge of my nose and exhale. He's just trying to get through today as much as I am. "Sorry, I just need the draft to go perfect."

"Have you considered he doesn't want to do this?"

Every damn day.

We might not have had anything permanent, but I came to care about Bishop. More than I should. Even after only two nights spent together, I know him better than most. What started as a connection forged through sex and limitless orgasms, ended with us talking until the morning light reminded us who we were and why we couldn't make it work. Me because

I was chasing my dreams and building a name for my philanthropy, and him because, well—I'm not sure he ever truly gave me a reason.

What I do know is he lives for the feeling of the dirt on his cleats and the sound of a perfectly framed pitch hitting his glove.

That doesn't just go away. Not even when lost in the overwhelming emotions that come with loss. And I've never seen someone more lost than Bishop. He's a shell of the man he was before.

I let out a sigh and turn to my uncle who, at my behest, has helped keep tabs on our star catcher for the last few months. Some nights going so far as picking him up after he's drunkenly started a fight at one of the many bars he frequents.

"He may be in a place where he's forgotten who he was. But I haven't. And I'm not about to let him throw it all away until he tells me he doesn't want to step on that field even one more time."

Graham's nose scrunches the same way it always does when we discuss Bishop. He hasn't said he suspects anything more than my actions being out of concern for a player on the team, but just like I know Bishop, my uncle knows me, and I'd wager he's not convinced.

He opens his mouth to say something but stops when George Falco, the MLB commissioner, steps up beside him. The Renegade President of Baseball Operations, Vaughn Logan joins him.

"What's the holdup?" the commissioner asks, eyes darting between Graham and me. "Everyone is seated and ready for us to start the draft."

Shit.

Plastering on the fake smile my mother made sure I perfected from a young age, I turn toward the two of them. "Almost. I'm just waiting for a few stragglers."

"What she means is she's waiting for Lawson," Vaughn mutters, giving the commissioner a pointed *I told you so* look.

These two have been trying to get rid of Bishop at every turn. Something about a clean slate. Unfortunately for them, the public latched onto his story of survival and if they push him out now, there will no doubt be an outcry from our loyal fans.

The Renegades might not officially be New York's team. That honor belongs to the NYC Liberty that plays in Manhattan. We have always been the *other* team across the river. But that hasn't stopped our fans from making us the Kings of Queens. They've always stood beside us with unwavering loyalty. It's a little shaky now, as all eyes are on us, but I have faith. The problem with being the center of attention is that it means all eyes are also on Bishop, who can't stay out of the tabloids to save his life.

I press my lips together to hold back the snarky response I'd love to deliver. It would only serve to further ostracize myself from the boys' club that is the upper management of this league.

To say they hate me is an understatement. Even though, aside from my stipulations surrounding Bishop and Graham, I've followed every bit of their advice and even made concessions I know in my heart my father would hate to meet their expectations. I might be business savvy in the non-profit realm and know the game of baseball like the back of my hand due to many summers spent at the ballpark, but I don't know the first thing about owning a team or its inner workings. I never imagined a day my father wouldn't be at the helm. Or that it would be my responsibility if he wasn't. Yet here we are. At the end of the day, it's more important to me to have my father's team and protect his legacy. Unfortunately, I need the support of the league to do that.

"Is he missing?"

"No," I stammer before Vaughn can open his mouth. "He's here. He just hasn't made his way to the press room."

I lock eyes with my assistant, Harold, and wave him over. In hushed tones, I order him to discreetly find Bishop.

He gives a worried nod before scurrying off toward the clubhouse.

Without missing a beat, Vaughn slides closer to me. His lips twist in a smirk like a kid who has just pulled one over on his parents. "Still stand by your decision to keep him?"

"Absolutely," I confirm, nodding to the commissioner reassuringly. Although I admit, in this instance, I wish Bishop would have proven them wrong.

A smirk lifts the corner of Vaughn's mouth as he gloats, "He's one major fuck up away from being released."

My jaw tightens, and I allow my gaze to fall if only to give me enough time to ensure my voice is steady. "I am well aware, but he's the best catcher in the league."

"If he can even still play." Vaughn's chuckle shakes his potbelly. "The press is reporting he's got permanent double vision from all the alcohol he consumes."

"He lost his entire team, Vaughn. What do you expect?"

Vaughn's green eyes slide to the commissioner, then narrow back on me. "It's Mr. Logan. Just because your father was my best mate doesn't mean informalities will be used at the stadium. And to answer your question, I expect him to act like the public figure he is."

Like a scolded child, my eyes find the floor, and it takes me a split second to remember I'm his boss. I lift my chin and smile sweetly.

"And while I agree with you," I continue, "I believe this organization can afford Mr. Lawson a little more grace. Don't you, Commissioner?"

Vaughn's lips part on a gasp, but it only lasts a second before he quickly schools his features and straightens his tie. George gives a slight nod, clearly not wanting to get involved with the war brewing between Vaughn and me.

Fucking coward. Not that I have any room to talk. Given my inexperience, I usually roll over and let Vaughn make decisions concerning the team. It's only where Bishop is concerned that I tend to forget the high society rules my mother ingrained in me.

Vaughn huffs and snaps defensively. "It's not your call to make."

"Who signs your paycheck, Vaughn?" Graham cuts in. I get the feeling he uses his given name only to see his face turn a darker shade of red. Which it does.

If his glare were daggers, I'd be dead.

While I appreciate my uncle standing up for me, we're playing with fire protecting Bishop and walking this fine line is bound to get us burned someday.

"You won't always be able to protect him," Vaughn sneers.

"No," I say with a resolute sigh, "but I can protect this team and the legacy my father would have wanted. As we previously agreed, Mr. Lawson stays through spring training. If at that time we, collectively as upper management, feel like he's a hindrance to our organization, we'll release him."

And he'll be forced to retire, is the part I leave off. Everyone standing there knows if Bishop is released to the trade waivers, no other team will pick up his hefty contract, and even if they are willing, he's only proven to be a liability since the crash.

A reporter from the front row of the press room tilts his head, eyes zeroed in on our group. He's far enough away I don't think he can hear our conversation, but I wouldn't put it past the press to have bugged the entire room with mics. By the way he leans in our direction, he's clearly picked up that something is going on.

Never has Major League Baseball had a catastrophe that resulted in holding a disaster draft. Especially one of this caliber, where every team must volunteer five players from which we get to choose one to restock our team.

It's all been building up to this moment. Even non-sports fans are invested in our story, waiting to see who will make up this iconic roster. And these reporters will do anything for the inside scoop.

We're making history.

Which is why I don't need this today. What I need is Bishop to keep it together—to stand with our organization as we redraft his team and get himself down to Florida for spring training. Then we can figure out what the hell we're going to do to get him back to the man and player I met a year ago.

"Ms. York," Harold interrupts. I didn't even notice him slide up beside me. He leans in to whisper in my ear, and I don't miss the way Vaughn and George subtly crane their necks at the same time to see if they can catch whatever he's about to tell me.

"Uh," Harold mutters, "Mr. Lawson is trashing the clubhouse locker room."

I pull back and whip my gaze toward my assistant, searching his face for any hint of a misunderstanding.

"He's what?" I whisper-yell.

Harold's eyes dart toward the door that leads to the clubhouse.

Shit.

Anger and sympathy war for dominance in my mind, but I keep my features a blank slate.

"Is everything okay?" Vaughn asks, his voice lilting like a cat ready to catch a mouse.

Plastering a picturesque smile on my face, I spin around and face him and the commissioner. "Peachy. Why don't you guys go ahead and get started with questions, and I'll join you with Bishop at the start of the draft?"

"You're sure?" George asks.

No, but at this point I've made my bed, so I've got to lie in it.

Nodding, I pray I'm not making a giant mistake.

He made it clear he didn't want my help. So for the past four months, I've given him space, allowing everyone else to be the ones to check in on him and keep him in line.

That ends today.

If he wants to live in the ruins of this team, I'll let him. God knows it would make my life easier.

As I make my way to the clubhouse locker room, memories of last New Year's flash through my mind. The way he talked me through a panic attack and challenged me to be more than what society demanded of me. He pushed me to be myself. Something I've forced myself to continue long after that night.

Bishop was once the only person who saw me.

Believed in me.

Now it's my turn to return the favor.

CHAPTER THREE
Bishop

I had every intention of staying in line. Showing up. Doing the press conference. Playing the part and building a team for Jackson to come back to if he wakes up.

When he wakes up, I correct myself.

Seven people survived the tragic plane crash. Jackson was one of them. But in keeping him, I still lost Norah. Tommy. My team. The rest of the survivors were flight attendants and team trainers. While their lives are important, the only one I care about is the man lying in a coma fighting to come back.

Out of habit, my feet carried me to the clubhouse, forcing me to come face-to-face with the reality of exactly what today meant.

I should've known I couldn't fake my way through this.

I've never been good at masking my emotions.

The splintered wood surrounding me is an indication of that.

It might be my first time back in the clubhouse since the crash, but nothing has changed. The same tables Jackson and I played cards at during every rain delay still lined the edges of the massive black and orange rug. The same couches sat in the center where I spent hours chatting with Tommy, not only about baseball, but about life.

But those aren't what set me off. It was the visual of all the empty lockers, with every name tape removed, ready to be replaced with a new name after the draft.

All except mine.

Set in the center of the left wall was my locker, nestled between where Tommy and Jackson should be, still filled with my uniforms and gear from last season.

A slap in the fucking face.

But the universe wasn't done reminding me of all I'd lost.

My eyes dropped to the swivel chair I sat in so many times, and I lost it. Sitting there was a small stuffed Stoney, our gargoyle team mascot. Tied to him was a deflated mylar balloon that read "Congrats" in bright orange letters and added beneath it, scrawled in Jackson's chicken scratch, was "on your divorce."

My best friend and teammates had wanted me to know I wasn't alone. I might not have been with them that night, but they went above and beyond to make sure I'd have a smile on my face during the end of my shit show of a marriage.

They had no way of knowing it was the last thing they'd ever do for me.

Shame and rage gripped my spine, and I blacked out. Even now, I can only make out flashes of what happened.

Tearing the uniforms from their hangars.

They're supposed to be here.

The crack of my bat against wood and glass.

I can't replace them.

Her hand on my bicep.

She shouldn't be here.

Her voice whispering my name.

Her begging me to come back to her—her strangled voice like a lighthouse to a sailor, a promise of safety. But it's only an illusion. I'm nowhere near land in the rough waters of my mind.

She's just like them. Playing their stupid fucking game.

My fingers around her throat.

They only want money.

Her fists pounding against my chest.

I came back to reality to the sounds of her gasping for air and the visual of my hands wrapped around her delicate throat.

"Fuck." I instantly drop my hands from where they are constricting her airway.

Willow slouches back, her blonde curls falling around her face as she struggles to force air into her lungs. When she peers up at me, her blue eyes are wide, like she's seeing me for the monster I truly am.

I haven't seen her in person since I left her standing on the steps of the courthouse after she told me about the crash. I denied every phone call. Every attempt at closure. She didn't do anything wrong. Until she did.

I work my fingers through my hair and grip the roots—the pain keeping me steady. Present.

What have I done? I'm not this person. I don't hurt women. Not unless they ask me to, and even then, it's always followed by mind blowing orgasms. This is barbaric. It's…shit who am I becoming?

My hands tremble as I stumble back and frantically drag my eyes over her to make sure I didn't hurt her. "Willow…you…fuck…are you okay? What are you doing here?"

Her eyes soften and a half-hearted smile tips her lips.

It slices through me.

How the fuck is she smiling right now? My fingers were around her throat, pressing her into a splintered locker while she gasped for air. There's nothing about this that warrants a smile.

"I was in the press room. Harold told me you were in here redecorating. I figured you might want a woman's opinion."

My mouth drops open as I try to process how the fuck she's joking around right now. She should be yelling. Cursing my name. Firing me. Any and all of the above. But no, this woman who has been the bane of my existence for one reason or another for the last year, who is now wearing my fingerprints around her neck, is smirking at me.

"Bishop. I'm okay." Her hands drift to straighten her skirt. "I shouldn't have snuck up on you."

My fists tighten at my sides, nails cutting into my palms. "It's not okay."

"I didn't say it was. I said I'm okay. Though, I'm pretty sure I saw a termite over there, so maybe you did us a favor."

She huffs a fake laugh and the insincerity of it momentarily reminds me this is not the woman who warmed my bed. She's not the woman who listened with reckless abandon to the stories of my life and inspired me to be a better man.

She's not endgame.

Not that I want her to be. Not anymore.

Endgame implies forever, and if there's anything I've learned in the last year, it's that forever is an illusion.

Mostly Willow York is someone I actively try to forget. If I'm going to survive this, I have to hold on to who she's become—a trust fund baby who wears a mask of indifference, indulges the whims of the league and the press, and only considers what the bottom line means for her business.

None of which is who I knew her to be.

My eyes narrow on the face I once found perfect and my voice hardens. "Happy to help."

Her stare clashes with mine, another reminder she's not the woman I remember.

Then she falters.

"Bishop." Her voice softens, wary and so full of pity it almost undermines the resolve I just solidified. "Are you—"

"No," I cut her off. "You don't get to ask if I'm okay. Not here. Not today."

She hesitates, and I watch as something wars behind her eyes before she nods. "Alright. Then I need you to get your shit together and get upstairs for the draft."

Ah, there they are. She might've been a pushover, but she's always had claws.

"Yeah, I'm not doing that." I scoff.

Her eyes narrow, and now that I'm not in the comedown spiral of my blackout, I take the opportunity to really look at her. It's been months since I've seen her, but she's still beauty wrapped in sin. Her soft coral blouse hugs her full breasts, and I can't help but remember what they look like cupped in my hands with my fingers teasing their sensitive nubs. My eyes wander shamelessly down her form, lingering on the curve of her hips in the skirts she favors, before falling to the open-toe heels she no doubt hates.

Fuck. Nothing about her or this moment should turn me on, but old habits die hard and I shift uncomfortably, willing my dick not to take notice.

Her hand finds her hip, accentuating her waist as I finally drag my eyes back to her piercing blue gaze. "You are. This team needs you."

This team.

I can't believe the fucking audacity of this woman. This isn't my team. It will never be my team, no matter who they sign. They will always be the replacements. The men who fell into this organization because of a tragedy.

Crossing my arms over my chest, my lips twist into an amused sneer. "And if I don't want to be a part of the dog and pony show?"

Willow doubles down. "Are you saying you're walking away? We both know that's not what you want. You love this game."

I do, but I'm not ready for this conversation. Especially not with her.

"Did they send you in here to manipulate me?" My voice is low, threatening.

It's the only thing that makes sense. Use my history with her to get me to do their bidding. Nothing else they've done has worked.

Willow sighs. "No, Bishop. They don't know about us, and I plan to keep it that way."

"Agreed. It was a mistake."

Willow swallows hard, and I swear her blue eyes go soft for a split second before her mask slides back into place, and she nods.

I chew the inside of my cheek, the flesh raw from the number of times I've needed to steady myself this morning.

How the hell is she so damn put together all the time?

"Good," I growl, ignoring the dagger to my heart. I don't want to be here with her. I don't want to think about her. She needs to stay in my past where I can remember who she used to be.

"Great." She clasps her hands in front of her and straightens her posture. "Now that we understand each other, can you please clean yourself up and get upstairs?"

I shake my head and lean down to grab the plush gargoyle at my feet—the last remaining bit of my team that I have—and head for the door. "The answer is still no. I'll let you figure out what story you want to spin to the press. You're an expert these days, after all."

"I dare you."

My eyes widen before they narrow into thin slits.

Those three words haunt me for so many reasons, but hearing them from her mouth—full of determination and spite—and the way she believes they will somehow convince me, it's both laughable and excruciating. They are the words Jackson and I taunted each other with for nearly a decade, always urging each other to be better under the guise of a competition. They are a reminder that someone believes in you. A challenge to believe in yourself.

They are the same words I used to inspire her just over a year ago.

A barked laugh bubbles from my throat, and I shake my head.

The joke is on her. There are a lot of things I will do for Jackson, but when it comes to Willow, my will to give a shit is gone. Or at least that's what I'll have her believe. Mostly because I'm teetering on the line of not knowing what the hell I'm supposed to do.

"So much for not using our past against me."

"I'll do whatever it takes to rebuild this team into something my father would be proud of."

"Still playing their game, I see." It's a low blow, but I don't care. She went for the knees first, and I'm not above calling it how I see it. It's about her father and the organization, not about the team. Not about me.

"What would you have me do, Bishop? Disband the organization? Fire the thousands of staff counting on us to reopen the stadium? Let the fans down that are counting on us to bring baseball back to Queens?"

My heart sinks as shame washes over me and I'm seconds away from walking out, finding the nearest bar, and drinking until I can't remember this interaction.

What's worse is that she's right. I hate that she's fucking right. This isn't just about me, but it fucking feels like it is. I'm the one on that field, not them. I'm the caged monkey in this shit show circus. I'm the one forced to play this game. A game that once consumed my soul and they expect me to do it without a hint of the spark that was once there.

Maybe the media is right. Maybe I need to retire. They haven't come right out and said it, but I'm not an idiot. It would be easier for everyone if I walked away. The fans would hate me, but it would give the team a fresh start.

You aren't ready to say goodbye, Bish.

Jackson's voice reverberates in my mind, and I roll my eyes. I wondered how long it would take for Jackson's voice to manifest in my mind. Ever since the crash, he and Tommy have become a sentient version of my fucked-up conscience. Every time they make their presence, I waiver between a twisted sense of joy at having them near and anger because they shouldn't be just voices in my head.

You love us. This time it's Tommy. *If you can't do it for you, do it for us. She's fighting for her father's legacy. Fight for ours.*

I'm going to regret this.

"I'll do it."

"Good. Now seriously, get cleaned up. You look like shit, and I need you to make the press believe we are one big, happy family."

I scoff. Clearly, she isn't fully acquainted with the new me because there's a fat chance in hell of that happening.

"Then I need you to head to travel to pick up your ticket for the spring training flight."

"I won't be needing it."

Her brow arches, and she sounds almost taken aback when she answers. "Excuse me?"

"I'm driving down to Fort Myers in the morning."

I silently pray she doesn't push the issue because it's not something I'm willing to budge on.

"That's twenty hours."

"And if I leave tonight, I'll have plenty of time to get there."

"Does Vaughn know you're doing this?"

I huff a laugh. "Vaughn isn't my keeper. He doesn't give two shits as long as I'm there when the rest of the pitchers and catchers report on Sunday night and ready to play Monday. Which you would know if you had any experience being an owner."

Just as I expected, this new version of Willow doesn't back down. Instead, she takes a step toward me and then another, until she needs to crane her neck to meet my glare. "I don't need experience to tell me you're a liability. One look at you or any tabloid tells me that. You can't be trusted to make that drive."

"I can. And I will," I say slowly, my words harsh through gritted teeth. "I'm. Not. Flying."

"What are you going to do the rest of the season?" There's a gleam of amusement in her eye, like she's caught me at my own game.

"That's assuming I'm playing this season." The corner of my lip twitches. "The real question is, what are you going to do? You're the owner now. You'll be expected to travel."

Willow winces as she studies me, her eyes cataloging my face with scrutiny, like she's trying to figure out the logic behind my actions. That's the thing, though. There is none. Logic went down with the plane that carried my teammates.

It helps that I know she has a debilitating fear of flying. I never understood the fear before, but now, the very thought of entering a death tube with wings makes my heart race and my palms sweat. I know I'll have to get over it eventually, but today isn't that day. Neither is tomorrow. Or the next.

"You aren't driving." She crosses her arms with confidence. "The team is responsible for getting you there."

"And what about you? I'm pretty sure I read you're driving down after signing new contracts, or is that not what you told *Vogue* when they interviewed you last month?" I silently thank Jackson's mom for leaving her trashy magazine in Jackson's room.

"I've always hated flying."

"Me too."

"Liar," she sneers.

I give a defiant shrug. "I'm not flying."

"You're a liability." Each word is pointed and precise. But even though she's stubborn, Willow is a habitual people pleaser. I watch as she chews her lower lip, silently considering the predicament I've created, until her brows raise and her lips tip in a smirk. I'm not sure if I should be intrigued or scared about what's going to come out of her mouth next.

"Take the private jet instead."

Definitely intrigued. Because in all her infinite wisdom, this is the only plan she could come up with to get me to comply.

I shake my head and huff a sarcastic chuckle. "What part of I'm not flying do you not understand?"

"The same part where if you don't do this, you'll forfeit your spot on this team."

My spine stiffens, and I don't dare look away from Willow's hardened stare. She's all business, but I can't tell if she's bluffing and this is a power trip or if she's actually serious. I might threaten the notion of walking away, but now that the reality of losing the Renegades is on the table, I'm struggling to force air into my lungs.

"You wouldn't." I don't recognize the low and menacing desperation in my voice.

I expected this from Vaugh. Even Graham would have grounds to threaten my position on the team, but this is the first time Willow has threatened my place here, and by the fierce look in her eye, she means it.

Fuck.

It's not even flying that scares me. It's everything else. The seat configuration alone gives me anxiety. Where is the safest place to sit? What happens if the engine goes out? What difference does the tray table being up make if we're in a death spiral?

How the hell am I supposed to just sit in my seat and *not* wonder who was sitting in that seat on the plane that went down?

Don't even get me started on landing.

None of it is logical, but my mind won't stop.

Out of everyone, Willow should understand, but of course she doesn't.

"Take the jet, Bishop." Her voice is strong despite its hushed volume.

I narrow my gaze on Willow, who's got just as much fire in her eyes as my own. There's a part of me that wants to tell her she's a good girl for standing up to me. The problem is there's a bigger part of me that needs to see her bleed as much as I am, because the fact that she has it all together is really pissing me off. Which is my only excuse for why I blurt out the worst idea on the planet.

"Only if you come with me."

If I have to suffer, so does she.

Willow inhales a sharp breath, and the wheels turn in her mind as she works out any other possible solution. "That's not an option."

I raise a taunting brow. "Then I guess I'm packing the truck and leaving tomorrow. The choice is yours, k—" I catch myself before I utter the nickname I gave a lifetime ago.

If she notices, she doesn't let it show.

"I wasn't planning on heading down there until the middle of next week. I can't leave tomorrow, but if I move some stuff around, I think I can leave the following afternoon."

I raise a brow, skeptical if this is her way to get me to avoid leaving with enough time to make the drive. Not that it really matters. I have no problem getting ripped a new one for showing up late to training. It's par for the course these days.

"Good thing I'm already packed. Text me the details and I'll be there with bells on."

"Oh, now you know how a phone works," she mutters under her breath, and I get the feeling it's payback for the almost-Kitten slip.

Willow shakes her head and pulls out her phone, tapping away in a hurry. When she's finished, she glares in my direction.

"Are we done here?"

"Yeah. We're done."

Willow turns on the heels she hates, but damn do they make her ass look good. She heads for the door, tossing one final jab over her shoulder as she does. "Don't fuck this up."

That's not a promise I can make, especially since I have no intention of attending the draft.

You're making a mistake. Jackson tries to reason.

I know.

But they want me to be Bishop Lawson, star catcher of the New York Renegades, and I'm not sure he still exists.

CHAPTER FOUR
Willow

We've been going in circles for an hour now. I don't know what made me think Vaughn would agree to allow me to escort our star catcher to spring training, but after witnessing Bishop tear apart the locker room and seeing the way his brown eyes no longer held any hint of hope, I knew I had to try to help. I've been silently berating myself ever since for not doing something sooner.

At the memorials, I avoided him because my heart wasn't ready to face him. Or maybe it was that I didn't want to accept what I noticed even then. The man who carved a piece of my heart out was no longer the man I remembered.

Seeing him again only confirms that's still true.

Vaughn slams his water down on the desk that used to belong to my father and stalks—more like waddles—toward the bar cart in the corner. Never mind that it's eleven in the morning or that he's pouring two fingers' worth of my father's expensive whiskey—the one he knows is saved for special occasions. I'm still unsure how it's possible my father considered this inconsiderate prick his best friend. I remember him being a jolly guy with a kind smile. Kinda like Santa—which checked out considering he sort of looked like him—but unlike the jolly Christmas icon, Vaughn doesn't like anyone. Especially me. My father always insisted he was a shark in the boardroom, but I've never seen that side of him. To him I've always been more of an annoyance—the offspring my father let freely roam the concourse.

Just like all of us, the crash changed Vaughn, and clearly not for the better.

His brows pinch together as he sips the smooth amber liquid and lets out a curt snort. "I don't care if he's God's gift to baseball. This team doesn't revolve around Bishop Lawson. He doesn't get special treatment. As it is, he missed the draft. I should release him based on that alone."

I wince. That was my fault. I shouldn't have let Bishop out of my sight after trashing the locker room, but I needed space. Being near him sucks the air from my lungs, making it hard to breathe.

I can't tell Vaughn that, though.

My gaze doesn't waver. "I don't need your permission."

"You're right. You don't. But it is my job to keep you in line and not let you destroy everything your father built."

Rage bubbles in my chest, but I stifle it down with a steadying breath. I hate that he thinks he has to keep me in line when I've done everything they've asked of me. Now I'm asking for one exemption and I'm the one destroying my father's legacy. Vaughn knows damn well I would never jeopardize that. It's why he still has a job. But this is something I'm not prepared to back down on.

"What's the harm?" I press, changing my tactic to one built on logic.

"Bishop's a liability if we allow him to drive. This way he's delivered to spring training without any issues, and hopefully he'll be happier when he shows up the next day."

It's wishful thinking and we both know it. One plane ride isn't going to fix Bishop. Especially with me, but Vaughn doesn't need to know that.

"Your problem is you think I give a shit what Bishop wants. He's been a thorn in my side since the crash. One fuck up after another and now he's trashed our clubhouse." Vaughn shakes his head and his nose wrinkles. "Not only that, but he did so when there was a room full of reporters just waiting for a story to unfold. He handed it to them. Now no one gives a shit about the fact we just made history. Instead, all they care about is our fuck up catcher and his latest antics. When are you going to see, you can't help people who don't want to help themselves?"

That's the thing. Bishop does. I saw it in his eyes. He's lost, but that's not a sin. I've been where he is. I know the way out. Isolating him from the only constant—the only thing he's ever truly loved—is not the answer.

"This team needs him."

"He's out of control. I'd sooner trade him than risk putting him on the field."

"You can't."

"That's where you're wrong, Willow. I'm the GM. That's literally in my job description. You might be new to this business, but your father trusted me to do this. You need to learn your place in this organization."

His words cut exactly where they're meant to, and I will the tears prickling the corners of my eyes to steer clear of falling. It's on the tip of my tongue to fire him right then and there. I'd be well within my right to do so, but that wouldn't come without repercussions of its own. I'm already on thin ice when it comes to public opinion. The world doesn't think I can do what my dad did because I wear a skirt and paint my lips red. If I were any man, I'd instantly be the hero rebuilding an empire, but because I've got a X chromosome, both the MLB and the greater public believe I couldn't possibly do a better job than the man in front of me.

So, I keep Vaughn around. What's the thing they say—better the enemy you know. Anyone else would have thrown me to the wolves. At least Vaughn pretends to placate me out of whatever remaining loyalty he has to my father.

I straighten my shoulders and latch onto the promise I made to honor my father. "Bishop isn't going anywhere."

Vaughn's lips twitch upward, and I swear he's holding back a smile. "Then he's your problem."

"What does that mean?"

"If you want him so bad, then you keep him in line. But know this is the final courtesy I'll be granting you. We agreed to re-evaluate after spring training, but that's no longer good enough. One more fuck up from Bishop, and he's gone. I'm done making excuses for him. We're on the verge of doing something historic, and I won't let him or you ruin this team."

I open and close my fists in my lap, registering his words for the threat they are. An ultimatum. When I finally find the strength to speak, my words are soft, and to my detriment, convey my utter devastation. "My father believed the Renegades were a family. Family doesn't leave family behind."

"That was your father's biggest mistake. This isn't a family. It's a business, and the sooner you understand that, the better. Bishop Lawson is deadweight that needs to be purged." Vaughn picks up his glass and makes like he's taking a drink, but mutters under his breath, "I still don't understand why he left you the organization. He should've left it to me like he always planned to do."

I blink. Once. Twice. Three times, trying to make sense of what he just said.

"I take it by the look on your face you didn't know. He changed his will a year ago, after the gala you held on New Year's. Something about you coming into your own. He believed you would be the best person to grow the Renegades if something were to happen to him. I didn't know he'd changed the will until the news broke after the crash. Otherwise, I would have tried to change his mind."

"He…" I struggle to find my voice. "No one told me."

Vaughn scoffs, his lips twisted in disgust. "Why would they?"

"I just…I'm sorry, Vaughn. I didn't know." The last thing I should be doing is apologizing to this man. He's been a pain in my ass since the moment I took over, but that doesn't negate that he lost something he held dear. If there's anyone who understands losing the future you planned, it's me.

"Are you—" A sardonic laugh fills the space between us, undermining my sincerity. "You're sorry. Geez, Willow, you're even softer than your father. You don't need to apologize to me. You need to figure out how to not suffer from the same delusional affliction as your father and stop acting like the pampered princess he raised you to be. If you don't, there won't be a team left to run."

My jaw clenches as rage floods my veins. "It's not a weakness to help people."

"No, but at what expense? As it is, you've already tethered us to a manager who will have to do everything to prove he's not cheating our way to the top. Now there's this shit with Lawson."

Grinding my molars, I try my best to keep calm. "Graham was

acquitted of all charges."

"But his name has never been the same since. He'll always be associated with throwing a World Series game."

I hate that he's right. My godfather didn't participate in the sign stealing, but he knew about it and said nothing. Still, hiring him is something I will defend till my dying breath. It's what my father would have done. He would always say this team is more than rumors and statistics—it's the fire inside each player. Another sentiment I'm sure Vaughn hates. Graham might not have a clean record in the MLB, but in his coaching career at many of the nation's top colleges he's shown he has the ability to inspire his players. Which was backed up when I called each of them, along with his previous teammates, in order to vet him.

My gut, along with their glowing reviews, tells me we need him. It also doesn't hurt that he's one of the kindest people I've ever met. At least off the diamond. Once he steps through the doors of the clubhouse, he's ruthless. Which is also something this team will need.

Just like we need Bishop. He's the heart of the Renegades—he always has been—even if he doesn't want to be just yet.

"I can see you wanting to deny it. If only you had that passion for the things that actually mattered." Vaughn shakes his head and runs his stubby fingers through his thin gray hair. "As I said. One more fuck up and he's gone."

Vaughn tips back his glass and downs the rest of its contents before walking over and setting the dirty glass on the center of my father's desk.

My desk.

"I'll keep Bishop in line," I vow.

Vaughn's laugh shreds my promise. "It's no sweat off my back if you don't."

He turns around and makes a swift exit, leaving me with a weight on my chest. My heart thunders against my rib cage, sharp pricks burning my eyes as I blink back the tears that always seem to pool, but I never allow to fall. Not since that day at the courthouse.

This isn't how I imagined my life.

I should be running my foundation, making a difference in the lives of children who have lost one or both parents, not grieving the loss of my own. I should be gearing up for spring classes at the new center in the Bronx and planning my trip to spring training to spend my birthday with Dad at the beach house. Summer would come and I'd split my time between the city and Camp Renegade Hearts upstate, because even though I'm the president and CEO of the foundation, I live to see the smiles on the faces of our campers. It's the only time I get to spend with my best friends, Indie and Leigh, completely uninterrupted.

Instead, I'm standing here, the epitome of fake it till you make it, wondering how the hell I'm not only going to eat, sleep, and breathe baseball for the next ten months, but also keep Bishop from ruining what he has left of his career. Especially with Vaughn breathing down both our necks.

A knock at the door pulls me from my thoughts and Graham pokes his head in.

"You got a minute?"

I swallow hard and nod. Picking up a pen from my desk, I twirl it absentmindedly in an attempt to convince both Graham and myself I'm not dangling on the edge of a cliff.

"You doing okay? I saw Vaughn as I was walking up the hallway. He looked a little too smug for my liking."

"I'm hanging in there." I offer him a weak smile, to which Graham rewards with a pointed look as he crosses my office and plops down in one of the winged back chairs my father favored.

Nothing gets by him.

"He's out for blood over Bishop."

My godfather cocks a brow, and his lips twist into a mischievous smile. "Do I want to know why you are going to these lengths for Lawson? He might be the best damn catcher in this league, but we both know this is more than any other owner would do."

I consider his words. It would be easy to say I'm motivated by our past—and there is a part of me that absolutely is—but it's more than that. Working with the kids at Renegade Hearts has taught me that sometimes all a person needs is to believe there is someone in their corner. And what are adults if not grown children? Somewhere along the line we just forget how to believe in each other. I believe in this team, and that includes Bishop.

Now I just need to convince Graham that's all it is.

"It's what my father would do. He always said the team comes first, the money comes second."

My uncle cracks a smile. "Ah, it makes sense then."

"What's that?"

Graham chuckles. "Why he left you the team and not Vaughn."

"You knew."

His lips pull together in a grim line as he nods, and I know he's remembering his best friend. It's the same expression I wear when I'm alone most days.

"Wills, he was so damn proud of you."

My eyes fall to the desk as I choke past the knot in my throat, once again fighting against the tears and heartache that so often threaten to overtake me. If there's anyone I should be able to fall apart with, it's Graham, but I just can't bring myself to do it. Some have called me callous or coldhearted, but if I let myself come undone, I'm not sure I'll be able to put myself back together.

My fingers fist the pen in my hand, desperate to hold on to his sentiment. "I don't want to fail him."

"You couldn't if you tried."

I wonder if he'd feel the same if he knew about my feelings for Bishop. Would he still believe in me?

"Thank you," I mutter, hoping he doesn't register the guilt dripping from my voice.

"Always, munchkin."

I roll my eyes. "Now none of that. I'm still your boss."

"And I'll follow where you lead." Graham gets up, rounds the desk, and presses a kiss to my forehead. "But you've got to get Bishop's head out of his ass."

"I'm working on it."

"Good. I'll see you down at training then?"

"Yup."

Graham heads for the door, and I shuffle the papers on my desk, trying to make myself look busy. Like I'm not going to sink into my chair the minute he leaves and contemplate every decision I've made over the last twenty-four hours.

"And, Wills?"

I look up to see Graham leaning against the doorjamb. "Yeah?"

"Don't work so hard."

"I'll try," I say, giving him a halfhearted smile.

Once he's gone, I slide back into the giant chair that made sense for my father but dwarfs my five-foot three frame, a mess of warring emotions.

It's been a fucking day—one I would sooner forget—but on the bright side, I officially have my team. The men who are going to take the field in black and orange and play a game that brings so many people together.

It's both exciting and terrifying, and I'm not sure if I want to spin in circles or throw up. Mostly I don't know how I'm going to do this—preserve my father's legacy, rebuild a team and babysit my ex situationship so he doesn't throw away the career he loves.

No pressure.

CHAPTER FIVE
Bishop

"Can you believe they chose Etchers over Tralenski?" I leave out the fact it's to replace Jackson at shortstop, in case he can actually hear me. "The fucker hates me. Not to mention, how the hell am I supposed to top our record of outs on a steal if he can't catch the broad side of a barn? It's a wonder the guy even got drafted in the first place."

I knew you couldn't keep up that record without me. I wince, imagining him saying it with a sardonic smirk on his face.

The doctors say it's possible he can hear me—that there have been plenty of coma patients who report hearing everything while they were unconscious. I should really ask them if it's normal that I hear the voices of my dead and unconscious teammates in my head.

I keep my eyes locked on the incredible view of the East River, sparkling in the last hints of sunset as the start of a hangover pounds against the inside of my temple. After my blowup at the stadium, I quickly found the nearest bar and managed to lubricate my mind. Many would say it's a problem, but it's the only successful way I've found to diminish the ache in my chest.

In the same manner a drunk finds their way home, I managed to find my way to Jackson's room at the long term care facility just as the highlights of the draft started on *Sports Talk*. I'd like to say it was because I wanted to check up on my friend, but my motivations were purely selfish. I needed to not feel alone, and these four walls have become somewhat of a sanctuary for me. They hold the last bit of hope that maybe someday things can return to normal. It's a crock of shit because even if he wakes up, the team is still gone. And Jackson will have to face that he not only lost them, but his wife too.

Jackson and Norah were soulmates in every sense of the word. They had a rough start but fought to be together, and their love is everything I thought I wanted. There was a time I believed I could find my person, and I thought maybe I had. But seeing Jackson and Norah ripped apart has been heart-wrenching. If this is the price for love lost—the crippling heartache and unsurmountable pain—I'm not sure I want it. I'm barely surviving losing my teammates. I couldn't survive something like that. If I could take her place on the plane I would, if only to spare my best friend and goddaughter even an ounce of this pain.

But I have to hold on to the hope that if he wakes up, at least we'll have each other. Because right now, I have no one that understands the dry drowning I experience with every breath.

The pain I have come to know intimately wraps its arms around me as I cross the spacious room and force myself to focus on telling Jackson about the rest of the draft. I gently pick up his limp left hand, wincing slightly at the lifeless weight of it, and lace my fingers through his. I study the tattoos on his skin, frowning at the burn scars that ruined some of the artwork. He'll be pissed about that.

Rotating his wrist in a circular motion the way the physical therapist taught me to help keep his range of movement, I give him the rundown of my new team. "Aside from Echers, the rest of the field drafted doesn't look terrible. We've got McCoy from the Blues and his solid arm on third, and Brooks from the Knights on second. Stone was a clutch pick for first, even though he's a bit of an asshole. Winters, Osborne and Luis complete left, center and right field. Just about every other player rounding out the roster are leftovers their club is grateful to get rid of."

I pause like I would if he were conscious, waiting for his comment on how we don't know they are just leftovers and even if they are, that doesn't mean they are at the bottom of the barrel. *Plus, the Renegades change people*, he would say.

I shake my head and let out a skeptical grunt.

Once upon a time, maybe. This team worked its magic on Jackson and me. We hated each other when we first met after he got called up. We didn't know then we were destined to be best friends—he grounded me, and I lightened him up. The tattoos that cover both his arms are evidence of that.

My eyes drift down to my leg, which is covered in ink beneath my jeans. A hint of a smile traces my lip as I remember the first time I took Jackson to my artist to get a tattoo for Norah. He walked in with bare arms and left with the start of a half sleeve. I'd never been prouder.

The problem is lighting doesn't strike the same place twice, and I'm not sure the Renegades have any luck left on their side.

"Come on," I reason, though I'm not sure who I'm trying to fool with my false bravado. "We both know Stone is one surgery away from needing a total arm reconstruction. You can't tell me that's not month-old leftovers."

Okay, so I'm exaggerating, but the guy is thirty-nine and even with one of the higher batting averages in the league, he's a ticking time bomb for injury and retirement.

"Not to mention he looks like he's got a stick up his ass ninety percent of the time. I'm not sure that guy even knows how to smile."

Well, I wouldn't smile at your ugly mug either.

I roll my eyes and finish with Jackson's left hand, ignoring the way it flops sideways before rounding the bed to do the same stretch to his right. "On the opposite end of the spectrum, we've got three rookies coming in hot from the farm team. Not to mention whoever they send up to test at spring training—don't worry, as far as I can tell, none of them have Tommy's penchant for theatrics. They'll go swell with our rookie coaching staff, though. It blows my mind Willow thought it was a good idea to hire staff that have a cumulative of five years in the majors all together. Then there's Graham Clarke as our new field manager."

Willow, huh?

Of course, that's his takeaway.

"I know you think I fucked that one up, but it's better this way. She's my boss now."

So, you talked to her?

I freeze like a kid caught red-handed before I remember I'm not actually talking to my best friend.

He doesn't know I've been lying to him for months. He has no clue that while I fulfilled my promise to forgo relationships and work on myself for the last year, I'd also met Willow at a party last year when we were at spring training. We talked all goddamn night, and I proceeded to fuck her on every surface of her beach house bedroom with party goers just below her balcony—and then jacked off to the memory nearly every time I showered since. He doesn't know I planned to find her the second our deal was up and demand she stop living rent free in my mind and take up a permanent residence. Because despite the fact we hadn't spent more than two nights together, Willow York was endgame.

Was.

The crash ruined all that. And thank fuck it did, because if our interaction today is any indication, I absolutely dodged a bullet there.

Dropping his hand, I flip up the blanket to cover him like a masseuse would during a massage, and make work stretching his leg. "No. We argued. End of story."

I leave out the part where I had my hands wrapped around her throat, followed by agreeing to allow her to escort me to spring training. Though, if he really is just a figment of my fucked-up conscience, he already knows.

If you say so.

"As I was saying, at least the staff showed some promise by going to bat against Vaughn during the draft. The prickly old bastard looked like he was going to have an aneurysm when they outvoted him and took Ramiro over Watts."

I hate that fucker.

A soft chuckle escapes me, the end morphing into a choked sob. "I wish you were here."

"He does too."

I drop Jackson's leg harder than I should and whip around and see Lana Roberts, Jackson's mother, standing in the doorway. She looks a hell of a lot more put together than I do, but the fluorescent lighting does nothing to hide the dark purple circles marring the space beneath her eyes, and it only highlights the nest of brown locks on the top of her head.

My eyes fall to the little girl with pigtails at her side, softening when she takes off in a full run and jumps into my arms.

"Uncle Bish!" Phoebe exclaims, nuzzling her face in my neck.

"Hi, Short Stack," I mutter, placing a kiss to the top of her mousy brown hair.

This little girl is the only light in this shitty situation. She's the one person I've tried to shield from my downward spiral. Once a week I go out of my way to make sure I see her, usually at my favorite donut shop down the street from their apartment. But never here. Never in front of Jackson.

It hurts too damn much to see her smile at me while holding Jackson's limp hand. That smile is an exact replica of Norah's and set below brown eyes with flecks of yellow that she gets from her father. Which is why when I come to visit, I usually arrive at precisely eight-thirty-one. It's the only way I can ensure Jackson's mom has left to take Phoebe to school.

I set the excited nine-year-old down and look back at Lana, who is taking her time looking me over. "You look like shit, Bishop."

"Swear jar, Nana," Phoebe pipes up.

Lana rolls her eyes dramatically and I can't help but laugh. Me and my mouth are one hundred percent the reason there is a swear jar in the Roberts household.

I cross my arms in an attempt to guard myself, knowing damn well it's useless. "I'm aware. What are you guys doing here?"

"Nana took me to Renegade Hearts and said we could come see Daddy after."

I turn away in the hopes neither of them sees how hearing about Willow's foundation or the fact my goddaughter was there affects me. As someone who wants the best for this little girl, I hate that Willow is able to provide her support where I can't. Mostly because I can barely help myself.

Schooling my features, I turn back to Phoebe. "Is that right?"

"Yup!" She pops the p at the end in the most adorable way. "Oh! Uncle Bish, I made you something!" Phoebe jumps excitedly on the balls of her feet before racing back to her grandmother.

Lana pulls an item wrapped in a dish towel with tiny ducks on it and offers it to her granddaughter, who turns around and dashes back so she can give it to me.

"I was going to leave it here for you, but now that you're here, I can just give it to you."

"Thanks, Phoebes," I say with a smile, unwrapping the gift.

Inside sits a handmade ceramic mug, painted with uneven flowers and a tiny ladybug. It's lopsided. The handle has a wonky curve, and the lip of the cup bows enough that any liquid would spill out.

I lift my gaze to Phoebe, who in all her innocence, stands there with her hands twisted in front of her, waiting for my reaction.

"I know you love dipping your donuts in coffee, so I wanted to make you something to put it in."

"It's perfect." I reach out and mussy the top of her head with my hand. "Thank you."

"Hey, Phoebes, why don't you go grab a hot chocolate for the both of us from the nurses station? I'm sure Greta will be happy to see you."

Phoebe gives her grandmother a narrow-eyed gaze that screams she's Norah's daughter. "Are you going to have an adult conversation?"

Lana returns with a pointed stare of her own. It's one perfected by moms everywhere.

Letting out a sigh far too exasperated for a nine-year-old, Phoebe crosses her arms and huffs toward the door. "Fine."

Once the little ears are gone, I pad over to one of the two chairs in the room and gesture for Lana to join me. "Why do I feel like you're about to ruin my day?" Adding a silent, *please, not today.*

I had to watch my entire team be replaced one fucking draft pick at a time. I'm not sure I can take much more.

Lana laughs as she lowers herself into the uncomfortable armchair beside me. "I think you do that well enough on your own, don't you?"

"Touché," I rasp. Over the last four months, she's never had an issue calling me out on my shit. It's one of the reasons I tend to take Phoebe out instead of hanging at the apartment. If I wanted to be mothered, I'd answer the dozen messages I've got sitting in my inbox from my own. That doesn't mean Lana hasn't tried. Lord knows the meals she's forced down my throat have been the only ones not heavily made up of alcohol and stale peanuts.

Her hands find her lap, twisting in the same nervous way Phoebe does. "Where have you been staying?"

I wish she would just put me out of my misery already.

"Did you really come here to make small talk?"

"No, I suppose not."

Her voice is soft. Too soft. It's the kind of tone people use when they are trying to prepare you for disappointment.

I bite my bottom lip hard enough to draw blood, as if that will somehow distract me from the tears slowly rimming her eyes. My chest tightens. I can't do this. I need to get out of there before the walls I've worked so hard to keep up come crashing down. Anger I can channel. Regret and guilt are my best friends. But the tears of my best friend's mom will break me.

Lana reaches into her bag and pulls out a manila folder, offering it to me. "Have you read this?"

I take the folder and open it. Scanning the title, I drop it into my lap as if it's burned me.

My lip quivers. "This is Jackson and Norah's will."

She nods past a sympathetic smile and reaches over, turning to a page marked by a bright pink post-it.

As if it wasn't suffocating enough to hold the final wishes of my best friends in my hands, I'm choked by the words on the page.

I tip my head to meet Lana's gaze, tears now openly falling down her face. "Is this real?"

She nods. "If anything happened to them, they wanted you to have Phoebe."

"Why am I just seeing this now?"

Lana winces, and I watch as this force of a woman shrinks back like she's been caught with her hand in the proverbial cookie jar. "Since Jackson isn't dead, there was a bit of confusion as to who custody would be given to. I asked the lawyers to let me talk to you first."

My jaw tics, and I'm not sure if I want to rage or cry. Mostly, I want my best friend to wake up and tell me what the hell they were thinking. Every reason why I can't be in charge of another human races through my mind. Especially one as precious as Phoebe. I can barely take care of myself most days. I'm a shell of who I was when they wrote their will. If I'm not using alcohol to chase the pain, I'm huddled in the damn shower where I can't tell the difference between my tears and the water washing them away. At the same time, I want nothing more than to protect her. To ensure she knows exactly how incredible her parents are and how much they love her.

Loved her.

Panic grips my spine as I try to reason how I can be what she needs, only to continuously come to the same conclusion. I can't.

I inhale a breath that's meant to steady me but only serves to further my anxiety. "Why are you showing me this now?"

"Because even though I think this is a terrible idea, Phoebe loves you and deserves to have a guardian who will put her first. Who is young enough to be there for her for the rest of her life. We aren't getting any younger, and I intend to respect my son's wishes."

"What does that mean?"

"It means I need you to do better. Not only for her, but for you."

"And if I can't?" My words are whispered. Defeated.

"Then we're going to petition the court for custody."

"And move her to Oklahoma with you." I finish her statement for her. If there's one thing I know about Jackson's parents, it's that they hate the city. It's too fast—too loud—all the things her son loves about this place.

Lana nods.

"But Jackson is still here."

"That's the other thing I need to talk to you about."

Fuck, the hits just keep coming.

"We want to move him to Oklahoma as well."

"And you need me to sign off on it."

Before Jackson and Norah got married, we gave each other medical power of attorney in the event something happened to us on the road. It's why I'm allowed to be here and talk with the doctors even though I'm not immediate family. Every decision is run through me. And they can't move him without my approval.

She nods again, solemnly.

"Lana, I—"

"Please. Don't say anything now. We don't have to make any decisions today. I just wanted you to know before you head down for spring training, so you can decide what you want to do."

No pressure.

"Okay." That's all I can bring myself to say. I can't even thank her for telling me, because how do you thank someone who has every intention of ripping away the last inkling of hope left in your life?

"I better get going. I need to get Phoebe before she inevitably talks Greta into sharing whatever sweets they have at the nurses station and ruins her dinner."

"Yeah. Okay." It's something I wouldn't have even considered.

Seriously, Jackson, what the hell were you and Norah thinking?

When I don't get an answer—not even from the fucked-up version of him that stalks my mind—I glance over to the still form lying in the hospital bed.

Please, wake up, I silently beg.

Without another word, Lana gets up and leans over to press a kiss to Jackson's temple and whispers something in his ear.

I look away, not wanting to encroach on this moment with her son. Out of the corner of my eye, I see her pause before she reaches the door, and I will the universe to make her go.

But I'm not that lucky.

"You're allowed to grieve, Bishop. Just don't lose yourself along the way."

Before I can answer, she's gone, leaving me alone with nothing but my thoughts.

No matter how hard I try to come to terms with everything I've done and learned today, I keep coming back to the same problem. I have no idea who I am anymore, only who everyone wants me to be.

The team wants me to be Bishop Lawson, star catcher of the New York Renegades.

Willow wants me to stand with them—lead them.

The press wants me to be their cover story.

Jackson and Norah want me to be a guardian to their daughter.

But none of those are who I am.

Because the truth is I'm lost.

I can't retrace my steps. I can only move forward. And fuck if I know what comes next.

59

CHAPTER SIX
Willow

This cabin isn't big enough for both of us.

Between the panic slithering under my skin, making every breath stick in my chest, and Bishop's continuous glares from where he's sulking on the other side of the aisle, I'm seconds away from suffocating.

I've always hated flying. Something about being twenty thousand feet in the air, in a tiny metal cylinder, doesn't sit well with me. I used to cling to the knowledge that aircrafts were statistically the safest mode of transportation. It's what got me through every flight, but now that I know exactly how *not* safe they can be, there's no rationalizing. Every bump, every sound has me wondering if this is it. Is this the moment we're going to meet the same fate as my father?

Bishop lets out a sigh and gets up from his seat…again. I do my best not to peek out of the corner of my eye and notice the way the denim of his jeans hug his muscular thighs or where his long sleeve green Henley hits his wrists, giving way to his very capable hands. There are lines I can't cross, and this is absolutely one of them. But I'm still a woman, and I can't pretend I don't know exactly what he looks like without all those layers on.

With the exception of takeoff, he's been all over the place. Pacing the length of the plane. Flirting with the flight attendant in the small galley. Visiting the tiny bar my father insisted on having installed at the rear of the cabin.

I roll my eyes. I may have asked him to arrive sober when I texted him the flight details—which he did—but he reminded me as soon as he got on the plane he made no promises to stay that way.

Another reason I have to ignore him. Because remembering who he was hurts too much and leads to remembering why he's not anymore.

This time, he heads to the restroom behind the workspace I'm currently occupying. He ignores me as he passes by, per usual. It's infuriating, and I almost wish I could write him off like everyone else has.

Unfortunately, my bleeding heart won't let me. That and a part of me understands why he's become this shell of himself. The part of me that's falling apart too. I just do so in the privacy of my office, where no one can see my tears or witness the crippling anxiety attacks.

It helps that I also have my therapist on speed dial. Honestly, Janet is probably the only reason I'm still standing. Where Bishop copes with booze and bad decisions, I'm a workaholic who crams my emotions in a box and cares too damn much about making sure everything is perfect. She'd argue neither is healthy, but at least no one has to babysit me on a daily basis.

Grief breaks everyone differently. The only constant is when she sinks her tendrils into your soul, you become her mistress. Something both of us know all too well.

I inhale a steadying breath—which is entirely for show if my quivering hands are any indication—and focus on my laptop and the full inbox waiting for me.

"Do you ever stop?"

I jump, Bishop's voice catching me off guard. It's the first thing he's said to me the entire flight. Craning my neck, I look up at him. "What?"

"Working? Do you ever stop?" His voice is playful with a hint of mocking.

Ignoring his jab, I click on an email marked urgent, informing me that Renegade Hearts has been chosen by the commissioner as the benefiting charity for the Orange League Gala. It's an annual event held for the Florida spring training league in which all the owners, managers, and star players attend to raise money for a charity usually associated with one of the teams. Fans pay big money to attend, rub elbows, and participate in the player auction for a chance to spend time with their favorite players.

I let out an exasperated sigh. Freaking Vaughn. This has him written all over it. After I explicitly asked him not to use my charity as a publicity stunt, he went and did it anyway. Once again, proving he'll do anything to keep the crash narrative and our team in the headlines. Even if it's at my expense.

My hands immediately find the keyboard and I work on crafting a response, not bothering to shy away from using my very best per-my-last-email tone.

"Willow."

"What?" I snap, my annoyance hitting an all-time high. "It's not like you have anything nice to say to me. We're almost to Florida. Can we please just continue to ignore each other?"

"I just figured—Wait. What the hell is this?"

His voice goes from slurred and playful, to low, and dare I say, deadly. I glance up just in time to see his nostrils flare, his eyes darting over the original email.

Shit. This isn't going to be good.

"It's nothing." I reach up and grip the top of the laptop with every intention of slamming it closed, but his hand snatches the top of the screen and stops me.

He yanks the laptop from the table and brings it up to his face. "Willow. What. The fuck. Is. This." Each word is punctuated with rage.

At least he's done trying to play nice.

Nice Bishop makes my knees weak. Asshole Bishop reminds me to keep my wits about me.

"I'm fixing it." I growl, trying and failing to grab the laptop from his hands.

Bishop throws himself into the seat beside me and scrolls through the message. His jaw tightens and if there was an open window, I can almost guarantee my laptop would be taking flight.

"Tell me this isn't what I think it is." His eyes are hard and filled with nothing but contempt as he shifts his stare to meet mine.

"I told you I'm fixing it."

"Fixing it?" A manic laugh slips from his throat. "You're going to use them. This is why you've been so involved. Not because you give a shit about the team. You're going to use their deaths to fundraise for your foundation."

"No, that's not—"

"I can't believe this shit. What happened to the woman I met who couldn't even talk to a room full of socialites without having a panic attack? The soft soul who gave a shit about other people? How did she become"—he lifts his hand and gestures up and down—"this."

She's still here, I want to say, but words fail me. I want to tell him I had to learn to channel that panic into something more. There wasn't room to be both. The crash didn't only take the lives of the dead. It took mine, too, and forced me to figure things out on my own.

Fuck him for using that against me.

Bishop shakes his head, and before I can figure out how to explain myself, he twists the knife he thrust in my chest. "I knew you'd allowed yourself to become cunning and manipulative, but I didn't think you were a fucking monster. For fuck's sake, Willow, they lost their parents. I know that's your whole schtick, but to use them as a way to make money? To use Phoebe?"

An image of the youngest Roberts forms in my mind and how she possesses more strength in her nine-year-old body than most adults. The way just yesterday she talked about Bishop like he hung the damn starts. My eyes prick with tears, and it takes everything in me to choke back the sob in my throat. How can he possibly think that's who I am?

"Bishop, listen, it's not what you think. I swear." My words wobble despite their sincerity. "It looks bad, I know, but I promise I didn't—"

"No, you listen," he yells, slamming the laptop closed before shoving it across the tabletop toward me. "This might technically be your team now, but they aren't yours to puppet."

"I know."

"You don't," he growls and for the second time this week, fear wraps around my spine and I shrink away from him, pressing myself into the window. "It's clear you don't know a damn thing about what it means to be a Renegade. Your father would be ashamed."

My head screams with the logic that he's lashing out in anger and pain, but my heart can't do the same. Not when it's him giving life to my greatest fear. My eyes find the table, and I do my best to ignore the gut-wrenching feeling swirling inside me. I've somehow managed to keep my walls up until now, but one flight with Bishop is enough to have them crashing down around me.

"Bishop, I—"

The plane picks that moment to jerk and my hands drop to the leather cushions of the sofa-like seats, digging in. I press my back straight and slam my eyes shut.

In for one. Out for two.

Breathe.

It's just turbulence.

In for two. Out for three.

As soon as the panic subsides to a dull roar in my chest, I open my eyes and find Bishop's eyes still on me, wide with fear of his own. He hasn't returned to his seat. He furrows his brow in a way that almost gives the impression he's concerned.

And the award for emotional whiplash goes to Bishop Lawson.

"You really don't like flying." It's not a question.

I shake my head slowly as frustration replaces anxiety. "No. I don't."

He's never had the pleasure of flying with me. Usually, I need anything and everything to either distract me or force me to sleep. That wasn't an option today since I'm on babysitting duty.

"And it has nothing to do with…It hasn't gotten worse because of…" His voice trails off and his chest sputters between breaths. "What happened."

I shake my head again, silently wishing he would just let me suffer alone.

There was a time I'd turn to him, to just about anyone, but I've become accustomed to my solitary suffering.

He opens his mouth then shuts it when the flirty flight attendant strolls up and places her freshly manicured hand on his bicep. With a sickly sweet smile, she croons, "We're starting our descent. The pilot also asked me to let you know there's a storm in Fort Myers, so it's going to be a bumpy landing." She turns on her heel and heads toward the galley, completely unaware of the death sentence she's just delivered us.

Okay, maybe that's a little dramatic, but this is exactly what happened four months ago. There was a storm. Errors made on landing. And they were gone. Sixty-eight souls.

"Shit," I mutter under my breath at the same time as Bishop sucks in a breath.

The plane dips and jostles to the side. My chest tightens, each breath a struggle as I attempt to quickly shove my laptop back in its bag, so it doesn't end up on the floor.

"Do you think they knew?" His voice is somber, barely a whisper above the roar of the engines.

I whip my gaze in his direction, simultaneously processing both his question and the horror etched on his face.

"What?"

"Do you think they knew that they were going to die?"

What kind of question is that? I thought I was losing it, but if this is what keeps him up at night, he's worse off than I thought. Bishop carries the weight of their souls on his back in a way I could've never have imagined.

"They didn't," I reassure him. "It was instant. Those that survived said one minute they were fine, the next they…"

Bishop winces but that doesn't worry me as much as the way he gasps for air.

He doesn't meet my gaze, but I can read the terror in his vacant eyes.

"Bishop?" I ask, but I know he's not hearing me. He's likely gone to the same place he went in the locker room. A place I've known many times in my life. First after my mom died. Then again, the moment I slid into the car after leaving the courthouse. It's a place where time and space cease to exist, and you're left with only the crippling presence of your twisted fears.

The seatbelt across my lap makes it hard, but I manage to twist myself enough that I can take his face in my hands and force him to look at me. "Bishop, breathe."

"Willow, they…they're gone…I should have…if I was only…"

"Bishop, there's nothing you could have done. Even if you were there."

"They're my team…mine."

"I know."

"I need them."

I'm not sure if he's talking about the team we lost or the team we gained, but if I had to guess, it's the former.

"You need to breathe, Bishop."

"I can't…I don't want to."

My heart aches for him as he shakes his head against my grip. I drop my hands to the sides of his neck, thumbs tracing the stubble on his jaw.

With each jerk of the plane, alarms sound in my mind, but I push them aside, focusing instead on the places our skin connects.

"Do it with me," I plead. "In for one, out for two."

"No." He swats my hands down, his eyes dark and distant. "How are you so fucking calm?"

I swallow past the lump in my throat. "I'm not."

"You are," he sneers. "Little miss perfect. Do you even care if they're gone?"

And we're back to anger.

I chew my lower lip almost to the point of drawing blood, to stop myself from letting my anger get the best of me. "Of course I care."

"Then why? Why are you letting them use them? How can you just sit by and let them manipulate this team into a cash grab?"

"The same way you keep running from it," I snap.

So much for not giving in.

His eyes go wide and his mouth parts slightly, like he's shocked I would say such a thing to him. Clearly, I'm the only one willing to.

"I'm one person. I'm doing the best I can," I stammer, each word a little bolder than the one before. "Can you say the same?"

Seconds pass like hours as he sits there, silently scrutinizing me until the plane makes a sudden drop. I gasp and dig my nails into the first solid thing they find. Which turns out to be his thigh.

Then he's there.

My eyes drop and zero in on where his hand tightly wraps around mine, his knuckles white.

When I tilt my head back up, his brown eyes have me in a chokehold. The corner of his mouth twitches, and he doesn't make any move to let go.

My traitorous mind punishes me with a truly agonizing thought.

This could have been us.

In another world, we could have clung to one another in the face of this tragedy. I'm the villain in his narrative. Not because I am, but because he needs me to be.

Bishop opens his mouth to speak, and closes it, thinking better of whatever it was he was going to say. His gaze drops when I part my lips and close my eyes, unable to stand his uneasy gaze.

"I'm not sure I can do this." His whispered words come out like a prayer. Or maybe a plea.

Or maybe that's what I'm hoping for—that this is the moment he asks for help.

In what I can only describe as a moment of weakness, he leans forward and presses his forehead to mine.

"You're not alone in this," I breathe.

He huffs a sound that is somewhere between a laugh and a sob. "How can you say that? I'm literally the lone fucking survivor from our team."

"There's still Jackson," I point out, though I'm not sure it helps because Bishop claps back, "Who is unconscious."

I give his hand a squeeze and whisper, "You still have me."

Bishop pulls away slightly, his brows raising a smidge. I hold the breath in my lungs, and I wait to see if he believes me. It's a lifeline. One I might regret giving him.

As if fate is laughing at us, the plane makes a sharp jerk, forcing me to fall in his direction. I press my hands against his chest to break my fall, and when I pull back, his lips are a hair's breadth away from my own.

His eyes search mine and I'm not sure what he's looking for, but whatever he needs, I'll give it to him.

"Fuck, Willow," he rasps.

"Bishop—"

I'm not entirely positive what I'm going to say, but it doesn't matter because I'm silenced by Bishop's lips crashing against mine.

He's kissing me.

Bishop Lawson is kissing me.

This is not what I meant when I said he still had me, but I'm helpless to force myself away.

It's not a peck or a chaste brushing of lips. No, what Bishop gives me is desperate, like a star on the verge of being sucked into a black hole.

Everything right and wrong about this floods my mind, the takeaway being I need to do something—anything—to stop this. Need is the operative word because tearing my lips from his is the last thing I want to do.

It's wrong.

So. Fucking. Wrong.

But just like every previous kiss from him, oh so right.

His tongue flits across my lips, demanding entrance, and it calms the chaos within me. My body moves of its own accord, opens for him, taking everything he's offering me. My fingers tangle in his hair, anchoring at the base of his skull, at the same time his reach down and dig into my hip with bruising force.

Something between a growl and groan escapes him, and I want nothing more than to memorize the sound forever. His teeth sink into my lower lip, and he tugs like I'm nothing more than a piece of meat to tear apart, melting me into putty in his hands. He's brutal, so unlike the rough but delicate Bishop I remember.

This isn't that.

It's possessive, the way he takes control of me, demanding my submission. He's ruthless, taking every ounce of his pent-up rage and frustrations out on my lips.

His hand slips from my hip and with one expert flick of his fingers, my seatbelt is off. He swallows the gasp of fear that escapes me and hauls me into his lap. Straddling him, I'm locked between his chest and the table. I teeter side to side, unbalanced by more than just the position, and Bishop tightens his grip—a promise he's got me.

Bishop slides his hands up my thighs, pushing my skirt to my hips and giving his fingers access to the flesh on my thighs. "Do you know what this skirt does to me?" he moans against my lips. "The way it hugs every goddamned curve. Every time I see you in it, I have to force myself to forget how perfectly you fit against me."

As if to prove his point, he rolls his hips, grinding his erection against the flimsy lace of my panties.

I whimper, and the world falls away, allowing me to chase the high he's giving. I need more—more friction, more of him. I've dreamed of this more times than I can count.

The plane tilts to the side, and somewhere in the back of my mind, I recognize it's making its final approach into the private airfield in Fort Myers. This is usually where I grip the seat and send up a prayer for a safe landing. This time, the only thing I'm praying is for Jesus to take the wheel and stop me before I take this mistake any further.

My hands search for skin as he deepens our kiss, eliciting an animalistic moan from him that I savor like a woman starved. I slip my hands beneath his shirt and hard, smooth muscles greet me. My fingers dance across his abs before gripping the sides of his torso and teasing his nipples with my thumbs.

I'm so focused on the harsh inhalation of his breath that I hardly notice as the plane touches down. It's the first time I haven't felt relief at the ground being firmly beneath my feet.

The fasten seatbelt sign dings off—startling me like Cinderella hearing the clock strike midnight.

The moment it does, Bishop snatches his hands back from my thighs, lifting them like a soccer player denying a foul. The problem with that is he absolutely drew the foul.

Pulling back, I slam my eyes shut, but I'm not fast enough to miss the dark look of regret that flashes over his features.

I wish I could say the feeling was mutual, but I'd only be lying to myself.

I miss him.

I miss this.

But I'm the only one.

"Willow." There's no hint of warmth in his voice.

I swallow hard, steeling my nerves before I press my hands into his chest, allowing for a healthy space between us, and open my eyes.

Bishop's features are once again hard and closed off. He glances down to where my soaked panties meet the bulge in his jeans and back up at me. "Do you mind?"

My jaw drops. *Do I mind? Yes, I fucking mind,* I want to scream. Remind him he's the one who started this, not me—but instead, I hold on to the bit of my heart that threatens to crack at the silent rejection. I can't break in front of Bishop. I can't even crack. Because as much as I'd hoped he'd hold me together, he just proved I can't trust him with any part of me... including the hurt he causes.

My limbs shake as I gracefully scramble back into my seat and straighten my skirt.

The plane slows to a halt outside the hangar as we sit in awkward silence. The moment the doors open, Bishop is out of his seat, grabbing his bags in silence.

All I can do is glare daggers into the back of his skull, because if I speak, I'm either going to burst into tears or rip him a new asshole. Neither of which is productive owner behavior.

Because that's what I am. His team owner—and he's my employee.

Fuck.

I'm supposed to be stopping him from fucking up, not helping him fuck things up for the both of us.

Just before Bishop reaches the door, he looks over his shoulder and smirks. "You make for a great distraction. Thanks for that."

Then he's gone.

My mouth drops open, and the second I am sure he's out of hearing range, I let out a frustrated yell and slam my hands on the table in front of me. The fucking audacity of that asshole.

He used me.

What's worse is he isn't wrong. Kissing him was the best distraction. Even if it was at the expense of my pride and integrity. It's the first time in months I've felt like myself. Free of all the bullshit that came when I was named the owner of this team.

Desperation to reclaim that feeling curls around the base of my spine, igniting the old parts of myself I fight to ignore. Only this time, the spark won't be put out. It's the same part of me that stood when we first met, locked on a balcony with the star catcher of the New York Renegades, and accepted his dare to be myself.

A truly terrible idea begins to take form, but with every second that passes, it solidifies into a plan I'm sure will end in mutual destruction.

I might not be the woman I once was, but much like my team, I have the opportunity to write a new ending.

But there's a chapter I need to close.

The one titled Bishop Lawson.

75

CHAPTER SEVEN
Bishop

There is one thought on my mind when I finish checking into the team hotel.

Forget.

Forget where I am. Delete the memories of walking through the silver doors behind me, laughing with my former teammates. Bury the discussion Jackson and I had at the hotel bar about him and Norah trying for a second. Wipe out the image of Luke picking up any and every cleat chaser with cheesy pickup lines. Most of which he hollered loudly solely for our entertainment and not for the woman vying for his bed. But mostly I'd like to erase the recent memory at the hands of the woman who gave me the only freedom I've felt since the crash.

Keep telling yourself that, Jackson quips, followed by Tommy's, *Right? He's delusional if he thinks he's walking away from this one.*

I shake my head—as if that's going to shut up the fucked-up peanut gallery of my conscience—and head toward the bar, tucked away on the far side of the lobby so it can't be seen from the entrance.

Two other men sit at the bar top watching sports center, and I'm instantly thankful the team plane doesn't arrive for another few hours. That's just enough time for me to drink and disappear, and then sober up for team meetings and physicals in the morning.

Guilt gnaws on me like a dog with a bone. Lana asked me to do better, not only for myself, but for Phoebe. I wish I could say it's enough to stop me, but the pending spiral is winning.

Tomorrow. I'll start tomorrow.

Spring training will be the official start of the new me. The version of myself that will be enough for not only Phoebe, but everyone else too.

Why put off till tomorrow what you can do today?

Fuck off, Tommy.

I take a seat at the opposite end of the bar from the others and wait for the bartender, a young guy probably mid-twenties, to notice me.

"What can I get for you?" he stutters nervously.

If his starstruck timidness is any indication, he's new to the hotel. It'll wear off in a week or two after serving the team every night, but right now I don't have time to reassure him I'm just a normal guy.

Normal my ass, Jackson quips.

"A shot of Angel's Envy. Neat," I grunt, bitterly.

The bartender's hands tighten where he grips the edge of the bar. "I'm sorry, Mr. Lawson, I can't serve you that."

"What do you mean? I can see the bottle right there."

"Yes sir," he stutters. "I mean, we've been advised not to serve you alcohol."

Annoyance flashes over my features. "By who?"

"I'm not sure. My manager only told me there was a phone call received and that we aren't to serve you any alcohol."

"Are you fucking kidding me?"

His eyes dart from side to side, likely looking for anyone to relieve him of this situation. "I'm sorry, sir."

My jaw tightens and everything in me wants to unleash a rage of "do you know who I am" mixed with a desperate plea to help me numb the emotions brimming within me.

It's not this kid's fault, a part of me reasons. Thankfully, it's loud enough to stop me from laying into him.

"Thanks for nothing," I snap.

Shoulders tense, I push away from the bar and head to the elevator, contemplating which of the upper management made the call. I punch the elevator button harder than I should, grateful when the doors open immediately and there's no one else inside. The last thing I need is prying eyes while I work through who is pulling the strings this time.

Not Vaughn. It's no secret he wants to see me fail.

Not Adrian. He fired me as a client after the second bar fight, and I've yet to confirm with the management company who my new agent is.

Possibly my unwanted emergency contact, Graham. He's been a constant thorn in my side throughout the off season, despite the fact that I've only met the man a handful of times. Admittedly, it's always been when he's trying to mitigate my fuck ups and I'm too intoxicated to care.

I reach the fifth floor and cover the short distance from the elevator to my room. Wrenching the door open, I let out a weighted sigh. It's nothing special, but it's home for the next month and a half. I stumble over my bags and head straight for the minibar.

The fridge is tiny, but I know they keep it stocked for their VIP clients. They want us to spend our hard-earned money, and I am more than ready to take the edge off, even if it costs me triple what the bar would. Picking up the glass from the top, I savor the thought of the burning liquid as it slides down my throat. Only when I open the door, it's empty.

Every. Single. Fucking. Bottle has been removed save for the water and club soda.

What the actual fuck?

It's one thing to starve me from the endless well downstairs, but to take away the option for release in the privacy of my own room too.

Who cares enough to do that?

The answer hits me like a ton of bricks. It's simple, really, and I'm a dumbass for not putting it together sooner. Who is the one person who has been the biggest pain in my ass since waltzing back into my life?

Willow. Fucking. York.

Everything always comes back to her.

I back away from the fridge and clench my empty fist. The need to hit something courses through my veins.

How dare she?

It's one thing to take over my team and exploit them in every interview and press conference imaginable. I'd even be willing to give her a free pass on her genius plan to use their children as a money-making ploy, especially if she is indeed going to *fix* it, as she claims. But to strip me of the vice that makes my very existence bearable is too far. It was fine when she was just the imaginary force pulling the strings—

Fuck.

It's been her all along.

The back of my legs hit the bed and I sink onto the plush pillow top, dropping the glass onto the bedside table beside me. My elbows find my knees, and I let my head fall into my hands, my fingers taking out some of my rage in the strands of my hair.

Graham always being the first call.

The fact I haven't been fined a penny by the league.

A private plane.

It's all been her.

Fuck.

Guilt for my actions starts to creep in before I actively shut it down. I can't think about that right now.

Maybe you need to.

"Fuck you," I yell at Jackson "And you, too, Tommy. I know you're there, too, you opinionated fuck."

Shit, I'm going crazy, yelling at the imaginary voices in my head. But I can't go down the path that leads me to scrutinize every action and inaction since the crash and if she had her hand in it. I can't consider that despite pushing away every single member of my family and friends, it's Willow who has been the one looking out for me—a silent life raft keeping me from drowning.

Not my siblings who stopped calling when I told them they'd never understand.

Not even my parents, whose love scares me the most, because one day I'll lose them too.

No.

It's goddamned Willow.

My chest constricts, and I don't bother to choke back the guttural sob in my throat as my mind continues to wrap itself around the notion it's always been her. Anguish morphs into anger, and I pick up the glass beside me and slam it onto the bedside table, shattering it into a million tiny pieces.

The sound of the crash reverberates off the sand-colored walls, and I'm instantly thankful the rooms on either side of me aren't yet occupied by my new teammates. They don't need to see me like this. No one does. I'm alone, which is how it needs to be. Phoebe can't get hurt if I'm not her guardian. I can't get hurt if I'm alone.

The blood catches my eye long before the pain begins to throb from where glass sliced my palm. I work my fist open and closed. It's not too deep, but it is my glove hand. Somewhere through the haze, I know I should care, but my first thought is at least every pitch thrown will ache. A constant reminder of just how fucked I am.

Teetering somewhere between self-loathing and rock bottom, I manage to get to my feet and stumble my way to the bathroom. Careful not to stain the countertop, I turn on the faucet and run my hand under the water, washing away any remaining shards of glass.

My mouth tightens as pain radiates from the wound and out of the corner of my eye, I catch sight of myself in the mirror.

That can't be me.

I catalog my features. Same brown hair and eyes. The signature scruff that has become a bit unruly as of late. The scar on my chin I got from falling off my bike as a kid and the tiny freckle at the corner of my eye that no one but me ever notices.

What's different is the permanent bruising under my eyes from lack of sleep. The hollow dips in my cheeks. The vacant stare of a man who has lost the will to fight.

I am just so fucking tired.

Tears rim my eyes, and I don't have it in me to stop them from falling. This stings worse than all the other times reality bitch-slapped me. At least I had the sense to be drunk first or plans to be drunk soon after. Grief when sober is infinitely worse.

My knees buckle and I hit the floor with a thud, my shoulder against the vanity is the only thing keeping me upright.

"Bishop?"

No.

Absolutely not.

This isn't happening.

She calls my name again, her voice a beacon—it always is—and because life is a cruel bitch, I'm helpless to do anything but let her find me like this, broken and sobbing on the bathroom floor.

The door creaks open, and in an instant, Willow is on her knees in front of me. "Shit, you're hurt."

Fucking understatement of the year.

She takes my hand in hers, concern marring her beautiful face. She's wiped away the smeared makeup I left her with on the plane. Not that she usually wears much, but I like that I can see the faint smattering of freckles that dot the tops of her cheeks. My eyes lock on the blonde curl that has fallen across her face. The curl that, not an hour ago, was wrapped around my fingers.

She shouldn't be here.

I was an ass. I pushed her away on the plane before I gave into the need to get lost in her presence. Because it's not real. She's not real. What we had before is now nothing but a daydream. That doesn't mean we aren't insanely compatible. We are. Chemistry has never been our problem. Fuck. She tasted as pure as I remember. Like stepping out into an empty stadium before a big game, all nerves and excitement. But it's not real. And I made sure she knew that with my dickish words.

Yet here she is.

"What happened?" Willow gasps, leaning in to get a closer look at my palm.

I look down numbly at where she's taken my hand in hers. It's bleeding again.

She turns around and digs in her purse, procuring a Band-Aid which she quickly opens and uses to cover the cut.

As soon as she's done, I snatch my hand back and hold it against my chest. My eyes fall to the ugly mosaic tile on the floor. "Please go."

"What happened?" she repeats, this time a little more forcefully.

My pulse pounds in my throat, resulting in my voice becoming unsteady. "I need you to go."

"I'm not leaving," Willow says defiantly. She shifts her weight, shoving her knees forward so they interlock with mine. Her hand raises and she uses her fingers to lift my chin, so my gaze meets glittering blue ones. It's in moments like these, like on the plane, laced in panic and fear, with a hint of self-loathing that it's hard to see the person she's become. When she looks at me like she is right now, I can almost believe she cares.

"Please," I beg, something I never do, but desperate times call for desperate measures. "I don't want you here."

She huffs a challenging laugh, and it might've warmed my heart in any other situation. "I'm done caring what you want."

Fuck, I just need her to go. Leave. I don't want to talk.

"You don't have to."

Shit, now I can't even tell what I'm saying out loud verses in my head. Maybe I am going crazy.

Her fingers trace the stubble on my jaw before sliding up, cupping my jaw. I lean into her touch, soft and delicate. Every moment she's got her hands on me, I lose a little of my resolve to throw her out. The problem is, I don't know what happens if she stays. I can't trust her. And I don't trust myself.

I open my mouth to tell her to go, but before I can, she whispers, "What do you need?"

My mouth gapes like a fish out of water, struck stupid by the question. It's the first time anyone has asked me that. They always ask if I'm okay. Or tell me what I should do, how I should feel. It's not that simple.

Willow sees that.

Before I can stop myself, my brain short circuits and word vomit takes hold. "I just want to be okay."

A weak smile tips her lips. "Okay is overrated."

"Says the woman who has it all together."

She shrinks back like I've slapped her. And a hint of something new flashes across her face. Anger. "Is that what you think?"

It catches me off guard. Aside from the obvious, what does she have to be angry about? She's got it all figured out. She's playing the game and winning.

Then again, if she's angry, then she'll leave. So, of course, I poke the bear. "Sure as hell seems like it."

Willow sits with my words for a second before her gaze falls and she lets out a weighted sigh. "Then you don't know me. Maybe you never did."

"You're right."

She leans back on her heels, creating the space I desperately need. At this point, I just need to push a little more and she'll leave. Shit, when did I become an expert in pushing people away? This isn't who I am. I've always been an open book. I don't hurt people—I welcome them. I was walking fucking sunshine.

You do what you have to in order to survive.

Tommy's right. That's all I've been able to do for the last four months. Survive. I'm sick of surviving, but I don't know how to do much more.

Despite the war going on in my mind between who I was and who I've become, I open my mouth to tell her again to leave, but Willow beats me to speak.

"Have you considered that maybe it's not about being okay?" she whispers, almost like she's afraid to say anything. "Maybe it's about figuring out how to live again."

"Oh, it's just that easy?" I groan. "It's as simple as saying I don't want to feel this way."

"And which way is that?"

I run my uninjured hand through my hair, tightening around the strands at the base of my skull. "Like I'm constantly falling short of who everyone expects me to be. Like I'm drowning with every breath. Like I'm the only one who remembers them. Like I can't move on."

Tears stream down my face, the weight of my plea heavy in my chest. I'm not sure why I keep letting things slip to her. She's not on my side. Not really. Everything she does is for the sake of the team. But there's just something about Willow that constantly catches me off guard.

She worries her lower lip, catching it between her teeth. "What if you could not feel it? Even for just one night?"

CHAPTER EIGHT
Willow

I chew the inside of my cheek and ignore the way my heart threatens to race clear out of my chest.

This is a terrible idea.

What the hell was I thinking coming here? And now I'm seriously considering telling Bishop to use me as a distraction.

He's looking at me like I'm an idiot. Like I couldn't possibly know the first thing about pushing aside the ache in my chest.

Then again, he thinks I'm doing just fine.

I really should take it as a compliment that the act is working. He has no idea the lengths I go to pretend like I'm okay in front of the world. Where he's always the extrovert, I've always identified as the introverted extrovert. I'd much rather stay at home and curl up with a good book than attend a gala. Not that the press would have you believe that. But that's what I want them to see. I know how to turn on the charm when it's needed and lock away the emotions that don't play into the narrative of the night. It's a perk of growing up the daughter of Adrianna and Richard York. The family motto is forever ingrained in my brain: Never risk the York legacy. But it always catches up with me. Usually in the form of a panic attack. Which then leads to me hiding in my work for weeks because when I'm lost in something else, the nerves and emotions can't touch me.

God knows how I cope with things is far from the right answer, but it's a step above the train wreck sitting in front of me on the bathroom floor with tears streaming down his face. Not that I haven't been there. Hell, I lived there for months after my mother died. And then a week after the plane crash.

I've been there and I know the way out—anger, distraction, indifference, acceptance, healing.

I'm on step two of my five-part plan, and I'll live there until it doesn't hurt as much to think of my father and the team. It might not be scientifically proven, but hey, it's what's worked for me.

I thought I was finally reaching acceptance when it came to grieving my relationship with Bishop. That's what tonight was supposed to be.

On the car ride over, I constructed and rehearsed the perfect speech, letting him know exactly where he could shove his distraction. I was ready to walk away and build the wall between owner and player. No more watching his back. No more fixing his mistakes.

So much for closing the damn book.

From the moment I heard the crash of the glass standing outside his hotel room, followed by his choked sob, I knew I wouldn't be able to shake this man. Then he opened his mouth and bared the tiniest bit of his soul with me, and I was a goner.

He needs this. But so do I. Especially if I'm to survive the next months—shit, the next week—of playing this never-ending game that is owning this team. I need something I can hold on to. A distraction that can live rent free in my mind.

And maybe, if I'm honest, a little closure on whatever it is that runs hot and fast between us.

Bishop is still scrutinizing my words when his brow raises, and he tilts his head curiously. "How do you propose I stop feeling this way?"

"You already did."

"What?"

A distraction."

His incredulous stare lets me know he's not following my logic.

"On the first night we met, you distracted me on the balcony. You kissed me, distracting me from the speech I had to give." I pause, a manic attempt to give myself a moment before I continue. He presses his lips into a line, nodding to spur me on. "Then on the plane you called that kiss a distraction."

"The best kind," he says with an annoying smirk that has me rolling my eyes.

"It would have been better if you finished what you started, but I'm not complaining." At least not out loud. What he did was a dick move, but I get it a little more now. We all do stupid shit when the emotions hit too close to home.

"You want to fuck the feelings away?"

My brows shoot up and I let out a stifled giggle. "That's not how I would've put it, but if that's what it takes."

"Shit." Bishop breathes, shaking his head. "I thought I was rock bottom, but it seems I've got a bit more falling to do if you believe that's what I need right now."

I arch a speculative brow. "You're telling me you didn't feel the freedom of what we did on the plane?"

He freezes, and I know I'm right. It wasn't just me. Whatever this thing is between us, this addiction to sharing stolen moments, it's not nothing.

I never told him the night he found me at the party at my father's beach house that I was falling apart. I'd just found out my father had been diagnosed with prostate cancer. Later I'd find out it was likely manageable with surgery and chemotherapy, but at the time I could only think about how I'd lose him. Bishop took one look at me and knew I wasn't okay. He didn't ask why I was teary-eyed or press for more information. For one night, he let me live in a moment that was just ours.

We live for these moments. This is just another between us. Because that's who we are—two very fucked up peas in a pod who don't have a chance in hell of making something meaningful work any time soon. I can see that now. But that doesn't mean for just one night we can't help each other move forward.

His brown eyes pierce me, and despite wanting to look away, I need him to see I'm in this.

"What do you get out of this?" he asks.

It's the same question I had the night we met. He told me he got a taste of the most beautiful, intriguing woman he had ever met. That night, he made me believe it was true.

Eyes locked on him, I whisper the honest and raw truth. "I get to spend the night with the man who's made me believe I'm worth more than my name, and then I get to say goodbye."

Bishop curses under his breath, and I wait for him to tell me again to leave. When he doesn't, I muster up the courage to glance up at him through my lashes.

"Willow, I…I can't give you…."

"That's your problem, Bishop. You always want to give. This isn't just about me. It's about you too. Take what you need. I'll do the same. No feelings. No commitment."

Or at least I'll do my best to forgo them.

"Just one night," he finishes my sentiment perfectly.

"Just one."

"No feelings."

"None whatsoever."

I roll onto my knees and stand in front of him and watch as his gaze travels up my body as he contemplates the offer I have just made.

The ball is in his court. We all have these moments in life. The ones where we can either climb the mountain alone or give up. Renegade Hearts was my first Everest. It was my solo climb to make something of myself when I didn't believe I could. Sure, I had help along the way, but it was my dream. My moment to overcome the bullshit belief my mother implanted. I was a woman and could only be the trophy wife on a man's arm.

I know Bishop is fighting to summit his own Everest. He can either follow me or stay in his pity party at base camp. But if he's willing to climb and make the most of the future he's been given—to fight his way through and learn to live again—then I have no doubt he's going to succeed.

And I want to be there to see it.

But I can't do it for him.

All I can do is give him the night he needs and pray he's ready to take the first step.

And then I need to walk away.

CHAPTER NINE
Bishop

She's a drug.

And I'm addicted.

Every part of me knows I shouldn't follow her out of this bathroom. She doesn't hold the key to fixing the shit show that is my life. Hell, if anything, she's the catalyst making it worse. Which is exactly why I absolutely shouldn't be considering taking her up on her offer.

But when in the last four months have I done what I should?

I roll from the floor onto my feet and clear the doorway in two easy steps. When I enter the room, Willow is standing beside the king size bed, hands twisting in front of her. Her gaze sweeps over me, full of heat, with apprehension billowing in waves.

I take a predatorial step toward Willow, and then another, until she cranes her neck so her stunning blue eyes can meet my gaze. Her hands fall to her side and I take another step forward. The faint outline of her nipples straining against the fabric of her shirt catches my attention before my chest meets hers. She sucks in a breath, catching her lower lip between her teeth.

Willow may have decided she's all in for one night, but she doesn't know what she's asking of me. I'm not the man she remembers. I can't be. But one night. No strings attached. A taste of the freedom I experienced for a split-second on that plane. I can be that man.

"Are you sure this is what you want?" I give her one more chance to walk away, but more than that, I need to hear her say it. I need her to give me permission. Because if I touch her, all bets are off. There isn't a flight attendant or a plane landing to stop me this time. If she says yes, I'm going to take what I need. I'm aware how selfish that makes me. But if what she says is true, she needs it as much as I do.

Willow is silent for a beat, then gives her reply by way of nodding.

My hand snakes up, hooking around her neck, and my thumb traces her jaw. Tugging her lower lip from where it's still caught between her teeth, I growl. "Words, Willow, I need you to tell me you understand what you're asking me for."

"I want one night." She nuzzles into my palm and whispers, "Forget everything else with me."

My heart pounds against my ribcage as my eyes search hers, begging, pleading for her to understand. "I won't be gentle."

Her hand covers mine and pushes it down, forcing my fingers to wrap around her throat. Swallowing hard against my palm, her lips tip into a wicked grin. "I'm banking on it."

Fuck. I don't deserve her taking care of me. But I'm an asshole—a greedy prick—and there's no way in hell I'm walking away now.

My dick twitches in agreement. Contrary to what the tabloids have reported, I haven't been with a woman since before the crash—specifically the woman in front of me nearly a year ago.

Willow rocks up onto her tiptoes and ghosts her lips over mine. "Lawson."

Lawson. No longer Bishop. And I remember what she said—this is goodbye.

I've never hated my last name so much.

"Stop thinking and fu—"

It's all the encouragement I need. I crash my lips against hers.

Inhaling, she eagerly wraps her arms around my waist, pulling me closer, deepening the kiss so I can taste her silent plea to deliver everything she's asked of me. An involuntary moan tears from my throat, and I drop my hands to grip her hips before running them over the fabric of the skirt that could bring grown men to their knees, down to the curve of her perfectly rounded ass.

A growl rips from my chest. "I've told you what this skirt does to me."

"I remember you saying something about them once. Can I tell you a secret?" She smiles against my lips and I nod, a part of me desperate for her to return the confidence I've given her. Willow reaches up and tugs me down so her breath caresses the shell of my ear as she whispers, "I wore it for you."

The little minx. The joy in her voice cripples me. It might not have been any sort of declaration like I've made tonight, but it proves one thing. Willow York has been thinking of me.

"Fucking hell." I dig my fingers into the offending fabric. "I should take you over my knee for the way you made my dick stand at attention for the majority of that flight."

"You wouldn't." She scoffs playfully, but pulls back enough to look to see just how serious I am.

In both our nights together, I didn't give into my need for control. I was just happy to count the number of times I could make Willow come on my face and cock. Now, though, the very thought of losing control has my skin crawling.

A mischievous grin tips my lips, and I lower my voice to just above a sultry moan. "Oh, I absolutely would. I'd love to see your perfect flesh reddened by my hand. But if I only get one night to distract myself, then I plan to spend it buried deep in that tight cunt of yours, not punishing you."

The tiny gasp that escapes her lips gives me life, as does swallowing it with my mouth. A mess of lips and teeth, our tongues fight for dominance, and I love the fight she's putting up. It only makes me want to possess her more.

One night, I remind myself.

My hands wander to the zipper at the small of her back. I lower it completely, fist the fabric on either side and pull, tearing the fabric to the slit. Willow gasps as the cool air of the hotel room hits her skin and the offending piece of cloth falls to the floor.

"Now it won't be a problem," I pant and silently add, *For me or anyone else.*

Willow's chest shakes with quiet laughter against mine, the curve of her lips a silent promise I know from experience means she'll exact her revenge in a way I never thought possible. But I'm too far gone to care.

I hate to admit it, but she was right. This is exactly what I needed.

My arm snakes around her waist, and when I lift, Willow instinctively wraps her legs around my waist. Her curves mold to mine and I love that when my hands find their way back to her ass, they aren't met with bone, but soft, supple flesh.

Wait, flesh.

Not lace.

Not cotton.

"Willow, where the fuck are your panties?"

Her laugh is like sunshine and sends a zap of lightning straight to my balls. She gives me a look of innocence that is all for show. "They were wet, so I left them on the plane."

I swoop down, my lips capturing hers, biting harshly on her lower lip until she lets out a sound that's somewhere between a groan and a gasp. "You absolutely deserve that spanking."

"It's a good thing you'd rather be buried deep in my cunt." She mewls against my lips before devouring them, bruising them in the bone deep way only she can.

Remind me again why I've lived in self-imposed celibacy for the last year?

Oh, that's right, because she's the only woman who makes my dick hard, and she hasn't exactly been an option. Fuck, she still isn't an option. But that's not a worry for tonight.

Shifting our position, I turn and drop her onto the edge of the hip-height bed, pushing her so she falls onto her back.

Willow giggles, her legs and arms bouncing on the mattress. Her eyes flit down to her legs, and like she knows exactly what she's doing, she lets her knees fall, revealing the pussy that has played a starring role in nearly all of my solo shower sessions. I bring my fist to my mouth, sinking my teeth into my first finger. She's a fucking goddess.

"Like what you see?" She props herself up on her elbows and begins to unbutton the flimsy blouse she's wearing. Her sultry gaze never leaves mine, even as I nod my agreement.

Willow toys with the fabric, pushing it just far enough that I can't see more than the strap connecting the cups of her bra. "You want to rip this, too, don't you?"

Holding her gaze, I take a step forward, edging myself between her legs. I lower one of my hands and tug on the bottom of her blouse. "Fuck, you have no idea."

She laughs again, and I swear it's magic. My gaze drops lower, following as her delicate fingers reveal inch after inch of her flawless flesh. She's wearing a white lace bra that pushes her breasts up and is sheer enough that I can see her peaked nipples.

"Fucking hell. If I had known this is what was waiting for me under your clothes, we would have never left the plane."

Willow shrugs off her blouse and awards me with a teasing smirk. "Choices were made."

A chuckle rumbles in my chest as I pull out my wallet, followed by the condom I keep there. Her eyes zero in on the foil packet and just before I tug my shirt over my head, I swear I see her wince. I've never used a condom with her. Usually because we've always been too caught up in the moment and I know she's on the pill, but that isn't a boundary I can cross tonight. I might need the distraction, but I also need to remember this isn't real. It's chemistry. It's a distraction. It's not Kitten and Bishop. It's Willow and Lawson.

By the time I'm shirtless, any trace of hurt is gone from her face, and I push it from my mind as I ditch my jeans and boxers.

Willow licks her lips, eyeing the proud display my cock makes. The piercings from my Jacob's ladder glint in the light from the single lamp in the room. She loves the damn piercing as much as I do, and I can't help but toy with her. "Don't lick those pretty little lips of yours like you deserve this cock between them."

She doesn't miss a beat. "No, I deserve it in my cunt where it belongs."

My eyes nearly pop from their sockets.

Holy shit, this woman.

A year ago—hell, even six months ago—she wouldn't have had the balls to meet me in the gutter with such confidence. She's always told me how she gets off on my filthy mouth, but asking for what she wants—demanding it without me having to coax it from her—that's new.

And I don't hate it.

Fuck, I absolutely don't hate it.

"Not mine," I mutter under my breath. Mostly for me, but when she answers "not yours", I'm left wondering if she needs the reminder too.

Fuck, we're quite the pair.

"Now"—her attention shifts from my cock to my face, and she arches a single brow—"are you going to fuck me or not?"

My balls draw up with desire, and I can't help the way my lips tip all the way up in a smile that feels foreign to me. "You've got a mouth on you, now."

Willow shrugs. "I learned from the best."

Her confidence is a breath of fresh air in an otherwise suffocating world, and not at all expected. "Are you trying to break me?"

"No, I'm trying to get you to break me," she quips.

Fucking hell, I'm in trouble.

"Lose the bra," I demand.

While she slips off the remainder of her clothes, I make quick work of sheathing my cock with the condom. I nudge her knees further apart and slide onto the bed between them. Running the length of my dick through her slick folds, I take my time teasing her and coating my dick with her arousal.

"You're so fucking wet for me."

"Mmmhmm." Her whimpers are a symphony, and when I tap the top barbell on the underside of my cock against her clit, she jerks her hips up to meet me.

Unimpressed with my antics, Willow arches her back and angles her hips so I'm notched at her entrance.

Her blue eyes blaze into me and something clicks. Something primal. Something pure. Something I shouldn't want.

I ignore the twinge in my chest. The one telling me this is a terrible idea, and I should absolutely get up and walk the fuck away. Right now. Do not pass go. Just leave Willow and whatever fucked up game we're playing behind.

But there's not enough blood for my brain, heart, and dick to all work at once, and I have no complaints over which is winning the war.

I'm aching. Desperate. My body needs this like it needs its next breath, and my mind is begging for relief. It's unconventional, but honestly, Willow's a goddamn genius.

Her sharp inhale goes straight through me, causing goosebumps to break out across my flesh as I hold on to her hips and push into her, painfully slow so I don't wreck her—or me.

A shared gasp is the only sound between us in the otherwise deafening silence of the hotel room.

"So goddamn tight," I grit out, sliding the final inch, so I'm completely seated within her.

She licks her lips and moans, her eyes baring her soul. "Just how you like it."

God, she's magnificent.

Willow's hand digs into my forearms, grounding her as I slide out and back in and I relish the pain. Living for the way it makes my nerves fray and my body come alive. I'm chasing the high, every muscle coiled tight as I work our bodies together.

"Fuck," I exhale, "you feel too fucking good."

"Yes," she pants, rocking her hips to meet my thrusts. "More."

More.

This damn woman always wants more from me. More leadership. More consideration. More understanding. For months I haven't been able to give her what she wants, but this—more of my cock—this I can do without the worry of failure.

Wrapping my arm around her, I flip us so she's on top and scoot us the short distance to the head of the bed.

"Hands on the headboard," I command, and though she raises a brow in question, she complies. Leaning forward until her breasts hang just above my mouth and only the tip of my length is left inside her.

"Hold on tight."

It's the only warning I give her before I thrust my hips up, hitting the deepest parts of her.

Willow throws her head back and lets out the prettiest scream, followed by a string of curses. "Holy fuck, Lawson."

My last name echoes like a gong in my mind, but it's easy to ignore as I watch her tits bounce from below, mesmerized by her flushed skin. Eyes closed, her blonde hair sticks to her forehead as tiny whimpers escape her swollen lips.

I lift onto my elbow, taking her nipple into my mouth like a man starved. My hand finds the nipple not occupied by my mouth and for every suck on one, I flick the other in time with the thrusts of my hips.

"Please," she begs like I'm her savior, saving her from whatever plagues her.

I should care. I should ask her why she needs freedom from the perfect little life she's made for herself. But I don't. I can't. Caring means connecting, and that's the last thing I want. Connecting only leaves you with the ability to lose. And I've lost enough.

"Please what, Willow?" I purr against her skin.

"Make me come."

Say less, Kitten.

I'm not sure where her body ends and mine begins, and the sounds she's making are so damn sexy. She's magic.

"Watch, Willow," I rasp between frantic thrusts. "Watch me fuck you. Watch yourself take every inch of my cock, so tomorrow you'll remember exactly who left you aching."

Her head drops, eyes locked on where we connect, but my gaze remains on her. The way she bites her lip when her pelvis meets mine and the way her mouth parts slightly, a low whimper slipping past her lips— she's a delicious mix of sinful and erotic.

My mind struggles to reconcile this is really happening.

That is until Willow locks her piercing blue gaze with mine. Her brow furrows, like she's trying to figure something out and can't quite grasp it. Once again, I'm hit with the memories of my old self. A time when I would question it, press until she told me what was bothering her, and figure out how to fix it. But I can't do that now. Not when her eyes are wide windows to a lost soul—a soul that matches mine.

As soon as the moment comes, it's gone, flitting away with the thrust of hips and rushing pleasure.

A shiver wracks her body and Willow stills, her cunt turning into a viselike grip on my cock as she attempts to force me out. My fingers tighten on her hip and my thumb brushes her clit in tiny circles. I hold her there until she throws her head back and cries out.

"Fuck, yes, Bishop."

My chest swells. She's fucking beautiful when she comes, and I have to fight not to join her too quickly, but my name on her lips is enough to undo me.

Tingles shoot down my spine and my vision doubles as she cries my name again, begging me not to stop.

I couldn't if I tried.

Two more thrusts and I follow her over the edge as she rides out the last spasms of her orgasm.

Willow collapses on me, her forehead pressed to where my heart pounds in my chest. When her breath grows steady, she looks up at me, her eyes glassy and full of satisfaction.

Slowly, I pull out and she takes that as her cue to roll off me. Only she doesn't stop in her usual spot—the crook of my arm with her head on my chest. Instead, she's a mile away on the other side of the king size bed, catching her breath with her eyes closed.

Well, that won't do.

If I'm not allowed to retreat and ruin this moment, then neither is she. This is about forgetting, and I'm not about to let reality seep in. Not after a spiritual moment like that. Reality can wait.

Carefully, I remove the condom from my deflated dick, tie the end, and discard it on the floor. A mess for later. I crawl across the bed, closing the distance between us and settle between her legs.

Willow jumps, propping herself on her elbows and attempts to close her knees, but I'm there stopping her, hands on her thighs. Her brows knit together before she gives in and her knees flop onto the bed.

I raise my brow. "Where do you think you're going?"

Pink tinges her cheeks. "I should go."

I shake my head. "You said I get one night. That implies in its entirety. Did you think we were done?"

"I figured—"

"I thought you said no thinking." My voice lilts, dare I say playfully, as I trace my fingers up the inside of her thigh until I reach the lips of her pussy, swollen and dripping from her release.

Something I can only describe as animalistic pride puffs in my chest with the knowledge that I did that to her. She could have asked anyone to free her, but she showed up at my hotel room.

"You want more?" Her words are breathy and filled with the trepidation that comes with spiraling into one's thoughts.

I wonder—nope, if she can't spiral, neither can I.

She sucks in a breath and fists the comforter when I slip a finger inside her.

"I want what I was promised," I say, removing my finger.

Her eyes are wide and zeroed in on my digit as I bring it to my lips, painting them with her arousal before taking it in my mouth and licking it clean.

Her lip catches between her teeth and she moans. "Fuck, that's so hot."

"Yes, you are. And the night is still young."

CHAPTER TEN
Willow

I woke up feeling more like myself than I have in months. That's not to say there isn't a part of me that feels guilty using Bishop like my own personal fuck toy, and allowing him to do the same before sneaking out while he was still asleep. There is. It's the same anxious feeling in my gut that knows it can never happen again, despite a very different part of me that wants just that. Last night was as I told him: a distraction followed by a goodbye of sorts.

Goodbye to the man who pushed me to be better. Goodbye to the attachment I've held onto for far too long. Goodbye to what was beginning, once upon a time, to feel a lot like love.

Don't get me wrong. Feelings are still there, but as long as I don't think too hard about them, I'm able to focus on the good that comes from letting go. Last night, he ignited a fire in the deepest parts of me, burning through the fear of failing and left hope in its wake. Hope that maybe I have what it takes to push past the grief and roadblocks and make this team something my father would be proud of.

Instead of showing up bright and early to the stadium, I let Vaughn know I'd be working from the beach house. I didn't let him know I'd be doing so in my bikini, soaking in the heat of the Florida sun. I'm sure he'd have a few choice things to say about me working on my tan instead of showing up. But I needed the day to myself. Plus, it's not like I need to be there for the first few days. It's all physicals, team meetings, and allowing the pitchers and catchers to get acquainted with one another before the entire team shows up next week.

The afternoon sun beats down on my shoulders as I roll over onto my belly and set my laptop in front of me on the plush outdoor lounge, reading over the plans I've spent all day organizing.

They're a pipe dream, a wish list of everything I want to do with the Renegades. They span from ideas on how to build a team of champions, to ways to get our fans excited about coming to the ballpark again. They fill in the holes left behind by my father, who had lofty dreams of making money in the sport he loved. While he was a fan from the day he was born and cherished this organization like it was an extension of his family, that sentiment didn't expand beyond the team. He was still a businessman, and while I completely understand his choices, the Renegades can be so much more. I want to see that happen.

My phone buzzes beside me, two short and one long, and I know before looking who it is.

INDIE: T-minus one month until I see your faces!

LEIGH: Willow's Birthday Palooooooooooza!!!

I roll my eyes and close the laptop screen before pulling myself up to sit cross-legged. I'm so lucky to have Leighton James and Indiana Lewis in my life. They don't ever come out and say it when they message, but this is them checking in on me. Since the crash, they've made sure there isn't a day that goes by that they don't call or text. Always under the guise of something else, never anything of importance, but they always check in, knowing it's something I need so I don't spiral. They ground me, not because I asked, but because that's what best friends do.

A stray thought hits me, and I wonder if Bishop has anyone checking in on him like this. My fingers hover over the button that will take me out of the girls' group text to where a text chain with him still sits. I'm itching to reach out, if only to remind him he's not alone, but then I remember that's not my job. Not anymore.

Another text from the girls comes through, and I force thoughts of Bishop from my head.

INDIE: What's on the agenda this year for birthdaypalooza? Beach? Books? Boys? Oooooh…you think she'll let me sneak into the locker room and get a peek at all those tight asses?

LEIGH: She's not even looking at those tight asses.

INDIE: A shame really.

LEIGH: Right? She's doing a disservice to women everywhere. Come on Willow, share the asses.

INDIE: <GIF of shaking butt>

LEIGH: <GIF of swaying butt>

I roll my eyes with a smile on my face as I reply.

WILLOW: Some of us are trying to work.

Ever since we were in school, we have tried to celebrate our birthdays together. Indie dubbed Birthdaypalooza the week before and after your birthday, all of which is fair game to celebrate. And this year they are going above and beyond to make sure I'm not alone.

INDIE: Work-shmork.

WILLOW: But also, I'm excited you two are coming.

INDIE: Asses Willow! Some of us are surrounded by tiny hands with large attitudes all day, every day. SEND US ASSES.

I chuckle at the visual of my two best friends up to their eyeballs in kids. Neither of them have ever particularly liked children, but in the last year both of them have been thrust into situations where kids rule their lives. Leigh became a mom unexpectedly after a one-night stand, and after the crash, she took over running Renegade Hearts for me. She splits her time in the city and at the camp upstate. Not because she needs to but because, like me, she knows what it's like to lose your parents and believes in our cause with her whole chest.

Indie, on the other hand, is a movie-star-turned-nanny. Well, that's how she describes it anyway. She's in Europe filming her next movie, which apparently is a rom-com set at some ballet boarding school where she is the new teacher, and all the students hate her.

Sounds like my life except replace students with the majority of the Renegade's upper management.

Smiling, I text back my response.

WILLOW: No asses. But I'll have plenty of sun, dirty books and alcohol waiting for you.

INDIE: Sisterhood of the traveling smut!

LEIGH: Bishop really did get it right giving us that name.

INDIE: oooooh Bishop is going to be there, right Wills? How's that going? Is he still being an asshat?

LEIGH: Oh, he's an asshat. An asshat with the face of a brooding alphahole. Holy shit did you see the death glares he gave those reporters when they tried to follow him out of the stadium?

INDIE: Oh fuck. No! Show me!

LEIGH: <sends link to The Foul Line>

INDIE: Tell him you'll kiss that frown off his face if he gets his head out of his ass. He likes when you do that.

WILLOW: <eye roll emoji> Trust me my kisses aren't effective in head-from-ass removal.

LEIGH: WILLOW MAE ARE YOU KISSING BISHOP LAWSON.

Shit. I instantly regret my fingers moving faster than my brain.

It's not that I don't want to tell my best friends about what happened between Bishop and me. I do. Usually, I tell them everything. But Bishop, our night, is something I don't want to let them in on. That moment is ours, and anything they say might taint the beauty in the sorrow I feel. I want to hold on to that. It's mine.

INDIE: Go on…

WILLOW: It's nothing. We kissed. He told me I was a good distraction. End of story.

LEIGH: Start from the beginning.

I begrudgingly recap the story of what happened on the plane, leaving out the part where I was practically grinding on his cock through his pants and the subsequent visit to his hotel room. It's selfish, but I'd rather they continue to see him as somewhat of the villain. It will help my resolve to end things if they aren't pressing me to explore things—hopeless romantics that they are.

INDIE: That fucker. When I get there, I swear he won't know his mouth from his ass because I'll have inverted them myself.

I love fired up Indie, but maybe I took this too far.

WILLOW: Really that's not necessary.

LEIGH: Okay, so he's an asshole, but also, I sort of get it.

INDIE: WTF Leigh?

LEIGH: He's grieving. He lost literally everyone. And flying sucks when you don't have the fresh reminder that your entire team died in a plane crash. Plus, Bishop Lawson has already proved kisses are his only form of distraction. It's par for the course.

INDIE: He's not the only one grieving though. He's taking advantage of our girl and that's a dick move.

LEIGH: I'm not saying he was right in what he did. I hate him for putting Willow through that since we both know she's not over him.

Fuck Leigh and her ability to see right through me.

I fire back.

WILLOW: That's not true.

It's totally true. 100%. No lies detected. But it's over. Time to move on.

LEIGH: <monocle emoji> Are you sure about that? You went out of your way to make sure he had a private jet to get down to Florida.

WILLOW: For the sake of the team.

LEIGH: Uh huh. I see you, Willow Mae.

INDIE: It doesn't change the fact he was an asshat and doesn't deserve your lips, let alone any other part of you.

LEIGH: I'm just saying. I don't think he meant what he said. We say a lot of shit when we're grieving. Remember the summer I shut you guys out after my parents passed? I said some horrible shit.

INDIE: I still haven't forgiven you for the comment you made about my hair being like a lion's mane.

LEIGH: It's a very pretty lion's mane. Brings all the boy lions to the yard.

INDIE: <middle finger emoji>

A weighted sigh escapes me, and I type and retype my response three times before I send it.

WILLOW: I hear you. I really do, but I'm his boss. It doesn't matter what happened in the past, there isn't a future for us.

It's the truth. And I need to hold on to that more than ever. We might have an insane chemistry that transcends the realm of reality, but Bishop and I are two fucked up sides of the same coin at the moment. We each need to figure out how to move forward, and we can't do that together.

INDIE: That's right Willow. Tell him to fuck off and maybe put a laxative in his Gatorade.

LEIGH: <face palm emoji>

WILLOW: I'll take both options into consideration.

LEIGH: Now that we've got that planned out, what dress do I need for the gala? Is there a theme or can I just go balls to the walls whatever makes me feel sexy?

Anxiety coils low in my stomach.

The gala.

It's the one aspect of my work I've been avoiding thinking about. I still have no idea how I'm going to fix the issues with the league gala. Bishop wasn't wrong when he said we were using the children of the victims of the crash. That was Vaughn's plan all along. And what's worse is the board of Renegade Hearts loves the idea. They ran the numbers and partnering with the league has the ability to generate millions for the organization. I'm the only one who sees a problem with it. Maybe because I was one of those kids once upon a time.

After my mom died, there was a period of time my dad didn't know what to do with me. I was shipped off to boarding school. When I came home on breaks, he expected me to continue being a present part of the York name—attending parties and fundraisers with him like before. But it was different. I was no longer Adrianna York's little progeny. I was the girl who lost her mother, and everyone made sure I knew that—with their pitying stares and half-hearted offers of condolences that would segue into questions about how they could get in good with my father. It wasn't until my dad realized I enjoyed spending nights with him at the ballpark more than dressing in frilly dresses that things began to change. I was no longer my mother's daughter but the daughter of Richard York, and no one messed with him.

I can't put these children through that. Especially when none of them have the York name to fall back on.

My phone buzzes again, pulling me from my worries back to my friends.

INDIE: Absolutely go for sexy, Leigh. Lord knows you deserve the night out.

LEIGH: You aren't wrong.

WILLOW: As long as it's formal, whatever you wear will be perfect, I'm sure.

INDIE: I have the perfect dress for you, Wills.

WILLOW: We both know anything you fit in I won't.

Where I am short, soft and all curves, Indie is a six-foot, African American goddess with the body to match.

INDIE: Oh contraire, my voluptuous bestie, this is one from a designer friend of mine and you are going to love it.

WILLOW: You really don't have to do that.

INDIE: It's already done. Think of it as an extra birthday gift.

WILLOW: NO GIFTS. How many times do I have to tell you guys I don't need anything?

LEIGH: Every year until forever.

INDIE: Too bad. It's already done.

WILLOW: I'm not sure if I should be excited or terrified.

LEIGH: Both. Definitely both.

INDIE: loooooooove yoooooooou

WILLOW: Right back at ya. Now I need to get back to work.

INDIE: No, what you need to do is go find yourself a cabana boy and get laid. But work is cool too.

The thought of finding a random hookup makes my skin crawl. But I can't deny that maybe Indie is right. Maybe it's time I put myself back out there. Even if it's only so I don't have to wake up each morning after dreaming of Bishop and help myself with a battery powered boyfriend.

I shake my head and roll onto my back, soaking in the sun on all the bits I keep hidden behind my skirts and power suits. Setting my phone down, I close my eyes and turn my focus back to the list I've created, making a mental note to email it to Nikki, our PR coordinator, with strict instructions to keep it between us but look it over and let me know what she thinks.

It's a lofty goal, but for the first time since taking over the Renegades, I feel like I'm finally on the right path. It's a good feeling to have hope for the future.

CHAPTER ELEVEN
Bishop

I'm a mess.

Annoyed.

And sober.

The last one I could have rectified easily with a trip to the nearest liquor store, but there's a part of me that wants to prove Willow wrong. Also, I made a promise to myself and Lana that I would do better. I only wish it wasn't so fucking hard.

It's been a week, and her words still play over and over in my mind.

"You've changed," I whispered, from between her legs, wiping her arousal from my chin.

She propped herself up and gave me a lopsided smile. "So have you."

"I don't hate it."

"Don't ask me to say the same."

It shouldn't bother me as much as it does. We don't owe each other anything. In fact, I should be livid she decided to insert herself into my life after I walked away on that plane, making it clear I didn't want her.

It's not that you didn't want her, Jackson's voice huffs and I can picture his signature annoyed eye roll.

I bend over and lace up my cleats, ignoring the jab. Mostly because he's not wrong. It's something I've known all along but refuse to give life to. I may have walked away from Willow that day on the courthouse steps, but it was days later that I decided I couldn't face her again.

She'd stood in front of me on what should have been the best day of my life—the day I finally divorced the woman who had made my life hell for a year-and-a-half—and delivered me the news, making it a day that would forever haunt me.

Time stopped.

I froze.

And then I ran.

I was a coward, but I couldn't look at her. I couldn't see beyond the dagger she thrust straight into my chest. It didn't matter that somewhere in the back of my mind I knew she must be hurting too. All I could think about was Phoebe and my team.

The memories after that moment are a bit hazy. My first stop was Jackson's apartment, where I held Phoebe as we both fell apart. I kept her away from the news and the press, protecting the innocence I so desperately wanted her to hang on to. There were phone calls and plans made, but I couldn't tell you what was said.

I ignored every single one of Willow's calls. Her desperate pleas for me to let her know I was okay.

I wasn't.

And as time went on, I realized I never wanted to be in that situation again. I never wanted to lose the people I loved. Which made the solution simple.

Don't love.

Don't feel.

Willow saw right through me on that. She's been the only one to see me because, as much as I don't want to admit it, she's in the same boat. The difference is we have two very different ways of approaching it. It's obvious now that she bottles it up, drowns herself in work and bad decisions, and releases with mind blowing sex while I find the nearest bottle.

Hindsight what it is, her way is much more fun. And surprisingly effective. I've been able to focus on that night. Anytime I find myself starting to spiral, I think of that moment on the bathroom floor. I still hate who she's become, but anytime I want to pick up a bottle from the liquor store up the street from the hotel, I think of sinking into her tight cunt and it's enough of a distraction to stop me.

But today is different.

Today would have been Tommy's thirtieth birthday.

He had big plans to have a funeral celebrating the death of his twenties filled with women, booze, and his best friends. He didn't know I'd be the one attending his funeral four months prior, and when the day came, I'd be the only one left.

I still expect you to celebrate, asshole.

My chest tightens as I glance up at the clubhouse that's slowly filling with my new teammates and the hopeful farm team guys. Over the last week, I've silently watched them from afar as they build a rapport with each other, while I remain haunted by the men who once stood in their place, unable to engage.

"So, you've got a date lined up for right after we're done, and then another in case that one blows up in your face?" One of the rookie catchers—I think his name is Noah Smith, but the guys have taken to calling him Smitty—asks Carson as they join me in the locker room.

Carson Whitmore, our ace pitcher, shrugs with a half-cocked smile. "When you put it like that, it sounds like I'm an asshole. I'm just ensuring that I can share my love with as many as possible on this fine Valentine's Day."

I grind my teeth as I finish lacing up my cleats. I've been so focused on Tommy that I forgot he shares his birthday with the one day I've come to hate.

I didn't always. It was once a holiday my family celebrated with reckless abandon. Growing up in the town of Cupid's Hollow, it was somewhat of a given. Each year there's a festival that spans the entire week of Valentine's Day and culminates with the lover's dance in the town square. There was a time I lived for that dance. I calculated and planned who I would ask to be my date and dreamed of the day I did so with my wife.

It's funny how plans change. The very idea of loving anyone like that makes my skin feel like it's going to break out in hives.

But as different as I am now, some things never change. Like Carson. He's still the same fuckboy he's always been. He might be the best pitcher this league has seen in twenty years, but chasing ass and breaking hearts are synonymous with his reputation.

"What about you, Bishop?" Smitty turns and asks, bouncing on his heels like a puppy wagging its tail. "What are your plans for Singles Awareness Day?"

My brows knit together, and it's on the tip of my tongue to tell him I plan to drink myself stupid so I won't remember the rookie that should be there instead of him, only to wake up tomorrow to be smacked with the reality that he's still not here.

Fuck, Bish, that's a little harsh, don't you think? He's just trying to get to know you, Jackson offers, ever the voice of reason.

You're right, but you'd think after a week of trying he'd have given up, or at the very least, realized I'm not looking to make friends, I reply in my head.

That's not very captainly of you.

We both know there's no official captains in major league baseball, but the sentiment isn't lost. I'm supposed to be the leader on this team. It was a job Jackson and I took on together in previous years. It feels wrong now without him.

Ignoring the rookie and his question, I grab my glove and gear and stand from the bench.

"I'll meet you out there," I say to Carson, who gives a slight nod and turns back to Smitty, murmuring under his breath not to take it personally.

The field is empty when I enter the training facility. Which is just how I like it. Baseball has always been the one thing that calms me and brings me joy. But stepping out into the practice field feels different now. The joy is a bit muted, and the calm is notably more restless. There are a million reasons I can come up with as to why it feels this way, but all of them are excuses. The truth is, I'm not sure this is where I'm supposed to be anymore. I love baseball and the idea of this team, but it doesn't feel like home. My only inkling of hope is playing the game gives me the foothold I need to push through.

I cross the walkway, where press and fans will inevitably line up as the spring training season continues, and enter the dugout. Throwing my gear down, I climb the two steps to the field and squat down, running my fingers through the dirt on the short warning track like Jackson and I do every practice and game. Superstitious fucks that we are. It's our version of saying hello to the fields we call home for nine innings at a time. Or in this case, our spring training home away from home.

My eyes burn with unwanted tears as I try to reconcile how I can hate this place and still love it with every fiber of my being. It's a constant reminder of the people who should be here but aren't, leaving the whole vibe off. Spring training is supposed to be fun. Almost like summer camp where you miss your friends in the off season, but now you're back together again. Only this time, they aren't here.

Tommy won't walk in full of swagger and confidence, and Jackson won't pull his seat out from under him to take him down a peg. Marshall won't blast reggae from his phone, and Fellows won't be there to hype us up before each game with a joke that would make even the most vulgar of us blush.

And yet, I'm supposed to just move on.

For the umpteenth time since arriving in Florida, I shake the memories of my fallen teammates from my mind, knowing if I don't focus there's a good chance I won't make it to opening day.

Maybe I'm not supposed to.

Maybe I'm supposed to move forward with Phoebe, protecting her until Jackson wakes up—because I have to believe he's going to wake up. But then what? What comes next for me?

I hate the thought as soon as it enters my brain, but it's one I keep circling back to. I may love this game, but I've learned the hard way love isn't enough. Not when it can be ripped away in an instant.

Carson slides up next to me, pulling me back to the job at hand. "You know he didn't mean anything by that question."

I sigh and turn to the only guy on this team I can remotely stand to spend more than five minutes with, and that's only because he's my ace pitcher and I have to. "What?"

"Smitty," Carson says, jerking his head back toward the clubhouse. "He's just trying to get to know you."

"I don't need to know him," I quickly bite back, not wanting to have this conversation.

Of course, that doesn't stop Carson.

"He could be your backup."

"And so could any of the other five other catchers still here." It's a harsh thing to say, but I'm not about to invest in anyone that isn't going to be here when the season starts.

That's what spring training is all about. Those who are already signed to the forty-man roster show up to get reacquainted with each other's styles, strengthen rapports, and set our signs and communications so that by the time games start in two weeks we are solid. Then there are those—like Smitty—brought up from the triple-A team. They are trying to impress the suits and slide into the big show. Most of them will get cut long before the season starts. The probability of Noah being one of them is high, especially considering there's some jackass currently riding the roster as my backup.

Sure, that's it.

I wince internally. I'm not sure how I'm going to make it with these jackasses in my head. They've had infinitely more to say now that I'm surrounded by the spaces I shared with them. And usually, it's calling me out on my bullshit.

That's because we know you want to do better.

I don't dignify the sentiment with a response.

Carson's eyes narrow, like he's trying to figure out if I'm serious. He runs an aggravated hand through his hair and sighs. "Okay then. You ready?"

"No" is on the tip of my tongue, but I shove it down and grab my gear from the bench and follow him onto the field. We go through the song and dance of stretching before starting with a simple game of catch as the rest of the guys trickle out of the clubhouse and do the same.

Everyone pairs off, mirroring Carson and me, but it's not like previous years where camaraderie flowed like beer on St. Patrick's Day. There's not an ounce of celebration or excitement in the air. Even after a week, it's every man for himself. The veteran players need to solidify their status on the team while the rookies make sure one slip up doesn't cost them their chance. Every day is a damn dog and pony show.

I throw the ball back to Carson harder than I need to.

"You okay, Bish?" he asks.

"Fine," I snap, jerking up my glove to provide him with a target.

His brows raise, proving I'm not fooling anyone here. "You sure? You just about took my hand off."

"Just throw the damn ball, Carson," I sigh.

We throw a few more warm up tosses and then slide over to the row of mounds where I squat behind a plate to catch Carson's pitches. I ignore the way my knee clicks and the burn of my thighs and calves, silently berating myself for not putting in the work during the off season. I may have been in the gym a few times a week, but I was more focused on pain and forgetting than I was on properly stretching. Now I'm paying the price.

We work on calls, signs, and techniques with the pitching staff and I'm thankful he's currently set to be our ace. He's exactly what this team needs. He might present himself as the class clown, but he's focused, adaptable, and easily one of the best pitchers in the league. I still have no idea how his name ended up on the list of draftees, because there is no way Atlanta didn't put up a hell of a fight to keep him. Though given the way the rest of these guys on the field are showing off for the staff, he's going to have a run for his money to keep his place at the top. They may not be my Renegades, but we've got a solid bullpen.

I slip my hand between my legs and Carson reads my sign. To his credit, he throws a perfect sinker, but instead of framing it, I flinch and the ball slips from my glove, hitting the dirt and rolling behind me.

A string of muttered curses slips free as I flip my mask off and pop up to field the ball. It's a rookie mistake and not the first one I've made since we slid over.

Carson shakes his head and starts toward me as I bend over and reach for the ball. If the way his brows are furrowed tells me anything, this will either be hilarious or end with my fist in his face. It's really a toss-up.

Carson tugs his glove from his hand and stows it under his arm, his free hand finding his hip. "You gonna tell me what the fuck is going on with you?"

Okay, so we're going with fists.

I stand up and offer him the ball, ignoring his comment. Mostly because this is a man who I respect a hell of a lot, and what I'm going through is none of his damn business.

"Get back on the mound, Whitmore."

He takes the ball and puts his hands up in surrender. "Listen, I know it's our first week back, but even I can see you aren't okay."

My jaw tightens and I grind my teeth as I grit out, "Drop it, Carson."

Hearing the lack of humor in my tone, he backs away and slips his glove back on, throwing the ball into the pocket a few times. "Fine. But I didn't come here to lose."

"What's that supposed to mean?"

Carson glares at me, making sure I know I'm the problem. "All I'm saying is I didn't work every back door deal to make it to this team in order to lose."

My mind works to process his words. Backdoor deals? When it clicks, my brows reach my hairline. "You volunteered for this?"

He narrows his gaze, but the smirk that paints his lips is one of a kid getting away with pulling one over on his parents. "Is that so hard to believe?"

"Why?"

"Get your head out of your ass and I'll tell you." Carson turns away from me and the mound and starts toward the opposite end of the practice field. "I'm going to throw with Smitty for a bit. Let me know if you want to talk or need help dislodging your head so we can get on the same page."

My mouth drops open slightly, but I catch myself and press my lips together into a tight line as he leaves me standing there like an idiot. He's drawing a line in the sand, and I can't blame him. As our starting pitcher, he deserves someone who can meet his level of dedication to this team and right now, that's not me.

Unfortunately for me, his actions will reflect who he believes should be behind the plate.

Fuck.

Do better. Jackson adds salt to the wound.

My gaze follows Carson as he joins a circle of pitchers and catchers standing at the opposite end of the practice field. They welcome him with open arms, but that's not what adds insult to injury. As they part to let him join the group, I catch a glimpse of the person they're surrounding, laughing like they're old pals.

Standing there in another one of her cock teasing skirts—this one in charcoal gray—and with her bouncing curls tied up in a pony is Willow.

She hasn't made much of a presence at the field over the last week, but the few times she has stopped by, she's made it a point to spend at least five to ten minutes chatting with the team. They flock to her, even the married guys. And not in a creepy or sexual way—those stares are reserved for me and me alone. They just can't help but be pulled into her vortex of infectious positivity.

Everyone except me. I keep my distance.

Every once in a while, I see her stolen glances in my direction. The trepidation in her eyes, not knowing if she should approach me or not. I know she's waiting for me to make the first move.

"Lawson," Graham yells from the dugout, and I look over my shoulder to where he's chatting with Ignacio Perez, our pitching coach. He tips his head, calling me over.

By the time I enter the dugout, Ignacio has stepped onto the field, leaving me to chat with our field manager alone.

Graham spits sunflower seeds on to the dirt and levels his gaze on me. "You haven't completed your physicals."

In any other situation, I'd force the innocent smile that has gotten me off the hook more times than I care to admit, but I was expecting this conversation sooner or later. So instead, I offer a half-hearted lift of my shoulders. "I did most of them."

Graham's stony gaze doesn't waver. "Most isn't all."

There isn't any doubt my astute field manager is talking about my session with the team therapist. It's not something I wanted to do on my first day back at spring training. Hell, it's not something I wanted to do, period. Which is why I have been putting it off every day since.

Every other season I've had no problem with the preseason check-in to make sure players are good to go mentally. This season, I'm not, and I don't need someone to tell me so. My own therapist already fired me, saying I needed a grief specialist to unpack all the trauma from the crash after she struggled to find a path to help me back to who I was before.

I was more than okay with agreeing to find someone else. Because what if that's not who I'm meant to be? She knew me when I was searching for love in all the wrong places, giving it to anyone and everyone because I saw the world with the rose-tinted glasses of a hopeless romantic. I don't think I can go back to that. I need someone who is going to help me navigate the future, not just the past.

But I can't say that without calling into question if I should be on the field to begin with. Baseball is the only thing giving me a hint of normalcy. If I lose that, I'm a goner.

However, if there's anyone aside from Willow who can smell my bullshit, it's Graham. He's had a front row seat to every one of my fuckups and isn't going to let me skate by without checking every single one of the boxes I need to be cleared. He wants me on that field as much as I want to be there. He said as much to me after our first team meeting.

Graham sighs and lifts his hand, running it along the back of his neck. "Listen, I hate this as much as you do, but you've got two choices. Get your ass inside and finish your physicals, including a stop at mental health, or ride the bench."

The fact I knew it was coming doesn't do anything to soothe the way my chest tightens as the weight of his words hit home.

This is the moment I've dreaded. From here on out, it's all or nothing.

My jaw tightens, and I nod.

"Good. Hit the showers. They're expecting you."

I pause and look out over the field at the men who are supposed to replace the ghosts that loom forever in my mind. Guilt washes over me.

All or nothing.

Do better.

The mantra's echo one after another.

Something has to change. This team doesn't deserve this from me, but neither does the team that left me behind. I'm at a loss on how to honor them and still manage to move on.

Then again, maybe Willow was right. Maybe moving on isn't the answer.

Just before I exit the field, I look up and my eyes connect with the woman whose wisdom haunts me. She's looking at me with every ounce of confidence she did in my hotel room, and I remind myself she's not here for me or to pick up the pieces I leave in my wake.

Fuck off, Bishop. We both know that's not true, the birthday boy sounds off. *She loves this team, but she showed up for you when you needed her. Every. Single. Time.*

Fuck.

She's the answer.

The second the thought crosses my mind, I know I should squash it and go see the damn therapist. But now that it's grown talons and lodged itself in my chest, I won't be able to think straight until I let it work itself out.

Willow is the only person who has made me feel anything more than pain, anger, or grief in the last four and a half months.

I called her a distraction, which she is, and that's all she should be. But the way time stopped when I kissed her—fucked her—has lived in that space rent free all week. What if I could stay there? Where every other emotion doesn't touch me. Maybe then I could focus and be present for this team just long enough to work out how to make it my future.

It's a crazy thought, but maybe crazy is what I need to get me through this. Nothing else has worked, and while seeing a therapist is absolutely the better option, I don't have the time to wade through the bullshit and be okay.

Opening day is right around the corner, and as much as I feel like I'm on the verge of needing to walk away, it's not something I'm willing to do without putting up a fight. I owe it to myself. I owe it to Phoebe. I owe it to my team.

Dead and alive.

I'm not naïve enough to believe this is a long-term solution. Someday I'll have to face my demons. But today isn't that day.

At least this time when I fuck up, I'm going to enjoy every minute of going down in flames.

Now, I need to see a woman about a plan.

CHAPTER TWELVE
Willow

"What do you mean he didn't speak to the team therapist?" I snap, as I try to focus on not poking my eye with my mascara wand.

Graham mutters a curse I can barely make through the speakerphone. "I mean, I told him to show up to the appointment or ride the bench. He then proceeded to show up, but he didn't say a damn word to her for the entire hour."

Freaking Bishop. I'm not sure if I want to be impressed with his malicious compliance or throw my phone at his head.

I really thought we'd turned a corner in the last week. While I've witnessed firsthand the distance he keeps between him and any of the other guys on the team, at least he wasn't showing up drunk or getting into trouble at the hotel.

We should be celebrating the baby steps but the league, or should I say Vaughn, waits for no one and not taking his therapy session seriously is absolutely something they would use against Bishop as grounds to trade him.

"I'll talk to him," I muse as I put the finishing touches on my face and run my fingers through the blonde curls I spent the last hour perfecting.

I don't know why I'm trying so hard. It's not like I expect this date to go anywhere. It was a mistake made in a moment of manic bravery when Indie asked me if I wanted her to add me to an elite dating app for celebrities. I'm not foolish enough to believe I'm anyone important, but the NDAs and privacy put my mind at ease, and I was feeling particularly alone that night.

Plus, it's time I get back on the horse. I might not be ready to let go of Bishop completely, but that doesn't mean I need to spend my nights alone with copious amounts of popcorn and reading about the love I wish I could find. Not to mention I could use the distraction. Especially after the five rounds I went with the board today, trying to get them to reconsider partnering with the league for the gala.

"Are you sure? You don't need to get involved." My uncle tries to reassure me, but he's wrong. I do.

Bishop doesn't trust anyone, least of all me, but we have a history. We might have only shared a few nights, but those evenings were filled with talk of nothing and everything between the rounds of downright filthy sex. He gave me a part of him that he gives to no one else. Just like he did a week ago. He'll hate every minute of my meddling, but my gut is telling me if there's anyone he'll listen to, it's me. I'm just sorry it took me months to realize it. Maybe if I had tried harder sooner, we wouldn't be here.

I just need to reiterate we're talking as owner and player and nothing more.

"I'll get through to him," I vow, smoothing down the hem of my beaded designer dress and picking my phone from the bathroom counter. "I'll be at the stadium tomorrow to welcome the rest of the team. Send him up to my office after morning work."

The doorbell echoes through the house loud enough that I can hear it from my bedroom in the back.

"You have company?" Graham asks, but the curiosity in his voice lets me know it's my uncle asking, not my field manager.

My eyes dart around the room, looking for the torture devices, also known as heels, that match the purple beading of my dress. "I'm going on a date tonight."

"I didn't know you were seeing anyone." His tone makes my heart stutter. It's the same one my father used to take with me when I would conveniently leave out details about my life he thought he deserved to know. He'd furrow his brow and give me a stern yet sing songy, "Willow Mae." And I'd melt and tell him everything. Because where my mother never learned to value my presence as more than a weapon to control, my father eventually took the time to care. He put in the work.

Tears burn the corners of my eyes. God, I miss him.

Slipping down to the mattress of my bed, I slide my feet into the heels and make quick work of the buckles, and I shake my head like both Graham and my father can see me rolling my eyes. "I'm not seeing anyone. It's a first date."

"On Valentine's Day?" Graham scoffs. "Ballsy of him."

My mouth drops open. I hadn't even realized that was today. My mind has been so wrapped up in plans for both the team and Renegade Hearts that I didn't make the connection. However, Shepherd's comment on the field about needing to send flowers to his wife makes a hell of a lot more sense now.

I roll my eyes. "It's just a day."

"Alright but let me know that you made it home safe."

"I'll see you tomorrow, Graham," I sass playfully to cover the way my lip trembles at the way he cares.

"Wills," he replies sternly.

"I'll let you know."

"Thank you. I know I'm not your father, but he'll haunt me if I don't keep an eye on you."

"Thanks, Graham."

"Have fun," he says before ending the call.

My phone screen jumps back to the dating app that was open before Graham called and shows the altogether too wholesome Hank, 35, CEO of Johnstons Enterprises. I'd been contemplating for the hundredth time if I should just cancel. Sure, I'd be the bitch who did so on Valentine's Day of all days, but I'm second-guessing if I can paste a smile on my face through a five-star Michelin dinner and pretend I'm the society sweetheart-turned-baseball-team-owner this man expects me to be.

But it's a step in the right direction, I remind myself. A step toward healing. And that's the only thing that has me inhaling a steady breath and moving toward the door despite my shaky hands.

I check my hair one last time in the mirror in the entryway and ignore the way the clicking of my heels against the hardwood reminds me of a ticking clock.

I can do this.

For me.

Lips turned upward in an award-winning smile, I swing open the heavy door, ready for what the night will bring.

Only it's not Hank staring back at me with flowers or some other stereotypical first date item in hand. Instead, I'm greeted by the last person I expected to show up on my doorstep.

"Hi," Bishop mutters, his eyes roaming freely over my done-up form, lingering on every curve a moment longer than is appropriate for a man who wants nothing to do with me. "I—are you going somewhere?"

My mouth hangs open, mimicking a fish out of water as I look him over, making sure he's okay. His eyes are clear, and he doesn't reek of booze. I'm fairly certain he's not drunk. He isn't bleeding and there isn't a police officer escorting him to my door. So, that rules out a fight. Which means there is no good reason for him to be standing here.

Eyes narrowed, my hands find my hips. "What are you doing here?"

"I—" He runs a hand through his dark chestnut hair. Something I've learned he does when he needs a moment to think. "I needed to talk to you."

I'm torn between being angry and welcoming him inside. It's the blurry line between head and heart, but I made a vow to say goodbye and as much as there's a part of me that wants to let him back in, I can't.

"Then make an appointment. You don't get to just show up here unannounced." I look past him to make sure my actual date isn't about to stroll up to find me on the porch with another man. "How did you even get past the gate?"

A wicked smile curves his mouth. "You really should change the code more often."

The thought never crossed my mind that he'd remember the code given to guests of the party last year. Normally it would've been changed after the event, but Dad must not have done so, and I didn't even think twice to change it when I arrived since I have a key card that lets me through the gates.

"Where are you going dressed like that?" he asks again, a hit of agitation in his tone.

I run my hands over the front of my dress, mostly to distract myself, so my words come out steady. "Not that it's any of your business, but I have a date tonight."

Bishop scoffs. "On Valentine's Day?"

I throw my hands up and let them fall. "Why does everyone keep saying that? It's not like the day changes anything. It's a made-up holiday for greeting card companies and restaurants everywhere to make a buck."

Bishop's lips draw back in a snarl, jaw tight, and his eyes darken. "Cancel it," he demands.

"What?" I heard what he said, but I need him to repeat it one more time because it sounded like he just asked me to cancel my date, and I know damn well he doesn't give a shit about me enough nor does he have the right to demand such things.

His eyes narrow, and he lets out a low growl as he steps forward so that I have to crane my neck if I want to meet his stare. Which I do.

"Cancel the damn date," he says again.

I keep my eyes locked on him in an act of defiance. "Why would I do that?"

My words come out harsh, despite the fact he's giving me the out I've wanted since I agreed to the damn date. I wanted to prove I could do it, not because I actually wanted to go. But now that he doesn't want me to, I'm pretty sure I'll go. Just because the petty is real, and he needs to know he can't expect me to say "how high" when he says "jump".

"I need to talk to you."

Digging my heels in, I double down. "You've said that. It can wait until tomorrow at the stadium."

I grip the door and start to close it when he suddenly stammers, "It's not a baseball thing."

That makes me pause, and my heart races in my chest, worry making its way to the forefront. "Is everything okay?"

Bishop sighs and I can see the anxiety etched on his face. "Yes, now cancel the date."

A piece of me aches to see him distressed, but I can't play this game with him. "You don't get to just waltz in here and demand that I cancel a date or listen to what you have to say. Not anymore."

I try to close the door again, and this time his hand juts out, stopping me. "Just one night," he mumbles.

Is he seriously throwing those words in my face? What the hell does he hope to accomplish? I huff a sardonic laugh. "Oh no, that ship sailed last week. I told you it was goodbye."

Bishop dips his head, and I stare up into the disarming eyes I once fell for. He takes another step forward, closing the distance between us.

My breath catches in my lungs when his chest brushes against mine. This close, I can see the stubble he's let grow to the point it's borderline beard. The tiny scar at the corner of his eye I've never asked about. The perfect curve of his lips I so badly want to taste again. He's too close for what would be considered appropriate for player and owner. And yet, ever the masochist of my own heart, I can't will my feet to move.

Say something. Anything that will shut this damn door.

"Bishop, I—"

"I'm here asking for help." He breathes like it's the hardest thing he's ever had to do. "Please invite me in and hear me out, and for the love of fucking God, cancel your date."

"You're an ass," I mutter, knowing damn well I'm not about to say no to him. "You told me I shouldn't use our past against you, and here you are doing the same thing."

"I'm aware," he replies, "but turnabout's fair play."

He's right. I did the exact same thing when I showed up at his hotel room to extract closure of my own. I hadn't meant for it to go the way it did, but it doesn't change the fact we used our history and each other to get what we wanted.

But it was supposed to end there.

Absolutely nothing good can come from this conversation. I've spent the last week keeping my distance and allowing him to do the same. I'm navigating the road to healing my heart and trying to move on by focusing on what comes next.

He can't be a part of that.

But he's here, doing the work and asking for help. He's making the first move of what I can only hope is allowing himself to do some healing of his own. Which is why I step back and extend my arm, granting him entrance. "Fine, but if we're about to talk about this. I need to change into some comfy clothes and make myself a gin and soda."

Bishop lets out a sigh of relief and gives me a lopsided grin. "Lead the way and don't lose the dress."

"Don't push your luck."

CHAPTER THIRTEEN
Bishop

The house is exactly as I remember it. Pristine. It reeks of money, excellence, and the kind of perfection those with a big bank account love to flaunt. I remember thinking it was completely unlike Willow the first time I visited. Now I'm not so sure.

She's shown me she's not everything I feared she'd become, but I'm not entirely ready to let my guard down. Not that it matters. Not for what I need from her.

What I hope she needs from me too.

Willow led me to her father's office and left me to wait while she changed out of the stunning off the shoulder purple dress and heels she greeted me in. It accentuated every single one of her sinful curves and left my dick twitching in my pants. That is until she told me it was for another man.

It's not that I'm jealous.

Okay, that's a lie. I am. But only because if she's shackled to another man, there's no way she can do what I'm about to ask her. It's jealousy by necessity.

Whatever you need to tell yourself to sleep at night.

Fuck. I don't need my jackass teammates in my head right now. Not when I know what I'm about to ask is a fucked-up drive into left-center. But I'm desperate for a little control over my life, and this might just be the answer to gaining it.

My eyes drift, taking in the room. It's impersonal and cold, and not what I expected from our warmhearted former owner, but it sets a precedent. One I'm sure Willow was aware of when she chose it for the setting of our conversation. I was hoping for the comfy sectional in the living room, but wish in one hand and want in the other.

The large mahogany desk looms in front of a wall of bookshelves that holds various law texts and baseball memorabilia. Adjacent to the desk, floor-to-ceiling windows overlook the setting sun on a private beach. The same private beach that each of the monstrous houses in this community boasts. I might be a professional baseball player with a multi-million-dollar contract, but this is more than even I could imagine. I keep scanning until my gaze lands on the bar cart in the corner.

Bingo.

Willow had the right idea. Drinks are going to be necessary. At least for her. I can't allow myself to indulge. If I do, I might not want to stop and I need to keep my wits about me.

See? I'm trying to do better.

I make quick work of pouring Willow a gin and soda with a twist of lime just the way she likes it.

When I've finished, a binder, tucked between the glass shaker and the lip of the drink cart, catches my eye. The leather is worn, a stark contrast to the perfection that drips from every surface in this room.

I'm not usually one to snoop, but curiosity gets the better of me. What could be so unimportant for the immaculate Richard York to leave out for anyone to find? My gaze darts toward the door to make sure Willow isn't standing there before I pick it up and carefully work the zipper around the edge.

I don't know what I expect to find, but it definitely isn't pages upon pages of baseball cards—rare ones at that.

My mouth drops open. It's the kind of collection any kid would dream of. Hell, any adult would too. There was a time I collected cards like these, but growing up in a house of eleven, expensive baseball cards weren't exactly a reasonable expectation to show up under the tree.

"Starting without me?" Her voice is hesitant but playful, and I hope that will carry over to the conversation we're about to have. I need this to go well. If it doesn't, I'm not sure how I'm going to make it through the coming weeks.

With one hand, I clutch the binder to my chest, like a kid who's just been caught red-handed, and I pick up the gin and soda I made for her as a peace offering.

I glance up to where Willow stands in the doorframe in leggings and an oversized Renegades sweatshirt. Her hair is no longer down, instead she's pulled it up into a messy knot on the top of her head with a few stray curls framing her face. It's a good look on her. Relaxed. Dangerously so. It's almost like by dressing down she's taken off the mask of being an owner for this conversation. And while that's the girl I remember, the girl I once started falling for, I have to remind myself that isn't who we are anymore. What I have to say won't change that. It can't.

"Just making sure you have what you need," I say, lifting the gin and soda in her direction. It's not a complete lie.

She raises a brow, and I understand the skeptical line she's pressed her lips into. I've given her every reason to question my motives.

Willow closes the space between us and takes the drink from my hand, her eyes zeroing in on the binder.

"Am I drinking alone?" she asks at the same time I say, "Are these real?"

I chuckle. "Yes. I'm taking a break from alcohol."

Her brow raises even higher, but she doesn't pry.

I let the binder fall open in my hands once more and run my fingers over the rare cards, and for a moment I almost pull them back because I have no doubt these should be in a museum. "You know what this is, right?"

Willow leans over and looks at the card I'm pointing at. She huffs a laugh. "Yes, I'm aware. It's a 1948 Leaf #79 Jackie Robinson rookie card."

My eyes go wide at the same time my cock takes notice. It's incredibly hot she's able to rattle off the card's name in its entirety. "So, you know what one of these is worth?"

"More than one with your face on it." She smirks and lifts her drink to her mouth, moaning as the alcohol coats her throat.

The sound is a flashback to the night in my hotel room and is like a lightning bolt to my dick. I shift my weight to hide the evidence of my blood rushing south behind the bar cart.

"Am I in here?" I tease, brow raised as I turn the page and marvel at each of the cards.

"Not a chance."

I bring my hand to my chest in mock hurt, loving the way her lips tip up in a lively smile. "I suppose even without my presence, this collection is incredible."

"Thank you."

"Were they your father's?"

Surprise smacks me in the face when her face falls and her gaze darts to the floor. "They're mine."

"Because you inherited them?"

Her jaw tightens, making me painfully aware I've said the wrong thing. "No, they've always been mine."

My mouth gapes, and she laughs. This time it's genuine. Something I haven't heard from her in some time.

"Is that such a surprise?"

"Sort of," I admit.

"Of course. I couldn't possibly know a thing about baseball, right?"

"I know you better than that." She knows the game better than anyone gives her credit for, and now that I think about it, so many of the conversations we've had tangled in each other's arms about stats and baseball history make more sense.

Her face scrunches, but she doesn't elaborate. "Now that you've satisfied your curiosity, can we move on?"

Willow turns her back on me and pads toward the desk, but I'm not ready to move on just yet. There's more to this story, and even though I promised myself I wouldn't push this beyond what I'm here for, I can't help but want to know more.

When I don't immediately follow her, she halts her steps and looks over her shoulder.

I shake my head. "Not until you tell me why you have these."

She sighs and rolls her eyes, and for a split second, I think she's going to tell me to fuck off. Which she's well within her rights to do. Instead, like always, she surprises me. "My father got me some every year for my birthday. First it was guys from the Renegades. Then from every team in the league. Soon we bonded over finding rare cards. Happy?"

No. Not even close.

Mostly because I am trying to reconcile how it's possible she can be both the woman who frustrates the living shit out of me with her calculated behavior and still be the innocent woman I met on a balcony.

I set the binder down on the bar cart and take a step forward, following as she continues toward the desk. She turns and leans against the front, gesturing for me to sit. As much as I'd rather stand, I choose to pick my battles and lower myself onto the plush leather Chesterfield chair. She looks down at me, and I can't shake the feeling that I'm about to be scolded in the principal's office.

Hell, maybe I am.

Willow takes a long pull from her glass, downing half its contents before setting it on the desk beside her. "What did you need to talk to me about?"

I swallow hard and my hand itches to tug at my hair, but I don't want her to pick up on my nerves, so I fist the fabric of my jeans instead. "It's not so much a talk as a proposition."

My eyes don't dare leave her face, searching for any hint of trepidation. But if she's surprised, her poker face doesn't let on and I'm hit with the realization that this is how she operates with the league.

With me, her eyes have always been a window to her soul, just as they were moments ago talking about those damn baseball cards. Right now, she's on the defense, and instead of allowing me access, she's hiding all the bits she feels like she needs to protect.

I shouldn't hate it as much as I do.

Willow nods. "I'm listening."

I want to tell her I don't want the business side of her, but the truth is, that's what I need. She's right to keep me at arm's length.

With this in mind, I relax my shoulders and come out with it. "I…I want another night."

She starts to say "no" at the same time I force "hear me out" from my lips.

"Fine," Willow grits out and crosses her arms across her chest.

"Last Sunday night was exactly what I needed to get through the next day. What you said, about not feeling, you were right. Sometimes it's not about moving on, it's about learning to live. And that night I felt alive."

She drops her hands to the side of the desk to hold her weight as she leans back and crosses her legs in front of her. "So, what are you asking me for?"

"I'm asking you to make my days easier."

Her stone facade cracks, and she closes her eyes, shutting me out. "I can't heal you, Bishop," she whispers, her voice strangled.

Can't. Not won't.

For fuck's sake, that's what you heard?

Leave me the fuck alone, I chastise my teammates. *You aren't here and I'm fucking trying.*

"I'm not asking you to heal me."

Willow's eyes pop open, and what once were stony pools of blue are now a raging storm. "No, you're asking me to let you use me."

"No. Fuck. This is coming out all wrong. To be honest, it made a lot more sense in my head." I run a hand through my hair, and I regret not making myself a glass of scotch. "It's crazy. I know that, but I'm desperate. I can't lose baseball, and I can't—talking isn't something I want to do. I need action. Something tangible."

"So, fucking the grief away is your answer? For how long? How long does that last?" Willow pushes off the desk and stands in front of me, her knees now inches from mine. "I gave you one night. I gave you your distraction. All I'm hearing is you, you, you. You think you're the only one who's desperate to run from these feelings? Well, let me tell you, Bishop Lawson, you're not. You don't own the cornerstone on grief. Some of us don't get the luxury of falling apart and coming up with half-cocked ideas to cope. Some of us only get the fleeting moments and then have to get up every morning, and put on our big girl panties, and figure out how the hell we're going to make something of nothing, knowing damn well we're going to hate ourselves for the bullshit games we have to play. Some of us have to learn to live while playing with one hand tied behind our back. When are you going to realize—" Her eyes go wide, matching my own. Except where I'm stunned into silence, she's choking on the tears streaming down her face.

I haven't seen her lose it like this since the morning she showed up on those courthouse steps. Even then, she held it together. First for me, and then for the team when that reporter showed up. Then on the plane, when her panic was as palpable as the air at thirty-thousand feet, she managed to keep it together enough to help me.

Fuck, I'm an idiot.

No shit, Jackson whispers, but I can't focus on him. Not when Willow has actively let her wall down in front of me.

"Fuck. I'm sorry," she stammers, her curse hitting me like a freight train. "I shouldn't be taking this out on you. It's just been a rough day."

She makes a move to step back, but I grab her wrist, keeping her in front of me. Her eyes dart to my fingers and then back to mine, and I give her a pointed look.

"Do you want to talk about it?"

Willow huffs a laugh. "With you?"

"We used to talk before," I say with a sheepish shrug, remembering all the hopes and dreams we shared under the umbrella of orgasms and stolen moments.

She yanks her arm and turns away, her eyes locked on the wood floor worn into what looks like a path from pacing. "Pillow talk with you is barely an almost when it comes to talking."

Hurt aches in my chest, accompanied by the spider web of grief—tangling, suffocating me with every passing moment. "I gave you a piece of me on those nights."

I did. Before our lives were upended, I gave her more than I gave most because I still had hope.

"And I treasured it." Willow scoffs, not bothering to hide her own hurt any longer. "Can you say the same?"

I want to say I did, I do, but my actions since then won't let me. Lost in my own emotions, I've failed her on every front since the crash.

The question is, what are you going to do about it now?

I suck in a gasp at the new voice making an appearance in my head. It's Norah. She was always the voice of reason. The person who never shied away from asking the hard questions. I suppose in death it wouldn't be any different. But I don't have an answer for her. I came here with a plan and even though it now seems half thought out, the weight of it still holds true.

One night wasn't enough to distract us—me—for more than a week. And I get the feeling it's the same for Willow. She wasn't joking in the hotel when she said she needed it as much as I did. She's not keeping it together—she's falling apart—and even though there's every reason we shouldn't do it together, I want to look past every single one.

I slide to the edge of the chair and rest my forearms on my thighs, looking up at where Willow stands. "Let me ask you this. Was your day better or worse after last Sunday night?"

Even though she still won't face me completely, her eyes slowly track to meet mine. I love that with her walls down, I can see her mind working as she chews on the question. She opens her mouth then closes it, repeating the movement once, then twice.

"Don't lie to me now, Willow. What's your gut say."

She lets out a sigh that feels a lot like she's trying to rebuild those walls. "That's not the point. I shouldn't have lost it on you like that. It's unprofessional at best and—"

My words cut off her nervous ramble. "Because me showing up here and asking to fuck the grief away is all sorts of professional."

Her shoulders slump forward and her curls sway as she shakes her head.

"Willow." Her name is a plea on my lips.

She throws her arms up and turns back to face me. "Okay, fine. It was better. Better than I've felt in a long time."

"Like you could breathe again. Conquer the shit you've been avoiding."

"Yes."

Moving slowly, so as not to spook her, I stand and take a step forward. Her head tips back to meet my gaze, and I can't stop my eyes from darting to where her tongue slips out, wetting painted red lips.

Her eyes track my movement and she sucks in a breath, letting me know she's just as affected as I am.

I raise my eyes to her sparkling blue ones and will her to hear, not only my desperation, but the plea to let me help her. "So, why wouldn't we try to feel like that again?"

Her eyes search mine. "Is this what you've been thinking about for the last week?"

"Among other things." It's a lie. I've only had the idea for the past seven hours. Which were spent pacing my hotel room trying to work up the courage to show up on her doorstep.

"We can't."

"Why not?"

"It's wrong."

"Says who?" I counter.

Uncertainty flashes across her eyes for a moment before she speaks. "I'm your boss, for one. And we—we'd just be scratching an itch."

"One that needs scratching."

"It's not real."

"It doesn't have to be if it helps us learn to live again."

Willow breaks her stare and glances at the window before taking a step back, which I allow. I might be willing to beg, but if she really doesn't want this, I'll walk away and respect her wishes. She turns back to the desk and reaches for her glass. Finishing off her drink, a weary silence fills the space between us.

I wish I knew what she was thinking, but I don't have it in me to ask, especially if it's all the reasons why we shouldn't. I know them. I've gone over them a thousand times, and I keep coming back to her words—don't move on, learn to live. I don't know the woman standing in front of me. Not like I used to. But I know there's some part of her that wants the same thing I do. She wants to live.

"I'm going to go," I say softly, causing her eyes to snap in my direction.

Her face is drenched in a mix of apprehension and guilt, but I could swear I see a hint of longing as well.

"If, and I do mean if, I consider this, what would it look like?"

I breathe a sigh of relief and answer honestly. "Whatever you want it to look like."

"Can I think about it?"

I nod. "Of course. Take all the time you need."

Willow presses her lips into a thin line and returns with a nod of her own, though her eyes tell me there's plenty she wants to say.

It's probably best to quit while I'm ahead. She might not have said yes, but she didn't say no and for now I'll take the win. Because if she does say no, I'm not sure what comes next for me. I don't want to fall back into alcohol and fights. I need to do better, not only for myself, but I'm not sure I can make it through on my own.

With that somber thought, I turn on my heel and head for the door.

I'm a little surprised when Willow doesn't follow me out like the good host I know her mother raised her to be, but it's probably for the best. If she did, I'm not sure I could stop myself from saying the one thing I should have. The one thing I owe her, but I'm not ready to give.

My apology.

CHAPTER FOURTEEN
Willow

My heels click with every step as I head down to the clubhouse. This morning is the meeting to kick off spring training with the entire team and my first time addressing the guys all together. Mentally, I go over all the things I want to say to them, the hope I want to instill within them. I've seen the stats for our team, and contrary to the reports that we were given, the castoffs from every team in the league, we've got a strong lineup. We might not make the playoffs the first season out, but we have a real shot at becoming a team to be reckoned with. That is, if we can get our shit together and play as a team.

Just another reason to give Bishop the distraction he needs to step up and be the leader I know he is.

Shit. A swarm of drunk bees takes flight in my stomach at the thought of seeing him.

My thoughts always come back to him. He might have left before the sun went down, but I spent the majority of the night with him on my mind. First trying to wrap my brain around what he'd asked me to consider, then trying to convince myself it's a terrible freaking idea.

I can easily make a case for saying yes. If only for him and what I know he's capable of. Because if he'd let go and allow himself to forge meaningful connections with this team, he'd be unstoppable. He needs them.

But what about me?

One day ruined our lives and changed us forever. Until yesterday, I haven't let myself even remotely fall apart. Not because I haven't wanted to, but because as a York, failure is not an option.

Once upon a time, that belief was challenged by Bishop. We might have only been a series of one-night stands, but in so many ways, he became the fleeting person I could let my guard down with. My safe place. Maybe that's why it was so easy to word vomit everything like I'd come down with a bad stomach bug. And he took it and held it safe. He didn't push or throw it back in my face like I thought he would.

Now he's asking me to be that person for him. He's asking me to hold his grief and distract him for more than just one night.

And I'm stuck warring between giving in and standing my ground.

On the one hand, it's a terrible idea. Not only am I his boss, but I'm not sure I can separate the feelings that are twisted up in him. He might see this as nothing more than a continuation of our one-night stands, but that ship sailed for me. I meant it when I said the last time was goodbye.

But just like with every argument, there's a flip side. In my case, it's the incessant hope that often gets me into trouble. He was right when he said this could be the thing we both need. I could stop living from low to low and live in the high that followed my last night with him.

I halt my steps in the middle of the stadium corridor outside Graham's office, when my eyes catch a glimmer of where my father's favorite quote is engraved on a silver plaque.

Success is in whatever you're avoiding.

I can't stop the sardonic laugh that bubbles in my throat. I don't think Bishop is what my father had in mind, but there's something to be said for it.

My eyes well with tears, and just like always, I blink them away. It does nothing for the ache in my chest.

My father should be here.

If he was, I wouldn't be. If he was, Bishop and I might've found common ground long ago, and far beyond just one night.

If.

Always if.

If we do this.

If we learn to live.

We can't live in ifs.

Nope. Not going there. I need to focus.

I knock on the door to Graham's office and poke my head in, praying he's already there so I can stop myself from continuing to spiral in my thoughts. "Good morning."

Thankfully, he's sitting at his desk buried under a mountain of paperwork, mostly notes from his staff, if I had to guess. I've told him more than once he needs to get with the times and move to a digital process, but he insists the information is more in depth when a person is forced to put pen to paper and consider their words.

Whatever works for him and his staff, I guess.

Graham looks up and offers me a warm smile. "Morning. You ready for today?"

"As ready as I'm going to be," I say with a shrug. Leaving the door open and crossing the room, I snag a seat in one of the plush gray chairs in front of his desk.

He slides his reading glasses from his face, setting them down on the desk. "Good. If you're nervous, just remember, they aren't anything special. Not yet."

I roll my eyes. "That's a glowing review for your team."

"No, it's honest. Right now, they don't give a shit about you or me. The starters just want to impress Vaughn and Ben enough to keep their spot on the team, and the guys from the farm team want to wow him enough to snatch those positions for themselves."

I'm no stranger to the game. I've watched players come and go from this team for the better part of my life. Cut days at spring training always leave everyone on edge. But unlike Vaughn or our GM Ben, I'm not interested in their stats. I want their heart in the game. We can work with players to make them better. We can't teach them to have heart.

A few of the players in question have started trickling down the hall, their rambunctious greetings echoing loudly.

"You've got a point," I conceded. "But I think they're going to surprise you."

Graham nods approvingly. "Just like you are."

I cock my head to the side in confusion.

A smile splits his face, and he lowers his voice. "Nikki shared with me your plans for the team."

"Damn it." I huff, annoyed. "She wasn't supposed to do that."

"Ah, don't be too hard on her," Graham reassures, though the blush that fills his cheeks has me wondering just how close he is with our PR manager. "She's behind you one hundred percent. She just wanted to check with me to see my plans for day-to-day schedules for the team during the season, so she could tweak and expand on some of your ideas. Then I might have strong-armed her into sharing the rest with me. Under the threat of death, I promised I would keep my mouth shut."

"And?" I ask, needing someone to put me out of my misery and tell me if they're brilliant or garbage before I share them with the rest of upper management. "What did you think?"

Graham scrubs his chin with his hand. "You'll have your work cut out for you. The league is going to put up a fight. And if they don't, you can bet Vaughn will."

"I know, but it's worth it." I defend it, and I realize just how badly I want this to work.

Of course, the boys' club will hate my ideas. Not because they aren't smart, but because none of them give a shit about more than money. They don't care about outdoor spaces that give fans a place to congregate and form connections. They don't care about upgrades, giveaways, or fan experiences with the team. They don't care that I'm looking to up our player salary cap, and at the same time, reevaluate how we build our roster to strengthen it over time. They just care about the bottom line and how spending more money—even if it is my own—will make them look bad.

"That said, I think they're great ideas that will strengthen our organization in the long run."

"Exactly." I let out a sigh of relief. "Which is worth the push back. This is my team and I believe in it."

"Keep that optimism, Wills."

I give him a pointed stare, causing my uncle to chuckle.

"Ms. York," he corrects with a snort. "That's going to take some getting used to now that we're going to be at the field more."

"Willow is fine," I reassure him playfully.

"Willow is fine," a deep baritone mutters from the door.

We both turn around to see Fransisco Sharpe standing in the doorway, only he isn't there for long.

A hand appears on his shoulder and yanks him back, and I wince when I hear the thud of his skull crashing into the wall outside the office door.

"What the fuck?" Sharpe bellows.

Graham is out of his seat faster than I thought possible for a man his age, and I quickly follow behind him to see what the hell is going on.

When we file into the hall, we are greeted with a wide-eyed Bishop with his forearm pressed against Sharpe's throat.

"Apologize," he growls, eyes narrowed on his teammate.

"I didn't—" Sharpe chokes out, and Bishop presses harder on his windpipe.

Instinctively, I reach out and place my hand on Bishop's shoulder, trying to deescalate the situation. "It's fine."

"It's not." Bishop side-eyes me with the same rage he wore in the locker room in New York, and I back off, dropping my hand.

Sucking in a breath, I hold it as if that will somehow encourage Sharpe to just apologize before this turns into an all-out brawl, effectively ending Bishop's season before it even starts. Because I have no doubt that's where this is going with a look like that.

"I'm sorry, Willow," Sharpe grunts, half-heartedly.

"Ms. York," Bishop corrects.

Sharpe rolls his eyes and repeats, "I'm sorry, Ms. York."

"If I ever hear you disrespecting our owner like that again, I'll make sure you never play in this league again."

Sharpe scoffs but doesn't put up more of a fight. "Message received."

Bishop shoves off Sharpe and shakes his hands out like he's offended just by the touch of him. The three of us watch silently as the backup catcher takes off toward the locker room.

"Thank you," I say softly.

Bishop turns, pinning his icy glare in my direction. "I didn't do it for you. We have standards on this team, and that guy is an asshat."

"Still," I murmur, ignoring the way my stomach flutters at his act of protection, "thank you."

Bishop blinks like he finally sees me before I'm rewarded with a muffled grunt as he shakes his head, following his teammate toward the locker room.

Graham's chuckle fills the silence between us. "Well, there's a plot twist."

"What?" I stammer, fully convinced my godfather has figured us out, and I'm about to be read the riot act for fraternization.

"That's the most I've seen Lawson give a shit since the crash."

"Oh. Me too," I mutter, wondering if our conversation last night had anything to do with Bishop's actions. Either way, I was just privy to Bishop Lawson's first show of leadership on this team. It's a good look on him.

I smooth down my skirt—yes, I wore it to aggravate Bishop—as Graham introduces me to the whole team. All eyes turn in my direction. All except the one set I wish would look. Bishop's gaze is glued to the wood floor as I push off the door I was leaning against and make my way to the front of the room beside my uncle.

The spring training facility is not as extravagant as the clubhouse in New York. There's one large table in the center of the room with chairs surrounding it, though those are all empty now. Everyone instead is seated in the folding chairs in front of each of the coveted cubbies that line the four walls.

As I walk, I look around the room, mentally cataloging the faces I recognize, their stories and those that I only know by name who, as Graham so eloquently put it, are hoping to make the team. Some are smiling, like one of our relief pitchers, Joshua Shepherd, while others like Elliot Stone, our first baseman, study me with open skepticism. Still others, like our farm team catcher Noah Smith, look at me like I'm their ticket to something they've dreamed of their entire life. Bishop's gaze remains on that treasured spot on the floor.

I want so badly to ask him what's wrong. There's no way he's still sulking about what happened in the hallway. Sure, he was pissed about Sharpe's comment, but that was honestly small dice compared to some of the things the press has written about me. I don't see him going after them. No, this is something else. There's something keeping him from looking up, and I want to know what it is.

But at the moment, I'm his owner, not his friend, and absolutely not his fuckbuddy.

Clearing my throat, I shake Bishop from my mind and offer my team a genuine smile.

"Let me start by saying I know this isn't ideal. Each of you planned to start this season with the teams I'm sure you've come to love and respect. Instead, you're here with us with zero sense of stability. I know I'm just the team owner and you don't have to listen to anything I'm about to say. After all, I just sign your paychecks. What do I know? But I'm here to tell you that even though I'm just a figure in an office on the concourse, I'm happy you're here. This team has been through a lot in the last year. We've lost great men and women who were the foundation of this organization. We were on our way to a pennant run, and that's not something you forget. But that doesn't mean we can't rise from the ashes and be great with the men in this locker room right now. You don't have to show up, you don't have to give it your all, and you absolutely don't have to believe in what this team stands for. But I hope you do, because even though you didn't ask to be here, you are and that makes you a Renega—"

A crack echoes through the otherwise silent locker room and all eyes whip to see Bishop standing, his helmet spinning in a circle where he chucked it at the ground. His chest heaves, and even though everyone is looking at him, his gaze is locked on me. Whatever goodwill he had for me when he walked in and defended me is gone.

Without a word, he kicks the helmet from in front of him. It hits the shins of one of the farm team pitchers across from him. Not that Bishop takes notice. He's already halfway to the exit.

The silence is deafening. Everyone's eyes dart from him to me, and back again until he's gone, and I can feel the rift tearing through the team I was moments ago trying to unite. So much for starting off on the right foot.

"I guess that's my cue to leave the baseball to you guys," I stammer, barely managing to keep the feeling of failure from my voice.

"The lady has spoken." Graham steps in. "You know the drill. Everyone needs to complete first day physicals and mental health screenings today. You're on your own today for workouts, and tomorrow we'll hit the ground running on the field."

For a heartbeat no one moves, then one by one the team starts moving, and I'm grateful when Graham takes it upon himself to usher me toward the exit.

Just before we reach the door, we're stopped by our starting pitcher,

Carson Whitmore. Graham gives me a look, silently asking if I want him to stay for whatever he has to say. I give him a curt nod letting him know I can handle it. I might not need his protection, but I'm happy to have him in my corner.

"Hi, I just wanted to introduce myself. I'm Carson—"

"Whitmore," I finish for him. "I know who you are. What can I do for you?"

Carson runs a hand through the curls of the shaggy blonde hair that reaches just below the nape of his neck. He's tall, not quite as tall as Bishop, and where Bishop is all muscle, Carson is more lithe and lean with bulk in just the right places. He's the epitome of a perfect pitcher's build.

His blue eyes soften when he smiles. "I just wanted to say I'm sorry for your loss. Your dad was an incredible man and a staple in this league."

My heart constricts, and my eyes rim with tears. "Thank you."

He's not the first to give his condolences, but he's the only one on this team, aside from Graham, to acknowledge that I've lost someone too. Not even Vaughn has gone so far as to ask how I'm doing. Everything out of his mouth is how I couldn't possibly be as great of an owner as my father.

Carson smiles, revealing two deep dimples in his cheeks and nods. I expect him to walk away, but then he hesitates. His shoulders hunch slightly and when he speaks, his voice is low. "Don't worry about Lawson. He's had a rough go of it, but the guy has a heart of gold. He'll eventually get his head out of his ass and when he does, he'll be unstoppable."

If you only knew the half of it, buddy.

"You know from experience?" I ask, more than a little curious to get a feel on how the team is reacting to our prickly catcher's hot and cold streaks.

Carson sighs, letting his hand fall to his side. He works his fists a few times before he continues. "We've played against each other for years.

Heckled each other for the majority of them. He's a sore loser, which was the driving force behind me perfecting my sinker. He can't hit them, and he hates it."

I laugh. "It's a good thing you're on our team, then."

Carson nods and offers me a reassuring smile. "It's also how I know he'll come around. He feels hard, but he always manages to pull through."

I nod. "I think you're right."

He lifts his head toward the exit that leads to the practice fields. "I should probably head out there."

"Have a good day."

"Thanks. I'll see you around."

I sidestep Carson and slip through the open locker room door. Focused on my phone and the mountain of emails that have come through in the thirty minutes I spent in the clubhouse, I don't notice the wall of a man standing in front of me before I crash into his chest.

Wobbling on my heels, Bishop reaches out and wraps his hand around my bicep to steady me. His heated gaze darts in both directions, and I only have a moment to right myself before he plunges me into the darkness of the nearest equipment room.

CHAPTER FIFTEEN
Willow

It smells like wood and oiled leather. Probably because this is the room that houses the extra bats and gloves for the team. I blink, my eyes adjusting to the dim fluorescent overhead. When they do, I'm greeted with the sight of Bishop, chest heaving paired with a heated stare that's eerily similar to the one he gave me earlier while defending me.

Once the door clicks closed, he unleashes on me. "What the hell was that with Carson?"

My brows raise and I smirk as my hands dig into the curve of my hips, fully preparing to poke the bear. "Oh hello, Bishop. Of course, I'd love to talk with you in this tiny equipment closet. Why was I talking to a member of my team? Oh, I don't know? Maybe because I'm the owner and he wanted to offer his condolences."

"You don't need to be talking with him," he growls. "Any of them. You don't need to show up to practices. It's a distraction."

His declaration catches me off guard, but I quickly catch up and refuse to believe the audacity he's displaying. "Oh, so it's only okay when I'm your distraction."

Bishop's jaw tightens. "That's different."

"Is it?" I press, not entirely sure how we got here, but I can't deny there's a small part of me that likes seeing Bishop unsettled. Not upset or spiraling, but on his toes, in a way I don't think very many people keep him.

Amusement sparkles in my eyes, and I wait for his snarky response. When Bishop remains quiet, I change the subject, hoping it will catch him off guard. "You want to tell me why you just stormed out of that meeting?"

He snorts and shakes his head. "Hard pass. Did you think about my proposition?"

"Nope, not until you answer me first."

Bishop's hard stare is as unwavering as my own. Tension crackles between us, neither willing to budge. Several seconds go by, and his chocolate eyes burn a hole straight through me as his jaw flexes. That's when I realize we can't keep circling each other. It isn't helping anyone, least of all us.

I take a step toward him, to which Bishop responds by taking a step back.

"Are you really not going to say anything?"

Another step for each of us.

"What do you want me to say?"

Another step. Only this time, Bishop is greeted by the rattling of bats as his back hits the rack.

A moment of silence stretches between us, but it's not enough to break the chasm of tension that sits in the mere inches separating us.

I tip my head, unwilling to back down now. "Tell me why you walked out. Prove to me you want this distraction to continue, because I can't agree unless we're in this together. You use me. I use you. But we have to talk to one another. I won't just be a fuck toy."

Bishop lets out a scoff, but I don't miss the hurt that flashes across his face. "Is that what you think I see you as?"

"Prove me wrong." There's no mistaking the challenge in my voice, but if you asked my heart, it would say it's more of a plea.

From the moment he asked for one more night, there was a part of me that wanted to say yes. I hadn't realized how big that part was until just now. But if I'm going to do this, I need to be more than just a one-night stand. It's playing with fire. It's asking to get hurt. If I'm going to do this, I need to know that I'm making a difference. I want to be his distraction, but I also want to know why he needs it. I want *him* to know why he needs it.

Bishop opens his mouth to speak but pauses, rubbing a hand down his face for a second before meeting my gaze. "The deal was physical, not honesty."

"Then there's nothing for us to discuss," I say softly and turn my back on him.

"I'm sorry," he mutters low enough that I can barely make out the words.

I pause mid-step and wait for him to continue. When he doesn't, I look over my shoulder at his slumped shoulders and vacant stare. "Me too."

"I just—" His voice trails off and I turn around, watching as he chews on whatever words he is trying to piece together. "You want the truth? Yesterday was Tommy's birthday."

My breath stalls in my chest as I see Bishop's eyes darken with defeat. I close the space between us and take his forearm in my hand. "I'm so sorry. I had no idea."

"He would've been thirty," he says softly. He stares over my head at the spot I previously occupied as he still clings to me, sliding his arm so our fingers intertwine.

I give him a soft squeeze, encouraging him to continue.

"I don't know how to play without them. I don't know how to walk into the locker room and not see their ghosts. Listening to you talk about them like they aren't a part of this team anymore—" He hesitates, and I'm left hanging on his every word. Savoring the pieces of himself he's giving me. "They might not be important to you or everyone else, but they're all I've ever known. I don't know how to be me without them. Fuck. This is why I came to you." He blinks and when he opens his eyes, they are locked on mine. "This is why I—Shit, I shouldn't have dragged you into this." He runs his free hand through his already tousled hair, and it takes everything in me not to wrap my arms around him and promise everything is going to be okay. Because I can't promise that. As much as I would like to, I won't lie to him.

"I'm sorry for my outburst. I shouldn't have taken this out on you in the middle of your speech. It wasn't what I wanted to do. I just needed to get out of there. I needed space to breathe. I just—" Bishop's chest heaves as he tries, and fails, to inhale deeply. "Does it ever stop?"

"What?"

"The pain," he clarifies, then adds, "is it the same as when your mom died?"

I swallow hard, stalling as I try to filter through the truth of his question. He wants an answer, but nothing I have to say is going to help. Not really.

"Yes. And no. Losing a parent is the hardest thing I've ever experienced." It's an answer I've rehearsed over and over. It's what I tell the kids at Renegade Hearts and the press when they ask. But for Bishop, I elaborate. "But, as much as I love my mother, it doesn't change that she was terrible toward me. My dad and I were much closer, especially in the last few years. Losing him hurts infinitely more."

"I'm sorry you lost him."

I'm stunned, frozen into place. I'm two for two on apologies today. Except, unlike when Carson offered his condolences, when Bishop says his first real apology, the tears fall freely.

Bishop is quiet for a moment, and I pray he doesn't ask the question I know he's dying to. It's the same question I asked my father over and over. The same question I ask myself on the rare occasion I allow myself to open the box I've got locked away tight in my mind and to grieve.

Of course, praying doesn't stop him from asking.

"Does it get better?"

I look away, but my entire body feels the weight of his stare. It's all I can do to nod once. Twice. Three times. Lies every single one of them.

Because while time does heal, the pain never goes away. There will always be moments when the universe reminds you they're gone. It plays tricks on you and forces the good memories to overtake the bad. Until the moment you remember everything they're missing. The birthdays and holidays they'll never celebrate again.

I bite my lip to stop myself from releasing the sob that threatens to overtake me. "It won't feel better for a long time. But eventually, you feel less like you're drowning and more like you've got an elephant on your chest. And then one day it's only a dull ache instead of a death sentence."

"How long?"

I can't stand the desperation in his voice. The silent plea for me to deliver encouraging news. But I can't.

"I'll let you know when I get there." A sad smile crosses my lips. "That's why I told you it's about learning to live. Not learning to be okay."

Bishop lets out a weighted sigh and leans forward, pressing his forehead to mine. "You're right there with me, aren't you?"

I nod softly against him, unable to put into words how right he is. I'd love to tell him there's a one-size-fits-all solution, but there isn't. Some days you're able to wake up, and for a few minutes, you forget. You live for those moments. Then other days are so debilitating you can hardly breathe. Some days you get the two-for-one deal and experience both before lunch.

Today is that day for me. The swing between considering Bishop's offer and missing my father, followed by Bishop's outburst, has me feeling weightless and like I'm drowning at the same time.

I look up, and this close, I can see the light brown flecks in Bishop's otherwise dark bronze stare. My tongue darts out, and his eyes track the movement before returning to mine.

"Distract me." The words are past my lips before I can think twice.

Bishop pulls back and searches my face. "Are you sure?"

No. Not even a little bit, but I think he's right when he says we can't do this alone. And even though I might regret this the moment we leave this equipment room, for right now I need this, and so does he.

We're doing whatever we have to in order to live.

The moment I nod, I'm stunned by the brutal force of Bishop's lips against mine. I've come to expect the change in his kisses. They are no longer the slow, sweet, and gentle kisses I received when we met and at the party. This is rough and passionate, carnal and demanding. My thighs clench when his tongue dives between my lips, not asking but forcing his way in, taking what we both want.

My hand comes up and cradles his stubbled cheek, holding him in place as I pull back. Bishop latches on to my lower lip and rakes his teeth over it, and I can't help the moan that escapes me.

He cocks a brow, and I smirk past breathless pants. "I think we need some ground rules."

Bishop wraps his arms around my waist and tugs me against his muscled torso as he huffs a laugh. "We've never been good at following those."

He's not wrong. Just one night was never just one night and goodbye wasn't goodbye. That doesn't mean I can just jump in with both feet and believe we'll come out of this unscathed. I might be a hopeless romantic, but I'm not stupid.

"First, no one can know."

He nods. "That's a given."

"I mean it, Bishop. If anyone finds out, it won't be you that's ridiculed."

"I wouldn't let them—"

I pin a glare in his direction, effectively stopping him mid-sentence. We both know it won't be him who suffers. The league may give him a slap on the wrist, but just like it has been with the takeover, I'll be the one they focus on as the failure. I'll be the woman who took advantage of her position and slept with a player. It doesn't matter that we have a history or that we're two consenting adults.

"Okay. No one finds out."

"Two—piggybacking on that to make sure it stays secret—nothing can happen between us at the stadium."

"You mean like this?" Bishop leans down and runs his nose along my neck and an almost feral growl vibrates against my flesh.

Goosebumps break out across my skin and a shiver tears through me. "Okay after this."

Bishop's chuckle rumbles against my chest, his fingers digging into the swell of my hips. He nips the lobe of my ear and rasps. "Well, there goes my plan to bend you over the railing of the owner's suite with a view of the whole stadium."

This man and his filthy mouth never cease to amaze me.

My thighs clench and I almost take back my first rule immediately. Bishop definitely has a thing about bending me over with a view. Times Square. The beach house balcony. And now the stadium. And I absolutely have an exhibition streak because I've come from the thrill every single time.

Something to consider for the future. Which brings me to my third point.

I shift between his legs, doing my best to ignore the way his jock strap strains against the tight fabric of his uniform pants. "Three. This has an expiration date. Opening day."

"Got it," he murmurs as his hands drift up the side of my torso and across the swell of my breasts to finger the buttons of my powder blue blouse. "What happens at spring training stays at spring training."

His hands work at the buttons from the top down, exposing the matching lacey blue bra underneath. "Fuck," he curses. "If it's not those damn skirts, these lace-covered tits are going to be the death of me."

I smile with the knowledge I thought of him when I picked my outfit today. I wanted him to squirm in his seat with the need to rip the skirt from my hips. I dreamed of a moment just like this. I never thought I'd be giving life to said dream. Or maybe I did. Manifest destiny and all that.

Running my hands down Bishop's torso, I untuck the gray and black practice jersey from his pants. "And the last one." The rule I know he's going to hate me for. "If we're going to do this, I'd like for you to agree to see the team therapist regularly."

Bishop's hands still against my stomach. "Absolutely no—"

Despite the fact my heart has stopped and I don't want to think past the sense of deep aching want, I shake my head. "It's nonnegotiable. No therapy, no distraction."

He hesitates, and I watch his heated expression as he clenches his jaw. He wants me—wants this—but is it enough to agree to help himself?

For a split second, I think it's not before he grits out. "Fine."

"Do you have any conditions of your own?"

"Only one." Bishop reaches up and tugs his jersey over his head. He drops it to the floor, standing in only his pants and cleats, proving he plans to do more than shake on this promise. "No feelings."

I wince, but before I can school my features, Bishop continues.

"As cliché as it sounds, it's not you, it's me. I don't want to hurt you."

"You won't hurt me," I say, looking away. Not because I believe he would hurt me, but because his rule is one I might struggle with.

"Not intentionally, which is why I want to make it clear this offer is for distraction only. I'll ensure we forget the bullshit of our day by making you come in every way imaginable. I'll even play by your rules and let you know why I need to be distracted, but I can't give you more than that."

Holding his gaze, I shrug off my blouse. Then I turn and walk the three short steps to the door and flip the lock.

I don't have more than a moment to react past the reverberating click before Bishop is there. He spins me and, with a hand on my chest bone, presses me into the cool metal of the door.

"Please tell me that's you saying yes."

"Yes," I breathe.

My confirmation is enough to light the fuse between us and in seconds we're a tangle of limbs and lips. His hand slips down to palm my breast while the other tangles in my hair and pulls my needy mouth to his. His touches are desperate but gentle. Fingertips brush my nipple, causing a ripple of pleasure at the same time as the hand in my hair tugs until I feel that delicious sting of pain.

"Please, Bishop," I moan against his lips. He sucks my lower lip as he pinches my nipple.

"Fuck, I love when it's my name you're moaning." He groans, dropping his face lower to suck on my pulse point. It simultaneously sends shivers down my spine and a zap of lightning to my clit. "Tell me what you need, Kitten."

I'm teetering on the edge and hearing him call me the pet name I've always loved sends me into a frenzy. "I want you inside me."

Bishop pulls back and smirks. "Have I told you how sexy it is that you now voice what you want?"

I laugh. "Noted." But my chest swells with pride. He has no idea he gave me the confidence to speak up. He was the one who inspired me to give into the things I need and fight for the things I want.

"Unbuckle my pants," he says as he flips my skirt up to reveal my matching lace thong. His hands roam the round of my ass as I work his belt and pants open and push them, along with his briefs and jockstrap, down to his knees.

I inhale a sharp breath when I see the tattoos on Bishop's left thigh. Each of the individual tattoos holds a special meaning to him. Each of which he explained to me. The bottom of his leg houses the ink he got to commemorate his family, while the space on his thigh is for the moments that have changed his life.

Just like when I saw him in the hotel, my eyes dart across his exposed flesh, looking for any new ink he might have added, but I find none.

"You like what you see?" Bishop grins.

Instead of dignifying him with an answer, I wrap my hand around the base of his cock and slide them from root to tip, dragging my fingertips over the metal bars on the underside of his shaft and eliciting a delicious hiss from Bishop.

"What do you need?" I whisper, echoing his question.

"This." His hand cups my pussy. "This body with these perfect fucking curves, reminding me the world might be burning around us, but I've got this to hold on to."

Fuck. So much for keeping my feelings locked tight. He can't say shit like that and expect me to stay impartial.

I'm about to tell him as much, but I'm rendered speechless when he dips his body, wrapping his free hand around my waist, and picks me up. The surprise move forces me to drop his cock and hang onto him so I don't fall. He presses me into the door at the same time he slides my panties aside and notches his cock at my entrance. "Wrap your legs around me, Kitten. Make room for me."

"Please," I beg, writhing my hips forward, seeking the friction only he can give me.

"Tell me again," he says, thrusting only his head into me.

"Fuck me." I whimper followed by another panted, "Please."

We're both panting as he works his shaft a little deeper with each thrust until he's completely seated within me, his piercings stretching me further than any other man ever has.

"Don't stop," I moan, only minimally aware that between my pleas and the sound of our naked flesh slapping together, we aren't exactly hiding what we are doing.

"I couldn't even if I wanted to, Kitten." Bishop rocks his hips harder and faster, his eyes darkening as he reaches up and wraps his hand around the base of my throat.

I tip my chin up, giving him more of me to hold.

"New rule," he growls, spearing me with his cock. "This pussy is mine until we're done with this arrangement."

I whimper, nodding against his hand as my orgasm starts to tug low in my core.

"Say it, Kitten," he rasps, his breath hot against my temple. "Tell me no other man will have this."

"Bishop—"

He angles his hips in a way that hits the deepest part of me at the same time as his pubic bone slams against my clit with every thrust.

"Oh my God," I cry, digging my nails into his shoulder.

"Say it."

"Yours," I moan. "No one else."

If only it were true.

He pulls back, a wicked smirk on his face. "Good girl. Now come for me."

Those damn words, paired with the way he tightens his grip, restricting my air supply, have me racing over the edge. My body trembles, my pussy tightening around him like a vise, and suddenly I'm floating.

Bishop pounds into me once, twice, and on the third thrust cries out, coming inside me.

When we're both no longer shaking, he slides from inside me and sets me on the ground. He pulls up his pants and buckles them before dropping to his knees to right my panties and skirt.

Not that it helps much. I can feel the evidence of what we just did seeping past the flimsy fabric down my thigh.

He stands in front of me and drops his forehead to mine, letting slip a small hum of appreciation.

He lingers a second longer, and I'm just about to ask what happens now, when he sidesteps me and unlocks the door.

It's like being doused with cold water.

Confusion laces my voice. "Where are you going?"

"I'm a man of my word. Which means if I want this to happen again, I've got a date with the team therapist." He tugs the door open slowly to give me enough time to move out of the way.

"Wait." I wrap my fingers around the door and stop him before he steps into what I hope is an empty hallway. I'm not exactly sure why I stopped him, but now I need to say something. So, I offer him a lifeline. "Would it help not to use the locker room for now?"

He tilts his head in confusion.

"You said earlier you struggle being in there because it reminds you of the past. What if I can have your things moved to another room that you can use as a makeshift changing room? That way there isn't the constant reminder, and you can hopefully focus better."

Bishop scrutinizes my words like he's looking for the catch. "You'd do that for me?"

"I'm pretty sure I just fucked you to help. This is little more than a call to the groundskeeper."

His mouth opens and closes again before settling on "thank you."

I glance up at him and nod. "I know it seems impossible, but you were you before them. You will be you after them. You just need to give yourself a chance."

He nods. "Can I come by tomorrow night after my appointment with the therapist?"

I hear the silent, *I might need it after the session* loud and clear.

"Yeah, I have a meeting at six, but I'll be there."

He nods again and slips from the room.

CHAPTER SIXTEEN
Bishop

Fuck the damn therapist.

There is plenty on my mind, none of which I want to talk about. Not why I chose not to speak during our first session. Not the way I stormed out of the team meeting yesterday. And absolutely not the round of mind-blowing sex I had with my team owner in the equipment room.

Not that Jolene asked about any of that. Instead, she's only asked one question.

Why am I there?

Over and over for the last hour.

Jolene is young for a league therapist, maybe in her early thirties, but I'd guess even her late twenties. She's a breath of fresh air compared to the crotchety old guy we had before who only cared to talk about stats and never actually did his damn job. And she's the exact opposite of the therapist I saw before the crash. The one who told me she could no longer help me because I wasn't the happy-go-lucky golden retriever I once was and believed I needed to see a trauma specialist. Which is what Jolene is hired specifically to help the team with the next three seasons as we adjust. She also made it very clear she isn't going to push me unless I push myself and has no problem telling Graham to put me on the injured reserve list.

At this point, I should just have a plaque added to the dugout to mark the spot where I'll be parked on the bench all season.

There's only five minutes left in my session, and yet again, we haven't made any progress. Only this time, I'm more confused than when I entered the room.

I've given her every answer I can think of to the question. I'm here so Graham won't bench me. I'm here because the league requires us each to have a baseline at the beginning of every season. I'm here so as soon as I leave, I can sink my cock into Willow's perfect pussy and forget for a minute that we've been dealt a shit hand.

Okay, so I didn't tell her that last one, but that doesn't make it any less of a driving factor.

I know what Jolene wants from me. She wants me to admit I'm there to work through the bullshit of the last six months. Hell, the last year. But if I admit that out loud, then I have to follow through. And I'm not sure I'm ready for that. Especially not after everything I unloaded with Willow yesterday morning. Not to mention everything I learned from her.

"I'll let you know when I get there."

That's what she said. Those eight words shattered the filter I'd unknowingly been viewing her through. Paired with all her actions—I'm a mess trying to reconcile it all. Fuck, she's willing to give me my own locker room just so I won't be in pain every time I walk into the stadium. And she's not okay. She lost her father. I can't even fathom what that feels like. Not that I'm currently speaking to my own, which is another can of worms I should explore in this therapy session. And yet, Willow is willing to let me fuck her senseless, not only so I can forget all these problems, but so she can too.

I don't know what to think, other than I don't deserve her.

And yet, I need her.

I need this ass backwards situation we've found ourselves in more than I need to sit in this chair and talk about my feelings.

"That's all the time we have today." Jolene sets her pen down on the notepad in her lap and looks up, offering me a smile. It's not condescending or high-handed, but it irks me nonetheless. She knows as well as I do that I have to be here, but I can see she genuinely wants to help. I'm just not ready. Because what happens when I'm fixed? What does that mean? I can't just forget my team. I don't want to. But is there a world in which I can remember them and be healed? Willow seems to think so.

The cut in my soul is deep, but I don't think I can survive bleeding out any longer.

I stand and head toward the door, but my feet turn to cinder blocks. Instead of taking a step forward, I sigh and shake my head.

"I'm sick of living a life where everything hurts." It hurts to admit it out loud, but surprisingly feels like a small weight has been lifted.

Jolene's brows raise, and a tiny smirk lifts the corner of her mouth. "What was that?"

"Fuck," I curse, rolling my eyes because I know damn well she heard me. "You asked me why I'm here. The pain is beginning to become a part of the fabric of who I am as a person, and while I could easily live that way, I'm not sure I want to."

Not after seeing the way Willow looked at me. The way she has multiple times, only I was too stupid to see it. Like I'm worth fighting for. I don't believe it, but there is a tiny spark in me that wants to, and for now, that will have to be enough.

Jolene hesitates, then gives a slight nod. "Thank you for sharing that with me. It tells me that you're less angry about attending these sessions and more angry about why you have to attend. Something for you to think about. I'll see you the day after tomorrow."

All that from one tiny admission.

My mouth gapes for a moment before I school my features and exit her office. If I stayed, I'd say something I couldn't take back.

How dare she blame the team? This isn't on them. It's because of my inability to control the ache in my chest. It's not their fault they died. They should be here. They should–

Fuck, I need a drink.

I'm halfway tempted to drive to the nearest bar and forget this whole day ever happened. Then I remember I have another way to forget.

One that's got soft curves and a delicious ass I'd love to smack.

The drive to the beach house is filled with screaming at the top of my lungs to my favorite 2000s pop punk playlist in the rental truck. The guys used to make fun of me, but the sounds of my youth just hit different, and right now, I need anything to keep me from spiraling into thoughts of healing and how much it all terrifies me.

I glance at the clock and see I'm an hour early, meaning Willow is likely still in her meeting. For a split second, I consider turning around, but going back to the hotel for an hour would absolutely lead to dwelling on all the revelations I've made over the last twenty-four hours.

Nope.

I need release.

I need a safe space.

And as much as I hate to admit it, Willow can give me both of those things.

Fuck, that woman has buried herself under my skin, and I'm torn as to how I feel about it.

By the time I pull up to the house and make my way to the door, I can't tell if my nerves are fried or shaking with anticipation. Maybe it's a little of both. It's not like I know what I'm doing. I've never done this before. No strings attached. Usually, I'm very attached and ready to declare my epic love by the sixth date. Willow and I are more than halfway there if you count New Year's and the party, plus the hotel and equipment room trysts.

It's a good thing you promised her no feelings, Jackson jests.

Exactly. Because I'm not even considering love or what type of ring would look good on her delicate fingers. I'm not even wondering how I'm going to convince her to move in with me. The only thing I'm concerned with is what color panties I'll be ripping from her tight little cunt.

Sure it is.

I know Jackson and Tommy don't believe me. Even if they were the ones who'd said I needed to play the field for a year and stay out of anything serious. They were also the two who heckled me the most about Willow. They knew she was different. They just wanted what was best for me.

We still do.

Before I can silently berate my dead and unconscious best friends, Willow answers the door and all coherent thought goes out the window.

I swear she only owns one thing because once again she's wearing the skirt I love, only in black this time. But that's not all I notice. It's like now that I'm no longer actively hating her, I'm seeing her for the first time.

She's still fucking radiant, a blonde goddess, but how did I miss the slight dusting of purple under her eyes and the crease between her brow? The way her cheeks hollow when her expression drops and the way her go-to stance is no longer one with shoulders pinned back in confidence.

Has it been like this every time I've seen her? Was it all just a show, and I was just too blind to notice?

It doesn't matter that my soul is torn where Willow is concerned. I don't think, only react, wrapping her in my arms and crushing my lips to hers, as if somehow this thing we share will protect her from whatever it is that plagues her. The same way it does for me.

Willow tenses before she relaxes in my arms and returns my kiss, her lips eager. Her hands tangle in my hair and a soft mewl escapes her. Fuck, I love the sounds this woman makes. That's one thing that's never changed—everything about her is intoxicating.

My hands find her waist and slide over her ass, my fingers digging into what is debatably my fourth favorite part of her body—preceded only by her mind, lips, and pussy.

"Willow?" a voice echoes down the hall from the office. "Everything okay?"

"Shit," she murmurs against my lips. "I'm still in my meeting."

I lean away and smile reassuringly. "I can wait."

"I told you I wouldn't be done until six," she whispers, and untangling herself from my arms, looks down and straightens her skirt.

"I…" I bite my tongue, stopping myself from telling her about my therapy session and why I didn't want to be alone. "Have you eaten?"

"No." She hesitates, and I'm immediately suspicious of the way she glances toward the ground. "I was planning to just order something later."

I'd bet my contract that's a lie, given what I know about Willow and the way she was raised by a mother who only cared about her figure. She's admitted to me before that when she's stressed, she'll forget to eat, mostly because that's how it was when she grew up. Her mother would be angry or too focused on whatever was the latest made-up socialite tragedy of the day and would cancel dinner for the household, forbidding the staff from making it. Her father would get home late, after Willow was in bed, leaving her hungry and alone.

How could I possibly believe Willow would allow herself to be anything like that monster of a woman?

Because you're a fucking idiot, Tommy snaps lightheartedly in my mind.

He's right.

I nod toward the office. "Go back to your meeting. I'll cook."

"You cook?" she asks, skepticism written across her face.

"I know. Incredible, right?" It's easy to forget that despite the fact we know each other intimately, there is still so much we didn't cover during those late-night rendezvous.

"I don't think—" She shakes her head and smiles sympathetically. "We have rules, Bishop. This doesn't feel like it constitutes as part of a distraction."

She's right. Cooking for her somehow feels more intimate than it should, but I shrug it off. "This doesn't break them. It's really for your benefit. I am going to need you fueled up if I'm going to fuck you like I want to."

Her eyes go wide, and I swear I see her clench her thighs. It's incredibly sexy and has the blood from my brain traveling south.

"Fine. I mean, I don't know what's in the kitchen, but you can have at it."

"I'll figure it out."

She sighs as she turns and heads back down the hall toward the office, and I follow, veering right toward the kitchen.

I'm appalled by what I find.

It makes sense she didn't know what was in the kitchen because there's not much. I'm going to have to MacGyver something from the meager pantry staples, frozen items, and my saving grace—eggs. For a split second, I consider pulling out my phone and ordering takeout, but if the containers in the trash are any indication, she's been living on whatever delivers to the house.

In this case, I'm thinking breakfast for dinner is going to be easiest. Omelets, to be specific. Mostly because one, who doesn't like breakfast and two, there aren't a whole lot of other options.

Willow's voice carries through the house as I thaw some turkey bacon and get the pan hot enough to sauté some veggies. Though I can't make out everything she's saying, I'm ninety percent sure she's on a call with the board of Renegade Hearts if the mentions of camp and dollars are any indication.

Which only serves to piss me off more.

I turn my attention back to the stove and force myself to loosen my white-knuckle grip on the wooden spoon I'm using to push the vegetables around. I'd love nothing more than to give that damn board a piece of my mind about their partnering with the league and using the crash victims' children to raise money. It makes my blood boil that they'd even consider doing such a thing. They're supposed to be protecting them. Not exploiting them.

The only reason I haven't barged in there is because I know Willow agrees with me and promised to do what she could to fix it.

Not wanting to hear another word, I pop in my headphones and press play on the same playlist I started in the car, setting it just loud enough to drown out Willow's voice. By the time I'm done with the first omelet, Willow is still in her meeting, so I eat it myself and wait to start on hers because cold omelets are the worst.

My eyes drift around the room. The kitchen decor is sparse—a few nautical themed knickknacks and a coffee pot on the counter. In the corner, there's a pile of cardboard boxes that looks like they've yet to be unpacked from a move. I'm about two seconds from starting to snoop when Willow's voice cuts through the house loud enough that I can hear her over my music.

"I understand the league will cut funding, but there has to be another way. We are not going to subject these kids to a gala full of pretentious assholes."

My eyes go wide and I'm instantly on my feet. I don't think I've ever heard her yell like that. And that's saying something, considering there have been plenty of times over the last two weeks when I rightly deserved that tone.

Quickly and quietly, I close the distance between the kitchen and the office, standing with my back to the wall just outside the door.

"The gala is in a few weeks. We're not saying—"

"I know, you're not saying anything!" Willow says, sounding exhausted. "You're just trying to do what's best for Renegade Hearts, I get that, but this isn't just money we're talking about. If that's all we care about, then we're no better than the league. They aren't dollar signs, Eric. They're children. Children who lost their parents. They are who we are fighting to protect—to help. I don't give a shit about the money."

Atta girl, Willow.

"But we can do more for them with this opportunity," a deeper voice chimes in. "Think how many more classes we can offer. We can expand beyond New York and coordinate sponsorships with the league in other cities with the respective teams. This could be the partnership we need."

"At the expense of the kids!" Willow bellows.

My shoulders slump as I process what I'm hearing. I've been so fucking wrong about this woman. It's been effortless to make Willow the villain even at every turn. Easier to have someone to hate—someone to blame—and she took it all.

And the worst part is I knew better. She's not innocent in all of it. She still played the game, but if I had looked closer, maybe I would have noticed everything she's doing to make changes for the better.

Having heard enough, I round the corner and stand in the doorway. Willow's gaze instantly connects with mine. She winces and lets out a deep sigh, knowing I heard every word of what she just said.

"Food is just about ready," I whisper just loud enough that she'll hear me, but the board members won't.

She gives me a subtle nod and I turn on my heel as she picks up right where she left off. "Find another way. I agree with you that we could use the support and the money the league gala will generate, but I will not agree to using the children."

Her words are final, reiterated by the sound of her slamming shut the laptop in front of her.

My mind spins on the walk back to the kitchen, working double-time as I pop my headphones back in and crack the eggs to whip up her omelet.

She doesn't deserve the shit her board is laying at her feet. Hell, she doesn't deserve the shit I'm laying at her feet. This woman might not be perfect and has made many mistakes, but as far as I'm concerned, she's a goddamn saint for putting up with the way each person in her life pulls her in a different direction.

It makes me wonder what else she's taken on since the crash that I don't know about. And how can I make it easier?

I shake my head.

It's not my job to care, I remind myself. We have an agreement. Live our lives. Fuck the grief away. Make each day a little easier.

That's what I'm doing.

I'm working within the confines of our agreement.

And tonight, I'm going to make sure she's taken care of in that regard.

CHAPTER SEVENTEEN
Willow

I should have told him to leave.

The last thing I needed was Bishop overhearing my argument with the board about having the crash victims' children present at the gala. I already know his thoughts on the matter, and I agree with him. I'm doing everything I can to fix it. That doesn't mean Bishop will see it that way. If there's one thing I have come to count on since the crash, it's when presented with the option of seeing me as the enemy, Bishop Lawson will.

My shoulders slump and I drop my head, a piece of hair falling in my face. Even if we did share a moment of clarity in that equipment room, he's not someone I can count on to stay rational. Not yet, at least. But I still have hope someday he'll get there.

Pulling back my shoulders, I find the last bit of resolve I have, tie my hair up, and eye the bar cart in the corner. There's a part of me that debates downing half a bottle before venturing out to find him, but I decide against it. One of us needs to have a level head.

I push away from the desk I've come to hate and drag myself toward the door. Might as well get this over with. I had hoped tonight would be a release—no strings attached sex with a man who knows how to please a woman—but given the circumstances an all-out brawl is more likely.

The moment I step into the kitchen, I'm hit with a heavenly aroma and my stomach lets out a hopeful growl.

When was the last time I ate a home-cooked meal? Leigh came over with Zach a few weeks before the draft and made me enchiladas. Has it been that long? I can tell you for certain I haven't had anything homemade since I arrived at the beach house. And today I'm running on empty. I think I opened a granola bar around lunchtime—ah, yes. I did. But it was interrupted by Vaughn demanding I get my shit together and stop insisting I review every single one of his requests to let players go or officially add them to our roster.

He's not going to like the notes I left in the margins or the veto stamp I bought just for the outrageous suggestions he makes. Not to mention he's absolutely going to hate the player I've got my eye on adding to the roster. Where he's focused on building a team, I've got dreams of building a legacy.

Bishop's back is to me when I pad into the kitchen, and I'm struck stupid by the sight of him swinging his hips to what sounds like the melody of Avril Lavine's "Sk8ter Boi" pumping through his headphones. I slide onto the stool at the island, my eyes locked on the way the hem of his Henley hugs the curves of his trim hips and gives way to the rounded ass and thick thighs made possible by the position he plays. He might be the reason I'll go gray before I turn thirty, but never let it be said that Bishop is anything but a delicious snack of a man.

"Like what you see?" He chuckles, not bothering to turn around.

I'm not sure how he does it, but he always catches me while I'm staring. And every time, the cocky bastard makes sure I'm aware he knows by asking that same question.

I lean forward onto my elbows and rest my head in my hands as I continue to drink in the sight of the man in my kitchen. "That depends. Are you going to rip me a new one as soon as this song is over?"

His dancing halts and Bishop looks over his shoulder, eyes narrowed. "I didn't come here to fight with you."

"No, you came here to fuck me, but it wouldn't be the first time you've jumped down my throat when we're supposed to be civil."

Bishop grunts something under his breath, too low for me to hear, as he turns back toward the stove. Flicking off the gas, he makes a show of transferring a perfectly crafted omelet onto a plate. My mouth waters as he grabs a fork from the drawer in the island and slides both in front of me.

"Eat." It's more command than a statement and only serves to spark something low in my belly. It's the same tone he uses when he demands I come for him.

And I do. Every. Single. Time.

Flavor explodes on my tongue with the first bite, and an involuntary moan slips from me. "This is delicious."

"I told you I could cook," he says and his lips curve into an unguarded smile that I haven't seen in some time.

I take another bite, savoring just as much as the first. "It's impressive, considering there was hardly anything to work with."

Bishop shrugs. "It's a gift. Just wait until you taste my kung pao chicken."

My heart stutters and it takes everything for me to focus on taking another bite instead of gaping at him like a fish out of water.

Who is this and what did he do with the man I had the pleasure of dealing with the last few weeks? I'm well acquainted with the prickly version of him that believes I'm the villain. And I've met the broken man who wants to forget. Arguably, my favorite is the man who needs a distraction and doesn't mind using my body to extract it. Or at least that was my favorite. Until now.

This playful, almost pleasant version is the closest I've seen him to the man I remember, and I can't decide if I want to kiss him, fuck him, or beg him to stay.

All of which are problematic for the exact same reason.

While I eat, Bishop cleans the pan and puts away leftover ingredients. I'm mesmerized by the way he moves with such ease through the kitchen. He's only been here once, and we spent the majority of that time hiding from the guests of my father's party and testing the structural integrity of the furniture in my room.

This feels different, almost domestic. There isn't a hint of the awkwardness I expected when he told me he'd be coming over. It's easy being around him when he's like this, so much so that I can almost forget the arrangement and the fact he's here so we can both ease the pain and forget the bullshit of the day.

Shit. Guilt floods me as I remember why he was coming here in the first place.

I'm not the only one who had a rough go today. Bishop was supposed to have his therapy session. Caught up after the argument in my meeting, I didn't even think to ask him how it went.

I finish the last bite of my omelet and round the island to put my dish in the sink so that I can make sure he's okay.

The plate barely touches the bottom when I feel the heat of Bishop's body pressing against my back. His large frame makes me feel small, but more than that, it makes me feel safe. He traces the tips of his fingers down my forearms until he reaches the counter, gripping the lip on either side of me. His breath on my neck sends shivers down my spine, and I clench my thighs in anticipation.

"Do you want to talk about it?" he whispers against the space below my ear.

"No."

"Good." He presses an open mouth kiss to the pulse point on my neck, sucking my racing heartbeat between his teeth. "Because I meant what I said. I don't want to fight with you."

My legs shake as I arch into him, nestling his hard cock against my ass.

"How was your therapy session today?"

He trails his lips over the crook of my neck to my shoulder and nips at the flesh where my blouse meets my flesh. "I don't want to talk about that either."

"Alright," I whisper. "No fighting. No talking."

"Not tonight," he murmurs. "Do you still have your bag of tricks?"

I let out a small chuckle, rolling my eyes. Of course, he would ask about the bag of sex toys I shared with him on our first night together. I'd been so nervous he wouldn't react well, but he shocked the hell out of me and promised we'd explore every inch of it and then some. We didn't get the chance that night, but it played a supporting role in many of my solo endeavors—with him as the star of my fantasy. I didn't think this is where we would be all these months later, so it remains nestled in my bedside table in New York.

"Yes," I whimper as he continues to pepper my skin with stubbled kisses, "but it's in New York."

"Well, that's a shame. We'll have to see what we can do about that."

Memories filter through my mind of all the ways he made my body sing, expertly utilizing the toys like he invented them just for me. My thighs clench together and my hips shift of their own volition, seeking friction.

"Mmmm," he moans against my skin. "You like that idea?"

"You know I do."

A growl of approval from deep in his chest vibrates against my back. His hands dig into my hips, their possessive grip turning me to face him.

A breathy gasp escapes my lips as he drops his mouth to hover above mine, inhaling my breath into his. He lifts me and steps forward to set me on top of the island.

My mouth yields to his kiss, parting to take him deeper, and his tongue ever so slightly sweeps across mine. It's not like in the equipment room, which was angry and hurried. This time he's commanding yet measured, like he's holding back.

He raises one hand, curving it around my throat to bracket the back of my neck while the other slides my hips across the granite countertop to meet his, bunching my skirt at my waist.

"Forget the Renegades board. We aren't living for them right now," he mutters breathlessly against my lips, his words piercing my soul.

My chest heaves uncontrollably and a small moan creeps up my throat as my palms find his shoulders, sliding down his thick arms to his torso until I can dig my fingers into his waist. I feel Bishop's lips curve up against mine, and I want to memorize the way it feels to have his smile. I want them all. Forever.

Fuck, I am so screwed.

The pads of his fingers slide down my throat and trace every ridge of my exposed collarbone before dipping to where the top button of my blouse meets my modest cleavage.

I know what he's about to do, but before I can protest, he grips either side of the delicate fabric and tears the buttons apart.

"Bishop!" I exclaim, at the same time he lets out an incredibly sexy chuckle.

"Add it to my tab."

"You mean the tab you still haven't paid?" It's not the first item of clothing he's destroyed—starting with the La Perla panties he shredded that first New Year's night, and most recently the skirt in his hotel room—and I get the strong feeling it won't be the last. The man has a love of tearing my clothes from my body, and as much as I fight him on it, I can't deny it turns me all the way on.

Though I wouldn't mind if he stocked my closet. Ideally, in items he wants to rip from my body. Shit. I shouldn't be entertaining the idea of wearing clothes just for him. Not that I didn't wear this skirt today because I knew it would drive him crazy. I absolutely did. I may have ordered three more just like it for the same reason.

Bishop pushes the destroyed blouse over my shoulders and unclasps my bra with a flick of his fingers. His eyes go wide as the lacey white fabric falls away. "Jesus, your tits give me fucking life."

My nipples tighten, and if I had to guess, it's not from the cool air. My tits may give him life, but I'm constantly living for this man's filthy mouth.

He runs his thumbs over the tight peaks, hard and sensitive for him alone.

"Do it again," I beg breathlessly.

He does so, this time rolling them between his fingers before pinching them.

"You like that?" he asks, though he doesn't need my response. If there's any man who could get me off from a little nipple play, it'd be him.

I nod, and he smiles wickedly before leaning down and swiping his tongue over the tip of my pinched nipple.

"Yes," I whimper, arching my back to give him better access. The movement causes my hips to slide further to the edge, my panty-covered pussy grinding against his hardened length.

Bishop swallows a gravelly groan of satisfaction. "Goddamn," he exhales, pulling away for only a second.

I'm so wet, so close, and my pussy pulses as it searches for the friction only he can provide.

He lowers one hand, cupping my ass to keep me in place as he ruts against me, his cock brushing against my clit with every roll.

"Bishop," I mewl, my hand dropping to the lip of the counter and gripping tight. I wish it was sheets I could twist and fist in desperation, but I'm also completely enamored by the fact I will never be able to be in this kitchen again without blushing.

He continues to slide against me, teasing my nipples with his fingers and mouth until I'm wound tightly and ready to come.

"Right there," I pant. "I'm so close."

Usually, I would be embarrassed by coming from a bit of dry-humping and nipple play, but with Bishop, I feel none of it. When it comes to sex, he's always pushed me to the edge of the things I never thought I'd enjoy, without reservation or judgment. With him, I can just let go. Which is what I need. What we both need.

Cool air pulls me from my thoughts, like a splash of water dousing the heat between us, and I realize Bishop has taken a step back.

I'm unable to swallow the involuntary whine. When I look up, I immediately want to smack the smirk off his face. "Why did you stop?"

Chest heaving, his eyes trail down my body, lingering on the wet spot between my legs. "If you're going to come, it's going to be on my face where I can taste what I've done to you."

I open my shaky legs a little wider, giving him a better view of his prize and savoring the way he catches his lower lip between his teeth and groans.

"Yes, please," I say, with a wink.

"So fucking polite when you get what you want." He runs his fingers up my thighs and hooks them in the lacy waistband of my thong. I'm about to protest that he better not rip them as they are one of my favorites. He must sense that because he lowers them, painstakingly slowly, setting off every sensitive nerve in my body until I'm bared before him.

"Fuck, I've missed this pretty little cunt."

"It's been twenty-four hours," I mock.

"Not since I've tasted you." He growls, but I get the feeling he wants to say more.

With expert fluidity, Bishop drops to his knees, his mouth reaching the top of the counter only because of his height. He rests my knees over his shoulders and runs his tongue up my inner thigh, his scruff the perfect scratchy sensation on my skin.

Nestling his nose into my sensitive flesh, he inhales and gives a sharp nip with his teeth. "To be clear, there is no time that could pass that would make me want this pussy less."

Even though I know he's just saying them because he's as lost in this moment as I am, his words register and tug at my heart. As if he knows I'm moments from spiraling into those thoughts, he wraps his arms around my thighs and gently strokes his thumb over my clit.

His name tears from my throat as I buck off the counter, but he's there to catch me, pinning me down with his arms as he uses his thumb to expose my clit. He flicks his tongue over it just once, but it's enough to shoot a bolt of pleasure straight through me.

My mouth opens to protest that I'm too sensitive, knowing damn well it will fall on deaf ears. When Bishop Lawson gets between my legs, his only goal is to please.

He licks again, this time covering me with his mouth and making long languid strokes, flicking my clit each time he reaches the top.

I fall back onto my elbows, feeling all control leave my body. My hips take on a life of their own, rolling in tandem with his tongue, chasing my orgasm on his lips.

He concentrates once again on my clit, relinquishing his hold on my hips so he can sink two fingers inside me, curling forward.

And that's all it takes.

I'm done.

Free falling off the edge as my release rips through me so hard I'm a quivering mess on the counter. Every muscle tightens, and I press my thighs against his head, simultaneously wanting to keep him there and push him off my sensitive bits.

Bishop hums his approval against my core, his tongue procuring every last shutter my body has to offer.

Somehow, I manage to make my arms work and push up so I can see him. "Fuck." I suck in a breath, but it comes out more of a moan. He looks so damn good down there, and I can't stifle the need to touch him, fist his hair as I ride his face to another Earth-shattering orgasm.

So, I do. And Bishop lets me use him until every last shake and shiver has left me a puddle on the countertop. I lower myself onto my back, my fingers still entwined in his hair, twirling the strands like they're a lifeline.

A sexy chuckle echoes free from his chest, and I take it as my sign we are moving on.

But apparently, Bishop has other plans.

The fingers still inside me pick up speed, hitting the spot deep inside me he's never had a problem finding.

"One more, Kitten," he growls. "Give me one more."

His tongue lashes against my clit, and I cry out. "No—fuck, I—"

His hands slip from around my hip and flatten on my stomach, holding me in place. "Don't you dare say you can't. You're thinking too much. Give in, let go."

The flutters in my stomach travel south and settle in my clit as he ramps me up faster than before, and in seconds I give in to his demands and let go for a third time, falling over the edge again, his name the only coherent cry from my lips.

My body goes limp, the cool countertop warring with the heat radiating from my body as I float in post-orgasmic bliss.

Bishop nips my thigh, and I barely jerk in response. He stands, giving me a lackadaisical smirk covered in my release. It's a good look on him.

Moving to the fridge, he pulls out a water bottle and grabs a towel off the freezer drawer. He cleans me up before wrapping his arms under me and pulling me against his chest.

My head feels heavy, nestling into the fabric of his shirt. The sound of his pounding heart grounds me, reminding me I'm not alone. We're forgetting together. And somehow that is both comforting and terrifying.

Bishop's fingers tip my head up, and he places a gentle kiss on my lips, his tongue piercing through so I can taste myself on him.

"Fuck," he rasps like it was him that just ran an orgasm marathon and not me. "It's such a joy to taste every part of you at once."

A shiver wracks my body, and he chuckles.

"Here, drink."

My gaze darts from his face to the water bottle and back. I open my mouth to argue that I'm fine, since this feels like more than just forgetting. There isn't a rule against letting him take care of me, but there should be.

I'm about to tell him as much, but I'm stopped by the harsh glare that forms on his face. I take the damn bottle.

Bishop nods, clearly satisfied as I down half the bottle. He steps back, and the moment I no longer feel his skin, the spell wears off and I get the distinct feeling we're back to being owner and player. Lawson and Willow.

He grabs his keys from beside the stove and starts toward the door.

My eyes go bug wide as I stammer, "Where are you going?"

"Back to the hotel."

"Why?"

"Because you need your beauty sleep and if I stay, I'm going to fuck you on every surface imaginable."

My head tilts to the side and I force a playful smirk. "Isn't that why you're here?"

His lips fall into a frown for a split second before he matches my grin. "I changed my mind."

Panic grips my spine and I search his face for clarity, finding absolutely none. "Why?"

"You needed this," he says as if it's the simplest thing in the world. "And trust me, getting you off does wonders for setting my mind straight."

Relief fills me. Well, mostly. He isn't saying he changed his mind about the arrangement, just about fucking me senseless. But the truth is, I want him to. I want to make him feel good too. For both of us.

"Bishop," I protest, the need to make sure he is okay setting off alarms in my head.

"I'm good. I promise. Demons at bay." He turns and pads toward the front door.

It takes me a moment to get my ass in gear and slide from the counter, haphazardly pulling my clothes back into place. I hurry after him, catching up as he opens the door.

He hesitates, and glances over his shoulder, looking too incredible for words with his finger-tousled hair and a satisfied grin. "I still hate the idea of using the kids, but I understand this partnership with the league could mean incredible things for Renegade Hearts. Instead of having them attend, have them record something that can be played throughout. Have the donors each sponsor one kid. Make them their own player's cards."

"I—" I'm speechless. Not only did he make me forget the problems plaguing my mind with his tongue, but he's managed to come up with a solution. "That's not a bad idea."

"I know," he replies smugly. Giving me a stern look, he raises his hand in a mock two-finger salute. "I'll see you tomorrow, boss."

I groan. "Nope. You can't call me that with my come still painting your lips."

The last thing I need is a reminder we could both lose our jobs if anyone found out about this fucked up little arrangement we have going on.

"No promises."

And then he's gone, leaving me standing dumbstruck in my foyer trying to piece together a single coherent thought about what just happened.

I retreat to my father's office and immediately draft a memo to the board, incorporating Bishop's plan for the gala. The more I think about it, the more I believe it could actually work.

The doorbell rings thirty minutes later and my heart jumps, hoping Bishop came back to finish what he started.

Instead, I open the door and find three giant reusable grocery bags filled with food and a note taped to one.

You need to take care of yourself, Kitten. Think of it as taking care of what's mine.
Next time I'll make you breakfast in bed after having you as mine.
-B

Butterflies take flight in my chest and my thighs clench.
I'm so royally screwed.

215

CHAPTER EIGHTEEN

BISHOP: You're not in your office.

WILLOW: That's a very astute observation. Am I supposed to be?

BISHOP: Our first game is in a few hours, so I assumed it was a given.

WILLOW: You know what they say about assuming.

BISHOP: Where are you?

WILLOW: I'm in Miami this week speaking at a conference. Where are you?

BISHOP: Your office. You hate public speaking.

WILLOW: And you hate me, yet sometimes we have to do things we don't like. Get out of my office.

BISHOP: Was that a joke?

WILLOW: Was it funny?

BISHOP: I don't hate you.

WILLOW: What do you need?

BISHOP: You.

WILLOW: Well unfortunately that's not something I can help you with today. Everything okay?

BISHOP: It's our first game, Willow. What do you think?

WILLOW: I've seen you at practice. You're going to do amazing.

BISHOP: I can't do this without forgetting.

WILLOW: Letting go is one thing, forgetting isn't something I can help you with.

BISHOP: You know what I mean.

BISHOP: Where are you exactly? Why didn't you tell me you weren't going to be here?

WILLOW: I don't have to tell you where I am.

You were at my house last night. Same with Sunday and Monday. I have the bite marks to prove it. I told you good luck last night.

BISHOP: I thought you meant t hat in the general sense.

BISHOP: Where are you?

WILLOW: Grabbing breakfast at the hotel restaurant. Get out of my office. The last thing we need is someone catching you there.

BISHOP: Go to your room.

WILLOW: As hot as that sounds daddy, I think I'll stay right here.

BISHOP: Fuck, Kitten. You can't call me daddy like that.

WILLOW: Why's that?

BISHOP: I was already half hard on my way up here thinking I'd get to sink my cock into your tight cunt. Now I'm rock hard and couldn't possibly leave.

WILLOW: Get out of my office.

BISHOP: I think I'll stay right here.

WILLOW: Bishop.

BISHOP: What happened to daddy?

WILLOW: Fine, I'm going to my room.

BISHOP: Atta girl.

WILLOW: Will you get out of my office now?

BISHOP: I can't go back to the clubhouse rocking a tent in my pants.

WILLOW: Tuck it up.

BISHOP: I'd much rather take care of this here. Maybe leave my mark all over your desk.

WILLOW: Bishop

BISHOP: Relax Kitten, there's no one here. Just me and this enormous desk. I'll even turn the lights down just in case.

BISHOP: …You still there?

WILLOW: Yes

BISHOP: What are you wearing?

WILLOW: One of the skirts you love.

BISHOP: Fuck. I really need to rip every single one of those.

WILLOW: Where's the fun in that?

BISHOP: I'll enjoy it. Now take it off.

WILLOW: Bossy.

BISHOP: You like it.

WILLOW: Done. Now what?

BISHOP: Lose the sexy white lingerie we both know you're wearing.

WILLOW: This seems a little one sided.

BISHOP: Are you asking me to take my cock out, Kitten?

WILLOW: At my desk? Maybe

BISHOP: No.

WILLOW: Why not?

BISHOP: Not until you tell me exactly what you want.

WILLOW: Fine. Take out your cock

BISHOP: Only because you asked so nicely.

WILLOW: Run your fingers along the bottom swirling the tips around the barbels like I would my tongue.

BISHOP: Fuck Kitten

BISHOP: That is quite possibly the hottest thing you've ever said to me.

BISHOP: I take it back. Yelling my name when you come is infinitely hotter.

WILLOW: Stroke my cock for me. Gently. You can't come until I do.

BISHOP: What will you do for me if I do?

WILLOW: Anything you need.

BISHOP: Are you naked?

WILLOW: And spread on the bed.

BISHOP: Fuck yes. Your body is perfection, Kitten. Every fucking delicious curve. Tease those beautiful tits. Feel the weight of them in my hands.

BISHOP: Take your nipples and roll them between your fingers. Slowly. Then pinch them and pull them out like I wish I was doing with my teeth.

WILLOW: Holy hell. I've never done this before. Why is this so hot?

BISHOP: Because we're magic, Kitten.

BISHOP: Fuck I love your hands on me.

WILLOW: I need more.

BISHOP: Slide your hands down the curves of your body. Slowly, trace tiny circles over your hip bones with your nails, feel my lips worshiping every inch of you.

BISHOP: Trail them across your pretty little pussy, but don't you dare touch your clit. Not yet.

WILLOW: Fuck. Please.

BISHOP: Are you wet for me, Kitten?

WILLOW: Yes.

BISHOP: How wet?

WILLOW: Drenched.

BISHOP: Fuck. You're such a good girl for me.

WILLOW: Touch me.

BISHOP: Beg for it.

WILLOW: Please, daddy. Please touch me. I'm aching for you to touch me.

BISHOP: Fuck, Willow I'm not going to last. I'm dripping.

WILLOW: You have to. Please. I need you to.

BISHOP: Goddamn, I love the way you beg. Slide those delicate fingers through your pussy. Get them nice and wet for me.

BISHOP: Now slowly dip two of them in your cunt. Feel me stretch you, making room for my cock. Then pull them out, and as you slide them up your pussy, circle your clit for me. Then do it again.

WILLOW: Fuck. Can you feel how wet I am? Spit on your hand and that's still not wet enough.

BISHOP: You really do have a filthy mouth?

WILLOW: I keep telling you. I learned from the best.

BISHOP: The thought of corrupting you alone could make me come.

WILLOW: Not yet. Almost. I'm almost there. Fist your dick and come with me.

BISHOP: That's it, Kitten. Work that sexy little pussy. Use your other hand to rub your clit and get yourself there.

WILLOW: Fuck.

BISHOP: Come for me, baby.

WILLOW: I'm

BISHOP: Me too, Kitten.

BISHOP: Fuck.

BISHOP: Kitten?

BISHOP: Willow?

WILLOW: I'm pretty sure I just saw stars. I've never come that hard.

BISHOP: Glad to have been of service.

WILLOW: Are you really in my office?

BISHOP: Will you be pissed if I say yes?

WILLOW: There better not be cum on my chair.

BISHOP: No, I made sure to aim for Vaughn's invoices.

WILLOW: Bishop.

BISHOP: I promise I didn't defile your office.

WILLOW: Thank you. You okay?

BISHOP: I am for right now.

WILLOW: Good luck today.

BISHOP: When are you back?

WILLOW: Late Saturday. Maybe early Sunday.

BISHOP: Expect a phone call before then. Next time I want to hear you come.

CHAPTER NINETEEN
Bishop

One more out and an at bat.

That's all that stands between me and the end of this shit show of a game.

With a full count, Bobby Townsend, the batter from the New Orleans Crescents, is jonesing to swing. His tell is his dancing feet. The guy can't keep still in the batter's box when he's been given the signal to swing away. Which is a problem because Townsend's a powerhouse hitter, one that will have no problem connecting with a perfectly placed fastball delivered from our relief pitcher, Dominic Morales.

The Crescents need this win as much as we do. Baseball may be a physical game, but it's also one hundred percent mental. This is the first game of many, but starting off strong, even in spring training, can set a team up to make a hell of a season run.

Too bad the Renegades didn't get the memo.

Carson set us up in the first five innings, containing the runs scored to three. Our offense did their job, scoring two of our own. Then things fell apart. It started with errors on the field only to be escalated by the two relief pitchers who have continued to shrug off the pitches I've called, as if they know the game and the players better than I do.

Not that I've given them any reason—aside from my ten fucking years in the league—to believe I know what the hell I'm talking about. To be fair, it's a miracle I even know the kid on the mound's name. He's one of the rookie relief guys brought up from the minors to see if he has what it takes.

For the record, he doesn't, and if I had to guess, this is his last week in the big show after his performance and the four runs he let in during this inning alone.

Maybe if you had spent more time with the relief guys instead of hiding behind Carson at practice, this wouldn't be a problem.

Not helping, I growl silently at Jackson's jab.

The Florida sun beats down miserably, causing sweat to drip from my mask down my forehead, which only serves to amplify the shitty atmosphere in the stadium. The fans aren't happy with what they're seeing. It's clear they were under the assumption we'd bounce back and be the team they remembered at the end of last season. How they thought that was possible is beyond me when I'm the only one on the field from that team.

A cackle from the seats behind home plate reaches my ears, and I can only imagine the trash being spouted. Now more than ever it's evident in a very public way that the Renegades aren't a team. We're a bunch of guys thrown together trying to play a game that doesn't work as individuals.

I press the button on the PitchCom for a slider, knowing Townsend can't hit them for shit. To no one's surprise, Morales shrugs it off. Mindful that the pitch clock is counting down, I call for a changeup, hoping we can fool the guy into swinging, but once again the rookie shrugs it off.

Fine, it's your funeral.

I call for the fastball he so desperately wants, and sure enough, Townsend's bat cracks dead center and delivers a beautiful drive to the pocket in left-center where there isn't a soul to catch it.

Mentally shaking my head, I pop up and prepare to protect the plate as Keller and Brooks—our centerfielder and second baseman—react quickly and hold him to a single.

When the next batter takes to the box, Morales finally listens to me and throws the slider I'd hoped would keep Townsend off base. The ball comes off his fingertips at an angle and veers right, forcing me to reach out to get it. My balance is off and that's the only encouragement Townsend needs to take off toward second.

The muscles in my thighs burn as I fumble to right myself, safe with the knowledge I have one of the quickest reaction throws in the league. I manage to pop up and send a beautiful throw to second where the ball lands moments before Townsend reaches the bag—and in the dirt. Etchers, our shortstop, isn't there to catch it. He's two feet in the opposite direction.

"Fuck," I mutter, my eyes darting to where the ball has continued its trajectory into center field.

It was my fuck up. I threw it as if Jackson was the player at shortstop receiving the ball. It's a play we've practiced a thousand times. So much so that it's ingrained in my muscles. That's where he stood. Every. Single. Time.

Etchers throws his hands up in my direction and curses instead of covering down. If he had, he would have seen Keller wasn't there to field the runaway ball. Townsend takes the opportunity and heads for third.

Graham's curses echo from the dugout as my team finally gets their shit together and gets the ball back to Morales on the mound.

The play is yet another example of our lack of cohesiveness. If *my* team were on the field, this never would have happened.

Except this is your team, Tommy whispers.

He's right—and he's wrong.

Nothing about this team feels right. It's easy to blame the fact that we're individuals trying to find our way in this shit situation, but I'm not sure that's exclusively the case for me. The rest of the guys were traded here, some of them because they wanted to be and others against their will. For them, it's absolutely the growing pains of a new beginning. For me, it's personal.

Lining up behind the plate, I look out at the eight men staring back at me, and I search for something, anything, that ties me to them besides the black and orange uniform we wear. There's nothing. And I get the feeling they'd say the same when they look at me.

We're fucking screwed unless something changes.

What surprises me is, I want it to change.

Maybe it's the fact I hate to lose and there is no way I'm going to sit through an entire season of this bullshit.

Then again, maybe it's something else. Something more.

And that scares the shit out of me.

To absolutely no one's surprise, we take the loss.

Despite the fact my muscles are screaming in protest for me to give them some sort of relief, I forgo any treatment and head to my private little locker room off the clubhouse, wanting more than anything to lick my wounds alone before I have to open new ones with Jolene at my mandated therapy session in a half hour.

I enter the tiny converted equipment room and change quickly before scrolling on my phone, trying to decide if Willow would prefer purple or pink. She doesn't really seem like the pink kind of girl. She's got too many layers for that. Layers I completely misjudged until she proved me wrong last weekend. And while I might have made her come numerous times since then, I feel as though I owe her to make up for my shortcomings.

Okay, it might also be because I still can't get over how hot our sexting was this morning, and I would love nothing more than to hear her come around a toy of my choosing.

You owe her a fucking apology, Jackson snorts.

I roll my eyes despite the fact he's right. It's something I've been putting off, mostly because I can't seem to find the right thing to say. Every time I open my mouth to start, the words feel hollow and disingenuous.

Could it be because you have feelings for her, and you're running from that too?

It's Norah again, always sliding in with the voice of reason. Except this time, she's wrong. I can't have feelings for Willow. I don't. Not because she isn't an incredible woman, but because nothing can come from this. She's my boss, and I'm in no place to give her what she needs.

Is that it? Norah asks.

Yes. No.

I run a hand through my hair, cursing my best friend's wife and her probing questions.

I know the reason. It's the fear at the heart of everything. I can't lose her like I lost them.

After I hit purchase, my phone buzzes and I see Lana's name flashing across the screen. I wince as I swipe to answer, praying she isn't calling to give me another lashing. The game was enough. I don't need to be reminded I'm failing where Phoebe is concerned too.

Thankfully, I'm not greeted by the face of my best friend's mother, but instead by the smiling, toothy grin of my goddaughter.

"Uncle Bish!" Phoebe exclaims.

I smile, my heart so damn full at the sight of her. "Hey Short Stack, how are you?"

"I'm good. I'm sorry you lost your game."

"You saw that, did you?"

She nods, her smile never faltering because to her the game is inconsequential. The only thing that matters is the man in front of her. Me.

Tears burn in my eyes at the realization. Damn, I needed this call.

Phoebe tilts her head to the side and frowns. "What's wrong, Uncle Bish?"

I swallow hard and blink back the emotion in my gaze, hating that they have the power to dull the sparkle of my sweet girl. "Nothing, Pheebs. I'm just really happy to see you."

"I'm happy to see you too!" She bounces in her seat, shaking the phone as she does. "Nana said I could call you and see if we could come down for a game when I'm on spring break."

"You want to come down to Florida?" I'm caught off guard. I assumed Phoebe would want nothing to do with the team after losing her mom and almost her dad, but as always, she's full of surprises.

"Uh-huh." She nods, her high ponytail sliding across her face. "Nana says as long as you are okay with it, we'll book the tickets tonight."

"Let your Nana know I'd love for you to come down for a few days, and that I'll take care of the flights if she sends me the dates."

"Okay! I can't wait to see you and meet the team."

Phoebe keeps talking, and despite the fact I nod along, I don't hear a word. I'm too consumed by the ringing in my ears and the metaphorical knife twisting in my chest.

I'm blown away. Stunned into silence.

"Uncle Bish?"

Her curious tone pulls me back to the moment, and I blink a few times and nod. "Yeah. That sounds great."

"Okay. Nana says she'll call you later."

I nod again and smile. "I'll be waiting by the phone."

"I love you," Phoebe says, and I feel its warmth through the phone.

"Love you, too, Short Stack. I'll see you soon."

"Byeeeeee!"

I swipe to end the call and let the silence of my haven away from the team wash over me, grateful they can't see me on the verge of falling apart after a five-minute phone call with my goddaughter.

Phoebe, my sweet, innocent, little flower child, looks at me like I hung the damn stars. She sees the world with rose-tinted glasses. She wants to meet the team like it's a simple fact of life, and they aren't the men who were chosen to replace her father.

I'm not sure if I want to feel betrayed or impressed that at nine years old, she has the emotional capacity to grieve her parents and still embrace this new team when, at thirty-four, I can't.

She's smarter than you, that's why. Jackson voice beams.

She is. I don't deserve her. And yet, after the conversation, I'm more determined than ever to ensure she stays a part of my life.

I have to figure out how to get my shit together.

Bishop

Jolene doesn't bother getting up from her plush, oversized armchair when I enter the office and gestures for me to join her on the sofa on the opposite side of the room. For a woman so young and in a field working with mostly men, she's got the intimidating stare down pat. Even so, the space she keeps is inviting. I have no idea if she had anything to do with creating the vibe, but I appreciate that it's cozy with a modern and fresh flair. Instead of motivational posters or candles burning, she's got tasteful black and white close-up photos depicting elements of the game—a ball on the foul line, the corner of a base, and a row of seats. Instead of walls lined with binders and psychology reference books, she's got a mix of classic literature and romance novels to keep her occupied during spring training.

I wonder if Willow knows about this literary treasure trove. She and her friends would probably take Jolene under their wing and invite her into the sisterhood of the traveling smut.

Settling into the plush leather sofa, I rest my hands on my thighs, so I don't fidget with them in my lap. I'm already on edge, and I have a hunch talking about my feelings isn't going to help.

Jolene looks over her black-rimmed glasses and starts our session the same way she always does. "Good afternoon, Bishop. How have you been since we last met?"

"Fine, I guess." It's such an open-ended question. One I never know how to answer. I can't just say, *"Oh you know, still struggling and hearing my dead and unconscious teammates in my head. On the upside, I've started sleeping with my boss. No big deal."*

She scratches notes in her journal. Something I've come to hate. I know if I ask, she'll tell me what she's written, but that would mean diving headfirst into the inner workings of what she thinks about me and that's not something I want any part of.

Jolene pauses her scratching and sets down her pen in the crease of the pages before glancing up. "Anything specific you want to discuss, or is it the dealer's choice?"

"Neither," I reply honestly.

"In that case, we'll go with my plan."

I smile, but sarcasm drips from my voice. "Great."

Jolene chuckles. "You say it like it's a bad thing, but have I steered you wrong yet?"

"No, you just make the walls of my heart chafe a bit."

"I'll take it." She snorts and pushes her glasses up her nose, brows furrowing as she does. "Today I'd like to talk a bit about solutions."

I cock a quizzical brow in her direction. "Solutions imply I can be fixed."

"You'll never be fixed, Bishop. That's not how grief works." Her words echo Willow's, and while I understand them, they're not what I want to hear. There has to be a way to escape the waters I'm drowning in, even if I have to claw my way up the rocks to shore. I can't live here forever. Even if, at times, it's starting to hurt less, I don't want to feel this at all. I have to be fixed if I'm going to be the person Phoebe needs.

I shake my head, knowing if I continue down that road, I'll end up in one of two places as soon as this session is done. Willow's bed or the nearest bar. One isn't an option at the moment, and the latter would undoubtedly end with me being traded, or worse.

"There's got to be a point," I say with a sigh, a desperate edge to my voice. "A goal. Something to work towards."

Jolene's concerned expression gives way to an easy smile. "That's exactly what I want to talk about. You've done great while at spring training, not turning to the unhealthy coping mechanisms you did during the off season."

She wouldn't be saying that if she knew about the deal with Willow. I can't imagine fucking your boss to feel an ounce of happiness counts as healthy coping.

"It's not like I have a lot of time to do much," I say with a casual shrug.

"Give yourself some credit." She leans forward in her seat and sets her notebook aside. "*You* are the one who makes the choice, not anyone else."

I only barely manage to stop myself from rolling my eyes. "So, I've managed to not completely fuck up since being here. What's next?"

"I saw the game today." Her words are as tight as the thin line of her lips, as if she's hesitant to bring it up.

I nod. "So, you know it was a bit of a shit show."

"It was the first game."

My chest rumbles with a laugh. "I believe Graham's exact words, when he ripped us a new one after, were he's seen little league teams play with more heart than what he saw out there today."

"Why do you think that is?"

"Because we can't play for shit together. But as you said, it's the first game." I can only hope it's not an indicator of how the whole season is going to go.

"That's an astute observation." She picks up the notebook again and writes a few words before setting it down once more. "How are you jiving with the team?"

It's a question we both know the answer to. I'm not.

Most practices have been spent with me showing up late and ducking out early to get a jump on any therapies I need before the guys flood the clubhouse. The short time I am on the field is spent using Carson as a shield in the bullpen or putting everything I have into drills, so that I don't have to communicate with the men trying to replace my team.

Jolene sighs. "I can see your mind working to try and find an answer that I'll be happy with, but that's not what I'm looking for here, Bishop."

Her prickly stare bores into me as I run my hand across the back of my neck and exhale heavily. "Fine. I'm not. There isn't a single part of me that wants to look up from behind the plate and see those men on the field."

"And what can we do to change that?" Jolene prompts, waiting for me to come up with a solution on my own.

Ah. Solutions. I get it now.

"That's why I'm here, isn't it?" It's a cop-out. Mostly because I know, even though I wasn't the sole reason we lost today, there is more I could be doing.

It's the gut feeling I get every time I step out on the field. Like I know exactly what I should be doing, but I just can't bring myself to do it. Sometimes it's fear that stops me. Other times it's anger. But every time the result is the same. I'm just not ready. Even if I want to be. Even though I know it's what I need. It's like there is a mental barrier I just can't break through.

"To a point, it's why you're here, but I'm not going to tell you what to do. As we've covered before, I can guide you and make suggestions, but I think it's better if you realize what you need and then we work together to come up with a plan."

She's right. That's why I'm here. It's why I've fucked Willow every chance I get. To learn to live. To feel something more than grief. But that's not a plan. It's not actionable. I'm still running with my tail between my legs.

The realization hits me like a freight train. Coupled with the weight of Phoebe's phone call, my chest heaves and I struggle to breathe. But damn do I want to. I want to breathe. Which is why I force myself to formulate a plan.

"Fine," I mutter through gritted teeth. "I need to figure out how to see them as my team."

Jolene nods, though her approval does nothing to soothe me. "Alright. So, what's step one?"

Fuck if I know.

I search my mind for an answer—anything I can hold on to that resembles a solid plan. How do I see a team?

My thoughts drift back to my first spring training after being drafted to the Renegades. I was the young, hotshot hopeful straight out of college. The manager made it clear I was the team's first line of defense behind the plate, and there was a lot of pressure on me to not screw up as I figured out how to lead our team to victory.

A manic laugh bubbles in my throat, but I manage to keep it at bay. The weight of it isn't much different than it is now. Except now I know too much. Back then, I was a cocky twenty-three-year-old with a love of the game and an even bigger love for life. I was fucking terrified but put on a brave face for everyone else. It wasn't until our ace pitcher took me aside and gave me a piece of solid advice that I came into confidence of my own.

"It's just a game," Peter said. *"At the end of the day, those nine innings are just that—nine innings. It's the people at your side when you walk off the field that matter. Win or lose, you do it together. So as long as you do right by them, you'll be okay."*

Fuck.

My chest tightens and tears prick at the back of my eyes. I do my best to blink them away, but one or two fall. I haven't thought of Peter Daily or his words in years, but fuck if they don't hit me right where it hurts the most.

But how am I supposed to do right by the men on the field when doing so means betraying the ones who they replaced?

We aren't on the field anymore, Bish, Tommy answers, as if it's plain and simple.

But you're supposed to be—is all I can respond with.

Shit. Why did today, of all days, have to be about the hard truths?

I'm unsure of how much time has passed reminiscing, but when I speak, my voice is barely a gravely whisper. "I need to do right by them."

"What does that mean?"

"I need to give them a chance to be my team." I speak the words, but every syllable digs the dagger of betrayal deeper in my gut.

"That's a good start," Jolene confirms. "What does that look like?"

I give a half-hearted shrug and sink further into the plush sofa. "Hell if I know anymore."

"I think you do." Jolene smiles as she continues. "The fact you came to the conclusion on your own, that it's about you making the choice to let them in, tells me you can see the disconnect. What about a team dinner? Keep it casual."

Just the thought of spending an evening with the team makes my skin crawl. It's not that I couldn't manage it, hell I see them every damn day, but dinner is too intimate. On the field, there is a distance between us, almost as if my catcher's gear is armor I can hide behind. At dinner, I have none of that. It's not seeing them that makes my stomach churn. It's having to come up with small talk when I have no interest in investing time in them beyond the game. They aren't my team. I don't want them to be.

God damn.

That's the crux of it. I don't *want* them to be my team.

It's not the first time I've had this thought, but it's the first time I've been struck stupid by the gravity of it.

It's me. I'm the problem.

"Bishop?" Jolene calls my thoughts back to her question of a team gathering.

I shake my head. "They aren't my team."

When she speaks again, her voice is soft, almost cautious. "What about one person on the team? Can one person be your team? Then maybe two. And so on."

Carson is the first person that pops into my head. He's safe—annoying as all get out with his positive attitude and snarky bullshit—but safe.

"Maybe," I rasp, even though I want to give her the bird and tell her hell no. But the image of Phoebe smiling keeps me moving forward.

"Before our next session?"

A half smile tips my lips, and I feel my shields sliding back into place. "Now that's pushing it, doc."

Jolene sighs and crosses her hands in her lap. The movement reminds me of a parent trying to explain consequences to a child even though the explanation will likely fall on deaf ears. "I understand this is hard for you. What you've been through isn't something to take lightly. Healing takes time. It might not be today. It might not be tomorrow, but someday you'll wake up and realize that some people can be trusted. Sometimes you just need to jump. Otherwise, you end up standing in the same place your whole life. I'm hoping maybe your team can be the first leap."

I'm absolutely regretting showing up for this session. Even worse is that I know she's right.

With every second that passes, my muscles tense as my anger rises—at Jolene for being right, at the team for dying in the crash and leaving me behind, but mostly at myself. It keeps rising until I snap.

"The problem isn't trusting them," I bite back louder than I intended. "It's trusting myself to be okay with losing them when they inevitably walk away."

"Or die," Jolene adds, her face a mask of calm and truth.

And there's the heart of it.

Jolene wants to make plans and find solutions, but instead we've found ourselves at the core of my hang-ups. I can't let them in because they are all going to leave me. It's the reason why I've pushed everyone away. Why I can't force myself to call my family and tell them I'm okay. I can't let anyone in because I don't want to hurt when they inevitably leave or die. It doesn't matter if that's years from now. It's like I see it and—I can't—fuck.

I stand and run my hand through my hair, tugging until I feel the pain radiate down my skull.

"Fuck you!" I yell, not caring that she shrinks back into her chair. "You think you know what's going on here and—I—I think we're done for today."

"Okay," Jolene stammers quickly, pressing her lips into a grim line. "We can put a pin in that and come back to it when you're ready."

"Fine," I growl.

"I'll see you on Monday. Good luck at the game tomorrow."

I don't bother thanking her. In fact, I don't say a single thing as I storm out the door, straight through an emergency exit and out of the stadium. The alarm blares, alerting the staff that someone has opened a door, but I don't give a shit. I'm sure this will count as one of those fuck ups Willow cautioned me about, but I can't go through the clubhouse right now. I can't look the Renegades in the eye and pretend I'm okay with them standing there.

Fuck.

This isn't supposed to be this hard.

Says who? I'm incredible. Of course you miss me, Tommy sounds off, and I can't stop the chuckled sob that wracks my body.

No one stops me as I exit the stadium, which is good because they'd probably get a fist to the face if they did. I'm not sure where I'm headed, but I know it's got to be far away from here. Far from the pressure of who I'm supposed to be. Who I want to be. Who I'm not sure I'll ever be again.

But fuck, I want to be that person.

I yank open the truck door and slide in, my hands white knuckling the steering wheel as I peel out of the parking lot and drive. It's not until I'm on the highway that I realize where my body has taken me. The sign reads one hundred and sixty miles to Miami. In silence I seethe at what this might mean, but ultimately give up on caring. Instead, I focus on nothing but the road ahead, leading me toward the only thing that will calm the storm raging inside me.

CHAPTER TWENTY-ONE
Willow

It doesn't matter how many times I give a speech—it doesn't get any easier.

Prior to last year, Leigh handled all speaking engagements Renegade Hearts was asked to participate in. I blame Bishop for the fact I'm here instead. If he hadn't dared me to get up on that stage and tell my story to that crowd last New Year's, I wouldn't have been asked to headline as many conferences. He encouraged me to share a piece of myself that night and it, in turn, inspired others. It's only gotten worse since becoming the owner of the Renegades. Organizations love to add that to the headline beside my picture in their event programs.

I hate it. But at the same time, I love it. Every time I step out on a stage, I still experience the trickle of anxiety, but getting to witness the wheels click for people who have never experienced loss is truly amazing. Seeing the change that comes from what I do, the difference it makes when it comes from me instead of Leigh, is breathtaking.

Smiling as I wrap my speech, I never lose sight of the clock on the back wall, specifically the number six. Bishop might be to blame for my rise in public speaking, but he's also the reason I can get through it without crumbling into an anxious mess. Focus on one thing, he told me. Something that isn't going to waiver. Then talk to it like it's the only thing in the room. Hence the number six at the bottom of the clock.

It's also the first digit in the number he wears on the back of his jersey, but I refuse to acknowledge the correlation.

The audience is engaged, hanging on my every word, and I'm thankful the press isn't involved at events like these. It would ruin what we're trying to do. Plus, they're far too busy working to weave a tale of fabricated lies to care about a conference for educators or my talk on guiding students who have lost a parent.

My new favorite press story is that I missed the team's first home spring training game because I had to get my bikini waxed for my date with Jensen Fox, the significantly older owner of the Boston Navigators. All because I ran into him as I was exiting a salon and we exchanged hellos.

Imagine if they knew why I really had a wax appointment.

I finish my speech, and I'm about to take questions when a shuffling at the back of the room catches my attention.

My heart skips a beat, and my stomach drops when my gaze connects with the desperate brown stare of the man whose number I've fixated on for the last hour. I let out an unintelligible mumble as I take in his bloodshot eyes and the bags beneath them. His hair is tousled like he's been running his fingers through it nonstop, and his shoulders are slumped forward.

What is he doing here? Doesn't he have a game?

My eyes dart back to the clock, and I remember this is the evening session. The game ended hours ago.

Mind racing, I quickly thank the attendees and apologize for not taking questions before rushing from the stage toward the exit.

My heart pounds against my rib cage as I search for Bishop in the crowd exiting the ballroom. I need to find him and make sure he's okay, even if I already know the answer.

He isn't.

I'm halfway down the hall, heading toward the lobby of the hotel when a large hand wraps around my bicep and yanks me into a small alcove.

Without a single word, Bishop tugs me against his chest. Clinging to me tightly, he nuzzles his nose into my hair and lets out a sigh of relief.

A few moments pass before I carefully pull back and tilt my head to meet his gaze. We can't be here like this, out in the open. Even with the press not present, all it would take is one person—the right person—to see us together, and we'd both be in hot water.

"Let's go talk somewhere quieter," I offer.

"Kitten, please." His words are a strangled plea, paired with a hefty dose of desperation framing his eyes.

Kitten. Not Willow.

Anxiety takes up permanent residence inside my chest. This must be bad.

I lace my fingers in his and pull him out of the alcove toward the elevator at the end of the hall. In the most un-Bishop-like fashion, he complies wordlessly.

In the safety of the elevator, we ride up to my floor in silence. He doesn't flinch. Doesn't move. Eyes glued to the door in front of us, Bishop's hands never leave my body, one wrapped tightly in mine while the other takes purchase on my hip, digging in almost as if letting go would have him losing whatever minuscule control he has left.

I glance up at him over my shoulder, anxiety coiling low in my belly at the same time my heart seizes in my chest. He's lost, but he chose to come here. This isn't like the nights he showed up at the beach house because sex made the next day easier. Those nights were a distraction. But this— this is something more. Like it was in the equipment room. He could have found the nearest bar, but instead he drove three hours to find me.

When the elevator doors open, Bishop lets me lead him to my suite. I quickly key open the door and guide him inside. The moment the door clicks shut, he turns to face me, and I watch as a flip switches and his eyes narrow, going from lost to pure carnal need.

"Bish—" I mutter, but I'm cut off when he pulls me forward, tangling his hand in the curls at the base of my neck, and his lips crash against mine. There might be more to why he showed up, but in that one moment, he's conveyed exactly what he needs. And I'm all too willing to give it to him.

He's not gentle, not like he'd been when he'd passionately made me come on my kitchen island. No, this is bruising, scraping, and biting— taking what he needs. He grips my jaw tightly, and I let out a tiny squeak, allowing him access to my mouth. I'm desperate to moan his name, but he refuses to relinquish control enough for my lips to part from his even for a second.

I wrap my arms around his neck and run my fingers through his hair as he spins me and pushes me back to the bed, tipping me so he falls on top of me. We're a mess of tangled limbs—him desperate to find an imaginary foothold while I'm left helpless trying to provide it.

Biting down on his lower lip, I savor the delicious moan Bishop lets slip and reward him with one of my own as he forces my skirt up to settle at my hips. He digs his fingers into my thigh and wraps my legs around his waist, grinding his lengthening cock against my lace covered pussy.

He finally breaks our kiss, panting unintelligible words under his breath. I let out a needy gasp and crane my neck to reconnect us, but he's not having any of it. His eyes are nothing but a thin line of brown around blown pupils, as wild and feral as his hands that he uses to pin me against the mattress.

"I need this," he rasps. "I'm sorry. I'm—"

Given the far-off look in his eye, I'm not sure if he's talking to me or lost in his head, but I'm not about to question it.

"It's okay, Bishop," I reassure him. "Take what you need."

My hands drift south to the waistband of his track pants, but he smacks them away, keeping control firmly in his grasp as he pulls them down on his own and frees his cock. With zero warning or preparation, he deftly slides my panties to the side and pistons himself forward, forcing me to stretch for him until he's fully seated inside me.

I cry out his name at the same time he curses.

"Fuck, Kitten. This pussy is—fuck." He buries his nose in the crook of my neck and thrusts his hips forward. Each one accented with words of ecstasy—tight, wet, deep, magic.

It's primal and fueled by the rage and pain that consumes him, and I'm here for it. Not because I want him to hurt, but because I'm the masochist of my own heart and relish the fact he shares this with only me.

My lower belly tightens, and I feel the familiar tingle where the base of his shaft beats against my clit. As if he can read my mind, or maybe because he's more in tune with my body than anyone else, Bishop slides his hand from my hip and thumbs the tiny bundle of nerves between my thighs, sending me over the edge.

Two more thrusts and he's there, too, grunting into my neck as his whole body tenses and gives into his release.

Our breaths come out in ragged spurts as we both cling to each other and bask in the endorphins of our post orgasm high. But what goes up must come down, and I pinpoint the moment Bishop crashes. He tenses in my arms and pulls back, his gaze locking with mine. Only instead of feral heat, there is nothing but fear and trepidation in his eyes.

"Bishop?" I whisper and worry when he shifts his gaze away from mine to where his cock is still embedded in me.

His lips twist into a grimace, and he fists the sheets on either side of my head.

I hold my breath, waiting for him to make a move or give any indication as to what he's thinking. What I don't expect is to hear an audible sob, followed by the heave of his shoulders.

"Bishop?" I ask again.

When his eyes finally track up to meet mine, they are wide and brimmed with tears. And I swear, for the first time, I'm seeing the soul of this broken man.

My heart aches as I reach and cup his stubbled jaw, guiding him back to my face so I can place a soft kiss on his tearstained lips. Then another on his cheeks—first the left, then the right.

"Tell me," I whisper, praying he can feel the sincerity in my words as I silently beg him to remember he's safe with me.

"I—" Bishop rolls off me, shaking his head free of my hand as he falls onto his back. He swallows hard, his bare chest shuddering as he fights against emotion. A choked inhale is the only indication I get before the dam breaks and a sob wracks his body. "She wants me to—fuck— Jolene asked me to make plans to get to know the team better and I…I know I need to do right by them, but I can't." He cranes his neck to look at me—fat tears rolling down his cheeks. "Willow, I can't. Every time I think about viewing them as my team, the knife in my chest twists deeper. They aren't my team."

Nodding in understanding, I pull him toward me until his head rests on my chest. My fingers immediately tangle in soft brown strands, tugging them slightly the way Bishop does when he's stressed.

He releases an audible sigh and sinks into me. Naked and vulnerable, there should be nothing attractive about this moment, but the fact that he is allowing me to hold him and be more than just a distraction is everything.

"I don't know how to be what they want me to be." Every word is quiet, damaged, and dripping with pain.

"You don't have to be," I say softly.

Bishop scoffs and props himself up, so I can see the scowl painted across his face. "How can you say that? Even you want me to be the man I was before."

My jaw drops open, but I quickly shake it off. "Is that what you think?"

Bishop nods and rests his head back on my chest. He brings his hand up and splays it across my hip, tracing circles around the bone with his thumb.

"You implied as much when you found me in the trashed locker room."

Shit. I did. Even if it's not what I meant, I was just as guilty of pushing him to be something he can't be.

"I'm sorry." My fingers stop running through his hair and coast down below his chin, tipping his head to meet my gaze. I need to ensure he hears me. "I want you to be the man I know you can be."

"Isn't that the same thing?"

Maybe there was a time when it was, but now I'm convinced it's not.

The Bishop I knew before was a glorified golden retriever. He was fierce and loved with everything he had—be it baseball, his team, his friends, or a one-night stand. The man before me still has those qualities, but fear has made him cautious. He holds on to the things he loves most with a death grip, and because of that, lashes out when he loses control. He might not be the same, but he's still a good man. He's shown me glimpses of that in the way he takes care of me and others. Even if it is under the guise of our agreement. He buys me groceries and comes up with ideas to support the children of the crash and Renegade Hearts. There is no doubt in my mind that pieces of the man I knew are still in there, but now more than ever, I'm convinced that's not who he is supposed to be. No, Bishop Lawson is meant to be a phoenix rising from the ashes. And when he does, he'll be something more—something hardened by grief—but still the fierce protector he's always been.

He just needs to realize it's okay to not be the white knight. Pristine and perfect. Sometimes it's the dark knight—hardened and damaged, but still honorable—who gets the girl.

Or in this case, the team.

"No." I brush away a strand of hair from his forehead. "Because the man you were before was flawless. Now you're not."

Bishop blinks repeatedly before rolling away from me, fixating his eyes on the ceiling like the tiles are infinitely more interesting than anything I have to say. "That doesn't make any sense."

"It does." I prop myself up onto my elbows and give him a pointed look. "You think you need to be that perfect man again and you don't. Screw whoever says you need to be. Including me. The only person you answer to is you."

Bishop closes his eyes and lets out a heavy sigh. "I can't do it."

I reach out and wrap my hand around his bicep. "You can. I believe in you."

He doesn't pull away but scoffs and gives me a side eye glare laced with the smallest hint of amusement. "And that's supposed to make it all better?"

"No," I admit, solemnly. "But it's a start. One day you'll get there."

Bishop mutters something under his breath, and though I can't be certain, it sounded a lot like "fuck one day."

"Right now, you just need to be here. Be present. Be with me." It's a whispered plea, cut off by a groan from Bishop, which only serves to muddy my thoughts. While he might think I mean as a distraction, my heart wants so much more. It's easy to keep those feelings distant and locked away when we're lost in carnal bliss, but when he's this close, looking at me like he can't go on, the truth seeps out of the cracks in my walls.

I need him to keep fighting.

I need him to find his strength.

I need him.

I. Need. Him.

And that's when my heart shatters all over again.

My eyes close, and I hope he doesn't see the tears that threaten to fall. I won't put this on him. He already has enough on his plate without my heart coming into play. We promised no feelings, but I lied from the start. I might be the queen of fake it till you make it. I might thrive in the distance I create to keep myself safe. But the truth is, I never stopped caring for him.

"I'm here, Kitten. Always here."

Kitten. That damn nickname I've loved since the moment he gave it to me, only to have it taunt me when I can't have it mean what it once did.

Bishop swallows hard past the thick lump in his throat and continues. "But I'm still—"

"No. Don't finish that statement," I snap, unable to stand him berating himself any further. I tear my eyes open and force every ounce of unrequited love into my stare. "You're done believing you're broken or somehow less than what you should be. You told me to take care of what's yours, Bishop. Well, I expect the same."

His eyes darken and narrow, and when he opens his mouth—likely to contradict me—I roll myself on top of him and straddle him, shocking him into silence.

"You're mine." The words pull at my heart, but despite the way it twists, I pour every promise and vow into them. "Right here, at this moment, you are mine. Mine to encourage. Mine to comfort. Mine to fuck." My eyes flicker to the door and back. "Outside these four walls, we live in a world where we've been dealt a shit hand. But here you don't get to continue to berate yourself. You can doubt me. You can even hate me, but you are done tearing apart what's mine. You asked me to help you learn to live, but you need to give yourself that chance. You are more than what the world says. I see it every time I look at you, and I am done watching you find every reason to believe them. You don't get to let them win. You are destined to live."

My lip wants to tremble, but I fight against the collapse of my heart as he continues to silently stare up at me like I have all the answers.

Fuck, I wish I did, but I'm just as lost as he is on a good day. This has become too much. I'm in too deep, but there's no way in hell I'm turning back now.

His lips tip into a curious smile, and for a second, I think I've lost him. "Kitten, you can't say shit like that to me while you're naked and straddling me and expect me to take you seriously."

I roll my eyes and frustration thrums through me. We both know what he's doing. He's using our distraction to put his walls back up. Well, tough shit. I'm not letting him shut me out.

He reaches for my hips, but I'm quick to slip from his grasp and slide from the bed. Padding across the hotel room, I grab the two robes from the closet and throw one at him before covering myself with the other.

Bishop shifts unto his elbow and grunts, giving me an "are you serious" glare, followed by a devious grin. "I didn't mean for you to cover up. I like the sight of you on top of me."

"I like being on top of you," I point out as I tie the sash in a knot at my waist, "but we're not done talking."

"Fine." His nostrils flare slightly at my words. His glare turns icy as he stands and wraps the robe around himself. Not that it does much to hide his six-four frame. It's tight across his chest, and what comes to my knees barely hits him mid-thigh, leaving his delicious tattoos visible. Each one is a beautiful, and sometimes haunting, representation of the story of his life. A story so few get to see because he's always in uniform or pants during the cold New York months. They are Bishop wearing his heart on his sleeve, or leg rather.

He slides back onto the bed and rests his back against the headboard, crossing his legs in front of him.

He knows damn well I'm a sucker for those catcher thighs.

Bishop lifts his arm in my direction. "Will you at least come back and join me? If we have to talk about uncomfortable shit, I'd at least like to have my hands on you."

I should say no. I should put as much space between us as possible and give my heart time to fortify its walls, but the damn thing flutters and

I'm helpless to do anything but nod.

His attention is glued to me as I round the corner of the bed. He lifts his arm to make room, and I slide in beside him. He leans forward and slides his arm under my knees, lifting my legs over his. "Better," he says, and I exhale a humorless chuckle.

His palm slides under the fabric of my robe and finds my thigh, fingers digging into the soft and supple flesh just high enough to send shivers through me, but not enough that I can't think.

I cover his hand with mine to halt his movement and look up to see his brows find each other, creasing his forehead.

"You say I'm destined to live, but how do I do that?"

My fingers intertwine with his, and I lift his hand and press a kiss into his palm. "You make this your team."

Bishop looks at me like I'm an idiot and didn't hear anything he said before. But I did. I know he's struggling to put the pieces together, but I have a plan. One that takes him away from me—and gives him the connections he needs.

"Take them to the Guardian," I say matter-of-factly.

"The bar?" he asks with a raised brow. "You do know I'm here with you, so I won't get drunk, right?"

"I do." I chuckle. "Drinking isn't exactly what I had in mind. Though, I happen to know Lou makes a mean Shirley Temple."

Bishop rolls his eyes and pinches my thigh, to which I let out a sound that is somewhere between a giggle and a squeak.

"How do you even know about The Guardian? It's supposed to be a team secret."

"And I am the owner," I point out.

"Your dad?"

I nod. "There might have been a few stories that were shared about the coveted team bar that probably should have been saved for when tiny ears weren't around."

The Guardian was indeed the best kept secret of the Renegades. I'd heard the stories of the spring training parties at the tiny hole-in-the-wall bar that raged into the early hours of the morning and resulted in more than a few games being forfeited in the name of hangovers over the years. It was a safe haven away from the prying eyes of fans and the media. A place for the team to let loose and bond. A place I knew for a fact Bishop had not shared with the team given that the owner, Lou, called me asking if I knew why the team hadn't been in yet.

Bishop presses his lips together and shakes his head, visibly holding back. "I can't take them there, Willow. They aren't—"

I hold up my hand, cutting him off. "Let me ask you this. Do they wear the black and orange?"

"Yes," he grumbles.

"Then they are Renegades as much as you are." Twisting so I can take his face between my hands, my thumbs trace the stubble on his cheeks. "You are so focused on how you are going to replace your team, but maybe it's not replacing more than welcoming them into the family."

Bishop's eyes widen as he processes my words before he settles into a worried silence. I'm desperate to know what he's thinking, but I don't dare say anything more. This is something he needs to work through on his own. I can lead him, but I can't do it for him.

"How do you do that?" he whispers, soft eyes searching mine.

"What?"

"Make things make sense when I can't."

I shrug, letting my hands fall away from his face. "It's a gift."

I move to settle back into his side, but Bishop is quick to tighten his grip on my waist. Using the knuckle of his free hand, he tilts up my chin and presses his mouth to mine. It's soft and intimate. A stark contrast to how we started this hotel endeavor.

He breaks our kiss, his breath still hot on my lips as he presses his forehead to mine. "Thank you."

"No thanks needed," I reply, searching for air between us but finding none that isn't charged with his presence. "I told you—we have to learn to live. Part of that is asking for help."

He chuckles. "Jolene said the same thing."

"Smart woman," I say, ignoring the fact that I'm the biggest hypocrite of them all, considering I would rather drown in these emotions than ask for help.

Bishop exhales and lets slip, "You are not what I expected."

"What did you expect?"

His hands find my hips and tug me so I'm once again straddling his lap. My arms wrap around his neck. His cock twitches beneath my pussy, separated only by the terrycloth robe I insisted we wear for this conversation. It's easy to forget we are nothing to each other when he looks at me like he is right now, with his lip caught between his teeth and fire in his stare.

Instead of answering my question, he does the last thing I expect.

He apologizes.

"I'm sorry." His deep brown eyes lock on mine.

I open my mouth to tell him it's okay, but he reaches up and thumbs my lip, stopping me.

"No, please let me get this out."

"Okay," I whisper as I manically try to rebuild the walls around my heart before the verbal battering ram of his apology blows through the last whims of my defenses.

"I'm sorry for everything," he rasps, gently. "For the locker room and the plane. I wish I had an excuse, but all I've got is an impossible amount of grief I've been hiding behind, but that's not your fault and you didn't deserve my anger."

Tears rim my eyes, and unlike every other moment when I try to keep it together for him, I don't have it in me to stop them from falling.

And like the knight he is, Bishop is there to catch them, wiping them away with his thumb the moment they stain my cheek.

He takes a deep breath, holding my teary gaze. "I'm sorry for hurting you and for shutting you out after the crash. I'm sorry for all of it. I don't deserve this agreement with you, but I'll forever be grateful for what you've done for me—what you are doing for me."

Processing his apology feels like going through a hurricane. In a convertible. With the top down.

On the one hand, I'm elated at the show of Bishop finding his way through the darkness and the promise of healing between us, but it's overshadowed by the selfish hurt that every apology he made was not what I wanted to hear.

I've long forgiven him for all those things. They are water under the bridge. What I want to hear is that he was wrong—that he wants me the same way I want him. I need him to say he's sorry, but he can no longer continue with our arrangement because there isn't a world in which I can only be a distraction to him.

Guilt floods me. And it takes everything in me not to scurry from his lap and hide my face. This is a huge moment for Bishop. He needs my support. He deserves it, but for the first time, I'm struggling to ignore the hole in my heart. The one longing for fulfillment. Love. All the things he can't give me.

God, I am such an asshole.

"Willow?" His voice brings me back to where I need to be, and I'm not sure how much time has passed since he stopped talking and I spiraled down the rabbit hole into the wonderland of my own desperate fears.

"I'm sorry too."

He leans forward and presses a chaste kiss to my temple, and I feel the easy smile on his lips. "You have nothing to be sorry for."

If only that were true.

CHAPTER TWENTY-TWO
Bishop

The drive back to Fort Myers is a quiet one, not unlike the drive to Miami. Except this time, it's not rage that keeps me company, but unsettled peace.

I could have stayed and driven back in the morning and still had enough time to make morning work before our game, but something felt off with Willow. She was still there for me, just like she always was, but her mind was a million miles away. And when I asked her about it, she told me she was fine, just tired after a long day at the conference.

I may not be the greatest when it comes to relationships, but I know that there is no iteration of the word fine that actually means a woman is okay. But I have to trust she'll let me know what's bothering her, the same way she gives me the space to come to her.

She insisted it was alright for me to stay, but I got the feeling we both could use some space after our heavy conversation. That's not to say we didn't go two more rounds before she walked me to the door and kissed me goodbye. But where she would likely pass out the second her pretty little head hit the pillow, I'm wound up tighter than a toy soldier.

For the first time in a long time, I have a plan. One that makes sense and feels like it could be the right next step. It might have taken a therapy session, a three-hour drive, and the forgiveness of a gorgeous woman to beat it into my head, but now that it's there it feels like a weight has been lifted off my chest. I can almost take a full breath.

Almost.

There are still a few more things I have to do before I'm okay.

Not healed, but okay.

I think both Jolene and Willow were right when they said I'll never be one hundred percent, but I can learn to be okay with where I am.

In the wise words of Willow York: I deserve to live.

———

It's late when I pull into the parking lot of The Guardian and text Carson, letting him know I've arrived.

Instead of responding, he steps out of a slick, black sports car parked three spots over and heads toward my truck. Unlike me, who is still wearing our team warm-ups, Carson is dressed like a damn model in dark jeans and a collared light blue shirt. It's casual, but screams he spent far too long getting ready after he took my call.

Seems I'm not the only one a little nervous about this.

I pump my hands open and close a few times to stop them from shaking before I open the door and give him a nod to follow me toward the alley that leads to the Renegade's safe haven.

Carson turns on his heel and gives a quick hop to follow. He catches up in a few strides and cracks an uneasy smile. "Where are we?"

I have to laugh because I remember having the same thought when the guys first brought me to The Guardian. The entrance to the bar is tucked away on the back side of a strip mall located a block from the river. During the day and in the summer months, the front side is packed with tourists and locals alike, but unless you know of the tiny bar, it's not likely to be found. Which is exactly why we like it. It also helps Lou is a transplant from Queens and looks out for us.

Cocking a brow in his direction, I give him a devilish grin. "Do you trust me?"

"That depends. Are you leading me into this alley to sell my kidneys on the black market?"

"I mean technically you only need one," I say with a shrug.

Carson lets out a nervous laugh, like he isn't sure what to make of my dark humor.

When we reach the nondescript door that could easily be mistaken for an emergency exit, I glance over at Carson and point out the tiny orange gargoyle painted just above the handle.

Shock colors his voice. "Is that a Renegade Gargoyle?"

I nod, loving that little touch and how it makes me feel like a sleuth discovering a secret hide out every time I've visited.

Opening the door wide, I lift my hand and gesture for Carson to enter first. As he does, I send up a silent prayer I'm not fucking up by bringing him here.

He hesitates, but ultimately pushes past the short foyer through two hanging black curtains.

"Holy shit," he mutters as I join him, eyes wide and mouth gaping. "What is this place?"

My lips twitch upward, and I want to tell him it's home. Because that's the immediate feeling that slams into me the moment I step foot on these hallowed grounds.

The establishment isn't very big, maybe twenty feet deep and another sixty wide. Nestled at one end is a bar with every liquor imaginable and a tap that is stocked with local brews and a few of the team favorites. There are a few tables scattered throughout the room, as well as a pool table, and shuffle and dart boards. At the far end is a tiny stage set up with a karaoke machine and projector to play music videos or games that might be on.

Overall, it's a typical bar. What makes it special are all the things that adorn the walls. From neon signs to framed photos and memorabilia, every inch is dedicated to the Renegades.

"It's about fucking time." A voice I'd recognize anywhere hollers from behind the bar.

I wince, mentally preparing for the verbal lashing I'm about to receive.

Lou rounds the bar and heads toward us.

The man stands at a whopping five foot five and has more muscle than Carson and I put together. Coupled with his slicked back, jet black hair and leather jacket, Lou looks like he could be the bouncer instead of the owner. He's intimidating any day of the week until you get to know him and realize he's got a heart of fucking gold.

Lou shakes my hand and pulls me into a hug, his deep baritone voice whispering, "I'm so fucking sorry, Bishop."

My chest tightens the same way it does anytime someone gives me even a hint of condolences. I never know what to say to them. "Me too" doesn't convey what I feel because I'm not sorry they died. I'm fucking livid. Though I've learned I can't say that either, because then I'm the bad guy who can't move on. Damned if I do, damned if I don't.

When Lou pulls away, I give him a tight-lipped smile and nod.

Thankfully, he doesn't push the topic any further.

Instead, he turns to Carson and grins, lifting his hand with flair as he nods to the bar behind him. "To answer your question, Mr. Whitmore, this is The Guardian. Spring training home of the Renegades."

"Fucking shit," Carson breathes, his voice dripping with reverence as he continues to take in every inch of Renegade haven. Then he turns and punches me in the arm. "You mean to say you knew about this, and we could've been here weeks ago instead of that shitty hotel bar?"

My shoulders slump at the same time Lou erupts in laughter. "Come on, I'll pour you a drink and put it on Lawson's tab."

"Water for me, Lou," I say as we head toward the bar.

"One water and a—"

"Coors light."

Lou scrunches his nose and tsks. "It's a good thing you're a phenomenal pitcher because your taste in beer is abysmal."

Carson grips his chest as if he's been wounded as he slides onto a barstool, but the smile on his face says otherwise. "Give me Coors or give me death."

I clap him on the back and take the seat next to him. "If Lou has any say, you'll be a beer snob before you know it."

Carson belts out a laugh and it settles in my chest, warm and welcomed.

The next hour passes with Lou telling stories of Renegades' of the past and Carson savoring every debauchery filled detail. Meanwhile, my gaze drifts from photo to photo, lingering longer on the ones that hold the memories of the team I lost.

Tommy belting "Living on a Prayer" at the top of his lungs during karaoke.

Jackson dancing with Norah in the corner, like no one else was in the room.

Celebrating a hard win.

The Rookie talent show.

Folston proposing to his then girlfriend because he didn't want to go a whole season without her being his wife.

So many great memories that will never be recreated with them again.

But even with nostalgia haunting me, there is also an inkling of something new, and dare I say, exciting. It started with the look on Carson's face when he walked in and has only intensified with every moment since.

Is this what moving forward feels like?

This is how it's supposed to be, Jackson whispers, and it cuts deep.

I know, I reply, *but I still miss you.*

We'll always be right here.

"Bishop?" Carson says, and if I had to guess, it's not the first time he's tried to get my attention.

I turn to face him and watch as Lou disappears into the office behind the bar, leaving just the two of us.

Carson lifts his beer to his lips and takes a sip with a refreshing exhale. "Why'd you bring me here tonight?"

"It was time." I shrug. He doesn't need to know the gritty details that got me here.

"What changed? This is…" His gaze dances from photo to photo. "I know it couldn't have been easy for you."

"It's not." I run my hand from the back of my head and scrub it down my face. "But it's what the team needs."

Carson chuckles and raises a skeptical brow. "So, then why is it just me here instead of all the guys?"

"Because I can stand you for more than five minutes?"

"Come on." Carson presses his lips together and tilts his head to the side like he's waiting for me to correct myself. When I don't, he smiles and huffs. "They really aren't all that bad."

I give him a resigned sigh. "No, they aren't. But this is me trying."

Carson nods and lifts his beer. "To baby steps."

I clink my glass against his and hit it down on the bar top. "Something like that."

"I can get behind it." Carson sips his basically-water beer and smirks. "So, again, I'm going to ask. What changed? Because two weeks ago you weren't ready to do this."

I should have known he wasn't going to let me off easy. Not when he's been a constant pain in my ass, reminding me every chance he gets that I need to do better. But this isn't him poking and prodding. There's genuine concern in his eyes, and it's that sentiment that has me answering honestly.

"Someone told me it wasn't about replacing the team I lost—but welcoming the new guys into the family. As much as I hate it, it made a lot of sense."

Carson wiggles his brows, lightening the heartfelt moment with his own brand of comic jackassery. "Would this someone happen to be a woman?"

I freeze. "Why would you think that?"

Fuck.

There's no way he knows about Willow, right?

"No reason." Carson shrugs and takes a sip of his beer. "But with a reaction like that now I'm certain it is."

"How did you guess?"

"You aren't that smart, but there's also the lingering flowery scent that I'm pretty positive doesn't belong to you."

"Okay, yes, it was a woman," I conceded. "No, I'm not telling you who."

"Fair enough." The implied "for now" goes unspoken, and I hate that I feel comfortable enough with this joker that I could see myself confiding in him.

Carson sets down his beer and turns. Resting his elbow on the bar, he spins to face me. "So, the next step is we need to get the rest of the team here."

Shaking my head again, I let out a half-hearted laugh. He makes it sound so simple.

"That's on you. That's why I asked you here. To help pick up some of the slack when it comes to team leadership."

Carson frowns, shaking his head. "Not a chance. It needs to come from you. And I think next weekend is perfect. We have a day off Sunday. We can bring them here Saturday night."

"That's almost two weeks away. You're saying you want to sit on this until then?"

He throws up his hands, holding me off. "I know. That's why it's step two in my plan."

I lift a suspicious brow. "Do I even want to know what step one is?"

"You're going to hate it, but that's why you're going to do it."

My face falls.

"Don't look at me like that. If you're serious about welcoming this team, it has to start with you. They look to you because you were the heart of the team before the crash. You know this organization inside and out."

"Maybe once I did, but nothing is the same."

"No one expects it to be."

I scoff. "Tell that to the top brass."

"Fuck them," Carson roars and from the office in the back Lou echoes, "Yeah, fuck them."

The two of us look at each other and hesitate before we both burst out laughing.

"Seriously though, aside from Graham and Willow, they all have their heads as stuck in their ass as yours was. This is our team now."

It grinds my gears to hear him call Willow by her first name, but I let it slide. Mostly because I'm shocked by the fact it doesn't hurt to hear him claim my team.

Our team.

I nod. "So, what do you propose?"

"For the next week, you're going to spend at least five minutes with each of the guys, getting to know them."

"Carson, I—"

"No, Bish." He cuts me off. "I know you didn't ask for this. Any of it, but like it or not, it's your job. Unless you want to let it happen organically, in which case we should get used to losing because this team needs something to bring us together."

Fuck, I hate losing and Carson knows it. Having used him as a shield to avoid the team, he's heard more than a few of my rants about us being unable to get our shit together.

"But why does it have to be *me?*" It's not lost on me that I sound like a spoiled child, but honestly, I'm only just figuring out how to take care of myself. There's no way in hell I can take responsibility for the entire fucking team.

Carson smiles like he's been waiting for me to ask this exact question. "Remember a few years back at the all-star week when Callahan and Zoriah had beef that carried over into the game?"

How could I forget? The All-Star game mid-season is supposed to bring players together from each league as a show of unity. But the two of them nearly came to blows in the dugout. Come to find out, it was over a fucking misunderstanding with a cleat chaser who ultimately ended up screwing them both over and giving them the clap.

"You sat them down and spent five minutes listening to each side of the story and helped them realize the broad wasn't worth the bullshit. Now look at the two of them. They're best buds."

I snort. "How is this relevant?"

"You bring people together."

"I did," I point out. "But we both know I'm not that guy anymore."

Carson shrugs. "So, you've got slightly less fucks to give. The fact that you invited me here tonight is evidence enough that you aren't completely a lost cause."

"Like I said, this is me trying." I take a pull of my water, wishing it was whiskey. "The thing is, they look to you as much as they look to me, so do me a solid and make this happen."

Carson leans in and bats his eyelashes. "Are you asking me to be your co-captain?"

I roll my eyes. "We don't have captains."

"Not officially, but you and I both know every team has them."

"Fine. But only after you tell me why you came to the Renegades."

His comment about volunteering for the draft has rubbed me the wrong way since that first week of spring training. Carson is a huge part of our team, but I need to know why he's here if I'm going to fully trust him to stand beside me.

He stills and it's the first time I've seen Carson visibly give off anything other than happy and go lucky. Whatever his reason is, it's something he keeps closely guarded.

"I'm not going to go into the details, but I volunteered for the Renegades so that when we win the World Series, my father won't be able to avoid seeing my face on every fucking bus and billboard across New York City."

My eyes widen, and I chuckle. "A revenge plot. I like it."

Carson shrugs. "You could put it that way."

"We'll make sure it happens."

"Together?" he asks, and I know exactly what he's waiting for.

I huff a dramatic sigh. "Fine. Carson, will you be my unofficial co-captain?"

"I thought you'd never ask."

Maybe it's the sly twinkle in his eye or maybe it's the fact that Carson is more observant than I've ever given him credit for, but for the first time this season I feel like I've finally got the tiniest bit of solid footing with this team. And as much as I hate to admit it, it feels good.

CHAPTER TWENTY-THREE

BISHOP: Lou says hello and thank you.

WILLOW: I take it you took my advice and took the guys to The Guardian

BISHOP: Just Carson.

WILLOW: And?

BISHOP: I'm not going to say you were right.

WILLOW: You basically just did.

BISHOP: Did you know Carson volunteered to be part of the draft?

WILLOW: I might have been privy to that information.

BISHOP: I asked him to be my co-captain.

WILLOW: Should I be worried you'll be asking him to suck your dick as a distraction instead of me.

BISHOP: Never going to happen, Kitten.

WILLOW: I've got to go. Good luck at your game today.

WEDNESDAY

WILLOW: You played like shit today.

BISHOP: You watched the game?

WILLOW: I watch every game.

BISHOP: Well there goes my theory that you watching the game is good luck. It must be fucking you beforehand that is the golden ticket to not playing like shit.

WILLOW: Ah yes, success by pussy.

BISHOP: It's been working in every other facet of life. Why not baseball?

WILLOW: Fucking as a distraction is not the same as fucking for luck.

BISHOP: And what would the difference be?

WILLOW: Fucking for luck requires a four leaf clover and dirt from the field in which you play.

BISHOP: You're making that up.

WILLOW: You'll never know.

BISHOP: You know baseball players are a bunch of superstitious fucks, you can't go waving around the keys to luck and expect us not to take advantage.

WILLOW: I'm aware.

BISHOP: When do you get home?

WILLOW: Late Sunday.

BISHOP: That gives me four days to find a four leaf clover.

THURSDAY

BISHOP: What are you wearing?

WILLOW: If I say one of the skirts you love will you drive to Miami and rip it?

BISHOP: Maybe.

WILLOW: Then definitely the skirt.

BISHOP: Is that your way of saying you miss me?

WILLOW: That would imply I have feelings and we aren't doing that.

BISHOP: Right. No feelings. But if you were to have feelings for just my cock, I think I could allow that.

WILLOW: Then I would say watching you come on my phone last night wasn't enough to satisfy me.

BISHOP: He misses you too.

WILLOW: How are things going withthe team? No distractions needed today?

BISHOP: You owe me a massive distraction when you get back into town.

WILLOW: Really, how have you been doing?

BISHOP: Okay. I've seen Jolene twice this week and Carson is forcin g me to spend five minutes a day with someone new on the team.

WILLOW: That's good. I'm proud of you.

FRIDAY

BISHOP: Hey, Lana and Phoebe are coming into town next week to catch a game during Phoebe's spring break. As much as I would love for them to stay at the team hotel, I don't want to overwhelm them with the guys. Would it be okay if they stayed with you? I might have promised Phoebe she'd get to see you while she was down here.

WILLOW: Absolutely. I'd love to have them.

BISHOP: I owe you. Thanks. They'll only be here two nights.

WILLOW: Lucky for you after this week, I'll gladly take payment in orgasms.

BISHOP: I think I can help in that department.

SATURDAY

BISHOP: Did you know Stone became a dad at sixteen and still managed to make it to the majors?

WILLOW: Was he your five minutes today?

BISHOP: I'm freaking out about taking care of Phoebe and I'm in my thirties. I can't even imagine at sixteen.

WILLOW: Wait, what do you mean taking care of Phoebe?

BISHOP: Shit. Can we pretend I didn't say that?

WILLOW: Not a chance.

BISHOP: In their will, Jackson and Norah stated they wanted me to take care of Phoebe if anything happened to them.

WILLOW: And you're going to?

BISHOP: First I've got to convince Lana I've got my shit together.

WILLOW: Phoebe will be lucky to have you in her corner no matter what happens.

BISHOP: I'm fucking terrified.

WILLOW: I believe in you.

BISHOP: I know you do.

SUNDAY

BISHOP: Are you home yet?

WILLOW: I told you it would be late. Are you okay?

BISHOP: Tell that to my blue balls.

WILLOW: So that's all I'm good for?

BISHOP: No.

WILLOW: Is that your way of saying you missed me?

BISHOP: I may have missed having you around this week.

WILLOW: I missed you too. I'll see you at the stadium tomorrow before you leave for Tampa.

CHAPTER TWENTY-FOUR
Willow

"It's preposterous!" Benjamin Harris, our team's GM, announces and slams the outline of my plans down on the conference table.

I've been back in Fort Myers less than twenty-four hours and already I'm back to public enemy number one in the organization. So much for not making waves at spring training like they'd asked.

Tucked away in their cozy high-rise offices in New York, every member of the all male executive board nods in agreement on the screen in front of us. Next to me, I don't miss the smug smile plastered on Vaughn's face. It had been his idea to have this meeting as soon as I got back from Miami. I had every intention of waiting to present my plans until closer to the gala when the board would be present in person. I should've questioned Vaughn's insistence on being helpful, but I'd been too excited to get the ball rolling.

That doesn't mean I wasn't prepared for some backlash. There isn't a world in which I thought this meeting was going to go smoothly, but I didn't expect an all-out mutiny.

Nikki offers me a soft smile from across the large conference room. She might agree with my plans, but she doesn't dare speak up against the boys' club who would have her replaced as public relations manager faster than one of Carson's pitches.

I press my lips together, silently wishing Graham was here to back me up, but he's in the clubhouse preparing with the team to travel the few hours to their game in Tampa against the Raleigh Aviators.

Inhaling a steadying breath, I tamp back the urge to yell and force my voice to be steady. "I understand it's unprecedented—"

"That's an understatement, Ms. York. You are proposing restructuring the entire financial plan for the year," VP of Finance Justin Baker interjects, "and if I'm honest, it's quite the misappropriation of funds. The budget has been set for months."

"And was approved by my father. Who is no longer the owner of this team," I point out even though everything I've said so far has fallen on deaf ears.

Benjamin lets out an exaggerated scoff. "That doesn't mean you can barge in and change it on a whim. You agreed to this two months ago when we planned the draft."

I understand their frustration. They expected me to sit and roll over. Instead, I pulled the pin from a grenade and said catch. But I believe in what I'm trying to do. These plans will make not only our team better, but it will set our organization apart from every other club in the league. We'll set a standard, one built on putting our fans and community first instead of only our players and finances, like my father did. I want to build on what he did, and this is the next step.

We've gone round and round for the better part of an hour. Which is why I say for the tenth time, "I'm allowed to change my mind. If you'll take a look, it's been meticulously thought-out and distributed over the next ten years and includes sizable donations from my personal funds."

"If the club lasts that long." Someone snorts softly from the left corner of the screen, and though it shouldn't bother me, it gives light to my biggest fears.

"I'm willing to make changes and find a solution that satisfies the board, but as the acting owner, I have the final say, and this is the direction I am taking the team."

"Your father would be ashamed." Todd Gibson, our VP of Operations and golfing buddy of Vaughn and Ben, delivers the punch, compounding my growing anxiety.

Burning pricks the back of my eyes, and my nose tingles with the onslaught of tears. I blink them away and swallow hard to avoid letting them see me falter. I don't want to be the babbling, irrational woman they think I am, but I can't help the deep-seated emotion that comes with anything related to the team. I might be able to fake it till I make it most days, but it hasn't been long enough since the crash to make me completely impervious to the grief and fear of failing at the one thing my father left for me.

"I disagree," I declare, though my voice has lost some of its confidence. "My father wanted this organization to be a family, and while he created that within our staff and players, I want to grow that family to include our fans, new and old. Upping our social media presence, adding incentives for our season ticket holders, increasing our giveaway days and options, and creating a space where our fans can gather before and after games are ways we can do that."

"And upping our player salary cap? The sponsored hotel you want to build at the edge of our property using team's funds? That's going to also create a family? How about putting feelers out behind our back to bring a player back into the fold that was ousted from the league for sexual harassment and rape?"

I wince internally. This was the part of my plan I'd been most hesitant about. Hell, I'm still not sure it's a good idea to begin with, but something in my gut is telling me to take a chance on Mercer Cohen.

"He was cleared of those charges and is a phenomenal player. He doesn't deserve to live in exile because he was wrongfully accused. Yes, Mr. Harris and Vaughn usually handle any and all roster changes, but this is something I feel strongly about, so I reached out to see if it was even an option."

"It's a legal nightmare," the head of our legal department, Mr. Fios chimes in, pushing the glasses that are too small for his face up the bridge of his nose.

"What? That he likes kinky sex?" I blurt out. If they ever found out about the bag of toys I keep nestled away in my apartment or the fact I've never come harder than when Bishop tightens his hand around my throat, I'd be ousted faster than I could count to five.

Vaughn's face twists in disgust. "He was accused of rape."

I pin a narrowed glare in his direction, challenging his allegation. "And it was found that the woman making the accusations staged the whole thing to extort him. Should he be punished for that? His livelihood taken away? All because one woman thought to take advantage of him? Should Bishop then also be banned from the league because his ex accused him of knocking her up and deserting her, even though a paternity test confirmed it wasn't his child?"

"It's entirely different." Vaughn huffs.

"Maybe, but we aren't here to judge what happens behind closed doors. We're here to build a team, and I want that team to be a legacy. I want champions both on the field and in the stands. I believe both those men are part of that vision."

"Bishop we can stand behind," Benjamin sneers, folding his arms across his chest like his word is law, "but no one will stand behind Mercer Cohen."

"So, you're saying you can get behind the rest but Cohen is a hard no." It's a stretch but if I can get them to agree to everything else, I can work on getting an exemption for Cohen through the league in the coming years.

"That's not what we're saying," Benjamin continues at the same time, Mr. Fios and Mr. Baker chime in, "It's franchise suicide" and "this is insane".

"Enough," Patrick Kincade bellows from the center of the screen, and immediately the entire room, both present and not, goes quiet.

A man nearly triple my age with white hair and receding hairline, he's a member of the executive board filling an advisor role. He's been with the Renegades since before my father took over and practically wrote the book for our business model. In this franchise, he's the sort of man that people listen to when he speaks, and unfortunately for me, he's got nothing but archaic ways of thinking to share.

"Ms. York," Patrick begins, his tone patronizing, "in one meeting you have managed to turn this entire organization into a shit show."

I grimace but keep my shoulders back despite wanting to crumble under his scrutinizing observation.

"Your youthful approach, while refreshing, is not the way business is conducted. I'm not saying you don't have the start of *some* good ideas, but this team has a legacy of its own to protect, and right now, *you* are its biggest threat. You've run a successful philanthropy, which is to be commended, but this is not a frat party or whatever you are trying to turn it into."

I open my mouth to argue, but he gives me a slicing gaze as he throws his hand up, wagging a silencing pointer finger at me. It's reminiscent of the way my mother used to muzzle me with one pointed look when I would argue I wasn't her doll to control.

Then and now, I'm reduced to feeling like nothing more than a child to be disciplined, and as a result, fail to do more than comply.

"This is a prestigious team," Patrick continues. "One that was on its way to a pennant run before tragedy struck. We are willing to entertain your ideas and even concede on some of them, if you are willing to meet us halfway and agree to some of the requests you've avoided. But understand this. You will not have the support of this board or your upper management if you continue on the road you're on. I suggest you think long and hard about your whimsical ideals and come to the right conclusion."

The audacity of this man.

And the worst part is, I have no doubt every single person—save for Nikki—agrees. This boys' club will never give any of my ideas a chance. They'll agree to the smallest bullet points and demand I fall in line.

If I was a man, they'd pat me on the back and meet me in the middle. They'd praise me as an entrepreneur, but all they see when they look at me is the same thing that Vaughn does—I'm nothing but a pampered princess who couldn't possibly know anything.

I chew the inside of my lower lip to stop it from trembling. The urge to argue wars with the instinct to back down and live to fight another day. I want to be the one who makes a difference and inspires change. But I'm only one person, and given the outrage from Patrick and the board, I don't know if it's enough.

An uncomfortable silence washes over the room as heads slowly shift to see my reaction. I don't want to let them win, but what can I do? I could fire them all and start new, but that will only shatter my standing with the league, and I don't exactly have friends in the industry who are willing to rush to my side and help pick up the pieces with only the hope of creating something great.

These plans were always a risk and maybe I bit off more than I can chew, but I believe in what I'm trying to do here. I just need more time to get the board to agree and somehow avoid becoming their glorified puppet.

"What do you want from me?" I ask genuinely, even though I know they are going to demand more than I can give.

Patrick once again speaks for the group, and a spike of jealousy rips through me. It must be nice to know everyone will fall in line behind you. "I agree. We need to step up our social media and marketing and bring the team into the modern age. The giveaways and fan space are a good goal to look into, but taking funds to expand our portfolio to hotels and event spaces out of the stadium is out of the question, as is bringing in a controversial player we can't afford. Our focus needs to be on maintaining what we have and who we are. That means embracing the tragedy of the crash and using that to our advantage. You have already railroaded us once by adjusting the gala to not include the children of the victims of the crash." I protest, "But they—"

"That being said, I have spoken to members of this board, and we believe the best way to move forward is to livestream the gala and require the entire team to attend instead of just our top players. Doing so will set us apart from other teams in the league. In addition, during the gala, we have organized a concurrent press event in which you and Bishop Lawson will sit down for an interview with Tanner Phillips of *The Foul Line* and ensure that everyone knows we are a team and one to be reckoned with."

I fist my hands against the wood of the table and shake my head. "Bishop will never go for that."

Nor am I going to let them use him like that. He is finally beginning to see the new guys as his team. In just the week I've been gone, he's taken Carson to The Guardian, and he's making the effort to talk to the other players and get to know them. I've seen a change in him I never expected. He's letting people in. Me included. I refuse to let the board take advantage of him like this. He might be the only surviving member of the team we lost standing on the field, but he's not a pawn to be sacrificed.

"You'll make him," Patrick states, as if the answer is simple. "From what I hear, you have the best rapport with him."

"And if I don't agree to this?" The weight of his stare is enough to let me know he's not asking. Shit, he reminds me so much of my mother it's scary.

"I don't make idle threats, Ms. York. You are a small fish in a big pond. One in which you know nothing about. We are here to guide you, but don't mistake that as you being in charge. This organization has worked as a well-oiled machine, and even if you were to let every single one of us go, we know the skeletons hidden in every closet from here back to New York."

He's careful not to say he'd ruin this team, but that's exactly what he's threatening. It's exactly what I was worried about and why I haven't proposed any major staffing changes to the executive board. Still, I can't help but wonder what skeletons he's referring to and if any of them are just waiting to bite me in the ass.

I look out the windows of the conference room to the empty practice field, defeat weighing on my shoulders. My father wouldn't have wanted this. I can't say for certain he would have loved my plans, but there's no way he would agree with this. He believed this team was family. And while the Yorks might have had a fucked up version of what that looked like, he always made sure the Renegades were solid.

But it's just me now.

"I'll do the interview," I murmur, turning back to face the firing squad that is my board of executives, "but I can't speak for Bishop."

Patrick's jaw tightens, and for a moment I think he's about to lose his composure, but then he takes a breath and calmly states. "That's not good enough. He's the only survivor on the field. People want his story. I suggest you find a way to persuade him if you don't want us to overrule your changes for the gala and go with our original plan."

Stuck between a rock and a hard place. I'm not sure he can actually do that, but I'm not about to find out. Unfortunately, saving the children means placing Bishop at my side when the guns go off.

My gut twists, and I hate myself for doing it, but I mutter a monotone "understood", sealing our fate.

"Then this meeting is over."

CHAPTER TWENTY-FIVE
Willow

The executive concourse is empty as I make my way back to my office. Which is good, because that means there's no one to see my tears or hear my sobs as they echo off the concrete pillars.

Fuck.

He's going to hate me for this.

There's no way he'll agree to the interview, and I don't blame him. The media is gunning for him to speak about the crash and his experiences after. They would love nothing more than to dissect each and every fight and spiral while claiming they give a shit about his healing. The board is setting him up to fail, and I have no doubt they're banking on him fucking up. Especially Vaughn.

It's not right. But I allowed it to happen.

Guilt claws at me as I consider the progress Bishop has made over the last week. He only just started to come out of his shell, and I'm worried I just forced him back in.

Selfishly, I'm worried he'll never trust me again. Because at some point he decided to let me in. He seeks me out, not only for a distraction, but to talk about the little things like his day or his conversation with whatever teammate he decided to befriend. He told me about Phoebe and how he's terrified.

And I threw him under the bus.

When I finally reach the door to my office, I slip in and shut it quickly. Closing my eyes, I sink against the cool wood, as if it will somehow give me its strength. Before another sob can crack through my chest, I hear the soft padding of feet on the carpet.

My eyes pop open to see Bishop pacing the length of my desk. Panic grips my spine.

Shit. What the hell is he doing here? Shouldn't he be in the clubhouse getting ready to head to Tampa?

Lost in his thoughts, he continues to pace, none the wiser to my presence. His team warmups accentuate the hard lines of his tense shoulders while his freshly showered hair clings to his forehead.

"Bishop?" I squeak, instantly praying my voice won't betray my state of mind.

He freezes for a fraction of a second before looking my direction, and I'm thrown back to the hotel earlier this week. His eyes are red and wide, but unlike in Miami, Bishop isn't lost to the vacant spots in his mind. He's hurting, but he's still with me.

God, I don't want to break this man again.

I close the distance between us, needing to make sure he's okay. To fix whatever has him tangled up. At least that's what I tell myself. It's absolutely not because I'm drowning under massive amounts of guilt.

A fraction of a second later, his arms circle my waist and he tugs me against his chest. His large frame encompasses mine, and even though I have no right to find comfort after what I've done, I do.

His fingers tangle in my hair, and he tips my head to meet his distraught gaze.

"Who made you cry, Kitten?" Bishop growls at the same time as I whimper, "What happened?"

His thumb traces over my tearstained cheek as a strangled laugh rumbles from him.

I force a half smile and shake my head, leaning into his touch. "It doesn't matter. Are you okay?"

"It does," Bishop insists, his brown eyes searching my face with far too much concern in their depths. "Tell me."

He echoes my request in Miami.

If this were any other moment, my heart would be jumping for joy that he cares. I'd overthink every word he says and probably convince myself that maybe I'm not the only one who would be okay with something more between us. But right now, it just makes me feel like shit.

Shaking my head, I close my eyes. It makes me the worst hypocrite on the face of the earth, especially when Bishop has so willingly given me his hurt and his grief, but I can't tell him. Not when doing so could break the trust we've built.

"Please," I whimper. "I can't give you details. Just let me help you."

His attention dances between my eyes and my trembling lip like he's debating if he wants to dig his heels in or give up and give me what I want.

Because he was here for a reason, and that reason wasn't me or my tears.

I dart my tongue out and wet my lower lip, knowing damn well I'm not playing fair and it will push him over the edge.

"Fuck, Kitten." He adjusts his stance, his cock lengthening against the hollow of my belly. His eyes darken and narrow as he speaks through gritted teeth. "We're not done talking about this."

I nod, letting him believe what he needs.

Because I'll fix this long before he'll ever hear about the interview. He won't have to know I let him down.

I'll fix it.

CHAPTER TWENTY-SIX
Bishop

Willow kisses me like I'm the only one who can chase away her demons.

Demons she refuses to share.

Something has her spooked, and I'm trying to respect her wishes and give her the space she needs until she's ready. The same way she always waits for me. But fuck, I've never been one for patience. Not when it comes to taking care of those I lo—

What was that? Jackson taunts, and I can feel his smirk curl at the edges of my mind.

Nope. Not going there.

Willow is a means to an end. She's the reason I can get up every morning and do the job I'm meant to without drowning in dark thoughts. Of course, I care about her, but I'm not about to examine those feelings any closer. Especially when I can taste her tears on our lips.

Willow's hands drop from my face and press against my chest.

When she pushes me back, I immediately miss the feel of her lips on mine.

She looks up, and I'm caught off guard by the wicked grin she gives me. It's a stark contrast to the pain and hurt she wore moments before.

With all the grace of a ballerina, Willow falls to her knees, and my mouth drops along with her. I know exactly what she has in mind long before she fists my warmups between her deft fingers and tugs them and my boxers down, situating them just past my ass.

A grunt passes my lips in protest. As much as I'd love a blowjob, I don't want this to be solely about me. She needs this too.

"You don't have to—" The words die on my tongue, replaced with a moan when her lips wrap around the head of my cock. "Oh fuck, Kitten."

My head falls back, and I reach out and grip the edge of her desk to steady myself as all the blood in my brain rushes south.

I take it back. I want this just as much as I want to please her. I want to let her worship me on her knees before I bury my cock in her tight cunt and wreck her until she's hoarse from calling out my name.

"I know I don't have to. I want to," she says with a smile before sliding my length into her mouth.

Forcing myself to think beyond my cock for two-point-five seconds, I read between the lines of her words. I absolutely believe she wants to. But I also believe she is one hundred percent avoiding whatever it is she doesn't want to tell me. It's exactly what I've done every time I need a distraction. She's playing me at my own game, and she's a fucking pro.

As if she knows my mind is wandering, Willow dances her tongue over the barbels on the underside of my shaft, pulling a needy moan from my throat.

Check mate, Kitten.

For now.

She lets out a low appreciative hum, taking me deeper before pulling back. Her tongue flicks around the crown of my cock, teasing the sensitive nerves below the head before taking me to the back of her throat again. The blonde curls I've come to love fall across her face and I curl over her, gathering them in my fist so I don't miss a moment of watching her devour me.

"Goddamn," I curse. She's entirely too good at this.

Willow's lips tighten around my shaft, causing my hips to thrust forward. She smiles around my cock like a kid with a lollipop and glances up at me. I nearly come at the sight.

Her hands wander over my thighs, squeezing the muscles as she keeps working me over, taking me so deep her nose brushes my pelvis. She's slow and torturous, but hell if she's not the most addictive thing.

Then she moans.

She fucking moans with a mouth full of my cock, and I absolutely lose it.

My grip tightens in her hair and I thrust, bouncing her at the tempo I need to chase my release. Willow's grip tightens on the back of my thighs and she whimpers, but she doesn't shy away from letting me take control. In fact, she relishes in it. Laying her tongue flat, she hollows out her cheeks, sucking like there are diamonds at the base of my shaft.

"Fuck, just like that, Kitten." My body sends a jolt of lightning down my spine, begging me to let go, but I want this to last as long as possible. I need this memory to get me through a bus ride and nine innings this afternoon.

The fucking little minx has other plans, though.

Willow slides a hand down, cupping my balls before she takes the backside of her nails to the sensitive skin. The contrast of sucking and scratching hurls me toward release.

Glancing up at me with those mischievous blue eyes, she begs me to let go, waiting and watching so she doesn't miss the exact moment I come apart.

And I want her to. At this moment, I'm a goddamn masochist living for her to be the one who breaks me.

What does that say about me?

It's a thought for another time because I can feel my heartbeat in my shaft, signaling I'm not going to be able to hold on for long.

"I'm gonna come," I pant, and Willow hums her approval.

That's all I need. My entire body tenses as I force Willow down on my shaft and come so hard my vision fades around the corners.

She rides my orgasm like a champ, and after the final jerk of my hips, I release her head from my grasp. Her sharp inhale sends a bolt of panic through me that maybe I was a bit too rough with her.

"Are you okay?" I rasp.

Willow sits back on her knees, tips her head back, and offers me a sultry smile. I'm about to ask again if she's okay when she shocks the hell out of me and sticks out her tongue, showing me my release pooled on her tongue.

My eyes go wide, and my dick twitches to life despite having just emptied. "Fuck that is the hottest thing I've ever seen."

Willow closes her mouth and swallows hard, then shrugs, like she hasn't just given me a gift. "I aim to please."

"That's a fucking understatement."

I'm seconds away from clearing her desk and showing her just how much I appreciate her skill set when a knock at the door freezes me in place.

My gaze darts to Willow. Her sultry eyes flood with panic.

She scrambles to her feet, straightening her blouse before leaning over and dusting off the knees of her pants. At the same time, I work my pants back up to my waist, my sensitive dick throbbing against the soft fabric.

"You can't be here," she snarls, running her hands through her hair, trying to tame her just been mouth-fucked curls.

She's right, but I don't know where she expects me to go. My eyes shift across the room to the glass door that leads to the private box open to the field. Not an option. Even without a home game, there are still plenty of people milling about who could spot me.

There are a few boxes piled against the bookshelves on the opposite wall that I could maybe crouch behind, but there's no guarantee whoever is at the door wouldn't see me.

"The desk," Willow hisses. "Get under it."

I glance at the giant wooden desk and back at Willow. It's not a terrible idea considering it goes to the floor, and I'd be completely hidden. That's if I can manage to get my six-four frame in the tiny space.

I shake my head. "I'm not hiding under your desk."

"Do you have a better idea?"

I give the room another once over, searching for any other viable option before succumbing to my fate and rounding the desk. It's a tight fit, but I manage to curl up enough that my head and most of my torso are crammed in the small square. All I can do is pray Willow keeps whoever is at the door on the opposite side of the desk.

"Come in?" Willow hollers.

"You alone? I thought I heard voices." I recognize the sweet voice belonging to our public relations director, Nikki.

"I was on call," Willow lies with ease.

"Oh good. I was worried about you after the meeting. It was—Well, let's just say I wasn't expecting it to go that way."

What meeting did she have this morning? And with who? Is that why she was on the verge of tears when she showed up?

Willow sighs. "That makes two of us. Though, I can't say I'm surprised, but I was hoping for better."

"They're good plans, Willow. I know you and I aren't close by any means—and forgive me for speaking candidly—but those crotchety old bastards don't know what they are talking about. Your father would have been proud of what you're trying to do."

Plans? What plans? And which crotchety old bastards are going to be meeting the business end of my fist for making her cry?

"Thank you for saying so," Willow offers, but by her voice she doesn't sound convinced. "Was there something I can help you with?"

"Oh, yes." There's a shuffling of papers before Nikki continues. "After the meeting, I went to my office and brainstormed for the interview with Bishop."

What fucking interview?

I jerk up and hit my head on the top of the desk and silently curse, while Willow sends herself into a coughing fit.

"Are you okay?" Nikki asks. "Do you need some water?"

Seething, I silently lean into the front of the desk, as if that will somehow make it easier to hear the conversation.

"No, I'm fine," Willow chokes out. "Just something tickling the back of my throat."

She definitely did have something in the back of her throat five minutes ago, though I'm surprised she was able to swallow past the lies she tells.

Because you always tell her the truth right off the bat.

Great, the peanut gallery is back.

But for once, they aren't spitting truths. I might not have given Willow a chance right after the crash, but I've given her all my worries since we started this arrangement. I'm not in the wrong to expect her to have done the same. Especially when it has to do with me. We were supposed to do this together.

Neither Jackson nor Tommy has a response, which hurts infinitely more, because it confirms I'm right.

Willow chose to shut me out.

"**I'll leave these with you,**" Nikki says. "**You can review the list of topics we will and won't allow** *The Foul Line* **reporter to ask about. It might also ease Bishop's mind when you inform him of the plan.**"

It absolutely won't. Nothing she says could possibly dislodge the knife of betrayal in my back.

Are you mad she agreed to the interview for you or that she didn't tell you?

Both.

If there's anyone I expected to understand why I don't want to talk to the press, it's Willow. She's seen me at my worst. How the hell could she agree to put me in front of a camera when I can barely talk with her about how I'm feeling?

"Thank you, Nikki. I really appreciate this." The defeat in Willow's voice is evident. She knows I heard every word.

"I'm here to help. Whatever you need."

"Sounds good."

As soon as I hear the door click, I slide from under the desk and storm toward Willow. "What the fuck was that?"

She has the good sense to take a step back, guilt plastered on her face. "I'm sorry."

"Sorry?" I growl, anger etched in my raised brow. "This is what you didn't want to talk about? Instead, you gave me a blow job to distract yourself from the fact you threw me under the goddamn bus." Turning away from her, I take up the pacing path I'd worn into the carpet before she arrived. I can't look at her. If I do, I'll lose it.

"I—you weren't supposed to find out like this," she stammers, her hand still very much caught in the proverbial cookie jar.

I roll my eyes, and I can't hide the disgust that drips from every word. "No, you were going to get all your ducks in a row and present a case as to why I'm going to do this."

From the corner of my eye, I see Willow drop her chin to her chest and wrap her arms across her chest, retreating into herself. "Actually, I was going to try and fix it before you ever found out."

I stop mid pace and drag both hands though my hair, completely baffled. "I'm not sure which is worse. The fact that you would agree to it in the first place, or that you left me out of the loop completely."

Her eyes snap up and lock with mine, tears falling freely.

I shouldn't give a shit that she looks like she's about to collapse with the weight of all this on her shoulders. I shouldn't want to scoop her up and reassure her that we'll fucking fix this—whatever it is.

But I do. I want to.

And then I want to punish her, so next time she'll think twice before she shuts me out.

"What exactly did you agree to?" I ask, needing to make sense of this before I can decide if I'm walking out the door or taking her over my damn knee.

"The board of directors asked—demanded, really—that you and I are available for an interview during the Spring Training Gala."

"And if we don't?"

She squirms under my unrelenting gaze. "I don't know for sure. They implied they'd find a way to get the children down here to bring the spotlight of the night back to the Renegades."

"Jesus, fuck. So, it's me or the kids."

Her lower lip trembles as she nods and confirms she'd fucked me over to save the kids.

I run a hand through my hair and tug at the roots. It's exactly what I would have done in the same situation.

"Essentially, yes." Overwhelming defeat lingers in her voice and hits me right in the gut. She sounds so much like me when I'm lost, haunted by my demons.

Damn it.

Every part of me wants to be mad at her, but I'm not. At least not for making the deal. She might have had every intention of deceiving me, but it was never done with malice in her heart. That's not who Willow is.

Willow protects people. She protects me.

I take a step back and lean against the lip of her desk. Opening my arms, I leave the choice up to her if she wants to take the same lifeline she's offered me time after time.

Her eyes search mine for any hesitation, and when I nod in reassurance, she doesn't think twice. In three short strides, she closes the gap and folds herself against me. I wrap my arms around her waist and hold her.

She fits perfectly in my arms.

This is where she belongs.

Fuck.

No.

I shut my eyes and resist the urge to nestle my nose in her hair and inhale her sweet scent.

Nothing more than a lifeline, I remind myself. She's a means to an end. I won't go there. Going there means risking losing her in the future, and I'm done losing people.

Tommy cackles. *You are so fucked, my dude.*

He might be right, but that's a problem for future Bishop. Right now, I want to prove I can be there for Willow the way she is for me.

"Tell me what happened, Kitten," I whisper.

Her anxiety is palpable, but she pulls back and puts on a brave face. "I was presenting my plans for the franchise to the board. They hated them, told me I was nothing but a pampered princess, and if I didn't get in line, there would be consequences. Then they blindsided me with the interview."

My jaw ticks and I nod. While I had major respect for Willow's father, the board has always been a thorn in the side of this organization. More than once, I walked past Mr. York's office and heard him yelling at one member or another about their outdated practices. But they generally gave him what he wanted, so I don't think he rocked the boat.

Not Willow.

Willow was made to make waves. She doesn't deserve to be put back in the box her mother kept her in for so much of her youth. She worked too hard to break free of that part of her life. I'm guilty of believing she fell back into that way of thinking. I'm not going to allow her to actually be put there.

We deserve to live.

I'm about to ask what her plans entailed when Skillet's *"The Resistance"* blares as an alarm from my phone, signifying I've got to head back to the clubhouse to make the team bus.

Shit. It's the worst possible time for me to have to leave. I didn't even get the chance to distract her, let alone impart some wisdom like she always manages to do.

"You've got to go," Willow surmises.

I brush a curl away from her face and nod. "I do, but I want to see your plans and Nikki's talking points."

She glances up, brows raised. "Really?"

I meet her eyes, memorizing the pools of blue. "Send them over and we'll talk tonight when I drop off Phoebe and Lana." I lean down and press a kiss to her cheek. "This conversation is far from over."

"Okay," she whispers, and maybe it's wishful thinking, but I almost hear an ounce of her confidence returning.

Paired with the anger that still simmers under my skin, it will have to be enough to get me through the next few hours. Because when I see her again, we are absolutely going to have this out. And then I'm going to distract the fuck out of her.

Whatever you got to call it to sleep at night, buddy.

Fuck off, Jackson.

CHAPTER TWENTY-SEVEN
Willow

Phoebe's eyes dart from the box of gourmet donuts to me and back, her head dropping when she realizes the sweet breakfast treats arrived without her uncle in tow.

"I know you're bummed you didn't get to see Bishop last night," I offer, wanting to pluck the sadness straight from her giant heart, "but he sent your favorite breakfast."

"They're only my favorite with him." Phoebe huffs, resting her elbows on the island. She dramatically lowers her head into her hands and lets out a weighted sigh.

It breaks my heart. Ever since she saw me standing at the airport last night instead of Bishop, Phoebe has had a rain cloud hanging over her head. I think she needed this trip more than any of us realized. She's kept it together remarkably well since the crash, but it's clear having Bishop away has taken its toll on her.

I'm ready to say screw it and drive her to the team hotel if only to see her smile.

"I'll tell you what, eat up and we'll head down to the field early so you can watch batting practice and morning work before the game."

"Really?" Phoebe looks up from her hands and a hint of a smile traces her lips. "Are we allowed to do that?"

"Not normally." I plop down on the seat next to her and open the box that smells too heavenly for words. "Lucky for you, I know the owner."

Phoebe giggles, appeased by my offer, and digs into the box, carefully inspecting each of the options available.

It wasn't Bishop's fault the bus broke down on the way back from Tampa, leaving them stranded for an extra three hours. By the time they were able to make it back to Fort Myers, it was late and Phoebe had already passed out on the couch. Lana made the executive decision that we shouldn't wake her and let Bishop know we'd see him at the game today.

He agreed, much to my dismay.

Not that I could blame him. He had no reason to come over. Still, selfishly, I wish he would have insisted.

After the fight we had yesterday, I'm not sure where we stand, and I hate being on unsolid ground. Especially with him.

I screwed up by aiming to keep the interview from him, but I really thought I could fix it. I still think I can. There isn't any reason why he should have to get in front of the press if he doesn't want to.

But that isn't the point.

Over the last week, Bishop and I have found ourselves in new territory, skating somewhere between fuck buddies and something more—friendly? Lovers isn't the right word. Still, friends doesn't seem like enough.

I told him he was mine, and I meant it. If that doesn't say more, I'm not sure what does.

Maybe we're an ass-backward version of fuck buddies with benefits—the friendly part being the benefit. But damn if it isn't a benefit I want.

I sip my coffee and shake my head to myself. If that's the case, I'm hands down a shitty friend because it didn't cross my mind to ask him for help with this.

Bishop has given me his trust, and I've done what I always do—fix things. I listen to him. Distract him. Protect him. Even if doing so breaks my own heart. It's the curse of giving a shit.

No one tells you that, when you give a shit about others, it becomes second nature to keep them at a distance. It becomes second nature to hide behind their problems and push your own deeper.

My therapist would tell me it's a coping mechanism, but for me it's surviving.

Most of the time, I don't even realize I'm doing it. I will give and give to those around me. I'll even allow them a glimpse at the things that break me. But I don't ever fully let them in enough to see me fall apart.

Bishop is a special case.

I accidentally let him in once. He didn't ask to witness me sink into panic and lose it on that balcony in New York, but when he did, he brought me back and pushed me to be more. Then I left, shoving him away like I do with everyone when they get too close. I never could have predicted our world would implode as it did. And now to let him in—let him help me again—feels more intimate than I'm ready for while still managing to protect myself.

Because that's what I'm doing with Bishop. Constantly trying to stop the traitorous organ in my chest from demanding more than either of us can give.

Not that it matters this time. I hurt him.

And now I might lose him.

Lana pads into the kitchen, pulling me from my thoughts. She eyes the box of donuts with a knowing smile. "Your uncle sent over an apology breakfast?"

Phoebe bounces in her seat beside me, and I preen, knowing my plan has lifted her mood.

"Yup!" Phoebe pops the p at the end before taking a giant bite of a frosted pink donut with Fruit Loops sprinkled on top. "Willow is going to take me to the field early to watch batting practice."

"That's a great idea," Lana says, snatching a glazed donut covered in Oreo crumbs before turning toward me. "If it's okay with you, Willow, I'll meet you guys at the field closer to the game. I've got a few calls I need to make, and honestly, I'd love to take a nap."

Phoebe's brow furrows in the most adorable way. "You just woke up, Nana. You don't need a nap."

Lana chuckles and ruffles her granddaughter's hair. "When you get to be my age, there are no time restrictions on naps."

Phoebe gives her a skeptical head tilt, making Lana and me laugh.

"Of course," I say, reaching for the carafe of coffee in the middle of the island. Pouring Lana a mug, I then top off my own. "It's not a problem at all. I'll give you the number for my driver. He'll pick you up whenever you're ready. And if you want to spend the afternoon by the pool, that's okay too. I've got Phoebe."

"Really?" Lana's eyes widen, exhaustion evident in the soft purple circles beneath them. She places her hand on top of my forearm like I'm offering her the lifeline of all lifelines. "Are you sure?"

I nod. There's no way I'm allowing Lana to go to the stadium today. This saint of a woman has taken on the role of both parents for Phoebe since the crash, and even though I don't doubt she'd do it over and over again for her granddaughter, she didn't ask for the level of exhaustion that comes with taking care of a nine-year-old. If anyone deserves a break, it's her.

"I insist. Let me take Phoebe. You relax today." I turn to Phoebe, who has a mustache of powdered sugar dusting her upper lip from the second donut she snagged when Lana and I weren't looking. Laughing, I hand her a napkin. "We'll have a girls' day. I'll even take you to pick out a jersey at the team store."

"Really? Do you think they'll still have my dad's jersey?" Phoebe asks excitedly, wiping her mouth and hopping from the stool.

I force a smile, keeping Phoebe's attention on me so she doesn't see Lana wiping the sudden tears from her eyes.

"I know for a fact they will," I assure her.

The smile on her face makes me glad I fought the board to keep the jerseys of the team we lost in the team store for one more season. They wanted to discontinue them and auction off the remaining stock for absurd amounts of money.

Her smile falls as fast as it appeared. "But what about Uncle Bishop? Do you think he will be upset that I'm not wearing his number to see him today?"

"I think he'll understand," I offer, knowing damn well Bishop will be happy to see Phoebe wearing her dad's jersey.

Her nose crinkles, and it's hard not to smile at the innocence of it all. "You're right. But I still feel bad."

The fact that this sweet child has lost as much as she has and can still manage to think of others is remarkable. Not even I was capable of that after losing my mom. I was a downright terror until I found my place in the world with Leigh and Indie. Even then, it took a long time for me to find my groove.

Phoebe just keeps moving forward like nothing has changed. I know she has her moments. She takes on the weight of the world because she thinks it's what she needs to do. She'd rather see the smiles of those around her than let them see her tears.

It's a slippery slope, one I know all too well. Which is why I'm vowing today will be a day of fun where she can just be a nine-year-old.

I slip my knuckle under her chin and tip her head up, so her eyes meet mine. "No feeling bad. We'll make sure Bishop knows we are there for him too."

She chews the inside of her cheek and nods. "Promise?"

"I promise. Now, why don't you go get dressed and I'll braid your hair? Then we'll head over to the stadium."

"Okay," Phoebe says, finishing the last bite of her donut before she hops off the stool and bounces down the hallway.

When she's out of earshot, Lana sighs. "Thank you for taking her. She really looks up to you."

I sip my coffee and offer her a tight smile. "I look up to her too."

"And thank you for keeping an eye on Bishop."

"Oh…um…" I stutter, caught off guard.

If it was anyone else, I would have been able to lie with ease. I've been doing it for weeks. But this woman has the uncanny ability to make me feel at ease, but at the same time gives off "don't fuck with me" vibes.

I suspect it's a talent honed by motherhood. Not that I would know, considering my mother never got the memo.

As if to prove my point, Lana raises a brow in a way only she can. It says *who do you think you're fooling* and *I was young once* at the same time.

"I haven't talked to Bishop much since he's been down here for spring training, but the few times I have your name always manages to come up, even just in passing."

"My father believed the Renegades were a family. We take care of our own." The lie tastes bitter, but still I give a noncommitted shrug, hoping she won't press further.

It's wishful thinking.

Lana presses her lips into a tight smirk, twirling her finger along the rim of her coffee cup in a playful manner that lets me know she's absolutely not going to let this go.

"And I assume taking care of your own entails being at the owner's house at four in the morning?"

"I…uh…" My mind races to find an explanation, something that makes sense and still keeps my promise to Bishop of no one finding out, but I've got nothing.

I let my shoulders fall with a resigned sigh. "How did you know?"

Lana smiles, easing my worry that she is not about to rip me a new one. "I've been worried about him, not only because Jackson and Norah wanted him to be the one to take Phoebe, but also because Bishop is like a second son to me."

"That still doesn't tell me how you knew he was here overnight," I reply.

"When he was spiraling after the crash, I enabled locations on his phone so that I could track where he was and make sure he didn't end up in a gutter choking on his own vomit. I was worried he would do the same thing here in Florida. So, I kept tabs on him. Imagine my surprise when I found him at the same house multiple nights in a row. Then when I arrived, it turned out to be this very house."

I shoot her an impressed grin. "Does Bishop know you're tracking him?"

She scoffs playfully. "Absolutely not."

"You're sneaky. I like it."

"Just like you, I take care of what's mine. Which is why I have to ask—is it serious?"

I force out a strangled laugh that shreds my heart. "No. Bishop isn't ready for serious. We have an agreement to help each other when the world feels like too much. That's it."

It's not a lie, but it's not the whole truth—that I absolutely wish it was serious.

Lana gives me a skeptical look but doesn't push. "I'm happy he has you. Even if it is just for right now. He seems like he's doing better."

"He is," I reassure her.

She nods toward the spare bedroom at the end of the hall where her granddaughter is getting ready for the day. "Enough to care for Phoebe?"

I nod without hesitation.

Bishop hasn't wanted to talk about Jackson and Norah's wish for him to take Phoebe since he let it slip, and I haven't pushed for him. But little comments he's made here and there when he updates me on the lack of progress in Jackson's condition let me know he's taking the request seriously. He wants to do better, not only for himself, but for Phoebe.

"He adores that little girl, but more than that, he loves your son and he would do anything to protect them."

My words bring Lana's smile to life, and I swear she's about to let another round of tears fall. "That's what I wanted to hear."

My heart cracks at her statement, opening in a way I didn't anticipate. I've been so focused on the short game when it comes to Bishop—getting him through spring training, fighting to make sure his next breath is easier than the last—I haven't even considered the long game beyond him playing for the Renegades.

What comes next?

Opening day will be here in two and a half weeks.

Then we go back to the real world, where he'll become Phoebe's primary guardian and his entire life will change. Again. He'll be responsible for homework and school plays. Will he even want to play for the Renegades anymore when he's essentially a full-time parent? Is that why he brought up Stone becoming a dad at sixteen and still making it to the majors?

"Slow down, Willow." Lana's voice pulls me back to my kitchen island.

"Huh?" I mutter in her direction.

"I can see your brain working a million miles a minute." Lana chuckles. "Care to share with the class?"

"It's nothing," I say with a resigned exhale.

Her gaze narrows, and she crosses her arms over her chest. "I raised Jackson as my son. He's the king of overthinking. I know the symptoms when I see them."

I roll my eyes, which only makes Lana's smile grow. "It's nothing. I'm just trying to figure out what comes next for the team."

She chuckles. "You mean what comes next for you and Bishop."

Nothing gets past her. But I can't confirm that.

"Nothing comes next for us."

Lana sets down her cup of coffee and rounds the corner of the island, stopping behind me. She places her hands on my shoulders and gives me a tight squeeze. "You both have been through so much. Too much, if you ask me. Enjoy your time together and worry about the rest later. Life's too short as it is."

There's whimsy in her voice, and I want to ask how she can possibly have so much hope in a world that is hell-bent on breaking us. Instead, I sink against her forearm and savor encouragement.

"Thank you, Lana."

"Anytime, my dear."

Her advice clings to my soul with a white-knuckled grip.

Life's too short.

"Alright." Lana gives another small squeeze and heads for the door. "If there's nothing else you need from me, I think I'm going to go take that nap. You girls have fun."

"Enjoy," I say, waving after her, my mind on the verge of spiraling once again.

Life's too short.

The truth haunts me and spurs me forward at the same time.

Thank goodness only a few moments pass before Phoebe comes bounding into the room with a brush and a hair tie, ready for me to braid her hair.

"I just had the best idea," she declares, taking up her seat next to me and handing me the hair tools.

Turning to face her, I gently start to brush her hair. "What's that?"

"I'll wear Dad's jersey and you can wear Uncle Bishop's!" she exclaims.

The way she says it so matter-of-factly leads me to believe she's been working through this problem the entire time she was in her room getting ready.

"That's…um…" I stumble, trying to come up with a reason I couldn't possibly wear Bishop's jersey, knowing damn well I'm not about to say no to this little girl.

"We can be twins!" Phoebe yells, bouncing in her seat and making it impossible to untangle her brown locks.

Fuck. I can't do this.

I shouldn't be the one twinning with her.

Norah, I never knew you, but give me strength to survive your daughter's innocence.

Phoebe's excitement is infectious, and despite the fact it's probably a terrible idea to wear the jersey of any of my players—especially the one I'm fucking on the side—I find myself agreeing to her little plan.

"Uncle Bishop is going to be so excited to see you in his jersey," Phoebe proclaims.

I'm thankful she's facing away from me and can't see my grimace.

Bishop is going to be something, that's for sure.

I can only hope his soft spot for Phoebe is greater than his contempt for me.

CHAPTER TWENTY-EIGHT
Bishop

"Are we okay?"

I glance up at Ford McCoy, our third baseman, as I hit the end of my bat against the bottom of my cleat for the tenth time instead of warming up my swing.

Yes. No.

Fuck.

How do I tell him his confession the day before sent me into a spiral that landed me in Willow's office, needing a distraction, which resulted in not only finding out she threw me under the bus but also unlocked a web of feelings I swore I wouldn't have for our owner?

The answer?

I don't because none of it is his fault.

Jackson snorts in my head. *Look at you being all grown up and mature about this.*

I know. I deserve a goddamn medal.

I glance sideways to where McCoy stands between me and the net set up around home plate for batting practice. He's like a fucking puppy with his sad eyes and hopeful smile—that is, if puppies were six foot three and made of lean muscle. He means well and takes up the helm of a fluffy golden retriever right alongside Carson. But where Carson is the class clown, McCoy is the quiet boy next door. Meanwhile, I'm the rottweiler in the corner.

What? All bark no bite? Tommy jabs.

I roll my eyes. *I was going to say the moody guard dog, but seriously, fuck you guys.*

You'll always be our golden retriever, Bish. Jackson assures me. *You just discovered you have teeth.*

I shake my head as my stare drifts past McCoy to our first baseman, Elliot Stone, at the plate. He shifts his weight and swings, sending a line drive out to left field. Unfortunately, he isn't quite finished with his bucket of balls, which means there's no way to avoid this conversation.

Damn it.

"We're good," I offer McCoy. "You just caught me off guard. I didn't know Martinez was your brother."

"Stepbrother," he corrects.

I roll my eyes internally. It doesn't matter. Brother. Half brother. Stepbrother. It doesn't change the fact that a member of his family was my teammate and died in the crash.

Before yesterday, I'd never taken the time to talk with McCoy. Though apparently, he's been trying to find a way to approach me since he arrived in Fort Myers. He didn't want there to be secrets between us, but also didn't want to upset me by bringing up the crash.

Which is valid. I've been a hot fucking mess on a good day and those still end with me in Willow's bed trying to forget. Never mind the days that I need her body in order to feel like I can take my next breath.

But the joke's on McCoy this time. I don't like to speak ill of the dead, but Tyler Martinez was a selfish fucking prick who only ever thought of himself. I didn't tell his brother that. Especially after McCoy admitted he volunteered for the draft so he could honor Tyler's memory and support his family.

I didn't even know Tyler had a family. He was always bringing different girls back to our hotels when we were on the road.

Again, not that I was about to tell McCoy any of that.

Instead, when given the chance to connect with him as a teammate, I bolted. It was too much to process, and I ran straight to—

"Ms. York," McCoy stutters but recovers quickly with what I can only describe as a panty-dropping smile. "It's so good to see you."

"You too, Ford." Her voice washes over me, sending a shiver down my spine. "I'm actually glad I ran into you. I spoke to Henry about making an appointment with you later this week to discuss your sister-in-law."

It's at that point three things happen in quick succession.

First, my dick takes notice, twitching against my jockstrap at the sight of her bare thighs that are usually hidden beneath those damn skirts she wears. It doesn't matter that I'm still pissed at her. I also want her under me, reminding her as long as we've got this arrangement, she's mine.

Which explains the second thing. I drop the bat in my hand and clench my fists, ready to take out my teammate for looking at Willow with stars in his eyes. It wouldn't be the first time I've defended her from a teammate. Sharpe won't even look in her direction without checking first to see if I'm around.

And third, the metaphorical bucket of cold water is thrown over me as I'm tackled from the side by the force of a nine-year-old tornado.

"Uncle Bish!" Phoebe yells.

Wrapping my arms around her, I swing her in a circle. Her giggle gives me life. A reminder that everything I'm doing is not just for me.

When I set her down, I'm finally able to lock my eyes on Willow.

If my dick stands at attention from just from the sound of her voice, it's ready to go into battle at the sight of her. Which is problematic considering we are in the middle of batting practice and my soon to be ward is standing at my side.

I can't help it though. Instead of her self-imposed uniform of a blouse paired with one of those skirts that leaves me itching to rip fabric, she's wearing a black pinstriped Renegades jersey. It's unbuttoned and opened, revealing a tight tank underneath. A pair of cutoff denim shorts hug her thick thighs. From her curled blonde spirals to her favorite black high-top Chuck Taylors, Willow is not giving team owner vibes. She's giving gorgeous single woman vibes, and fuck if I'm not ready to lock that shit down before anyone else takes notice.

But as good as she looks, the first thing I see when my gaze returns to her face is the way her smile doesn't reach her eyes. She's holding it together remarkably well, but the signs are there that she's not okay. Arms protectively crossed over her chest. Fingers drawing circles over the smooth skin of her biceps.

She's nervous. Or maybe anxious.

To stop myself from interrupting Willow's conversation with McCoy to make sure she's okay, I tug my hat from my head and plop it on Phoebe's. "What are you guys doing here so early?"

Phoebe's cheeks tinge pink above her infectious smile. "I missed you, so Willow said we could come down early and pick out jerseys to wear and watch batting practice."

"I thought that might be a new jersey on you. Let me see." I lift my hand and spin my finger around. "Give me a twirl?"

Phoebe giggles as she spins in front of me, showing off the jersey she picked with Jackson's name and number on the back. It's a punch to the gut to see it, but on his little girl, the sting doesn't last quite as long.

"It's perfect, Short Stack."

"Thank you."

"And who is this?" Graham asks as he joins us standing behind the net.

"This is Phoebe Roberts, Jackson's daughter. She's here with Willow for the game today."

"Well hello, Phoebe," Graham says, squatting down and offering Phoebe his hand. "I'm Graham Clarke."

Phoebe puts her hand in his and gives it a firm shake. "Hello, Graham."

"So do I have you to thank for finally getting my goddaughter in a jersey and out of those stuffy skirts she likes to wear?" he asks, nodding his head in Willow's direction as he stands up.

My brows raise at seeing this softer side of Graham. He's usually such a hard ass in the dugout that it's almost creepy to see him engage in this playful manner with Phoebe. It's unexpected, especially since I'm pretty sure he's never been married or had kids.

Phoebe's eyes go wide as she bounces from foot to foot. "Willow is your goddaughter? I'm Uncle Bishop's goddaughter."

"You know I wear them because it's professional and I'm the owner." Willow steps forward and nudges Graham with her shoulder, adding playfully, "Uncle Graham."

"He's your uncle too?" Disbelief colors Phoebe's voice, her gaze darting quickly between Willow and Graham.

Willow laughs and nods. "Kinda like how Bishop is your uncle. He was my dad's best friend."

"Those are the best uncles," Phoebe declares.

"I agree."

"Me too," Graham confirms. "Now, would you like to try giving the bat a swing, Phoebe?"

Phoebe looks to Willow and then over to me, and my heart pounds against my ribs. "Can I?"

"It's fine with me as long as you wear a helmet," Willow says, and Phoebe turns to me for confirmation.

I tug my hat from her head and slide it backwards on my own. "Knock it out of the park, Short Stack."

"Eeeeek," she shrieks, following Graham to the net before looking over her shoulder. "You'll watch me, Uncle Bish?"

"Absolutely." I nod, swallowing past the lump in my throat that reminds me Jackson should be doing this with her, not me. "I'm just going to talk with Willow for a minute, and then I'll come over and we'll hit a home run together."

Phoebe squeals again and hurriedly joins Graham, who has a helmet waiting for her. She slides it on and takes the too big bat before situating herself at the plate.

Graham heads out to the mound, grabs a few balls, and sets up halfway between so he can toss them to Phoebe.

I laugh. Jackson would love this, but Norah would be positively beaming. Phoebe was her pride and joy.

Tears burn the backs of my eyes as I silently look up at the fluffy white clouds littering a crisp blue sky and wonder if she's watching this moment.

You know I am. She speaks in my head. *Take care of my family, Bishop.*

I swallow hard because it sounds like a goodbye, and somehow, I know she's not going to be making an appearance in my head any longer.

I'm not sure what that means, especially since it's my own fucked-up conscience at play, but there's a peace that comes with it. Like there was at The Guardian. And once again, I'm left asking myself if this is what it feels like to move on.

Except it's not moving on.

It's living.

I will, I promise her. *Always.*

CHAPTER TWENTY-NINE
Bishop

When I turn to talk to Willow, she's already walking away. Craning my neck, I watch as she heads toward the brick wall separating the field from the stands behind home plate.

That's when I see it.

My breath catches.

L-A-W-S-O-N stitched in orange and lined up perfectly between her shoulder blades above the number sixty-eight.

My breath catches in my throat, and I struggle to keep it together. It's the number I adopted this year in memory of the sixty-eight souls lost in the crash. It won't be released as my official jersey until opening day.

No one has worn that number paired with my last name except me. Not my family. Not any previous girlfriends. Not my ex-wife. Only Willow. And damn if she doesn't look good wearing me.

Every possessive bone in my body flares as I swallow the space between us, vaguely aware McCoy is still watching from a few feet away. I should care that the field is littered with my teammates and coaches, but it's the last thing on my mind. Right now, I only see Willow wearing my name. Mine. And the only thing I want to do is claim what's mine.

Willow reaches the wall seconds before me, and when she turns around, she chokes out a gasp at my proximity. Her eyes dart side to side, cautious of those around us, before she tips her head back and meets my narrowed gaze.

"Bishop." Her voice is breathy and little more than a murmur. It's a statement laced in a question—a plea to follow our rules.

"You're lucky we're on this field, Kitten, and that Phoebe is here." My voice is gravely and barely a whisper. "Because if we weren't, you'd already be bent over, taking my cock in that pretty little cunt of yours while I relish at the sight of my name across your back."

Her eyes go wide and pink colors her cheeks. "You want to—"

"God yes, Willow," I growl. "Why the fuck wouldn't I?"

"I figured you'd be pissed off I was wearing your jersey after what happened yesterday," she stammers. "But Phoebe felt bad wearing her dad's number when she was here to see you, so she had this idea that I should wear your jersey, so you didn't feel left out."

"Willow," I say, smiling, but it doesn't halt her nervous ramble. An adorable trait I hope she never loses. But at the moment, I need her to hear what I have to say.

"And I don't know if you've ever tried saying no to her, but it's damn near impossible. And I really am sorry for agreeing to the interview for you. I just—"

"Willow, I'm going to need you to stop rambling, or I'll have to stop you and you won't approve of my methods." My gaze falls to her painted red lips, and I watch as she puts meaning to my words.

"Oh," she mutters. "Um, yeah, that probably wouldn't be a good idea here."

"No, it wouldn't." I should take a step back. There's no reason for me to be crowding her like this, but before I do, I want to make sure she feels the weight of my words and lets them sink in. "I'm not mad about the jersey."

"Really?" she breathes, her chest brushing against me.

"No," I reassure her. "And I plan to show you just how not mad I am later, but we've got a few things to clear up between us first."

She presses her lips together, and her eyes drop to the floor beside us. "Yeah. We do."

As much as it pains me to disengage, I slide to the side and turn, leaning against the brick wall. Willow joins me, close enough that we can talk and not have to worry about anyone overhearing us, but not as close as I'd like. My only saving grace is the space between us where our hands grip the wall is small enough that, if I wanted to, I could reach out and lace my pinky finger with hers.

We stand there in silence, eyes forward, watching Graham walk Phoebe through the mechanics of swinging like her father wasn't a pro player himself. Phoebe knew how to swing a bat before she could walk, but she patiently lets the old guy walk her through setting her feet at the plate and the art of a perfect follow through.

McCoy trots over to help along with Stone and Winters, and I can't help but smile. Phoebe already has this team wrapped around her little finger. Just like she did before. Now all we need is her dad to wake the fuck up and join us.

I swear I hear Jackson whisper *I'm trying*, but I write it off as my mind hoping he's going to wake up.

My palms sweat and I'm suddenly nervous to have this conversation. It's not like talking with the guys on the team. While we struggle to connect sometimes, there's nothing lost if we don't jive right away. Team bonding takes time. But with Willow, we're already more than a team. We're—fuck, I don't know, but the thought of losing her makes my heart pound against my ribs. Right now, we are not on the same page, and I need us to be.

Willow glances over at me, clearly waiting for me to take the lead.

Here goes nothing.

"I read your plans on the bus yesterday."

Her shoulders fall, and she lets out a sigh of relief. "Yeah?"

I nod. "They're incredible. And I understand why you did what you did. Not just agreeing to keep the kids safe from being used, but also for the Renegade organization on the whole. These really are good ideas—innovative and forward thinking—but you've got an uphill battle if you ever want to see them come to fruition."

"I know. You aren't the first to say so," she agrees. Her lips pull into a tight line. "I'm sorry you got caught in the middle."

"I don't give shit about that." Willow huffs a laugh and gives me a pointed look. I concede, "Okay, I mean, at first I did. But given the circumstances, I get it, and I've been dodging press questions about the crash for months. I'm more pissed you didn't trust me to help you the same way you've helped me."

"But it's not the same." Willow's lips fall into a frown, her gaze finding the ground once more. "You did help distract me in my office. Keeping this from you wasn't a distraction. It was to protect you."

"Was giving me my own locker room a distraction?" I press, needing her to hear what I'm saying. "Was suggesting The Guardian a distraction?"

Her shoulders pop half-heartedly. "I suppose not."

"As much as I appreciate it, I don't need you to protect me."

That comment awards me a side-eye glare and I can't stop the chuckle that shakes my chest. "Okay, maybe I did need it before. But not anymore." I close the distance between our fingers and wrap my pinky around hers. "And we both know you've done more than just be my distraction. What I'm saying is, you took away my chance to do the same."

Her gaze falls to our connected hands before she trails it up to meet mine. "I didn't know you wanted that."

"I didn't either," I admit, and the truth stings in a way it shouldn't. I'm not afraid to admit that I want Willow to wear my name across her back for the foreseeable future. Seeing it there today cemented that. But realizing it also fans the fear in my heart that if I give into this, I'll inevitably lose her too. The same way I lost Corrine. The same way I lost my team. I'm barely learning to survive on my own.

Willow's brow furrows in confusion, and the question shines in her eyes before she asks it. It's a punch to the gut I'm not ready for, despite knowing it's coming.

"What does that mean?"

I wish I had an answer for her. One that would vanquish the anxiety in her electric blue eyes. But I don't. I could tell her what I know—that this isn't a fling. That nothing about us is detached like we planned. That ever since we met on that balcony in New York, I've wanted to know what it would be like to call her mine.

But if I tell her that, it still wouldn't be the whole truth. Despite all those things, there's not a future for us. Not right now. Not while she's my boss and there's a wall around my heart.

So, I don't say any of those things. Instead, I sigh and offer the only thing I can. A resounding, "I don't know."

"Do you want to find out?" Her voice cracks a bit, her vulnerability shining through. "Or is this you asking to end our arrangement?"

"No," I blurt, and quickly clarify. "I mean, I don't want to end our arrangement. And to the other question, I don't know."

Willow's lips lift into a goofy smile I'm not expecting. She squeezes my pinky with hers and nods. "Okay."

"Okay?" I ask, confused.

I expected more. Willow has never been one to shy away from questioning me, or at the very least pushing me to consider why I'm struggling to come to a conclusion. But this she's willing to let be? It doesn't sit right, but who am I to look a gift horse in the mouth?

She nods again. "Our arrangement stands, and when you're ready, we'll figure the rest out. But for the record, I'm all in."

I swear time stands still as those words leave her lips.

"You are?" Goddamn, my heart thunders against my chest and there's a part of me that wants to bolt, while the other demands I pull her into my arms and never let her go.

She's all in. She wants this. Me.

Willow chuckles. "Don't stress yourself out, Bishop. You don't need to say you feel the same."

Biting my tongue, I wait for her to continue because as much as I want to say that's what I want, too, I can't. There are too many unknowns. Too much could go wrong and end with me spiraling all over again.

"You said you wanted me to let you in," she continues. "I don't have a very good track record when it comes to doing that. Not just with you. With anyone. It's one of my fatal flaws."

I roll my eyes. "Because you have *so* many of those."

She shrugs and tilts her head playfully. "I forget to put the cap on the toothpaste too."

"You're a savage," I say on a laugh, my eyes trailing down her body as I try to figure out how the hell I got so lucky. "What made you change your mind and decide to trust me with the knowledge you're all in?"

"Someone made me realize I don't want to lose you again."

It's on the tip of my tongue to say "me too", but I can't bring myself to utter the damn words. Grinding my molars, I try my best to keep myself from spiraling by keeping the mood light and far away from actually addressing my feelings. "Who do I need to send a thank you gift to for making you realize that?"

"Lana, actually."

"Really?"

"Alsooooooo," Willow playfully drags out the word and smiles. "You should probably turn off location tracking on your phone. She's aware you've been at my house most nights since you got here."

"That fucking sneak." Though the more I think about it, it makes sense. It absolutely answers the question of how I always seemed to make it home after a night of binge drinking at one of the various pubs I frequented after the crash.

"I know." Willow chuckles and tucks my favorite strand of hair—the one that always seems to fall free—behind her ear. "She might be a saint, but that woman also terrifies me just a little bit."

"Me too," I admit, but I owe that woman a thank you. And probably an apology. She stepped up and took the role of the mother I needed when I shut mine out because it hurt too much to give even the smallest piece of myself to anyone.

Fuck. I really need to call my family.

"Bishop, get your ass out here," Graham calls from the mound.

"Swear jar!" Phoebe yells and the entire team erupts in laughter.

I push off the brick wall and spin, catching Willow as she bites her lower lip, her eyes trained low where my ass was. Arching a brow, I live for the blush that creeps up her neck. "So, we're good?"

"We're good," she confirms.

"No more shutting me out."

She throws three fingers up and smirks. "Scout's honor."

"You were never in the Girl Scouts."

"No." She smirks, eyes clear and bright in a way I haven't seen in a long time. "But you'd be surprised with the survival skills I've learned up at Camp Renegades. I even know how to tie knots."

"Do you now?" I tease. "Maybe you can show me sometime."

"I'd like that." She hums in acknowledgement. She lowers her voice and the most discreet tilt happens at the corner of her lips. "Then maybe you can punish me like you promised."

Fuck. She's trying to kill me. Right here on the field in front of my entire team, I'll die with a raging erection and the knowledge this woman wants me for everything that I am and everything I'm not.

I take a step toward her, ignoring the hollers from the guys on the field beyond me.

"Have you been naughty, Kitten?" I whisper, fisting my hands so I don't reach out and touch her.

She flutters her lashes and looks up at me. "Yes."

"Fuck. You have no idea how incredibly sexy it is when you ask for what you want."

She arches a perfect brow. "Noted."

Evanescence's "Bring Me Back to Life" fills the space between us and it strikes me how perfect it is for Willow. Except she's the one bringing me back to life—slowly—and I'm glad she isn't giving up on me.

Willow leans sideways so she can pull her phone from her back pocket. She tilts it in my direction, revealing Lana's name across the screen. "I should probably take this."

"Tell her I said hi. I'm going to make sure my goddaughter hits a home run."

I turn and stride toward the net, feeling a little bit taller than I did before and soaking in the moment of perfection. Willow wants me. Phoebe is here. I'm on my way to accepting this team.

Is this what moving on looks like? I sure as hell hope so because for the first time in a long time, I don't feel hopeless.

I round the net and place my hand on top of Phoebe's helmet. "You ready to show them how it's done, Short Stack?"

She looks up at me and giggles. "Graham pitches too slow."

My manager laughs from where he stands in the grass between the plate and the mound. "How was I supposed to know she's been hitting off the machine since she was six?"

I chuckle and tell him to turn it down to half speed and let it rip.

Graham makes his way behind the shield net that will keep him safe from any line drives and lifts a ball above his head, letting us know he's ready when we are.

I slide up behind Phoebe and crouch down, placing my hands over hers on the bat. Jackson and I have done this with Phoebe for as long as I can remember. It started when she was far too small to hold the bat up by herself, and one of us would have to help her while the other pitched. But as she got older, she still wanted our help. She claimed she hits harder with us. It's a load of shit, considering she can easily smash a ball to the outfield on her own. But neither of us could deny this little girl. The same way neither of us would ever admit we'll be upset the day she doesn't need our help anymore.

"Alright, you ready?" I whisper in her ear.

She nods and sticks her tongue out of the side of her mouth, as if that's going to help her concentrate on the ball.

I turn my head and give Graham a nod. He feeds the ball into the machine.

The ball sails towards us, and I tighten my grip around Phoebe's hands and guide the bat around.

The crack of the wood echoes through the empty stadium, and the ball soars between third and shortstop.

"Run, Phoebe!" I yell, but she's already taken off toward first.

Stone, who was watching from the outfield, makes a show of fielding the ball and throws it to where McCoy has taken up a position on second.

Phoebe rounds first base and is almost to second when McCoy lets the ball bounce off the tip of his glove and chases after it into right field.

"Keep going, Phoebes!" I yell. She giggles and pumps her arms faster.

McCoy gets the ball as she rounds third and looks to me at home plate. I throw my hands in the air, giving him a target.

He throws the ball, and I catch it just before Phoebe reaches the plate. It should be an easy out, but Phoebe is just as competitive as her dad and she plows right into me, knocking me on my ass. I purposely drop the ball.

"Home run!" she yells, and all around the field, my team echoes her cheer.

I stand and brush off the dirt before picking her up and spinning her in a circle.

When we stop, Willow is there. The smile on her face doesn't radiate the way it had before as tears stream down her face.

Panic floods me, and I close the space between us in two strides. "Are you okay?"

"Yeah." Her words say one thing, but those tears don't match. She reaches up and wipes her eyes. "You and Phoebe need to grab your stuff and come with me."

"Why?" I ask, anxiety gripping my spine and overtaking the joy of playing

the game I love with my goddaughter. "What happened?"

"Jackson woke up."

CHAPTER THIRTY

BISHOP: Just landed. Thanks for letting us use the jet.

WILLOW: How was the flight?

BISHOP: I much prefer it with you in my lap.

WILLOW: Next time.

BISHOP: I still don't understand why you didn't come with us.

WILLOW: Well for starters, there's nothing low profile about me running back to New York with you. And second, you need this moment with Jackson on your own.

BISHOP: I need you at the hotel for after the moment.

WILLOW: You don't.

BISHOP: Is this part of your plan on learning to live? Slowly denying me access?

WILLOW: Your logic is flawed because I'd be denying myself too.

BISHOP: That's true. You're addicted to this cock.

WILLOW: You think too highly of yourself.

BISHOP: Admit it.

WILLOW: I'm pretty sure I already did.

BISHOP: Say it again.

WILLOW: I'll show you how much I enjoy it when you get back to Florida.

BISHOP: Tease.

WILLOW: You'll survive.

BISHOP: What if he hates me?

WILLOW: Why would he hate you?

BISHOP: Because I'm here and Norah's not.

WILLOW: Do I hate you because you're here and my dad's not?

BISHOP: No. But it's different.

WILLOW: Convince me.

BISHOP: It's his wife. The love of his life.

WILLOW: He's my dad. The only family I had left.

BISHOP: I hate when you do this.

WILLOW: What? Defy your logic?

BISHOP: You have a family in the Renegades. And with Lana. And Indie and Leigh.

WILLOW: I know.

BISHOP: I'll call you after we leave the care facility. You better be in bed without a stitch of clothing.

WILLOW: Yes, daddy.

BISHOP: Fuck me.

CHAPTER THIRTY-ONE
Bishop

"Stop fucking crying," Jackson snaps at me, and I'm thankful he's got one arm wrapped around Phoebe and the other doesn't have anything within reach to chuck at my head.

Honestly, I would stop if I could, but every time I see his lip moving and realize his voice is not in my head, I can't stop my damn eyes from leaking.

"Swear jar, Dad," Phoebe squeaks, pulling her feet up further onto the hospital bed. She snuggles into her dad's side.

Jackson leans over and presses a kiss to the top of her mousey brown hair and my heart clenches.

My best friend might be underweight with dark purple circles beneath his eyes, but the smile that splits his face every time he looks at Phoebe is like hitting a grand slam. You feel the weight of it in your soul. Only this grand slam comes with a side of the ump calling it foul instead of fair—because there is one Roberts missing.

It's the invisible elephant in the room that Jackson refuses to acknowledge. He had seven hours alone with doctors and nurses to process the news of the crash and his condition. That's seven hours to spiral and lock away the parts that feel like they're going to rip him from the inside out. Seven hours to decide what the world gets to see. Jackson decided to take the route of the Olympic sprinter—running from the feelings like he can escape them.

Since we arrived, he's used Phoebe as a shield—not wanting to upset her by talking about Norah's death—which is comical, considering Phoebe has handled her mother's passing better than the rest of us.

After the doctors updated us on his extensive road to recovery, including mental and physical therapies, Jackson has focused any and all conversation on us. What is Phoebe learning in school? Is Lana still participating in book club? Did the bodega down the street from their apartment raise enough money through their Kickstarter to remain open? Did I end up divorced?

Lana finally had enough of the pussyfooting and decided she needed a shower. She offered to pick up dinner from Jackson's favorite Thai restaurant. She tried to take Phoebe with her, but Jackson wasn't about to let his daughter out of his sight.

If I had just woken up and learned I lost my wife and team, I wouldn't want to lose sight of the one thing I had left in this world either.

Is that why you want to pick up your phone and text Willow? Tommy chides, and instead of acknowledging his observation, I silently wonder if I'll only hear his voice now that Jackson is awake.

I close my eyes to hide the tears that once again threaten to leak from the corners of my eyes.

"Tell me about the team, Bish," Jackson presses, unable to let silence fall over the room for more than a few moments at a time.

Blinking my eyes rapidly, I force a half smile while trying to decide where to start. So much of my own spiral is woven in the fabric of our team. I don't need him to know the depths to which I fell, especially when he's fighting to keep his own head above water.

Fortunately—or maybe unfortunately—Phoebe takes my hesitation as her cue to insert herself into the conversation.

"Uncle Bish has a girlfriend," she sputters, like she's been dying to share the information.

I glare at the little girl who holds my heart and mouth, "Traitor."

Her grin confirms she knew exactly what she was doing.

"A girlfriend, huh?" Jackson raises an eyebrow and tips his mouth into a smug smile. "That didn't take long."

Fuck. This is the last topic I want to discuss with him. Not when Norah is gone and I have no idea what the hell I'm feeling for the woman we're talking about.

So, I deny it's even a thing.

"She's not my girlfriend," I declare, running a hand through my too long hair.

"That's not what Nana thinks," Phoebe quips, ignoring the glare I give her.

That's it. No more donuts for her. Or Lana. She should know better than to have any conversations in front of this sponge of a little girl.

I press my palm over my eyes and shake my head.

Jackson lets out a hollow chuckle. "So, what's her name?"

"She's not my girlfriend."

Phoebe shifts side to side, biting her lip like she'll burst if she doesn't say her name.

"Don't you dare."

"It's Willow," she blurts out.

Jackson's eyes go wide. "As in York?"

I never stood a chance at keeping this secret. I can only hope she didn't tell the entire team when my back was turned.

"Yup!" Phoebe pops the p at the end and beams up at her dad. "She's the best too. She got me a new jersey with your name on it, since mine from last year doesn't fit anymore."

"That was really nice of her."

Phoebe nods and twists so she can look up at her dad without craning her neck. "She also lets all the kids from the crash come to Renegade Hearts whenever we want, so we can play together."

Jackson's brow furrows, and he immediately looks out the window. I recognize it as the need to hide from his daughter the burning desire to shut down. Phoebe doesn't know any better. She's excited to share any and all aspects of her life with Jackson. The problem is every aspect of who we are now is intertwined with the crash.

There's no escaping it. Something I have learned all too well over the last five months. I wish I could spare Jackson the painful lesson.

When Jackson doesn't snap out of his daze, I offer him a reprieve. "Hey Short Stack, why don't you go ask Greta if we can have three of her famous hot chocolates?"

That does the trick. Jackson snaps his dagger-like gaze on me and then softens when he looks down at Phoebe. "I don't think that's a—"

"It's right outside the door," I insist, giving him a pointed look. "I think we could all do with a pick me up."

"Yes!" Phoebe exclaims. "You have to try it, Dad. It's reeeeally good."

"She'll be gone ten minutes tops," I reassure.

"I—" Jackson chews the inside of his lip, and I can see just how much he wants to say no. That is until he looks down at Phoebe's wide-eyed *please* face and he melts to her will. "Fine. Ten minutes tops."

Phoebe hops off the bed, and we watch as she scurries out the door.

She's not gone two seconds when Jackson asks, "So, Willow York?"

It's not lost on me that he's changing the subject, so he can avoid talking about everything that's happened.

I pick up the pen on the small table beside my chair and twirl it through my fingers. "It's nothing."

"You made it a year," Jackson states, but I can hear the hint of a question behind it.

He's the reason Willow and I didn't start anything after New Year's. I promised him I wouldn't date anyone seriously for at least a year. Technically, I kept my word.

"I fucked her at that party at her father's beach house during spring training last year."

He hit me with an unimpressed eye roll. "I know."

I stop twirling the pen and focus on him. "You did?"

"Of course," he huffs, smoothing out the blanket in the spot where Phoebe just vacated. "You're a shit liar."

"But you didn't say anything."

Jackson shrugs. "We agreed one year no dating. You weren't dating her."

"I'm not dating her now."

"Why not?" Curiosity brims in his eyes. "You two were good together, from what I remember."

It's my turn to look out the window in avoidance. We were good together. Maybe we still are. But I hold on to the fact we can't be. "She's the owner of the Renegades."

"Yes, but is she your aisle seat like you thought?"

I roll my eyes and toss my hands up before letting them fall back into my lap. "Fuck, not this shit again."

Norah had a crazy theory that the person you're meant to be with will want the aisle seat to your window seat—or in my case, vice versa. She and Jackson loved to remind me how none of the women I've previously dated would be willing to give up the aisle seat for my large frame. Which always left me crammed up against the window because I was nothing if not a gentleman.

Not Willow, though. I think back to the flight down to Fort Myer and how she curled herself up against the window while reading her plans. It might not have been for me, but I get the feeling she'd be more than content with letting me take the aisle. Even better, she'd be happier in my lap sharing the damn seat with me. I would be too.

Shaking my head, I stare at the ground, knowing damn well there's no conviction in my voice when I declare, "It doesn't matter."

"Because she's your boss."

I snap my head up and look him square in the eyes. "Our boss."

My stomach drops out of my ass when Jackson sprints right past my clarification without acknowledging his tie to the team. "The Bishop I knew wouldn't have cared if she was the President of the United States. He'd move mountains to be with a woman he loved."

I put a pin in my need to confirm he's still a part of our team and address his statement. "Red flags hold a little more weight now."

He inclines his head. "Why's that?"

My hands itch for a distraction. Anything to remove myself from this conversation. It's one thing to be self-aware of the man I've become. It's another thing entirely to admit it to my best friend. Before this moment, I could be anyone. I don't want to be broken Bishop who had to crawl back from damn near rock bottom. I want to be a rock Jackson can lean on, because God knows he's going to need it.

But you couldn't be that without drowning first.

Fuck you, Tommy.

I chew my lower lip before releasing a heavy sigh. "Because the crash fucked me up, okay? I'm not the same guy you remember. I lost everyone in one night. I went to sleep thinking we were one series away from the postseason only to wake up, get divorced, and find out the price of said divorce was losing my entire team."

Jackson's jaw ticks and fire dances in his eyes, though I'm not sure if it's fueled by anger or desperation. "But I'm still here."

"Now you are." I scoff, silently cursing myself for getting defensive. "But until today, you were nothing but a body in a bed and a snarky piece of shit voice inside my head that I couldn't imagine living without."

"What?"

"My fucked-up psyche turned you and Tommy into my voices of reason." I swallow hard so I don't mention Norah also was a part of their trifecta.

His eyes flick to the window and back. "And what did I say?"

"Mostly, you lobbied for me to get my head out of my ass."

"Checks out. You tend to get it stuck there often."

I laugh for the first time since entering his room and feel hope spark in my chest. "Fuck, I'm so happy you woke up."

Jackson hesitates for a beat too long before offering a half-hearted. "Me too."

Silence washes over us, and immediately Jackson's hands begin to intertwine nervously in his lap.

And just like that, guilt douses that small incineration. Looking at him is like looking at myself in a mirror five months ago. The silence weighs on him. Even a split second leaves space for thoughts to break free from the cages we locked them in. It's why I found myself in a pub most nights before Willow took that avenue away from me.

Just like I took away the crutch Jackson was using by sending Phoebe away.

"Truth or dare," I say, throwing him a lifeline.

Jackson arches a brow. "What are we? Twelve?"

I shoot him a look, asking him to humor me.

"Fine. Seeing as I'm tethered to this damn bed," he says, lifting his IV arm to drive his point home before continuing, "truth."

"Why the hell did you and Norah name me Phoebe's guardian?"

"Who else were we supposed to trust to raise our kid? You're our best fucking friend," he says without hesitation, like it's the simplest answer in the world, and I'm floored by his conviction.

Before I can tell him what a terrible fucking idea it was, he turns the tables on me. "Truth or dare."

I jut out my chin and choose dare, knowing damn well if I said truth we were going back down the road of Willow York.

Jackson's lips lift into a maniacal smirk, telling me I'm screwed either way. "I dare you to tell me why you aren't dating Willow."

Fuck me.

I should have seen that coming.

"Willow and I have an arrangement." One I'm questioning by the hour. "We are nothing more than fuck buddies." Well, to me, that's what we are.

You're so full of shit, Tommy confirms. It almost feels like the three of us are standing in the locker room having this argument.

I am. But this isn't the time or place for me to work through whatever the hell it is I'm feeling for Willow. Today is about Jackson. I only have today with him.

Jackson doesn't back down. He raises his voice and the vein at his temple pops. "Wrong. You're everything. My best friend would already know that. He'd be convincing me. Not the other way around."

I work my hands in my lap. Fisting my fingers and releasing them in an effort to keep my cool. "Maybe once upon a time."

"Nope. I don't buy it."

"Why are you pressing this?" I grit out.

"Because I don't fucking understand!" he yells, chest heaving against his blue hospital gown.

My eyes flick to the door, waiting for a nurse, or God forbid Phoebe, to come running in. When neither do I level with Jackson. "I told you. I'm not that guy anymore. I can't look at the world with rose-colored glasses and pretend love conquers all. Love can't stop planes from falling from the sky. It can't stop the press from tearing us apart. It can't stop the league from trading me. It can't stop hearts from breaking. Love isn't enough."

My chest constricts, and I'm seconds away from bolting from the room to give us both the space to cool off, when Jackson sighs and a single tear stains his cheek.

"No, but life's too short not to experience every ounce of what love has to offer."

"Is that really what I sounded like before the crash?"

Jackson runs a hand through his hair and tugs at the strands. The itch to mirror the same action consumes me, but I sit still, wondering if he grips hard enough for the pain to take the edge off the bullshit life has dealt us.

"No, you were our hopeless romantic. I'm the man who might never know that love again. But if I had to go back, I'd do it all again, even knowing I was going to lose her. I'd do it a hundred times over just to know her love."

My chin hits my chest with a thud and I murmur, "You're a stronger man than I am."

"No. Just smarter."

"I'm afraid to lose her."

The weight of my whispered truth hangs between us. Only it's not stagnant. It never has been. It swings with my emotions—like a pendulum. Sometimes hitting the peak in the space where I want to cling to her and never let her go. Other times it's the opposite and I can't run away fast enough. The thing about a pendulum is it eventually comes to rest. And when it does, I'll have to decide which I want. Am I all in or not?

"Bishop." Jackson's lip quivers. "You can't live life in fear just because one shitty thing happened. Otherwise, one day you'll wake up and realize you're seventy and still lost everything anyways, but there's no one to blame but yourself."

There's a sharp pang in my chest.

He's right.

I consider all the things I've allowed myself to lose since the crash because I've pushed them away. My team. My family. Willow. Myself.

It's at that moment I realize I want them back. All of them.

"How the fuck are you able to give sound advice when you lost more than I did?"

Jackson shrugs. "I'm fairly certain whatever meds they have me on are keeping reality from sinking in. When they do, I'll probably be in the padded cell they should have kept you in. Ask me again in a few months and see if I've got the same answers."

I want to believe he will, but he won't. He's on day one of the journey I've been trekking for almost six months. In that time, I've lost myself more times than I can count. I've suffered denial alone and nearly drowned in the waves of my anger until I crashed on the shores of bargaining for my team to be returned to me. I begged for life to take me instead. Moments of depression littered my days, and I've learned acceptance doesn't equal healing. It's a never-ending journey.

Jackson has the fight of his life ahead of him, but I'm vowing—here and now—to be there every step of the way. The same way Willow was for me.

"You aren't alone," I say, but the reminder is just as much for me as it is for him.

Jackson nods, but the way his eyes cloud over I guess the weight of everything is already starting to set in. His jaw clenches and he sighs. "I dare you to be fearless."

"Only if you do the same."

"Okay," he agrees, shaking his head. "We're absolutely pathetic."

I laugh and slump back into the uncomfortable hospital chair. "No doubt. We'll never speak of this again."

Jackson gives me a tight-lipped smile, followed by a nod in agreement. He picks at the spot where his IV enters his left hand. "Thank you for taking care of Phoebe."

"Always."

"Now"—he pauses for dramatic effect, a hint of mischief glimmering in his eyes.—"how are you going to get your girl?"

CHAPTER THIRTY-TWO
Willow

"Wills, is it a whiskey or tequila kind of day?" Indie hollers from the kitchen, but before I can remind her I don't need to be showing up to the stadium already sloshed, Leigh ends the call with her one-year-old son, Zach, and responds, "Whiskey makes her frisky but tequila makes her clothes fall off."

Indie's maniacal cackle echoes through the beach house. "That doesn't really answer the question."

Shaking my head, I savor the simplicity of the moment. I forgot just how much I missed these two. The last two days have been a whirlwind of getting Lana, Phoebe, and Bishop to New York, tweaking my plans for the team to better align with the board's wishes, hammering down the interview questions for the gala, getting the house ready for Leigh and Indie, and coordinating getting Bishop back from New York this morning.

Vaughn wasn't happy I'd approved his leave of absence for two days' worth of games and made sure I knew he blamed me for the team's losses both days. Of course, that's not the story he gushed to the press. Oh no. To them it was all his idea because Jackson is still a part of the Renegade family, and we support our own.

All that to say, I absolutely need this time with my best friends.

Leigh smirks at me in the mirror above my dresser as she finishes braiding her long brown hair, and I apply the finishing touches on my makeup. She makes the executive decision. "Definitely tequila. This woman needs to get laid."

A blush creeps up my neck, and I wince as if slapped with the memories of just how many times I've been laid in the past few weeks. Not because I regret it in any way, but because I still haven't told Indie and Leigh about Bishop.

My best friends are two of the most supportive people in my life, and with that comes a level of over protection that rivals the secret service. I have no doubt they will support Bishop and me—eventually—after lots of groveling on his part and maybe mine for lying to them for so long.

But I told Bishop I was all in, which means it's time to rip off the bandaid.

I take a step back and smooth down the front of my skirt. "Actually, I am doing just fine in the dick department, thanks."

Leigh cocks a brow and tilts her head. "Is there a dick I don't know about?"

When I don't immediately answer, she gasps and clutches the invisible pearls at her neck. "Indie, get in here. Willow has a dick."

I roll my eyes and smooth down my skirt, chuckling at the sound of Indie barreling through the house. You'd never know she's a world-renowned actress and professionally trained in ballet by the clumsy stampede running through my house.

She pokes her head through the door of my room, her tight dark curls falling over her shoulder dramatically. She smirks. "I'm really hoping you mean she's got a dick she's riding and not that she's suddenly sprouted an extra appendage."

Leigh and I tip our heads back, absolutely losing it when she fully enters the room swinging her hips as if she were trying to do the helicopter.

From the moment I picked up Leigh and Indie at the airport, it's been nonstop laughs. Which is exactly what I've needed to keep me from stressing.

Indie crosses her arms over the white designer Renegades tank that perfectly complements her dark skin and pops her hip, a wicked smirk painting her lips. "Before I get to the dick situation, you're not really wearing that to the game, are you?"

I look down at what Bishop deemed my owner's uniform—a light short sleeve blouse and the pencil skirts he loves so much. This time it's gray.

"I'm the owner of the team. I need to dress the part," I counter. As much as I would love to wear Renegades gear and shorts like the two of them, I'm already on thin ice with the exec board after showing up to batting practice in Bishop's jersey. The only reason they stopped was because I did it for Phoebe, and the photo the press caught of me walking in with her came across in a positive light. Still, I don't need them spouting off at the mouth again about how unprofessional I am.

"I'll let it slide, but I still think you should be able to dress it down with your best friends."

I wish, but if there is anyone who gets the double standard, it's Indie. She lives in the spotlight as America's sweetheart. When she does something, it's embraced by the masses to her face and torn apart later on the internet.

"Now about this dick."

"It's not Bishop, is it?" Leigh asks too quickly for her not to already be putting the pieces together.

I turn away immediately to hide the flush on my cheeks at just the mention of his name. "It's nothing. Just casual."

Indie snorts. "That wasn't a no."

Leigh's blue eyes narrow, and I know I'm in for it. "Willow Mae York, are you—"

The doorbell rings and all three of us swing our attention toward the front of the house, interrupting what I'm sure was going to be a riveting explanation of why any and all dick needs to be run by them, no matter how casual. Especially if that dick is attached to one Bishop Lawson.

Ignoring their demands for an explanation, I slip from my room and head for the door. When I open it, I'm surprised to find a package sitting on the porch since I don't remember ordering anything.

The box is discreet without any indication of where it came from, and aside from my name and address, there isn't a clear business name.

By the time I reach the kitchen and start looking for a knife to open the package, Indie and Leigh have settled around the island. Indie is busy crafting the perfect pregame drink while Leigh has buried herself in the pages of the bodice ripper romance I gifted her when she arrived.

She looks up over the top of the book, curiosity piqued. "What's that?"

I shrug. "I have no idea."

"Open it—quick," Indie says between shakes of the ornate gold and glass cocktail shaker my dad loved. "We've got twenty minutes before the driver gets here, and I'm planning on the three of us taking at least two shots of this outrageously expensive tequila Papa York left for us."

A smile edges through as my heart simultaneously breaks, wrecked by the paradox of being happy my best friends loved my dad as much as I did, but also crushed that he isn't here to laugh at our expense and give us a playful fatherly pep talk about behaving like ladies at the stadium.

"Here." Leigh offers me a knife from the block in front of her with a sympathetic smile. Her gaze narrows, letting me know she sees me.

We are the three musketeers, all having complicated parental relationships or really lack thereof. But where Indie is estranged with her parents because they are even more shitty than my mother, Leigh is in the same boat as me—orphaned too soon.

I shake off the melancholy thoughts and slide the knife through the blue tape. A loud pop of one of the packing bubbles startles me, causing me to knock the box off the counter and onto the floor. Leigh and I laugh and lean over the island, staring at the contents that tumbled out of the box.

"Is that—" Leigh snorts. "Holy shit, that's a dick."

It is.

And not just any dick.

There on my kitchen floor, is an eight-inch purple and veiny dildo with a suction cup on the bottom, and it's not the only toy littering my floor. There's a butt plug, a second dildo—this time orange—and a little, green u-shaped silicone toy. I get the impression it's meant to hit the clit and g-spot at the same time. And those are just the toys that fell out. There's still a colorful array of things left in the box.

My face heats as the butt plug with a shiny green jewel at the base rolls and hits my foot.

"I think I'll take that shot now," I mutter, wishing a hole would open in my kitchen floor and swallow me.

"Who is it from? Is there a note?"

Leigh's voice is excited as I reach for the box, but she's faster. Picking it up, she examines the outside before poking around inside until she pulls out a small slip of paper.

She holds it up and reads in a sultry tone. "Now you have a bag of tricks for the beach house."

My hands find my face, hiding me away from my best friends. I shouldn't be embarrassed. These two know I read books filled with smut and kink—they read them too—but I haven't told them about living out my fantasies with Bishop or all that he has opened my eyes to.

Let's just say it's thanks to him I have a penchant for five finger necklaces, spanking, and I'm no longer opposed to butt stuff.

Fucking Bishop.

"Oooooooooh," Indie sing-songs as she stretches out her arm and offers me the shot I requested. "Is this a gift from the casual dick?"

Without thinking, I take the shot and down it, grimacing as the tequila burns the back of my throat and warms my belly. "It would seem so."

"Are you going to tell us who the mystery guy is? Or should we continue guessing?"

"I—" My throat swells as I try to figure out how to word everything that's happened. Suddenly it doesn't seem so easy to rip off the bandaid. What the hell am I supposed to say?

I lied before and I'm totally fucking Bishop, but it's not what you think. You were right when you said I wasn't over him after the flight down here, but then we sort of agreed to be fuck buddies, and I fell for him all over again. He's not ready to say he's all in. But I think he feels the same. He's just scared. I am too. I don't know what this looks like. I could lose everything. But I don't want you guys to hate him for that. We've been through a lot. But I think he's it for me. Maybe. I don't know. I think I want him to be.

"Willow." Leigh's voice pulls me out of my spiral. "You're doing that thing where you freak out in your head. Just tell us what's going on."

I blink rapidly at her and blurt out, "I need a minute."

As soon as I'm locked in the safety of the half-bath off the kitchen, I yank my phone from my pocket and fire off a text to the catcher responsible for the flush on my cheeks and the anxiety in my chest.

WILLOW: Did you send me a package?

BISHOP: So it arrived.

WILLOW: What the fuck Bishop?

BISHOP: <smirk emoji>

WILLOW: That's it? That's all you have to say for yourself?

BISHOP: How about thank you daddy?

WILLOW: Considering I just opened the damn package and everything fell out on the floor in front of Leigh and Indie, I'm not sure you deserve that thank you. Now they have questions.

BISHOP: <Laugh crying emoji>

BISHOP: <Skull emoji>

BISHOP: I'm dead.

> **WILLOW:** What am I supposed to say to them?

> **BISHOP:** Tell them I know how to take care of you.

I imagine him saying it with a cocky tilt to his lips, which only makes my heart thunder harder against my rib cage. It's one thing to decide for myself to tell them, but having Bishop claim me to my friends is a huge step. One I shouldn't read too much into, but damn if I don't want to. And if the way my pussy clenches is any indication, my body wants to as well.

Three little bubbles float across the screen, and I hold my breath, waiting to see what he says next.

> **BISHOP:** Pick your jaw up off the floor, Kitten. I told you, for as long as this lasts, you're mine.

> **BISHOP:** Plus, I told Jackson about you. It's only fair you get to tell your friends.

> **WILLOW:** You did?

> **BISHOP:** Yes. Now, before you go tell your friends all about us, I need you to do me a favor.

> **WILLOW:** Anything.

> **BISHOP:** You might regret saying that. (smirk emoji)

BISHOP: That little green toy…I need you to slip it between those pretty pussy lips of yours and turn it on before you head to the game.

WILLOW: Absolutely fucking not.

BISHOP: Oh there will be fucking, but not until you're sufficiently wet and aching for me.

WILLOW: I'm the damn owner of the team. I'm not wearing a sex toy to a game.

BISHOP: We both know you're wet just thinking about it.

He's not wrong, but that's not the point.

BISHOP: Consider this the punishment you asked for.

WILLOW: I meant a spanking.

BISHOP: That can also be arranged.

WILLOW: I'm not wearing it.

BISHOP: The choice is yours. But we both know if you don't wear it, you'll be thinking about wearing it the whole time. Just know my cock is painfully hard in this cup and it will be torture for me the entire game, knowing you're wet because of it.

WILLOW: I hate you.

BISHOP: And I adore the idea of you hate fucking me later.

WILLOW: This conversation is over. I'll see you after the game.

Nervous tension radiates off me as I take cool water and rub it onto the back of my neck. It does nothing to stifle the heat coursing through me. This man has me strung tighter than a rubber band and ready to snap.

From the beginning he's pushed my limits, carefully taking note of the things that turn me on. Exhibitionism being one of them. Not that I want to have sex in front of a room full of people—I don't—but I have never been more turned on than when he fucked me against a glass window over Times Square. It was safe—the windows were tinted appropriately so that no one would see—but that thrill that they could was unlike any other. This was taking it a step further while adding another element. Could I keep my composure? Would I give myself away? I can't even lie to myself and pretend I'm not completely turned on by the challenge.

But I'm the goddamned owner. Owners don't act like this. Owners don't wear specific player's jerseys. Owners also don't fall in love with members of their team, yet here we are.

While drying my hands, I reassure myself this is a terrible idea and there's no way I'm going to follow through with it.

When I return to the kitchen, I find Indie and Leigh have already taken their first shots and poured another one for each of us. I grab my shot glass and raise it in the air before they can ask me any more questions.

"Champagne to all my real friends," I say with a grin, knowing damn well they'll complete the toast we fell in love with the year we turned twenty-one.

"Real pain to all my sham friends," they yell in unison, and we all hit our glasses on the table before downing the clear liquid.

Before the burn subsides, I pull up my big girl panties and unleash the story of Bishop and me onto my best friends, not pausing for a single second until I've finished the twisted tale.

I'm out of breath by the time I'm done, and Indie and Leigh sit with their eyes wide and their jaws hanging slack.

"Well shit," Indie mutters.

"So you're all in?" Leigh asks, caution lacing her voice.

I dip my head and smile. "Yeah. I'm not crazy, am I?"

"No." She slips from her chair and rounds the island to where I stand, pulling me into a hug. "I'm just sorry you have been dealing with this alone."

Sinking into her, I return her embrace and swallow past the knot in my throat. "I'm sorry I didn't tell you guys sooner."

Indie slides behind me, towering over us, and wraps her arms around us both. "You've had a lot going on." She presses a kiss to the top of my head. "But no more secrets, okay?"

I nod, and for the second time this week, I make the promise to stop shutting out the people who care about me. It leaves me feeling inexplicably lighter on my feet, steeling my spine with confidence.

Indie gives us a squeeze and pulls back, wiping a stray tear from my cheek. "So, I guess this means we won't be adding laxatives to his Gatorade in retaliation?"

A wet chuckle escapes me, and I shake my head. "Probably not."

"Unless he hurts you," Leigh adds. "Then all bets are off."

"Deal."

"Good. Now go put on that Lawson jersey I saw hanging in your closet," Leigh demands with a wink, like she's known the whole time and was just waiting for me to come clean.

I shake my head. She's too damn observant for her own good.

"I can't wear that." I untangle myself from their arms and grab the box from the island. "I still have a reputation to uphold as the owner of the Renegades."

"You also have a duty as the girlfriend to support your man."

"I'm not his girlfriend, and this isn't some romance novel."

"TomAto, TomAHto," she says with a shrug. "You're his girl."

I roll my eyes. "Fine. I'll slip it on top."

Indie's phone dings and she lets us know the driver is here.

The girls head for the door, and I make a slight detour to take the box to my room and grab the jersey. As I set it down on my bed, the box jostles and the universe taunts me by issuing its own dare in the form of the little, green u-shaped toy sitting perfectly nestled at the top of the pile.

My core tightens, and I silently berate myself as I pick up the toy and examine it. One end is thick and bulbous and tapers into a thin pliable bend before expanding into a smaller bulb. It seems harmless enough. Essentially, just a placeholder to tease me until I can get the real thing. And now that it's in my hand, I find I'm already wet. My resolve to walk away and leave it in the box waffles.

Man up and just wear it, I tell myself. *If anything, you'll be so turned on by the end of the game that even if Bishop doesn't follow through and fuck you wearing his jersey like he promised, you have a box full of toys to handle it.*

"Come on, Wills," Indie hollers.

Shit. It's now or never.

Fuck it.

I yank up my skirt and slide my underwear down before sliding the toy through my wet pussy, letting out a hiss as it enters and settles inside and presses against my clit.

This might be a bad idea, but it is by far not the worst decision I've made in the last month.

I turn it on, but nothing happens.

"Willow!" It's Leigh yelling this time.

I shrug and grab my phone, quickly snapping a picture. The angle reveals the tops of my panties pulled down just enough that he'll see the green top of the toy resting on my clit.

> **WILLOW:** (picture inserted)
> I hope you're uncomfortable the entire game.

> **BISHOP:** FUCK KITTEN.

Serves him right.

CHAPTER THIRTY-THREE
Bishop

Uncomfortable is an understatement. I've had a raging erection from the moment Willow sent me that scandalous picture. Lucky for me, I'm riding the bench today, so I'm spared the task of having to rearrange my cock in a cup between repeated squats. It also means I can focus on the woman behind home plate.

My eyes lock on Willow, seated ten rows back, right behind the plate. Usually she watches the game from the owner's suite, but her friends asked to be closer to the action. Her blonde hair is pulled back in a tight pony, her curls falling down her back. God, she looks good. She's still dressed to the nines in a blue blouse, that no doubt makes her eyes sparkle, paired with one of those skirts I love to fucking hate. Anything less than professional would be grounds for people to look at her like she doesn't deserve to be the team owner.

It's bullshit.

But this time, she added my jersey to her game day uniform.

Mine.

And in nine torturous innings, I can rip every inch of that uniform from her body and properly claim what I should have weeks ago. Jackson's right. Life is too short.

Graham climbs onto the bench next to me and plops down. "How do you think he's going to do?"

I tear my eyes from Willow and glance over at my manager. "Smitty?"

"Mmm," he hums with a nod.

My gaze tracks back to where the first batter of the game has stepped into the box and waits for the rookie to call the pitch. Carson nods and lets a fastball fly. It's a good call. The same I would have made.

"He's got good instincts," I offer Graham.

Of all the guys I've talked to in the last few weeks, per Carson's request, the farm team hopeful is the one who has been easiest to get on with. He's quiet, only speaking when he's got something worth saying which I appreciate. It also means he sees more than he lets on, a skill important to catching. He exudes a willingness to learn by spending his free time watching films of not only our team but our opponents.

"I agree. And it helps Whitmore seems to have taken a shine to him. Now he's just got to convince our GM he's the better choice."

I let out a weighted sigh. "Noah just needs to keep his head in the game, and he'll be fine."

The rookie has his work cut out for himself if he wants to be my second. Sharpe, the guy currently slated for the position, has experience and his nose so far up Ben's ass he'll be smelling shit for a lifetime.

It's why Graham came up with the idea to have them split the game today. The first five innings belong to Noah and then Sharpe will play the last four. All the while, Graham and I watch to see who's the better fit for the team.

Vaughn and Ben threw a conniption when they saw the lineup. Especially since Sharpe played the last two games and made a handful of shitty calls behind the plate. But Graham stood his ground, claiming he didn't think Sharpe was the right fit. I'm also pretty confident he wanted to make sure I was in the right headspace coming back from New York before getting me on the field.

Graham gives an approving grunt, something I've come to appreciate as his standard practice. When he doesn't immediately get up and return to his post at the opposite end of the dugout, I glance his way. His brown eyes soften, his chest moving with an exhale. "You doing okay?"

"Yeah, why?"

"No reason. I've witnessed you trying with the team over the last two weeks. Just wanted to check in." What he doesn't say is he's worried about my headspace after my trip to New York. I'd put money on that being the predominant reason he concocted the plan for me to be on the bench today.

"I'm fine." I give him a reassuring smile.

"Famous last words," he says with a chuckle, adjusting his hat. "Just— keep doing what you're doing."

He wouldn't be saying that if he knew the reason you picked that seat was so you could see his goddaughter wearing a toy you can control from your phone.

I swallow the snort that bubbles in my throat, and it comes out more like a cough. "Uh, thanks. Will do."

Graham nods and shuffles back to his post at the other end of the dugout.

My smile is painfully big as I shift and reach for my phone in my back pocket, tucking it between me and the end of the dugout. It's an unspoken rule to leave all devices in the locker room, but seeing as I'm not playing today, no one is going to say anything if I'm caught.

I flick my gaze to where Willow is sitting.

BISHOP: Are you ready?

Willow picks up her phone, and I nearly fall off the bench when she sees my text and smiles. She glances my direction before tapping out her response.

WILLOW: For what?

I thumb the button on the app, turning on the toy to the lowest setting so it vibrates against her g-spot.

A shit-eating grin takes over my face when she jumps in her seat and both her friends turn toward her to make sure she's okay.

Her fingers fly across the keyboard on her phone.

WILLOW: You're evil. I wouldn't have worn this thing if I knew you'd be controlling it.

BISHOP: Settle Kitten. We both know you're soaked at just the thought of being at my fingertips.

WILLOW: That's not the point.

BISHOP: That's exactly the point.

WILLOW: Don't you have a game to be paying attention to?

> **BISHOP:** Lucky for you I'm great at multitasking.

I return my attention to the game, watching as Smitty makes another two solid calls, resulting in the third out of the inning. The team floods the dugout, and the rookie catcher takes up root next to me.

"How was that?" he asks, the glint of a puppy looking for approval in his eyes.

"You did good, pig."

"Pig?"

"*Babe?*"

His brows reach his hairline as he tilts his head in confusion. "What?"

"The movie?" I clarify, then shake my head the moment I realize he has no idea what I'm talking about. "Fuck, I'm dating myself."

When did all these rookies get so damn young?

The same time you got old. Tommy snickers.

"You're calling me a pig?"

"No—just—never mind. You did good, kid. Keep an eye on your framing. You're a little late when you come up from the inside corner."

"Thanks."

Something twinges in my chest, almost like a physical ache, but it's different. It's not like before where I'd find myself missing Tommy. I still miss him and the teaching moments he used to share with Jackson and me. This is more of a swell with something like pride—the kind that gives way to joy. It's foreign, but not completely unwelcome.

The Renegades have a solid at bat, resulting in two runs coming across the plate. It's not until they're out in the field again for the top of the second that I feel my phone buzz at my side.

WILLOW: Did you forget about me?

BISHOP: I could never forget about you.

WILLOW: This isn't much of a punishment.

BISHOP: Oh Kitten, that was only the first inning.

CHAPTER THIRTY-FOUR
Willow

It's the eighth inning and I'm eating my words…and squirming in my chair.

The first seven were easy enough, kicking off with Bishop upping the intensity of the vibrations of the bulb nestled deep in my pussy. By inning four, he added the clit stimulation on the lowest setting. The low thrum was enough to make me wet, but not enough to make me come. More like having an itch I couldn't quite scratch. Inning five, he added vibrations—that I am affectionately calling "the wave"—to the inside, paired with a low pulse on my clit.

Then things escalated quickly from an itch needing to be scratched to an insane heat coiling low in my belly—in point-five-seconds. I clenched my thighs, seeking friction, but it still wasn't enough to send me over the edge. The sixth inning, he upped the intensity at the most inopportune moment. I was in the middle of a conversation with Indie, who looked at me like I was crazy when I doubled over in my seat, thighs clenched in an attempt to fight off the mini orgasm rendering me speechless.

All the while, I could see his smug smile in the dugout. This is my punishment for shutting him out, and he's absolutely loving every minute of torturing me.

"Are you okay?" Indie asks.

I manage a strangled "mmmhmmm" that comes out more of a moan as my pussy flutters around the toy.

When it passes seconds later, I look up. She has her brows raised.

Stuck between a rock and a hard place, I debate breaking my promise and telling her it's just cramps.

"I, uh—" The buzz on my clit ramps up, and I pin a glare in Bishop's direction. "I'm about to come," I whisper.

Leigh's eyes go wide. "You're what? Here? Now?"

"Ahhh." I chew my lower lip, heat filling my cheeks from both embarrassment and pleasure. "Toy. Bishop. Controlling."

Her eyes dart from Bishop to me and laughter bursts past her lips.

"What's so funny?" Leigh asks.

"Bishop's got Wills here wearing a toy, and she's seconds away from showing us her O face."

Leigh's eyes follow the same path Indie's had and she mutters, "Holy shit. That's fucking hot."

My little exhibitionist heart thuds fiercely against my ribs. I shouldn't be so turned on that my friends know I'm on the edge of coming, but I am.

I pick up my phone, warring with if I should beg him to stop or not.

BISHOP: How you doing, Kitten?

WILLOW: Indie and Leigh know.

BISHOP: And how do you feel about that?

WILLOW: Mortified and more turned on than I've ever been.

BISHOP: Do you want to come?

WILLOW: If I say no will that stop you?

BISHOP: Not a chance.

A stupid smile stretches across my face, and I can only imagine what I look like, smiling like an idiot at my phone and squirming in my seat.

"Who's that?" Indie asks, twisting in her seat.

I follow her gaze to see who she's looking at and notice Luca Donati, owner of the Los Angeles Monarchs, has entered our aisle with his gaze locked on the seat beside Indie.

Shit.

The last thing I want to do is schmooze with anyone right now. It's one thing to have an orgasm when it's just my best friends around me, it's another entirely to have to put on a professional face.

And yet I'm wet at the thought.

Fucking Bishop. I'm going to both thank him and kill him for this.

I mutter for Indie to switch seats with me, and we swap just as Luca does the same.

"Willow, it's so good to see you." Luca offers his hand, which I shake.

"It's good to see you too. Surprising, though. Shouldn't you be in

Arizona?" I shift my weight, thankful when the toy jostles enough that it's not directly on top of my clit.

"My brother and I thought one of us should be in town for the gala. We're very interested in partnering with Renegade Hearts and wanted to show our support. We'd love to speak with you about a partnership and getting something similar set up to what you have with the Renegades on the west coast."

My phone buzzes in my hand, and it takes everything in me not to look and see what my devious catcher has to say.

"Absolutely. We're happy to have you. I know we've spoken before about setting something up, but then with the…" My voice trails off. The last time we spoke was before the crash.

"We were very sorry to hear about the team, and your father. He was a good man."

People throw around the word sorry like it's nothing, but the way Luca bows his head, I'm inclined to believe he means it.

Bishop amps up the vibrations, and I can feel his smug stare on the back of my neck.

"Thank you for saying so," I manage to say without a hint of a moan.

I'm seriously going to make Bishop pay for this.

"I'm eager to hear about your plans for the team."

That makes one person. Luca and his brother, Enzo, are two of the younger owners in the league. Of the two, Luca is the charismatic one. Always being photographed by the paparazzi with a new woman on his arm at every event opening and nightclub he enters. Enzo, on the other hand, is more reserved. Definitely more my speed if I had to guess. The two of them are a force to be reckoned with. They shook things up when they bought the Monarchs five years ago. While none of their ideas have been quite as ambitious as mine, they might be a good duo to bounce ideas off of. That is, if I can ever get them past the board.

I offer him a tight-lipped smile. "I'd love to chat with you about them."

Luca's megawatt smile reveals two small dimples in each of his cheeks. Having been a ballplayer himself, those two little indents are just the cherry on top of a stunning man in a suit.

Am I seriously sitting here checking out one of the other owners of the league?

I fully blame the toy in me for ramping up my sex drive to ungodly levels.

I focus back on Luca just in time to see his gaze trail back up the length of my body and lock with mine.

Shit.

My lips part and I'm about to tell him to let me know when he and Enzo have some time, but Bishop picks that moment to ramp the toy on my clit up to ten.

My soul leaves my body as I jump, causing me to fall out of my seat, flat on my ass.

"Oh shit," Luca says, before reaching out to help me up.

Oh shit, is right.

Leigh and Indie lose their shit behind me, and I pin a glare in their direction.

"I-I—Thanks," I stutter, taking his hand. "Should probably get these seats inspected."

I don't even know what I'm saying, only that if I don't get out of here fast, I'm going to come in front of this very attractive colleague. My clit takes a beating as I shift my weight and the toy slides right up against it. I swallow the moan that begs to be released and force a smile like nothing's wrong.

Thankfully, Indie takes pity on me. "We could use a refill on drinks. Why don't you go get us some and check on that knee?"

I look down and see a small scratch across my knee where I must have hit the arm of my chair.

"Um. Yeah." I turn back to Luca. "Here, let me introduce you to my CFO, Leighton James. She's been heading up Renegade Hearts while I get the Renegades season underway."

"We've met," Leigh growls from two seats down, and if I didn't know any better, I'd say she's not happy about the introduction.

I tilt my head and silently ask her what gives.

She shakes her head as if to say "we'll talk about it later".

"Leighton? Is that really you?" Luca asks.

My head whips between him and Leigh.

"You've met?" I grit out, trying to focus on anything except the tightly coiled ache in my belly ready to explode.

"We—" Luca starts, but Leigh cuts him off.

"A long time ago."

The tension between them is so thick it could be cut with a knife. I hate to bail on her now, but I really don't want to come in front of Luca.

"Great. I'll leave you two to talk. He and his brother want to partner with Renegade Hearts to get a center started in Los Angeles."

"Wait, I—" is all Indie gets out before I turn on my heel and hightail it out of the aisle and up the stairs to the concourse.

The second I'm safely behind the staff entrance to the clubhouse, I sink against the door and let out a moan. Now that I'm no longer focused on fighting it, I'm so close. The tingling starts low in my belly and travels to where the toy massages the sensitive spot behind my clit. It's almost as if my orgasm is trying to wring itself from me through that spot. My phone buzzes again, and I mewl as I pull up my messages.

BISHOP: Who the fuck is that guy?

BISHOP: Willow.

BISHOP: Are you ignoring me?

BISHOP: WILLOW

BISHOP: If you come in front of him, I'm going to wreck you so hard after the game. I'm going to torture that tiny little pussy of yours until you can't come anymore because you gave away what belongs to me. That orgasm is mine.

Fuck. He's so damn hot when he's worked up like this. I love his possessiveness. He might not claim me the way I want him to, but I'll let him have my orgasms any day.

My fingers shake as I type.

WILLOW: You jealous?

It's cruel, but I can't help but tease him a little. He's played with me the entire game. It's my turn to punish him a little.

BISHOP: Yes.

BISHOP: Did you come?

WILLOW: No but I'm about to.

The second I send it, the vibrating stops.

I can't stop the whine that falls from my lips or the fiery text I send in response.

WILLOW: WTF

BISHOP: Who was that?

WILLOW: Luca Donati.

BISHOP: The Monarch's owner.

WILLOW: Yes. Now turn it back on.

BISHOP: No.

WILLOW: No? I thought the whole point was to come in public.

BISHOP: No, the whole point was to punish you by keeping you on the edge of coming until I'm good and ready to give you the orgasm you deserve.

WILLOW: Turn. it. back. on. Bishop.

I'm not above begging. My body feels like a goddamned live wire. The slightest touch will send an electric orgasm through me.

BISHOP: There's only one more inning. Come find me after you ditch the entourage.

WILLOW: Or you could come find me in the clubhouse right now and make good on your promise.

BISHOP: No. I'm going to leave you wanting, Kitten. And trust me, I'm wanting too. But I plan on taking my time with you. And you're not coming unless it's on my cock.

WILLOW: And if I do it myself?

We both know I'm not going to, but I love his filthy mouth and I'm not above taunting if it means I get more of it.

BISHOP: What I said before about wrecking you? It will look like child's play if you take what's mine. I doubt you'll be able to walk for at least a week after.

Fuck me.

CHAPTER THIRTY-FIVE
Willow

Bishop Lawson is a sadist of the best kind.

And I'm his willing masochist.

He took mercy on me when the game ended and returned the toy to the lowest setting. A torturous reminder of just how turned on I am and that there isn't a damn thing I can do about it until I get out of here.

Sitting at the postgame media table listening to Graham and Noah answer questions about his stellar performance, movement at the back of the room catches my eye. I zero in on where Bishop has slipped in. He's changed out of his uniform and into jeans and his team hoodie with a Renegade hat pulled low over his eyes. A smile quirks at the corner of my lips. I don't know who he thinks he's fooling. Everyone in the room knows what he looks like. He's not fooling anyone.

His dark gaze connects with mine. It's intense and possessive. I shift in my seat, jostling the still vibrating toy in my pussy.

Is this damn press conference over yet?

His lips twitch, and I watch as he pulls his phone from the pocket of his sweater and swipes. Seconds later, my phone buzzes on the tabletop and I don't have to look to know it's him.

I shouldn't acknowledge him, especially in a room full of reporters, but I can't help myself. I glance down at my phone and see his name and the preview of his message.

BISHOP: You are so fucking gorgeous up there. I wonder if I…

Heart thundering against my ribcage, heat fills my cheeks, and I don't need to read the rest of the message to know the threat. My eyes dart to the back of the room, and I'm greeted by a wicked grin. He's got his phone in his hand, his thumb raised, and the look in his eye tells me he's seconds away from edging me in front of this entire room of reporters.

I should be furious, but I'm far too turned on for that.

"Ms. York."

Hearing my name breaks me out of my lust filled haze, and I search for the person who called it.

A hand shoots up belonging to Ellis Monroe, a reporter from *The Foul Line*.

"Yes, Mr. Monroe."

"I was wondering if you would comment on the plan you presented to your board that would not only misappropriate funds for the team but also see the Renegades welcoming accused rapist Mercer Cohen to the team."

No.

No. No. No. No.

This can't be happening.

My mouth drops open, and I could swear all the oxygen has left the room. It's quiet enough that the only sound I can hear is the low hum of the vibrator in my pussy.

Then that stops too.

My eyes dart to Bishop. His eyes are locked on me, and though they are soft in a way that I have no doubt is meant to offer me strength, his mouth is pinned in a straight line, revealing his anger.

How the hell did the media get a hold of my plans? There was an NDA signed. The whole thing was embargoed until we decided what was going to happen next.

I don't even want to look down the table at Graham or Nikki, who I am sure is spiraling, trying to figure out how we're going to spin this.

Bishop nods and I swallow hard before returning my gaze to Mr. Monroe.

He blinks at me expectantly, waiting for my response.

I straighten in my seat and fold my hands in front of me on the table, trying my best to hide the panic that shakes them. "I am not sure how you got a copy of embargoed plans, but I am not prepared to comment on them at this time."

His lips twitch. "How about the evidence faxed to my office this morning accusing your father of bribing umpires last season, resulting in wins for the Renegades and allowing them to clinch a playoff position?"

"What?" I exclaim. "Who told you—"

"That's all we have time for today," Nikki interrupts my outburst. "We take any and all accusations seriously and will look into these and have a statement ready as soon as we've received all the facts."

My world tilts. Chaos takes over the room. Reporters jump to their feet, shouting questions while they simultaneously scour on their phones for any additional information.

A hand grips my shoulder and I'm tugged from my seat and cradled against a broad chest. When I look up, I'm greeted by Noah's sympathetic green eyes.

"I've got you, boss," he mutters. I nod and allow him to guide me, pressed between him and Graham, towards the exit.

We make it to the end of the slightly raised stage when a reporter jumps in front of Graham, pushing him to the side to demand answers from me.

I open my mouth to say no comment, but before I get a word out, a hand appears on the shoulder of the lanky reporter and yanks him out of the way. Graham and Noah usher me the short distance out of the press room, but not before I see Bishop push the reporter up against the wall. His eyes are filled with rage, and I'm helpless to do anything but send a silent plea for him to keep his anger in check. The last thing I need is another incident when our house is already burning from the inside out.

The walk from the media room to Graham's office is a blur of Nikki and Graham yelling at anyone who will listen to find out who the hell leaked my plans and what the evidence against my father is.

I don't give a shit about my plans. Let them rip it apart—rip me apart. I've had to defend my position since the day I took over. It's nothing new. But my father—

I feel like I'm going to throw up as I desperately try to make it make sense.

Any of it.

All of it.

My father rigged the game.

My father.

The man who cared about this team more than anything. More than even me.

When we reach the door, Noah gently hands me off to Graham, who wraps a hand around my waist and ushers me into his office. Out of the corner of my eye, I see Bishop pressed against the wall, his hands balled into fists, eyes pleading for—I'm not sure, but it almost looks like he's asking for permission to be there. I give a quick but subtle shake of my head, and he hesitates before storming off toward the locker room.

I hope he knows this isn't me shutting him out. There is no way he can be here without outing our relationship, and I can't add that to the clusterfuck right now.

Graham's office door clicks shut, and I let out a weighted breath as I sink into the chair, praying for relief. It doesn't come. We might be away from prying eyes and questions, but it does nothing to assuage the pressure from the elephant that has stomped on my chest. I close my eyes and cross my arms, my fingers drawing small circles over the skin of my biceps in an attempt to ground myself.

"Willow." Graham's voice is soft, yet stern in a way I didn't expect.

When I open my eyes, I see he's standing with his hands on his desk, eyes narrowed on me. "I have to ask. You didn't leak your plans, did you?"

My brows shoot up and I visibly shrink back. "No. Why the hell would I do that?"

He lets out a heavy sigh and softens. "I didn't think so, but I know the board disagreed and releasing the plans so that they had to acknowledge them is exactly something your father would do."

He would? It didn't sound like the man I knew. Then again, maybe I truly didn't know him at all. Is this one of the skeletons in the closet the board mentioned? Are there more?

Graham lifts a hand and runs it through his short salt and pepper hair.

"Fuck, this is bad."

"Which part?" I don't recognize my own voice. It's hollow. Defeated. An extension of my broken heart.

"All of it. They are framing you as reckless and irresponsible. At the same time, they are tarnishing your name through attacking your father."

"You don't think he—"

"No. There's no way in hell your father would fuck with the integrity of the game." Graham has never been one to curse in front of me. To his team? Absolutely. But never in my presence. I've always known him to keep cool, calm, and collected no matter what has been thrown his way.

But at this moment? He's just as shaken as I am.

"They have evidence," I state, clinging to the minuscule facts we have.

"Allegedly," Nikki pipes up from where she leaned against the wall by the door. She's got her phone in her hand, still scrolling as she crosses the room and claims the seat beside me. "We haven't seen the proof, and they haven't released it yet."

"But they have it," Graham argues. "They wouldn't have brought it up if they weren't certain. No one would dare go after Richard York unless they had irrefutable proof."

He's right. Me? Absolutely, they'd go after me. But my father has been a beloved member of this league for years. And after the crash, they would have to be crazy to tarnish his legacy.

"It doesn't matter," I whisper, realization setting in. Both sets of eyes focus on me, waiting for me to continue. "The damage is done. Whoever released this information, regardless if it's true or not, has gotten exactly what they wanted. Even if my father is proven innocent, there will always be the question of if it actually happened. We've seen how allegations of cheating have ruined teams in the past. Especially if action wasn't taken within the organization to rectify the claims. I don't know who leaked the information, but the damage has been done. And by leaking my plans, which I am sure will happen in the next hour, I'll be the daughter who took over and attempted to run the team into the ground.".

"Your plans were sound, Willow. Just because a bunch of bastards didn't like them doesn't mean—"

"It doesn't matter!" I yell, cutting Graham off. Leaping from my chair, I nearly knock it over. My body hums with the need to do something—anything—to stave off the soul-crushing weight of my life falling apart.

One foot in front of the other, I begin to pace the length of the office. My hands pump open and closed, searching for something tangible to grasp.

Graham and Nikki watch me with matching concern as I try to work out what I'm feeling.

Anger. Fear. Distraught. Helplessness.

All things I promised I wouldn't give to the people who doubted me. But I'm running on fumes. I can't fake it anymore. I'm done playing their game. I've done nothing but try to make this team not only my home, but a home for everyone—the team, my staff, the fans—and while so many have been appreciative, it's not enough to sway those who protect the status quo.

There will always be something. Sleeping dogs will never lie. Because I'm not who they want.

Tears prick the corner of my eyes, and as much as I want to let them fall, once again I force them away. After all, there is no crying in baseball.

I swallow past the lump in my throat and stop mid pace to turn toward Graham and Nikki. Grabbing on to the tiny sliver of strength I have left, I relax my shoulders and exhale. "They—this is what they wanted. This is—I'm exhausted. So, if this is what they want, then they can have the team. I'm not going to watch my father's legacy fold like a house of cards because of me. Even if the allegations are true, they will look past it because he's dead. The blame will fall on me."

"But you didn't know."

"It doesn't matter."

He's right. I didn't know, and I might not have any proof that this was a power move by the board, but my gut is telling me it is. I provoked them with my plans, and they retaliated.

Graham opens his mouth to counter me again, but I silence him by continuing. "You forget I grew up playing these games. I've witnessed these tactics time and time again. It's my fault for believing this organization and league had more integrity than a bunch of uptight society families. I should have remembered the only solid lesson my mother ever taught me."

Graham winces, his eyes falling to his desk as he rasps, "Everyone has a price, and no one gives a shit about you."

I huff sarcastically. "So, you've heard the wise words of Adrianna York."

"A time or two, yes," Graham grits, clenching his jaw. "I wish I could tell you you're wrong, but that doesn't mean you aren't meant to lead this team."

He put it together much faster than Nikki, who let out a gasp. Graham might not have always been around to be the godfather I needed, but when he was, he made sure to pay attention. He knows me better than most and has seen me at some of my lowest moments. He recognizes the look of defeat on my face.

"Wait, what?" Nikki looks between us, disbelief etched in her features. "You're leaving?"

"No. Not yet, maybe not at all," I try to reassure her, but my mind is ninety percent made up. "I want to see the evidence against my father before I make any decisions. Until then, I'd like to refine my talking points for the gala interview and prepare a statement for the press."

"I'll get right on that."

"Graham, I need you to give the team a heads up that no one talks to the press until we have more information. Schedule a team meeting first thing in the morning."

"Done."

I nod, fighting the endorphins of the press conference as they start to crash within me. "Okay. If you don't need me, I'm going to head home."

They both look like they want to say more or stop me, but neither do. They only nod silently.

"Thank you. Keep me posted."

I should stay and help, but my moment of clarity is passing, swiftly being replaced by depression's guillotine. I need to get out of here before I either go full Bishop on the clubhouse or sink into a puddle of tears.

I make it as far as the door when Graham calls my name, and I look over my shoulder.

His face sinks into a sad smile. "Don't give up, kiddo."

"I'm not."

It's a lie and we both know it, but it wouldn't be the first or the last time I put on a brave face for this team. I'm the port that holds safety for so many and that doesn't change just because a category five storm has wrecked my shores.

CHAPTER THIRTY-SIX
Bishop

My knee bounces, shaking the table in the corner of the hotel bar. I sit alone, mostly because of the don't-fuck-with-me vibes I'm giving off, but we're all there—the whole team—waiting anxiously to hear anything about the accusations made.

There are a few reporters camped outside the hotel waiting for anyone associated with the team to come or go so they can get a comment. Not that they will. Graham vowed he'd have our cleats if any of us utter a single word, and no one is willing to test him.

I hung back at the stadium for as long as it made sense for me to be there. I just needed to know she was okay. But there was no reason to stay once the rest of the team finished with therapies or extra work outs and cleared out.

My phone buzzes on the tabletop, and just like every other time it has in the past hour, my heart races. I flip it over only to have my stomach sink when I see it's not Willow, but my sister, Sutton. It's not that I'm not happy to receive her message. I am. Rebuilding the relationship with my family is something I'm challenging myself to do, but right now, my mind is focused on the fact I haven't heard from Willow.

> **SUTTON:** You okay? I just saw the reports.

No. I'm not okay. My world is fracturing. The legacy of the team I lost is being called into question, and the woman I love is being torn apart in the press.

So you admit it then, Tommy whispers. *You love her.*

Fuck.

Now is not the time for groundbreaking realizations.

I type out a snarky reply but instantly erase it. Sutton doesn't deserve my anger. God knows she's had enough of it over the last year. Not only that, it would be counterproductive to repairing what I've broken between us.

> **BISHOP:** Thanks for checking in. I'm as okay as I can be. Let the family know I'll call as soon as I can.

Just as I hit send, another text comes through from Jackson.

> **JACKSON:** What the fuck is going on down there?

> **BISHOP:** As soon as I know for sure I'll let you know.

JACKSON: Are you with Willow?

BISHOP: No

JACKSON: WHY THE FUCK NOT??

That's a great question. Maybe because I have no idea where she is. Or if she even wants me there.

I ignore him, not needing the berating I am sure is coming.

Setting the phone back down, I glance across the bar to the TV we've commandeered, playing the highlight reel of the press conference.

Over and over, I've watched the footage. The glint in Willow's eyes that was just for me. It screams of the passion we share. A moment existing only between us when she was at my mercy. Her pussy filled with my toy. Then Monroe asks his fucked-up questions, and that passion is instantly replaced by sheer terror.

I have never wanted to kill a man, but I was damn close in that moment.

A torso blocks my view, and I look up to find Carson standing there. He's not wearing his signature smile. It's the first time I've seen him look almost despondent.

"As your co-captain, I feel as though it's my duty to tell you we need to do something about this. The team is getting antsy. None of them want to head up to their rooms, but sitting here isn't going to get us answers any faster and rumors are starting to spread."

He voices everything on my mind.

"You think I don't know that?" It's the only reason I'm still here and not tearing through Fort Myers to find Willow. I have to trust she's in good hands with Graham and Nikki and if she needed me, she'd let me know.

The team, on the other hand, is my responsibility.

They haven't exactly been quiet with their comments. There's anger from some. Whispers that their former teams could have made the playoff last season if they were given fair calls. There's apprehension from others about inviting someone like Mercer Cohen back into the league, let alone onto their team. Some are going so far as to question if Willow knew all along. Overall, they trust her as an owner, but the few that don't, like Sharpe, are working hard to sow seeds of doubt through the team.

"I know you do." Carson runs a frustrated hand through his hair. "You look like you're ready to murder someone."

"I am," I growl.

"Would this have anything to do with a certain blonde-haired owner?"

"No, why would it—"

Carson holds up a hand, halting my denial. "Don't play dumb with me. I'm your co-captain. And you've shown up to one too many practices smelling of lavender and lemon."

"I—" Fuck. Willow's going to kill me. "How do you know what she smells like?"

"It's a curse, really. Nose like a damn bloodhound." He falls into the seat beside me and lifts his glass like he's goddamned Vanna White. "I can also tell you that this beer has hints of orange and an undertone of cloves mixed with the hops. And Julian is sleeping with the concierge."

My brow raises, silently asking if he's fucking serious.

"Even if I didn't smell her on you, there's also the fact that any time the two of you are in the same room, you look like you're going to devour one another."

Do we? Did I? Shit. I—I want to blame it on our arrangement, but even I know that's a lie. Even if I hadn't been fucking her every which way for the last month, I'd still look at her that way. New Year's and knowledge of how she sounded coming apart on my cock solidified that. Now, though?

You love her. Tommy says the words I won't let myself believe.

Until now.

Fuck. I do.

It hits me like a ton of bricks. Willow is my aisle seat. She's seen parts of me I previously reserved for the hot showers after a night of trying to forget—the breakdowns, the tears, the undiluted rage that consumes me.

Consumed me.

Past tense. I'm not delusional enough to believe it's not still there, but it's nowhere near where it was a month ago. She showed me it's okay to feel it, let it go, and do it all over again the next day. Because that's living after tragedy. She challenges me to be who I am, not who I was.

She's all in.

And now he gets it.

"You can't tell anyone," I murmur to Carson, hating the way my chest tightens when I do.

I've been such an idiot.

Carson scoffs. "And betray the brotherhood of co-captains? Never."

I shake my head. "I—I'm worried about her." Because that's all I can say. I'm confident Carson won't say anything, but I can't say the same for everyone else in the room. Anything more could cost us both our jobs.

Not to mention Willow deserves to hear how I feel before I tell anyone else.

"Listen, it's none of my business"—he pauses to sip his fruity beer—"but if you care so much, then why are you still sitting here?"

"Because she's my boss, and the team needs me here."

Carson grunts, but it comes out more of an annoyed laugh. "I'd be willing to wager my left nutsack that she'd be happy to see you, regardless."

"Your left one?" I clarify with a pointed look.

Carson shrugs. "Yeah, righty is the more dominant one. I need him if I'm ever going to have kids one day."

"You are so fucking strange."

His lip twitches upward. "You love it."

Unfortunately, the bastard's right. He's growing on me.

Carson takes another sip and cocks a brow. "So, you want to be here for the team?"

"Come on, man, don't do that. I'm trying."

"I know, but don't hide behind us just because you're too scared to be there for the woman you're clearly interested in."

Tommy snorts. *I like him. Keep him around when I'm gone.*

My chest tightens, and I struggle to force air into my lungs. When he's gone. When the fuck is that? I've already lost Norah and Jackson as my conscious interlopers. Am I going to lose Tommy too?

Eventually, you have to let me go. I have to move forward. Just like you.

What if I don't want to? I might pretend I hate their constant interjections, but having this piece of them has been a lifeline in the midst of all the bullshit.

Tough shit. Now go find Willow.

"Bishop?" Carson's voice and his hand on my forearm pull me from my spiral. "You okay?"

No.

"I—yeah. I'm fine."

His eyes narrow, and I'm not sure he believes me. Hell, I wouldn't believe me. I'm a grown ass man sitting here talking to the voices inside my head.

"Okay." He nods. "If you're sure."

"I am." I sip from my beer and focus on Tommy's advice. "Can you cover for me tonight? Keep the guys in line?"

Carson awards me with a disbelieving stare. "Are you, Bishop Lawson, the broody extraordinaire, going to make reckless decisions, sneak out on a school night, and trust me as your co-captain to handle our merry band of men?"

He says it as if I haven't been doing every one of those things for the entirety of spring training.

I nod. "I'm going to figure out what the hell is going on."

He leans against the table and pops a brow. "Annnnnd."

"I'm going to track down our fearless leader."

"Fuck yes." He lifts his hand for a high-five. "Go team Carship. No, Bishon. Whitson? No, Lawmore."

"What?"

"Our ship name."

I pinch my brow and dip my head to hide my smile before reluctantly lifting my hand and slapping his. "I fucking cannot with you."

Carson lets out a rough laugh before flashing me a wicked grin. "Go get your girl, Bish."

My heart skips a damn beat. I like the sound of that.

Unease grips my spine as I wait for someone to open the door. I count the planks that make up the wooden porch to stop my mind from circling back to my feelings for Willow.

The whole drive here, I rehearsed everything I want to tell her, but nothing seemed like enough.

I'm pulled from another rendition of laying my heart on the line when the door creaks open, and I'm greeted by Leigh. She's still dressed in her Renegades t-shirt from the game, but her ash blonde hair is pulled up on top of her head instead of down.

She looks me up and down and smirks. "So, the casual dick finally decides to show up."

I pop a brow up. "The what?"

"Never mind. I'm guessing you're here to see Willow?"

Indie steps out from the hall that leads to the kitchen. Unlike Leigh, she's changed from her Renegades gear into a pair of sweats and a tank. "Do my ears deceive me? Bishop Lawson is here?"

"Why is that so surprising?"

Indie rolls her eyes. "It's not. I just lost the over-under on how long it would take you to get here."

"I'm sorry I lost you money."

"Oh no, we are far past monetary exchanges. You just lost me the first crack at the newest hockey romance Leigh procured for our little smut club."

Confused, I ask, "Can't you just buy your own copy?"

Indie scoffs and rolls her eyes again and glances at Leigh, as if to say *this asshole*. "And miss the annotations that come from Leigh's filthy mind? Absolutely not."

I huff a laugh. "Can I please come in?"

"Nope." Leight throws her hand out and blocks the door frame. "We've got a few questions for you first."

An expectant look is etched on both of their faces, and I know I'm in for the "whole hurt her and I'll kill you" speech. "Okay. Fine. Let's get this over with."

Leigh smirks. "First off, you get points for the box of toys."

"Um, thank you. I think."

"But you lose points for being a complete asshat before that," Indie interjects.

"That's fair." I dip my head and rub the back of my neck. I deserve that title, and probably a bit more for all the things I put Willow through.

"Tell us. Why are you here?" Leigh presses.

"I need to make sure she's okay."

"I'm not convinced. You have been a whole pain in her ass since she took over the team." She glances at Indie, who nods in agreement.

"I know. But you also know we've become a whole lot more since arriving in Fort Myers," I argue.

"Sure. I know she's all in, but you? You're in—" Indie turns to Leigh and asks, "—what's the equivalent of a cleat chaser but for the owner of a team?"

"Skirt chaser?"

"Definitely not as sexy, but we'll come up with a better name." Indie snaps her gaze back to me. "She's got no one but us now. Which means she's ours to protect."

"Are you going to break her heart?" Leigh fires.

"No. I—"

Indie doesn't let me finish. "Because if you are, you can turn your happy ass around and head back to where you came from."

"I'm falling in love with her." I groan, dragging a hand through my hair. "Are you happy with that answer?"

"Fuck," Indie curses. "Really?"

"Yes. Okay?" I shift my weight, hoping it's enough to get them to let me in, but by the dumbstruck looks on their faces, I'll need to elaborate a bit more. "I have been since the first night. Ever since I found her on that fucking balcony. She came in like a damn wrecking ball and consumed all my thoughts, and I wanted her. But I wasn't ready. Neither was she. We both had things we needed to accomplish before we could ever be more. And then the crash. Fuck that fucking crash. I know I was an asshole. I fucked up in every possible way and shut her out. But Willow, the fucking goddess that she is, chipped away at every piece of me until I had nothing left and then she selflessly gave me pieces of herself to replace them with."

"Shit," Leigh whispers. "You really do love her."

"Yes." I drop my hand, not breaking eye contact with her. "Can I come inside now?"

Their shoulders relax and Leigh drops her arm from the door, signaling I've passed their little test.

When I cross the threshold, Indie mutters, "She's a mess right now. We had to make sure."

"I know." I sigh. "She's lucky to have friends like you in her corner."

That earns me a smile from Leigh. "Can I give you a piece of advice?"

"I'll take all the help I can get."

"Willow will hear you say the words, but she won't believe them. Her parents did a number on her as a kid and because of that, she will bend over backwards to help the people she loves. On the flip side, she struggles to believe she deserves the same. You say you're falling in love, but she'll be quick to believe you're just like everyone else and that love comes with a price. Her mother loved her as long as she was the perfect little debutant. Her father as long as she shared baseball with him."

I nod, committing her heartbreaking words to memory. "So, what are you saying?"

"Say the words, but back them up with your actions. Make sure she sees it. Feels it."

Chewing over her words, I realize she's right. Willow seeks action. It's in everything she's ever done. She made sure I got down here. Warned me about being on thin ice with my place on the team. Stopped me from ruining my career with my drinking. Even the advice she gives is all rooted in action. Learn to live. Take Carson to The Guardian. Go to New York to be with Jackson.

My girl speaks in action.

I nod, working it over in my brain.

"She's up in her room," Indie tells me. "She got an email from Nikki and told us she just wants to be alone."

Fuck.

"Do you know what it said?"

Indie grimaces. "It was the evidence."

"So, it's true?" I ask, even though I already know.

Leigh sighs and gives a half-hearted shrug, but her eyes hold something back. "It's not good. They have messages between her father and the umpires he bribed, in addition to bank statements for offshore accounts and wire transfers."

"And what do you think?" I press.

A pensive look crosses her face. "If you ask me, it seems too clean. Mr. York was a lawyer for years. He knew the ins and outs of the law. If he wanted to do this, there's no one better to get away with it. But the evidence is there, and I can't argue with that."

"Fuck." I exhale. This news would be a tsunami to Willow's heart. She believes in this team more than anyone I know, including the guys that make up the field. This on top of having the press tear apart her plans and making her the villain will have decimated her confidence.

"Will the guys stand with her?" Leigh asks softly, and I can read between the lines. She's asking if she'll be fighting this war on two fronts.

"I don't know," I say honestly. "I think most of them will, but until they hear the whole story, I can't say for sure."

Willow didn't have a single hand in this aside from her plans. I want to believe that if we tackle the cheating head on and let them hear the vision she has in her own words, the team will see she has their best interest at heart.

"We're here to help in whatever way we can," Indie reassures.

"Thanks."

"Now go get your girl."

I plan to.

CHAPTER THIRTY-SEVEN
Willow

The silence of my room overwhelmed me, and I retreated to the balcony. Leaning over the railing, I stare out at the infinite darkness of the sea. The sound of the waves the calming constant I need right now.

A soft knock filters out from the bedroom, but it's not enough to make me turn from my view. It's probably Indie or Leigh wanting to check on me. They're worried and only want to help, but all I want is to let my tears fall without being the rock for everyone else.

Because if I was out there, or at the stadium, or at the hotel with the team, that's what I would do. It's what I've done every single day since the crash—no—since before then. It's all I've ever done—try to keep it together because other people need me to. My dad, after my mother died. The kids at Renegade Hearts. Leigh. Indie. The team.

Bishop.

I'm so fucking tired, and for the first time in a long time, I can't just pretend it's going to be okay.

It's not.

The evidence is damning.

No.

Not just damning. It's a sledgehammer to everything my dad built—everything I've worked to build in the last six months.

There's nothing that unites people more than a scandal. And this is one that will no doubt be etched in Major League history.

This will be my father's legacy.

My thoughts race as my panic ebbs and flows like the waves, and I'm not sure how it's possible I still have any tears, but alas, they continue to fall.

"Willow?" His voice is soft yet commanding, and I can't stop the heat that fills my cheek or the way my thighs clench.

Then I remember my father's actions have torn apart the memory of his team. They will forever be the Renegades who didn't deserve their place at the top of the leaderboard. He has every right to be upset with me and the organization.

I freeze in place, cold washing over me despite the balmy Florida night, bracing for whatever version of Bishop I'm about to encounter.

"You're here," I whisper in disbelief as he joins me on the balcony.

"I am." He slides up next to me but instead of facing the ocean, he leans his back against the rail, the sleeve of his hoodie brushing up against my bare skin.

"Are you okay?" I ask, looking up to search his face for any hint of despair and finding nothing but a comforting calm.

His chest rumbles with a half-hearted laugh. "After the day you've had, are you seriously worrying about me?"

Of course, I am. That's what I do.

I frown. "Shouldn't you be with the team?"

"I came to find our leader," he says, his lips lifting in a soft smile.

A sardonic laugh falls from my lips, and I focus back on the vast ocean, unable to stand the weight of his stare. "You came to the wrong place then."

I silently plead for him to relent. To leave me be. But he doesn't let me hide.

Bishop reaches out, his hand gently wrapping around my biceps, and he tugs me between his legs and against his chest, almost like he knows that's where I need to be. He buries his nose in the slicked back hair just above my ear and whispers, "I came to find you. Talk to me, Willow."

Willow. Not Kitten.

I wish I knew what that meant. I don't know what we are anymore. We're a stark contrast from the last time the two of us shared this space almost a year ago. He was buried deep inside me while party goers mingled below. I suppose we have an affinity for balconies. And hotel rooms. Maybe it's not the location at all, but the invisible string that's managed to wrap itself around us and force us together at every turn.

Still, that doesn't answer the question of what we are to each other. And right now, I need to know. I need something to hold on to. Not that I'm about to ask him. Mostly because I'm not sure my heart can take any more of a beating if it doesn't match the Bishop-shaped hole in my chest.

When I don't answer, he continues, peppering soft kisses to the shell of my ear as he does. "I'm not going to ask if you're okay. We both know you're not."

A visceral sob wracks my body and I melt into him, my tears staining his hoodie. "I'm not."

His arms tighten around me. "What do you need?"

Every muscle in my body tenses. It's such a simple question, but it throws me off passing from the lips of the man currently holding me. This version of him is selfish, and rightly so. He's got walls up to keep his heart safe. But this question is so altruistic and so unique to the Bishop I met on another balcony what feels like a lifetime ago.

It's a tease.

His grip on me loosens, allowing me to pull back enough to look up at him. My gaze catches on his lips for a fraction of a second, and I consider kissing him to avoid answering. The thought floats away, though, as I remember I promised not to hide things from him.

"I need—" I hesitate even though my mind screams exactly what I want. Him. All of him. It's not fair to ask for. Not when he wants to distract me, and I want to keep him.

Bishop's eyes drop to my mouth, his Adam's apple bobbing as he sucks in a breath. "Tell me."

"You." I breathe, my eyes connecting with his. "I need you."

He brings his thumb across my lip and rasps, "Not a distraction."

Bishop reads me like a damn book.

It's not a question, but a statement. He sees I'm not completely whole, and while I might want a distraction, that's not what I need.

My hands shake as I fist his hoodie and he dips his head, urging me to allow him to be the tangible thing I'm desperate to hold on to.

"Say it," he whispers.

"I need you, not a distraction."

His eyes are windows to his soul as he utters the words I've been longing to hear. "You have me. All of me."

A choked breath escapes me, but he's there, inhaling my relief. His soft lips, paired with a hint of stubble, are the perfect amount of pleasure and pain as he seals his promise with a kiss.

"Fuck," he moans against me.

His hands drop to my hips, and he lifts me like I weigh nothing. I lock my legs around his waist, the evidence of how much he wants this positioned at my core.

He carries me inside, kissing me like I'm the oxygen he needs to survive, until we're at the foot of my bed. He slides me down his body until my feet hit the floor. I've never wanted to be off solid ground more than right now.

My hands trace the planes of his chest and I glance up, losing myself in the depths of his vulnerable stare. His broad frame towers over me as he fingers the hem of my silk sleep tank and pulls it over my head.

"Fuck, Kitten." Bishop growls, his eyes falling on where my nipples are tightened into peaks. "You're perfect. So goddamned perfect."

His head drops to the crook of my neck, teeth grazing my goose pimpled flesh as he kisses his way down my collar bone. He takes one nipple into his mouth while he rolls the other between his thumb and forefinger.

The dual sensation sends a bolt straight to my clit. I tip my head back and a throaty moan fills the space between us.

"Those sounds," he rasps, swirling his tongue and nipping the sensitive peak with his teeth before switching to take the other nipple in his mouth, giving it the same attention. "I live for those fucking sounds. They are the fuel for every one-handed fantasy I've had for the last year."

"They are?"

Bishop falls to his knees, his hands slipping beneath the silk of my shorts and kneading my ass. "Fuck yes, second only to the sound of you screaming my name as you come on my cock and directly before the taste of you."

A smirk curls the corner of my mouth. "You really know how to turn a girl on."

"My girl. Only mine. No one else matters."

His.

I suck in a breath, and he tips his head back, his gaze colliding with mine. "I've been so fucking stupid, Willow. You've been it for me for longer than I care to admit. You've taken care of my heart all this time, and I was reckless with yours. That ends now. I need you to hear me when I say this. I am on my knees for you. Only you." His breath hitches, and he bites his lower lip to stop it from quivering. "Willow, I love you. God, I love you so much it feels like it might kill me and that terrifies me. The thought of losing you—"

I silence his words with my mouth. Sliding down to the floor, I hold his face between my hands and kiss him with everything I have. I'm ravenous despite the tears rolling down my face. He meets me with the same passion and determination, his hands roving over my half naked body. Firm yet gentle, he gives me the support I need while silently promising to protect what's his.

"I love you too," I say against his mouth. "I love you. You aren't going to lose me."

Our beating chests rise and fall in sync, echoing the sentiment that we are finally on the same page. Together.

"Never again."

Bishop moves slowly, lifting me up so I'm once again standing before him. He slips his fingers in the waistband of my shorts and slides them down, taking my panties with them. Leaning forward, he presses his nose to the apex of my thighs and inhales. With anyone else, it would be mortifying, but I widen my stance, giving him full access.

"Hmmmm," he hums. "Are you wet for me, Kitten?"

I rasp, "Always."

"Damn straight. Lay back on the bed for me, knees apart, and let me see what's mine."

I follow his instructions, loving the way his eyes never stop devouring me as I do.

He stands and lifts his team shirt over his head. His abdomen ripples, giving me a show—raw, intense, and perfectly sculpted. Just like the heart of the man beneath.

My fingers dig into my palm just to prove to myself this is really happening.

I watch as his deft fingers find the button of his jeans and, in one flick, he pops each of them open before pushing his pants to the floor.

My eyes trace the tent of his boxer briefs, and I lick my lips, following the tight fabric down to the ink on his left leg. Every time I get the privilege of seeing his tattoos, I'm left breathless. They're his life in art. The carefully chosen mementos that remind him of his family. The tributes to the moments that changed him. They're a reminder of how deeply Bishop feels when he lets himself—how beautiful his soul is.

His fingers dig into the waistband of his briefs, and he pushes the fabric down, his cock bouncing free against his abdomen. Usually, the barbells of his Jacob's ladder are what capture my undivided attention, but this time, my eyes are drawn to two fresh tattoos on his upper thigh.

My mouth drops open, and I'm stunned into silence. The skin is raw and the colors vibrant.

On the outside of his thigh there's a gargoyle, much like the one he got to commemorate his induction to the Renegades. Only this one has two bats crossed behind it and has a tiny circle of stars surrounding it.

And I knew—without needing to count—there are sixty-eight. One for every soul lost in the crash.

But that's not the tattoo that renders me speechless.

It's the tiny portrait of a cream-colored kitten with bright green eyes, surrounded by purple morning glory flowers on the inside of his thigh.

"When did you add that?" I murmur, my heart battering against my rib cage.

"When I was in New York. I paid my artist double to make room for me."

"But when you left, you alluded you weren't all in." I work through the timeline in my head and come to a conclusion. "Jackson?"

Bishop nods. "He reminded me life's too short."

I chuckle because it's exactly what Lana told me too. "Like mother, like son."

He smiles and runs a hand through his hair, resting it on the back of his neck. The pose makes him look like a damn Greek statue—chiseled to perfection.

"I realized that no matter what happened between us, you played a part in my story and I needed to have you with me forever."

"I'm honored," I say, my voice breathless. "It's beautiful. Both of them. But I don't have green eyes."

"No." He laughs, a sly smile lifting at the corner of his lips. "That's a reminder of our first night together."

Realization dawns on me, and my chest shakes with laughter. "The jewel on the butt plug."

"You trusted me to take care of you, this"—he gestures to the tattoo—"was my way of hoping you might trust me again."

"Yes," I blurt out too quickly, making his smile grow. "Anything. I'm yours."

"Fuck, I love hearing you say that."

"I'm yours," I repeat, pouring every ounce of my love into the words.

Bishop's eyes darken, and he eyes the box of toys on the bed exactly where I left it before the game today. He steps forward, sliding between my legs. "Then let me take care of you."

I'll let him do so forever if he asks.

CHAPTER THIRTY-EIGHT
Bishop

Splayed before me on the bed, I hone in on Willow's pretty, pink pussy lips, parted and glistening with her arousal—just for me. I love her.

And she loves me.

It's something I knew before she uttered the words. Her actions over the past months speak volumes, but hearing her say them is better than what I imagine a World Series win feels like. Not that I don't still want that win. I do, but that moment would be a snapshot. Willow's love for me transcends space and time. It fills the cracks in my heart, promising that if they grow, she'll be there to fill them.

I want to be that for her too.

That want is rapidly growing to become a need. I may have only just admitted to myself that I do indeed love her, but seeing her on that balcony opened the damn floodgates of my heart.

Sliding between her legs, I drop my cock on her pussy, savoring the gasp that escapes her when the top barbell on the underside grazes her clit. I rock forward, sliding through her slick folds, coating myself in her arousal.

As I do, the small blonde kitten tattoo catches my eye. It was an impulse decision. One I will never regret. She's as much a part of my story as every other moment inked on my skin. And I love that from this moment forward, every time I look down when I'm buried deep inside her, every time she takes my cock into the back of her throat, it will be there. A reminder of our beginning. A promise of the future I plan to give her.

Reaching over, I pull the box of toys from the corner of the bed until it's nestled beside me, and I formulate a plan.

"Please, Bishop." Willow mewls, lifting her hips to find friction against the studs on my dick.

"As much as I love hearing you beg"—really it makes me feral— "I want to take my time with you. I want you to remember this in the days to come, when shit hits the fan, and you need something to cling to."

She presses her lips together in a defiant line, shaking her head. "I told you. I don't want a distraction."

I reach down and tuck the stray curl that has fallen from her pony behind her ear. "Not a distraction, sweetheart, a lifeline. An anchor in the storm."

That's what she's been for me. She's been my lighthouse. My way home when the world became too much. That's what she needs. And if she lets me, that's what I want to give her.

"Okay," she whispers, nodding her head.

Willow watches as I peruse the box, fingering through the toys. So many fun options, each carefully picked with her pleasure in mind.

The heat of her gaze fuels my fire, and I have to remind my twitching dick that this is about her, not us.

"Did you know," I say with a grin, "as a catcher, I have to be able to explore all my options. I am the first line of defense when a new batter steps up to the plate."

She hitches a curious brow. "What does that have to do with anything?"

"Stay with me, Kitten," I urge, and she awards me with a giggle that zaps straight through me.

Wrapping my hand around the first item in the box, I continue. "My first step is always research. Knowing the batter who steps into my box."

I slowly pull the pink dildo from the bag and gauge her reaction. Nothing. Not a single twitch. I set it down on the bed beside her.

"Sometimes what excites me isn't the answer. It's all about what will make my opponent succumb to me."

Her tongue darts out and wets her lips.

"Yes, Kitten, I mean you."

Next, I pull out the nipple clamps. Her eyes widen, and she sucks in a sharp breath as I finger the metal chain between them.

A smile ticks at the corner of my mouth. "It's all about knowing what they want and using it against them."

Her eyes follow the tiny silver clamps as I set them down on the bed on the opposite side of her.

When they collide with mine again, I've already got the next toy out.

"Sometimes fast and hard is the answer," I rasp.

Her thighs clench around mine as she eyes the magic wand, and it joins the nipple clamps.

"Other times a slider, low and inside, is the most effective tool."

I pull out a toy similar to the one she wore all day at the game but has a much stronger vibration and suction as it's not meant to be discreet.

Willow grimaces and I let out a soft chuckle and add it to the "no" pile.

"And then there's my favorite. The change up. The single pitch, that if executed correctly, can trip up a batter and leave them walking away in pieces."

Willow cranes her neck to see what I'm going to pull out next. When I lift the silver butt plug with the emerald stone at the base, she lets out a strangled moan.

God, I'm addicted to the sound of her. Especially since I know exactly why she made it. This is the toy I've been dreaming about using with her. The toy that started it all. The toy I've memorialized on my thigh.

I grab the bottle of lube and set it in the pile with the other toys I plan to use to make her scream my name.

Willow lifts herself onto her elbows and smiles, her eyes twinkling. "You've always been a tease, Bishop Lawson, but come on, play ball with me."

The pairing of my name and a baseball reference has my balls tightening with need.

"Oh, I'm ready to play, Kitten," I tease. Sticking my hand back in the box one last time, I pull out the final piece of my plan and twirl the silky little blindfold around my finger. "And just like the batters in my box, you'll never see what's coming."

I lean forward, sliding my cock through her slick folds as I do, and slip the blindfold over her eyes. She flinches at the same time as she lets out a cross between a sigh and a moan.

"What's going on in that pretty little head of yours?"

When she hesitates, I run my hands down the slope of her shoulders to her torso, reminding her I'm there with her. When she still doesn't answer, I give the inside of her thigh a tiny pinch.

She squeaks, but still doesn't answer.

Control is something she prides herself on having. She's a planner. An executor. Giving it up is unnatural for her.

Once upon a time, she gave me her trust. She let go with reckless abandon. Before tonight, I hadn't earned that trust back. I hope to change that because fuck, if I don't crave it like my next breath.

Leaning over her so we're skin to skin, I ghost my lips over hers. "Kitten, I asked you a question."

"I'm thinking about which toy you're going to use first."

I stroke the side of her face and whisper, "Do you have a preference?"

"The clamps."

The image of her tits tortured between the tiny metal clamps...

"Good choice," I whisper. Wrapping one hand around her wrist, I bring her hand above her head before doing the same with the other. "Now don't move these until I say so."

A shiver wracks her body, and I pull back and admire the sight of her splayed out beneath me.

Her brows furrow under the blindfold. "And if I do?"

"I'll tie you to the bed."

She writhes beneath me.

"You like that idea?"

"Maybe."

"Don't hold back on me now, Kitten," I say with a smirk. The thought of her tied up and helpless has my cock dripping. "I love hearing you tell me exactly what you want. All the ways you want me to make you mine."

"I want you to tie me up." She breathes. "Not tonight, but someday. Tonight, I want you to torture my nipples, slide that plug in my ass, and fuck me, so I never forget who I belong to."

My hips jerk forward, and I swallow hard. "Goddamn, Willow."

This woman is going to be the death of me, and I'll go willingly as long as she's at my side.

I shift and take her nipple in my mouth, pulling the already pert peak with my teeth. She gasps and arches her back.

"I need you to pick a safe word, Kitten," I say as I grab the metal clamps with one hand and pinch her nipple with the other.

Her chest gives a shaky rise and fall. "A safe word?"

"If you say that word, everything stops."

She thinks for a moment and a smile spreads across her face. "Emerald."

I laugh. "Like the stone?"

"Like our beginning."

If I thought she was meant for me before, her safe word just solidified it times ten.

"Fine. Emerald it is." I drag the chain up her abdomen and across her nipples, loving the way they are peaked and needy and waiting for me. "Now breathe for me. Focus on each breath."

She does, each one a little less shaky than the one before. On her fifth breath, I pinch her nipple between my forefinger and thumb and tug it up before replacing my fingers with the clamp.

"Fuck," she rasps, her hips jerking once, then twice, riding the friction of my cock alone. She exhales, her body shuttering as her thighs clench around mine.

"Holy shit, Kitten, did you just come?"

Her chest rises and falls, rapidly flooding with the same pink that paints her cheeks. She gives a sheepish nod.

"Words, Willow."

"Yes," she admits, heat filling her cheeks. "It wasn't enough, though.

Almost like hearing the beginning of a song and waiting for the drop, only it never comes."

"Damn." I groan. "As much as I want to be angry it wasn't on my cock or tongue, that was quite possibly the hottest thing I've ever seen."

"Really?"

"Fuck yes. And I'm filing away nipple play as one of my new favorite pastimes."

"Please, fuck me," she whines, gyrating her hips in search of the friction only I can give her. "It wasn't enough."

"Patience, sweetheart. You still have one more nipple in need of jewelry."

Her groan makes me chuckle.

I love this side of her. When she crosses over from playing the perfect little debutant and gives in to every filthy fantasy she keeps hidden behind her manicured smiles.

Leaning over, I repeat the same process on her other nipple. She whimpers a stifled "please" again, but there's no release this time. Though, if the way she squirms beneath me is any indication, she's close.

I briefly consider tugging the chain connecting her nipples, but I don't want her coming again on anything but my cock or my tongue.

The thought spurs me to slide back and drop onto my elbows. Her pink pussy lips glisten in front of me with her arousal, and I see the darker pink of her asshole. I swallow a groan, remembering the sight of it with an emerald jewel popping out.

Soon.

First, I need to taste her.

I smooth my hands down her thighs, willing her body to relax while using the connection to remind her it's just me and her.

When her breathing evens out, I strike, sealing my mouth onto her pussy.

"Oh God." She hisses, her thighs snapping up to cradle my head between them.

My hands dig into the supple flesh and force them down so I can devour her. I work my lips and tongue, humming against her clit until she's bucking against my face like a damn bronco.

"Ahhh, that's—that feels amazing. I'm gonna—"

I back off, staving off her orgasm by blowing cool air on her swollen lips.

Willow wines and I slide my fingers inside her, keeping her on edge as I let them play until they are dripping with her.

"Please, Bishop," she begs. "I need to come."

"Soon, Kitten," I growl, sliding my coated fingers down to paint the rim of her asshole.

She tenses and mewls a string of unintelligible words as I sink the tip of my finger in, stretching the tight ring of muscles.

Willow gasps at the intrusion, the sound turning into a savage groan as she twists her hands above her head where I told her to keep them.

"You're doing so good, Kitten. Letting me play with this little asshole," I praise, and she preens, arching her back and thrusting her hips up toward my face.

"You like this? You like my finger in your ass?" I drop my mouth and tease her pussy with long lapping strokes, working my finger slowly in and out.

"Yes. More," she pleads, her hips meeting my tongue stroke for stroke.

It takes everything in me not to reach down and wrap a hand around my painfully hard, weeping cock. She has no idea what she does to me, begging me for more. I want to give it to her. All of it. Every inch of me aches for her in the most desperate, primal way.

My tongue flits across her clit as she rides my fingers, chasing her release. I pick up the pace with my mouth and I add a second finger. She pushes back, desperately seeking more.

"Right there—oh God, Bishop—I'm going to—"

"Fuck yes, Willow." I growl, "Let me taste you. Give me life and come all over my tongue."

Her hips jerk, and she forgets the instructions I gave her, threading her fingers through my hair. The moment her thighs tighten around my head, I seize the opportunity and slip a third finger in her ass. She clamps around them, crying out my name as her body bows off the bed and convulses through her release.

Chest heaving, her breasts jiggle, jerking the clamps as she shivers and moans again.

"That was perfect," she mutters, breathless.

I slowly pull my fingers from her ass and reach for the plug and lube. When I pop the top, she cries out, "Wait."

I immediately still.

Heat fills her freckled cheeks. "Don't put the plug in."

"Whatever you want," I say, dropping the plug back onto the bed.

"No." She rips the blindfold from her eyes and blinks a few times until they've adjusted to the dim light of the room. She looks up at me, flushed from her orgasm, and smiles. "I mean, I don't want the plug. I want you to fuck my ass."

My brain short circuits. "Are you—are you sure?"

She nods, giving me a gorgeous lazy smile. "You told me the first night we were together that you loved the sight of my fingers in my ass and couldn't wait until it was your cock instead."

I did?

How the hell does she remember that and I don't? I mean, it sounds exactly like something I would say. I wanted everything with Willow, even then.

"You don't have to—"

"I want to." She grabs my wrist and laces her fingers through mine, reassuring me. "I want this with you."

An involuntary moan tears from my throat and heat blooms in my chest. "I love when you ask for what you want."

"I know." Her blue eyes sparkle with false innocence. "Which is why I am asking you to fuck me. Please."

Fucking hell, I don't deserve this woman.

She squeaks when I smack her ass hard enough to leave a mark and smirk. "Because you asked so nicely."

I reach for the bottle of lube and offer it to her. "Get me ready for you, Kitten."

She snatches the bottle from me and sits up. Squirting some in her hand, she licks her lips before wrapping her hand around my length.

A strangled moan escapes me as she works me root to tip, dragging her fingertips over each of my piercings until she reaches the head and circles it slowly.

"Fuck, Willow, if you do that again, I'm not going to make it to your ass."

She giggles until I tug on the chain between her breasts, and it morphs into a sinful moan.

"Squirt some on your asshole."

She leans back onto the bed and I grab a pillow from behind her. Tapping her thigh, she lifts her hips so I can slide it underneath.

Once she's situated with her legs spread wide, I rake my eyes down her body, worshiping the sight of her splayed before me and genuinely moved by the gift she's about to give me.

She brings the bottle between her legs, dripping a generous amount of lube on her ass before tossing the bottle aside.

My body thrums with anticipation. I run one of my hands down her thigh and latch onto her hip, steadying as I fist my cock with the other. "Tell me if I hurt you."

She nods enthusiastically.

I open my mouth, and she rolls her eyes.

"I know, words," she sasses with a cheeky smile. "I promise I will tell you if, at any point, you hurt me."

"And you have your safe word. Say it and this all stops, no matter what."

"Bishop," she purrs, my name. "I know. Now fuck my ass."

I give her a two-finger salute. "Yes, ma'am."

My cock is desperate for that first squeeze as I slowly press the tip against her hole, smearing the lube.

"Relax," I whisper, "and bear down."

She exhales and her hands fist the sheets as she sinks her hips further into the pillow.

"Atta girl, let me in."

I tease the tip in and out, working my cock in little by little. When I reach the first barbel, I stop and check in with her.

"You okay?"

"Mmhmm," she mutters through tight lips.

"Good girl." I commend, focusing all my attention on her and not on the grip she has on my cock. "Now I need you to play with yourself. Tease the tip of your nipples, tug on the chain, circle your clit, whatever feels good. Can you do that for me?"

She stares up at me with pure adoration. "Yes, daddy."

My hips jerk, forcing the first barbel past the entrance. I mutter a string of curses. "Fuck, Kitten, you can't say shit like that and expect me to be gentle."

"Then don't." Fire fills her eyes, and I recognize the challenge in them. "Fill me. Fuck me. Wreck me."

"Fuck." My hand tightens around the base of my cock. I have to breathe to stop myself from coming right then and there. Willow has told me time and time again she got her filthy mouth from me. I've created a monster and now I'm reaping the consequences. But fuck if it isn't the sexiest thing I've ever witnessed.

I close my eyes so I can't see her, but it's no use. She consumes me.

When I open them again, Willow wears a satisfied grin. She's already started to follow my instructions. One hand tugs on the chain, pulling her nipples taut, while the other works her clit with two fingers.

It's a sight to behold, especially with the tip of my cock in her ass. There's no way I'm going to last longer than a few thrusts.

She whimpers and I sink deeper, watching her ass swallow every inch of my cock until I'm settled against the curve of her body.

Holy hell.

Nothing prepares you for the first slide home in the ass of the girl you love. It's fucking magic. I take another deep breath, wanting to move my hips, but knowing she needs time to adjust.

"Bishop," she moans.

"That's it, sweetheart, you're so goddamn tight," I mutter, dropping my head back. "You take me so well."

She lets out a little mewl of contentment. "You feel amazing. But I need you to move. I need—fuck—I'm so close."

Words fail me, and I grunt in response as I slowly work a few short thrusts.

"Yes," she pants, "Oh God, yes. Please, more."

A wicked smile tips my lips as I pull halfway out and reach up with both hands and release the clamps without warning.

Willow cries out, the blood rushing into her tortured nipples as I white knuckle her hips and slam back into her ass. She arches her back and tightens around me, coming with the full force of a fucking hurricane.

"Bishop!" She cries my name like it's a goddamn spiritual path. Like I'm her god and I've delivered her from her sins.

Fuck.

I reach for the final piece of the puzzle, the magic wand, and flipping it on, I swat her hand away from her clit and slam it against the swollen bud.

"Shit!" she screams and her whole body freezes, except for the tiny flutters of her ass around my cock.

"Fuck, Kitten. You're strangling my cock."

Willow opens her mouth, but no words come out as she rides the waves of her pleasure.

I do my best to hold on, thrusting through her continued release as my own coils tightly in my gut. My balls tingle, heavy with need, and I know I'm not far off.

Her body starts to relax, and I go to move the wand from her clit, but she stops me. Wrapping her hand around mine, she shakes her head.

"Don't you dare fucking stop. It's still—fuck—there's another one behind it."

A sheen of sweat covers her body as she hooks her heels behind my thighs and lifts her hips to meet each of my thrusts. "I want it. It's right there."

My eyes go wide in disbelief. She's still fucking coming. And who am I to interrupt the orgasm of a lifetime?

"Take it," I growl, leaning over her, sucking her lip between my teeth and tugging it until she moans. "It's fucking yours, Kitten."

Every thrust of my hips sends us closer to the edge, and I'm overwhelmed by the moment. Us. Here. Skin to skin. Finally. This is how we're supposed to be.

"Oh God," I moan, trying to do anything to stop the inevitable, but I can't. "I'm going to come."

"Yes," she screams, digging her nails into my back. "Come with me. Come in my ass."

"Willow," I cry as she tightens around me and I slam into her, my release claiming me like a bomb detonating.

I collapse on top of her, and she holds me against her. White spots dance in my vision, and even though it feels like I've been ripped apart, I feel whole at the same time.

"Holy shit," Willow murmurs, over and over, and I love that I've reduced her to profanities.

When I'm no longer dizzy, I lift myself from her chest and press a gentle kiss to her lips. "You were amazing."

She beams, her lips lifting in a lazy smile. "I didn't know I could come like that."

"Me either."

Willow winces as I slip from her and immediately a shiver wracks her body. I tug her up into my arms and situate us at the head of the bed.

She snuggles into my chest and lets out a weighted sigh.

Worry claws at my chest, and I fear that might have been too much for one night. "Talk to me, Willow."

"I just—that was a lot."

With two fingers, I lift her chin to look at me. "Good a lot or bad a lot?"

"Good. Definitely good." She glances away, and I know she's holding back. I'm about to press when she lifts her head and asks, "Are you really all in?"

It hurts that she feels the need to ask after what we just shared, but remembering what Leigh told me, I try not to take it to heart. Willow needs action—reassurance—and I'm sure this won't be the only time.

I brush away my favorite stray curl and smile. "Willow Mae York, I love you. And I'm yours as long as you'll have me."

"You might get sick of me."

"Not possible."

She chuckles, and I take it as a sign we'll be alright.

CHAPTER THIRTY-NINE
Willow

Last night was…perfect, magical, everything I've hoped but never dared to dream.

I can't help the way my lips twitch upward every time I think about every delicious moment.

Bishop loves me. He's all in.

After we cuddled, we showered and talked some more until we eventually fell asleep in each other's arms.

It still doesn't feel real, like I'll wake up and the other shoe will have dropped. Maybe that's because I was forced from our little cocoon where reality couldn't touch us. What I wouldn't give to go back and crawl into bed beside Bishop and live in make believe a little longer—the place where we aren't a forbidden pairing and the world isn't falling apart around us.

But the Earth keeps spinning and scandal waits for no one.

I left a note explaining I was called in to an emergency meeting with the executive board, and promised Bishop I'd make it up to him if I didn't see him before the team meeting later this morning.

Now I'm sitting to the right of the commissioner at the head of the table, feeling as though I've been pawned off for him to babysit as the rest of my board sits at the opposite end of the conference room.

Vaughn and Patrick Kincade lead the firing squad, much like they did at the last meeting, quick to comment on every point of evidence Nikki presents against my father.

It sucked to hear about them last night. It sucks even more to see the photos taken at various league parties of my father talking with the umpires who went to the press, saying he bribed them to call games in the Renegades' favor. That's how *The Foul Line* knew about the scandal before we did. The photos themselves aren't damning, but paired with the slew of texts from a burner phone the umpires claim belonged to my father and a multitude of monetary transactions from an offshore account, it's bad.

They're saying it's an open and shut case and Commissioner Falco agrees. As a result, pending the official investigation, the Renegades will be fined five-million dollars and will be forced to give up our first and second round draft picks for the next two years. In addition, anyone found to have knowledge of the cheating will be penalized accordingly.

So much for building the team of my dreams.

Not that any of them hold a flicker of a chance anymore. It's also been decided that all my plans will be put on hold until we're able to do damage control and assess our standing within the league.

Never mind that, now more than ever, we need to solidify our trust with the fans and the general public. We need to create a space that's welcoming and indicative of turning over a new leaf. We need to show we are a new team and not to be punished for the sins of our predecessors.

But I don't say any of that. Even if I did, the board has proven it would fall on deaf ears.

I sit quietly with my hands in my lap, well aware that this isn't a battle I'm going to win. They've insinuated more than once it's my father who landed us here and I'm not to be trusted. Which is fine. I'll bide my time. Especially because I have a bigger battle ahead when news breaks of my relationship with Bishop. I can only hope that when it does, we're able to come out unscathed.

Wishful thinking, I know.

"If that's everything…" Nikki hits her stack of papers into a uniformed pile on the table. Her gaze lingers in my direction, as if she's waiting for me to put up a fight. I give her a slight nod to continue and her face falls. "Okay, we'll adjourn for today and hand over everything we have of Mr. York's to the league's investigators. We'll reconvene Monday after the gala this weekend."

Her declaration is met with nods and a few grunts of agreement before the room erupts in a shuffling of chairs as the board attempts to hightail it out of there for their nine AM tee time. I heard them talking about how they'd have just enough time to play nine holes and still make it back for drinks at the game after lunch.

My stomach twists, and I swallow the bile that threatens at the back of my throat. None of them care about this team as long as they receive a paycheck and can continue their memberships at the country club.

How the hell am I supposed to fix this? At every turn, I take one step forward and two steps back.

Bishop was my win, and even though I'm ecstatic we're on the same page, I still want this. This team is my future as much as he is.

"Willow?"

I glance up at the commissioner. He hasn't moved from his seat.

Hands flat against the tabletop, he looks at me with a hint of pity I don't want or need. What I need is for him to step up and do his damn job instead of rolling over for the boys' club he only barely has a leg up on.

Calm and collected, I address him with a flat voice. "Can I help you, George?"

His eyes dart around the room, like he's looking to see if there's anyone in earshot. Once the room clears out, he speaks. "I just wanted to say I'm sorry this is happening. You have a good head on your shoulders and don't deserve this."

I chew my cheek to stop my mouth from dropping. The words are hollow and filled with inaction, but at least he said them. That's a step up from where we were even a month ago.

"Thank you for saying that. I hope the league will keep that in mind moving forward."

George nods, slides his chair back, and stands. He hesitates, wrapping one hand around the fist of his other, and shakes his head like he's warring with himself. His eyes track back to mine and the pity is replaced by determination. "When this all blows over, I'd like to discuss your plans without the board."

"I—" My words stutter as I process what he just said. "I'd like that."

"Good. They may not be suited for the Renegades, at the moment, but some of them are heading in the right direction and I think the league will benefit from considering the fans who support us."

Then he's gone. Leaving me to sit in stunned silence.

What was that? Did I just witness the beginnings of George Falco growing a spine? Was this my small win?

Relaxing into the plush conference room chair, I exhale a sigh. This entire meeting was nothing but a power move by the board, but if I walk away with an ally in the commissioner it will have been worth enduring.

I check my watch and see that I have about forty minutes until the team meeting in the clubhouse. Just enough time to find Bishop and update him—or invite him to my office to pick up where we left off last night.

Definitely the second option.

I shoot off a text asking Bishop to find me, grab my things, and head out into the executive corridor with a renewed pep in my step. That is until I see Vaughn leaning against the wall just outside the door, clearly waiting for me.

My stomach churns. Nothing good can come from the wry smile on his face. Why can't he just leave well enough alone?

"Willow," he says. "A word?"

My mouth goes dry, and I don't miss how his smile stretches higher when I swallow hard. "What now, Vaughn?"

He pulls something out of his inner coat pocket, offering it to me.

The stack of photos might as well have been a live grenade. My ears fill with the sound of my pulse as I flip through them, each one more damning than the next.

Bishop and I walking up the steps of my private jet.

Me entering his room at the team hotel.

Him entering my gated community.

Bishop's hand wrapped in mine as I lead him into the elevator in Miami.

The two of us on my balcony kissing.

It doesn't take a genius to figure out Vaughn had someone tailing Bishop, probably to catch him doing something that could be grounds for trading him.

We handed Vaughn his golden opportunity.

Dragging my eyes from the evidence of our affair, I meet Vaughn's Cheshire grin. "You had him followed?"

He shrugs callously. "Unlike you, I take care of my team and protect it from situations that have the capability to ruin us."

Ruin us. I refuse to believe that's what Bishop and I are doing. If anything, we've made each other stronger. But that's not how the world will see it. Not if Vaughn has anything to say about it.

"What's it going to take for you to forget these exist?" I ask, stretching my hand out to give him back the photos.

"Those are yours to keep. I have copies of my own." He pushes off the wall and crosses his arms over his chest, offering me an unapologetic smile. "As for what I want, it's simple. I can either use these photos as grounds to trade Lawson, or you can step aside and make me the acting owner like your father and I always planned in the event something happened to him. It will look as if you decided, after the allegations against him, you realized you were in over your head. You can go back to your little philanthropy project and everyone wins."

The slimy prick. His greed knows no bounds. Especially when he holds all the cards.

That's when everything clicks into place and I gasp, "You were the leak, weren't you?"

Vaughn's brow pops, and he lets out a sardonic laugh that makes his belly shake. "Of your plans? Absolutely. The board wouldn't do what was needed to take you down a peg, so I did."

My jaw tightens, anger coursing like lava in my veins. I want to yell and demand he tell me why the hell he would do that, but I already know. Vaughn only gives a shit about himself. He wants what he believes is rightfully his.

Shit.

It all makes sense.

Relaxing my shoulders, I lift my chin and ask the question I pray I'm right about. "And the deal my father made?"

Vaughn barks a laugh. "Ha. Undoubtedly. Your father wasn't smart enough to put that plan in action. We needed to win. We were hemorrhaging money trying to get butts in seats. If we had known the crash was going to happen, we would have left well enough alone. Now everyone wants to be a part of the team who came back from tragedy. I'm not about to let you or anyone else jeopardize that with ideas of grandeur."

His words exonerate my father, but do nothing to stop the tightening of my chest. I fist the photos in my hand, crumpling them.

We.

He didn't do this alone.

I can't help but wonder how deep this betrayal runs. Is this the skeleton in the closet Patrick Kincade referred to? Not the scandal itself, but the orchestration. How many more secrets are there I don't know about? I don't want to live constantly having to look over my shoulder waiting for one of them to pop up.

"You're in over your head, little girl," Vaughn sneers.

I lift my head, hoping he can't see the way my lip threatens to tremble or the tears that prick the corners of my eyes. "You're disgusting."

He shrugs. "Maybe, but I play to win. You have until tomorrow to decide what you'd like me to do with those."

"How do I know you won't use the photos against Bishop even if I decide to step down?"

"I guess you'll just have to trust me," he says with a wink and pushes off the wall, stalking past me in the direction of his office.

When he's gone, I let out a loud and long, "Fuuuuuuuuck."

"Ooooh, she cusses!"

My eyes dart up to see a giddy Carson, rounding the corner at the end of the hallway opposite the direction Vaughn headed.

Luca steps out beside him, his brow furrowed and hands fisted. It's all I need to see to know they heard every word.

God, could this morning get any worse?

CHAPTER FORTY
Willow

"What are you guys doing up here?" I ask, frantically hiding the incriminating photos behind my back. Not that it matters if they heard it all.

Carson raises an inquisitive brow, but lets it fall. "I ran into Luca in the parking lot and while we were catching up. He said he needed to chat with you, so I offered to show him where your office was."

It checks out. The baseball world is incredibly small, and the two of them played together for Los Angeles before Carson was traded to Atlanta and Luca bought the Monarchs.

"We didn't mean to overhear your conversation. But I'm glad we did." Carson lifts his phone in his hand and shows me the screen. It's opened to the recording app where there's a seven-minute file.

"So, you guys heard all of that."

Each of them winces and nods.

"It's bullshit," Carson says.

I glance at Luca who, of the two, has the power to take this all the way up to the commissioner and get me fired as an owner. He scrubs a hand over his face and looks at the floor.

"You don't look surprised," I say to him.

"I'm not."

Carson whips his head toward his former teammate and steps toward me in solidarity, so it's the two of us facing Luca. "What are you hiding?"

"Vaughn caught me as I was leaving the field after the game yesterday. He wanted to grab a drink and discuss the future of the league and my thoughts on a few things." Luca shifts his gaze to me, but nods toward Carson. "That recording isn't admissible in court, but mine is."

"What?" Carson looks at his phone in disbelief, his shoulders deflating.

"Florida is a two-party state. Meaning, even if I knew you were recording that conversation, Vaughn didn't. So, if we were to take this to the commissioner and it went beyond the internal investigation, none of it would be admissible in court," I explain. "But what do you mean, yours would?"

Luca smiles devilishly, a twinkle in his cool gray eyes. "At the beginning of our conversation, I let him know that I like to record my business meetings so that I can revisit them later. I'm shit with details after the fact. He agreed and then forgot after a few drinks."

Hope infiltrates Carson's voice. "What did he say?"

"Nothing as point blank as what he just told Ms. York, but he alluded to the fact he's taken measures that would lead to him taking over the team. He implied the scandal was bigger than even the press knew, and he'd be at the top of his game if everything panned out, and I should align myself with him if I wanted to get ahead in the league." He lifts his chin, nodding toward Carson's phone. "Paired with that recording, it's enough to have the authorities look into his involvement. Vaughn is the kind of man who likes to count his chickens before they hatch. He just didn't know I'm above his bullshit."

I huff a laugh. "It's why he was bursting at the seams to tell me everything he's done. Making sure we were alone when he did."

"Exactly."

"So, what do we do now?" I ask. It's not like I can just go to the commissioner. Not if I want to protect Bishop. We're in the wrong and Vaughn has proof.

"Nothing yet," Luca says cryptically.

Carson curses and runs a hand through his hair, fisting his blonde curls. "But we can't let him get away with this. It's a no-win situation. He's proven he's a snake. There's no way he's not going to trade Bishop and ruin Willow."

My eyes fall to the ground, and I blow out a slow exhale. "I'm going to lose the team either way."

"Maybe," Luca muses, "but I don't think so."

I snap my eyes up at Luca and scoff. "There's a no fraternization policy. We broke that."

First thing this morning, I double checked to see if there were any loopholes. There aren't.

Luca nods. "Yes, but I think we can prove it won't matter. You don't handle his contract. And you've never done anything to favor him."

I flinch. That's not entirely true.

"Shit," Luca curses. "What did you do?"

"I flew him down here on my private jet because he—" I stop. It feels wrong to out Bishop, not only in front of his teammate but another owner in the league. I'm stuck between a rock and a hard place with Luca's involvement, but that doesn't mean I trust him.

Luca nods as he puts it together. "He was afraid of flying after the crash."

"Yes."

"Any good owner would have done the same," he reasons with a reassuring smile. "And if we get enough of the other organizations to back us up, we just might have the grounds for the league to accept the two of you being together. It's not unprecedented."

I'm not sure what he means by that, but he's handing me a lifeline and I'd be stupid not to take it. Still, I'm skeptical. "Why are you helping me?"

His eyes grow distant, and he breaks eye contact, looking toward the open conference room door. "Call me a romantic as of late. Also, Vaughn fucked over my twin brother once upon a time. I'd love nothing more to see him burn."

I narrow my gaze and want to press, but it's not my place. Not when, at the moment, he's the only viable option I have at fixing this mess. The enemy of my enemy is my friend.

"A romantic, you say? Are you holding out on us, Lucky?" Carson chuckles. "Who is she?"

Luca's wistful gaze hardens, and he cuts a glare at Carson. "Apparently no one." He shifts his gaze back to me and continues. "From this moment forward, you and Bishop will have to be squeaky clean. Keep clear of him until I can figure this out."

That's going to be a problem, considering I just told him to find me.

I tug out my phone and fire off a text, letting him know something came up and I'll see him at the meeting.

Then I realize it's not just me and Bishop Luca has to worry about. I know what's at stake. Carson's our wildcard. He's loyal to Bishop, as he should be. If he lets this slip when he gets down to the clubhouse, I'm afraid it will be like setting off a one-man EF5 tornado. Bishop has fought so hard to get to where he is. I don't want him to have to choose between me and this team. Because I know who he'll choose, and I'm afraid it'll break him all over again.

I turn to Carson. "Are you going to tell Bishop about this?"

"Tell me about what?"

My whole body tenses as his deep timber washes over me.

Damn it. I guess the universe isn't quite done shitting on me quite yet.

In five large strides, Bishop traverses the length of the hallway and joins us. His head swivels between Luca, Carson, and me, each of us wearing a guilty expression.

"Tell me about what?" he repeats.

I inhale a jagged breath and suck my lower lip between my teeth. I promised I wouldn't shut him out, but I had hoped to have a more cohesive plan before having this conversation.

Hurt is etched in Bishop's furrowed brows when I look up at him and hand him the photos. "Vaughn knows about us. He's going to use it to get me to give up the team or trade you to another one."

"Fuck," he curses as he fingers through the glossy evidence of our affair. "Who knows about this?"

"As far as we know, just the three of us. But Vaughn has already been trying to recruit people, like Luca, to support him."

His brows furrow, his brown eyes boring into my blue. "Were you going to tell me?"

"I just did."

"Don't play stupid with me, Willow," Bishop snaps. "If I hadn't interrupted this little powwow, were you going to tell me or were you going to tell Carson not to?"

Uneasy under his unrelenting stare, I shift my weight. "I was going to tell you after the game today, once Luca shared his plan with me."

"What plan?" he deadpans.

"I'm going to make a few calls, cash in a few favors, and see what we can do to soften the blow."

I'm still uneasy about Luca's involvement but have to trust he wants to help us.

"Okay," Bishop answers, seemingly satisfied with our answers. He takes a step toward me, wraps his arm around my waist and presses a kiss to my temple. "I'm sorry. I thought you were keeping things from me again."

I was, but not because I wasn't planning on telling him. That's the difference and I'm happy he sees that. But I'm not out of the woods yet.

"There's one more thing," I say, leaning into his touch for strength.

"Fuck," he growls, "What else?"

"Vaughn is the one who orchestrated the cheating scandal."

"Fucking bastard." He looks over my head at Luca and Carson. "So, why aren't we pinning him to the fucking wall?"

"We need to get our story straight and make sure our proof is solid and has weight behind it if we're going to take him down," Luca explains. "We can't fuck this up."

"Fuck this." Bishop jerks his hands back from my waist and grabs my wrist, tugging me in the direction he came from.

I'm helpless to do anything but follow.

"W-where are we going?" I stutter, struggling to keep up in the heels I insist on torturing myself with.

When he doesn't answer, I look over my shoulder at Luca and Carson, who are both just as confused. They snap out of it when we're half-way down the hall and jog to catch up.

Bishop slams his fist against the button for the elevator, and it opens immediately.

We all file in, and the three of us watch as he hits the button for the clubhouse.

The elevator jerks its descent, and he turns to face us. Fire and determination are in his eyes. "Luca, get your damn plan together. I'm sick of people using me and this team as a fucking pawn in their game. That stops today. Right now."

So much for stopping the tornado.

CHAPTER FORTY-ONE
Willow

Bishop leads us through the club level and drops my hand when we reach the door to his tiny personal locker room. He throws open the door leaving Luca, Carson, and me standing in the doorway. We watch in stunned silence as he grabs his gear from the makeshift metal locker and yanks the magnetic name plate from where it had been stuck a month ago and storms back toward us.

We move out of the way for him to pass, but Bishop halts and shifts all his gear to one arm so he can grab my hand again.

I look up at him, my eyes pleading for him to give me something, anything to let me know where he's at right now and how I can support him—or maybe stop him from decimating our already burning world.

His hardened expression doesn't falter, but eyes soften at the edges. He squeezes my hand and glances at the door of the clubhouse locker room. "All in, Kitten?"

That single question holds so much meaning for the two of us and yet makes my stomach flip with anxiety as I put together what he's thinking.

It's not quite decimation, but it's a risk. He wants to tell the team about us—take away Vaughn's power over us and gain the support of those who matter most. Exactly what Luca wants to do on a larger scale, but this holds significantly more weight. This move allows us to get ahead of the inevitable fire inside the house. No matter what happens, Bishop needs his team on his side. It means more to him than the public or the press. Without them, he crumbles—and me right along with him.

But it's not just about the team or Vaughn. This is Bishop putting his money where his mouth is. It's the sort of move Bishop a year ago would pull—loud, flashy, and every bit the hero in a romance novel.

My knight in shining armor proving he's all in with me.

Carson and Luca swivel their heads between us, flies on the wall to this private moment.

"Yes," I answer without reservation. "All in."

Bishop squeezes my hand and grins before pressing a soft kiss to my lips. "I love you."

"I love you too."

"Awww," Carson sing-songs, and Luca just rolls his eyes.

Flinging the door to the locker room open with a bang, Bishop charges inside. Every head in the room turns to watch us. Even Graham pokes his head out of his office door and follows us.

"Team meeting starts now," Bishop yells.

Luca and Graham stay at the back of the room, but Carson follows as Bishop leads me to the front, his hand never leaving mine. When he reaches the vacant locker beside Ford's, he throws his gear inside and slaps his name plate to the space above it. It's a move that makes my throat thicken and my stomach flutter. With that one action, he's claiming his spot on this team.

Bishop squeezes my hand and leans over to press a kiss to my forehead. He then drops my hand and jumps up onto the bench in front of his locker.

The faint whispers in the room drop, leaving an uneasy silence.

Bishop glances around the room, not a hint of apprehension in his gaze as he silently dares each of his teammates to protest his leadership. When they don't, he begins.

"This team gave me the shot we all dreamed of as boys. It gave me a place to continue playing the game we all love. I've been protective of it. But I shouldn't've taken it out on you by ignoring your place here. I've tried over the past couple weeks to rectify that, but I still owe you an apology. I'm sorry."

A few of the guys nod in agreement, but there isn't an ounce of malice directed at their unofficial captain. Bishop has put in the work to earn their respect. They might not trust him yet, but they believe he deserves to stand at the helm of their team.

"Most of you didn't ask to be here. A shitty situation and a draft no one expected brought you to this team." He glances down at me. "A person I admire tremendously reminded me that regardless of how you arrived here, you wear the orange and black, and that makes you Renegades. That makes you family."

The weight of his words lingers in the air, and my chest swells with pride as Bishop publicly lays his insecurities on the line for his team. When I look at him, I can still see the hardened lines that are etched in his soul as a result of the crash, but instead of being sealed tight around his heart, there are now tiny cracks of light allowing the man he was before to shine through. His scars are healing, and I love the man he's becoming.

"Just like any family, we aren't perfect," he continues. Lifting his head, he slowly connects with every man in the room. "When it should have been me welcoming you into my home, you all turned the tables and welcomed me onto your new team. I'm really fucking glad you did."

"Here, here," Julian Garcia hollers.

Bishop lifts his hand in the right fielder's direction and nods his thanks. "Yesterday, our family had its integrity called into question. I can say with my full chest, none of us on the field last season had any knowledge of the accusations being made. But that doesn't change that the evidence presented against us and our organization's involvement in cheating is solid."

I wait for him to continue, to exonerate my father and tell them it was Vaughn all along, but he doesn't. My gaze tracks to the back of the room to where Luca stands, and he shakes his head, signaling I shouldn't speak up and say anything.

"Not yet," he mouths.

I clench fists at my side and nod, reminding myself patience is a virtue and there are still too many unknowns to bring everyone on board completely. That doesn't mean I'm not ready to pin Vaughn's balls to the wall and make him wish he was on that plane instead of my father.

"You've seen the evidence?" Russel Brooks, our second baseman, speaks up.

Bishop's mouth falls into a tight line, and he nods. "Not myself, but I've been made aware of what it is and it's viable. We're likely going to take some heat from the press and the fans."

There's a few muttered curses and a sea of shaking heads.

Fucking Vaughn. I wish I could take this burden away from them. None of them deserve to be taking the heat for this, not when they've already gone above and beyond to make this team their own.

"Is that why you called us here?" Ford asks.

"Yes. And no. There's some additional news that's going to break that I need you to be the first to know, and I hope you'll support me in it."

Knots tangle in my stomach as Bishop looks down and offers me his hand.

This is it. All in.

I place mine in his, and he tugs me up onto the wooden bench with him. He looks down to where our fingers are intertwined and lifts our hands for the team to see. "A year ago, a woman tied a string around my heart. She dodged my love, and I let her go so I could become a man worthy of her. Life had other plans and after a loss that broke me, she became my boss. I hated her, but she never gave up on me. I was a fucking idiot."

Laughter echoes around us, but it's lost on me. I'm too busy blinking away the tears that rim my eyes as I look up at the man who owns my heart.

"I love this woman. And by some miracle, she's agreed to be mine. Does anyone have a problem with that?"

I dare to look out at our team and see a vast array of reactions—jaws dropped, rolling eyes, smiles spread wide.

Bowen Marcos, our relief pitcher and one of the few married guys on the team, huffs a loud, "Fucking finally."

That's all it takes for the team to erupt in a cacophony of cheers.

"Kiss her already," Carson hoots.

It's all the encouragement Bishop needs. He drops my hand and tangles his in my hair. The other wraps around my waist. He dips me like we're lovers in a movie and crashes his lips to mine. This kiss breathes life back into me. It gives me hope, not only for us, but for this team. We are exactly what Bishop said, a family. And for a girl who doesn't have any living blood relatives, I'll take all I can get.

Before I know it, the team crowds around us and Carson yells, "Who are we?"

"Renegades!" the team yells back.

"Who the fuck are we?"

"Renegades!"

I laugh, breaking our kiss.

Bishop presses his forehead to mine and smiles. "Renegades, baby. We protect what's ours."

CHAPTER FORTY-TWO
Bishop

The stadium is packed for this afternoon's game, everyone wanting to see the team at the heart of a major scandal.

I knew we'd be tested as a team, but I didn't think it would come so soon and not in the form of retaliation from the umpires on the field. Every close pitch, on both offense and defense, is being called in favor of the Atlanta Thrashers. It's been an uphill fight since we stepped on the field. We're currently up by two, but we only got those runs by the skin of our teeth.

"Strike three!" The ump calls, and I watch from the railing of the dugout as my team jogs across the field for our at bat.

Smitty is the first to enter and slides up next to me, wiping the sweat from his brow. "You ready for your manhood to take a beating?"

I chuckle. He's played the first six innings of the game, and I'm playing cleanup on the last three. Not that I need to. After management released Sharpe this morning, the rookie has found his groove behind the plate and it shows. He could easily take my place in a year or two once he's got a bit more field time under his belt.

"Brent still muttering bullshit under his breath?" I ask.

Brent Colson is by far one of my least favorite umps in the league. He's a hot head and likes to make sure you know he's got the power to fuck you right where it hurts. Given the recent cheating allegations, he's taken it upon himself to exact justice for umpires everywhere.

Smitty scoffs. "Every other fucking pitch."

I open my mouth to respond, but Carson storming into the dugout makes me pause. He tears off his hat and throws his gloves at the row of bats leaning against the railing, sending them clattering to the ground.

"Fuck!" he yells before throwing himself into the corner of the bench. Running his hands through his hair, he fires off a few more curses.

I drop down next to him. "You okay, co-captain?"

The fact there isn't a joke about his role at my side tells me this runs deeper than just being pissed off about the umpire situation.

"No, the fuck I'm not. As if Brent and his bullshit calls aren't enough, Travers is spouting off at the mouth from the dugout and that fucker knows right where to sucker punch."

I glance across the field to first base where Carson's former teammate is chatting with his second baseman, his eyes darting in our direction with every other word.

Fucker.

Chirping is a part of the game. We've all done it and all had it done to us, but there's a line you don't cross. Travers is widely known for crossing it on a daily basis.

"Your dad?" I whisper, loud enough for only him to hear me.

Carson nods, his eyes vacant, like he's a million miles away.

"You wanna talk about it?" I ask.

"Not a fucking chance."

I cock a brow, but he doesn't bother looking in my direction. "I'm here if you want."

"I know," he growls with a hint of defeat.

A commotion at the other end of the dugout grabs our attention, and Graham bursts from his spot on the top step, charging at the plate like Brent is a bullfighter holding a red cape.

Shit. The hits just keep on coming.

Carson and I jump up and hit the railing of the dugout for a better view.

"Are you going to keep fucking us?" Graham yells, the vein above his eye bulging in a way I've never seen before.

He's usually the calm and collected voice of reason, but it appears even he has a breaking point.

Brent rolls his eyes and gets set for the next play. "Get back in the dugout, Graham."

"No." Graham steps up, his chest brushing the umps chest pads. "That pitch was outside."

"It was on the plate," Brent growls.

"The fuck it was. It was outside."

"I made a fair call."

"Bullshit. Do you need your prescription checked? It was outside and you keep fucking us."

"Get back in the dugout, Graham," Brent warns.

Graham steps to the side and draws a line exactly where the pitch crossed on the far side of the batter's box. "Does that look over the plate to you?"

Oh fuck. I've seen a lot of things in my tenure in the major leagues, but I've never seen a manager draw a diagram for an umpire like he's a damn toddler.

"That's it." Brent throws his hand up and cocks his elbow, yelling. "You're out of here!"

Graham's eyes widen as he turns back to Brent. "Are you fucking kidding me?"

I'm not sure what Graham expected to happen after making Brent look like a fool in front of thousands of people, but I applaud him for doing it. Even if it's only going to make our lives a living hell for the next three innings.

There's a satisfied glint in the umpire's gaze as he nods. "You're out. Get off my field."

"Fuck!" Graham yells, and the crowd boos in response. Though it's hard to tell if they're booing because they agree or disagree, either way it's not a good look for the Renegades.

Graham tugs his hat from his head and storms off the field, disappearing into the clubhouse without a word to the team.

The guys are looking around at the other managers and bench coaches, but all of them are shaking their heads and don't have anything to offer.

I nudge Carson and tilt my head, but he shrugs me off, still lost in his head.

Alright, guess it's just me.

Clapping my hands, I call the attention of the team. "Alright guys, we're on our own now. Let's keep our heads in the game. I know we're up against bullshit calls, but we're still leading the scoreboard. We're better than them. Let's prove it."

The team nods, but the dejected murmurings reverberate loudly in the dugout. The damage has been done.

After that display, the rest of the inning goes as expected—three at bat, three strikeouts, all questionable pitch calls.

I grab my gear and head out to get set behind the plate, stretching out my muscles as I do. Carson and I toss a few warm-up pitches. He hits the glove every time, but his head isn't in the game. Usually, he's got a running monologue after every pitch that is both entertaining and annoying as shit for batters. At the moment, he's nothing more than a brick wall—looming and silent.

There's no way we're going to squeak out our first spring training win if he doesn't get his head in the game.

I slide behind the plate and get set for the first batter to take the box. Julio Travers steps in.

Fuck.

Of all the players to take the plate, it had to be this one.

Carson's jaw tightens. Maybe this is exactly what he needs. Throw some heat and psych himself up.

The back of my neck tingles, and I turn and look up at the owner's suite where Willow is with Indie and Leigh. She's standing behind the two rows of seats with her hands twisted in front of her, worry painted on her face.

The cards are still stacked against us. After telling the team and witnessing their acceptance of our relationship, it's easy to forget we still have to convince the Major League Baseball community to accept us. No matter what we do, there will be people who believe it's unethical for us to be together, but as long as we have each other and our team, that's all that matters.

Life's too short. I want my aisle seat.

When Willow sees me looking, she smiles, and it hits me straight in the chest.

Yeah. I'm good as long as I have her.

I flash a wink up at her, holding on to the memory of her writhing beneath me as I dig my cleats into the dirt and lift my glove.

Carson throws the first pitch, a fastball low and on the inside, but well within the strike zone.

"Ball!" Brent yells.

I bite my tongue hard enough to draw blood as I throw the ball back to Carson, noting his continued silence.

Come on, big guy, give me something, anything to help get you back in this game.

Brent mutters under his breath behind me, but all I catch is "cheating bastards".

Fuck, this is going to be a long three innings.

Travers resets at the plate and glances down at me. "Might need to work on that framing, Lawson."

"Scoreboard," I grunt.

We're still up. One inning at a time. I repeat the mantra over and over in my head, so I don't give in to the anger coiling around my spine and wipe the smug smile off Travers' face.

He shrugs. "We'll see."

My thumb finds the PitchCom on the back of my thigh, and I signal a curve ball to Carson, who nods from the mound.

It's another close pitch. Another ball called.

"Shake it off," McCoy calls from third base.

"Let's go, Whitmore," Brooks encourages from second.

Carson wipes the sweat from his brow with his gloved forearm while the hand that holds the ball twitches at his side. He's used to being the best and seeing results. This entire game he's been throwing the pitches, but not being rewarded for the work. It's messing with his head. Not to mention the asshole in the box knows where he's weak.

I call for another fastball. Carson delivers and is once again not rewarded. Ball three.

"Fuck!" he bellows, catching Brent's attention.

"This is the only warning you're going to get, Whitmore."

Carson brings his glove to his face, and I would bet my entire signing bonus he's muttering a few choice words into the leather.

There we go. Get mad. Get your head in the game.

Travers swings his bat in a circle, a wicked grin splitting his face. "Daddy would be so disappointed. Oh, wait."

Carson takes a step toward the plate, and for a second, I think we're about to have a bench clear on our hands.

I shoot to my feet and shake my head, silently begging him not to take the swing I know he desperately wants to. Fuck, I want to for him. Travers is an ass, but we're already on thin ice.

His jaw ticks as he resets, only this time when he stares me down there's a glint in his eye. One that reminds me of the night he told me his presence on the Renegades was a revenge plot.

God dammit.

The second the ball leaves Carson's hand, I know it's not the changeup I called.

The ball rockets toward us, miles from the plate, and hits Travers in the thigh.

Before I can get my mask off, Brent is out from behind me and heading toward the mound. Carson's wearing a shit-eating grin, not even pretending to care he's about to get tossed from the game for his little stunt.

I glance at the dugout where our assistant manager gives me the nod to call for a relief pitcher. Lifting my right hand, I pinch my fingers together, signaling for them to send out Efren Watts, one of our right-handed pitchers.

Travers grins, dropping his bat dramatically. He leans over and unstraps his shin guard, tossing it toward the Atlanta dugout.

"That's how it's done, Lawson," he muses, his eyes lit with amusement. "Fuck 'em up and send 'em home. You should tell your owner that. Pretty little thing like that, maybe if she sucks the commissioner off, your little cheating problem will—"

I don't let him finish his sentence before my fist connects with his jaw.

Travers hits the dirt, cupping his face.

The crowd goes wild. The fucker got a free pass when he went after my co-captain. We're trained to put up with that shit. The thought that I'm a hypocrite for hitting him crosses my mind, but I don't give a damn.

He went too far with Willow. Even if she wasn't mine, I'd have punched him.

She's a Renegade, and she's innocent of everything but loving me.

"Keep my team out of your mouth, fucker," I spit. "Or *your* pretty little face will wear more than just the imprint of my knuckles."

I don't get more than a moment to revel in Travers' split lip before I'm shoved from behind. If there's one thing baseball does well, it's a bench-clearing brawl.

When I look up the field is a sea of Renegade orange and black, mixed with Thrashers red and white. The manager from the Thrashers tries to rein in his guys, but it's no use. Graham isn't there to stop us, and our other bench coaches are taking their sweet ass time. Everywhere around me there are curses flying and shoving matches being exchanged. It's clear my team has had enough of being the punching bag.

I've never been more fucking proud.

McCoy grabs the back of my chest protector and pulls me back from the center of the fray. "What the fuck, Lawson?"

I shake him off. "Jackass had it coming."

"I heard what he said."

"Good, then I'm leaving you in charge when Carson and I are ejected."

The crowd is electric, on their feet chanting "fight" as Brent and the field umps try their best to get in the middle and break up the skirmish.

When the teams finally begin to disperse, it's no surprise Carson and I are thrown from the game. We head to the clubhouse and are greeted by an irate Graham.

"What the fuck happened out there?"

Carson strolls past him and tosses his glove and hat in his locker. "Travers was going to be walked regardless of what I pitched. I just gave him something to remember me by."

Graham turns to me. "And you?"

I shrug. "I just gave Travers what he deserved."

"Yeah, a knuckle sandwich." Carson snorts.

It's good to hear his sense of humor is firmly back in place. I was worried I'd lost him to his thoughts out there and was going to have to drag him back like he did me.

Graham rolls his eyes. "Enough. I saw the fight on the live feed. Why'd you do it?"

"He was a dick to Carson. Then implied Willow could suck the commissioner off to get us out of the scandal."

"Should have punched him twice." Graham grunts at the same time Carson exhales, "Fuck him."

I huff a laugh. "Renegades protect what's ours."

"Damn straight," Carson adds, offering me his knuckles.

I pound mine against his, and wince when I realize it's the hand I punched Travers with.

Whatever. The pain was worth it.

Graham shakes his head. "Hit the showers. Press is gonna be a shit show, and I expect the two of you to play nice."

"Yes, sir," we say in unison.

I retreat to my locker and begin peeling off my gear when I catch Carson still standing beside me.

"You know Vaughn's going to use this as grounds to trade you."

His words are a sucker punch to the gut. Despite the terrible calls and over the line chirping during the game, I've been allowing myself to live in the calm before the storm—the high of not only my team accepting Willow and me but also finally allowing myself to accept this team as mine without letting go of those that came before them.

My work here is done, young Padawan, Tommy quips like a goddamn force ghost.

The hits just keep on coming.

Not yet, I silently plead. *I can't lose you while there's still a risk of losing this team and Willow.*

I'm not gone, he says. *We'll always be on that field with you. And you aren't going to lose her, jackass. You're going to fight for her like she's always deserved. The team too. Renegades and all.*

He's right.

I lift my head and turn to Carson. "Vaughn can fucking try."

I've got my team. I've got my girl. And there's no way in hell I'm going to let either of them go. But it is time to let Tommy and the rest of my former teammates off the hook. They deserve the same peace I do.

CHAPTER FORTY-THREE
Willow

Indie and Leigh block my path from exiting the suite. This isn't how I imagined spending birthdaypalooza with them. Sure, baseball was always on the agenda, but the anxiety of possibly losing my team was not.

"Move," I growl.

"No." Indie plants her hands on her hips, broadening her stance so I can't pass through the glass doorway behind her. "What part of keeping your nose clean didn't you understand? If you go rushing down to the clubhouse right now and someone sees you, the press will have a fucking field day. Especially after the news of you and Bishop releases."

"They're my team," I counter.

"Let me ask you this," Leigh interjects, always the voice of reason. "Are you doing down there for the team or for Bishop?"

"You didn't go running down there when Graham was thrown out of the game," Indie adds, softer this time as she reads the agony twisted on my face.

They're right, but Bishop is the other half of my heart. I need to make sure he's okay.

Panic grips my spine, and I feel the telltale signs of an anxiety attack rising—my heart rate spikes, my mouth goes dry, and my mind spins. Bishop just wrapped a reason to trade him in a bright, shiny bow and handed it to Vaughn. It doesn't matter now if I sign over the team. He got what he wanted and has no reason not to out us too.

I wrap my arms around myself and smooth the skin on my biceps, pretending, if only in my mind, that they are Bishop's arms. His hands.

Breathe, Kitten, he'd say. *We have a plan. I'm not going anywhere.*

But he can't possibly know that.

I drop my chin to my chest and heave a defeated sigh.

"Three more innings, Wills, then you can go be the hero. But right now, Luca's right. You need to keep your nose clean and let the team handle Bishop."

Out of the corner of my eye I see Leigh grimace, and I assume it's from Indie's mention of a certain tall Italian owner.

"Are you going to tell us why you hate Luca so much?" I mutter, grasping for something to occupy my mind. There hasn't been a chance for me to press her about the reaction she had to him yesterday at the game, or his claims they've met before.

She exhales a heavy sigh. "No."

"Not even if it distracts me from staging a jailbreak and heading down to the clubhouse right now?"

Leigh lets out a ragged exhale. "Remember how you didn't tell us about Bishop because you needed to protect your heart?"

I wince. That's not exactly how I said it, but Leigh can read between the lines.

"I need that space in regards to Luca."

Stepping forward, I wrap my arms around her, burying my nose in her blonde hair. "I get it. We're here when you need us."

Indie joins our hug and snorts. "You guys and fucking men. This is why you won't see me waste more than a night on a trouser snake."

That has us all giggling.

"Really? Trouser snake, Indie?" Leigh snickers.

Indie shrugs and untangles herself. "Real men get the luxury of having a cock. And even then, never for more than one night."

I shake my head. Being an actress, Indie has had a rough go in the men department. Too often, they only see the stars next to her name and a social ladder to climb. It breaks my heart that it's jaded her. I hold on to the fact that I know she still believes in romance. Deep down, in the part that clings to the romance books we read, she yearns for more. Hopefully someday, someone will give her the love she deserves.

"That was a bullshit call," a gruff man with a beer belly bellows from the seats in front of our suite.

We turn to see the end of the inning, with Elliot Stone shaking his head as he walks back to the dugout.

Two more and I can head to the clubhouse.

"Come on." Indie leans in and bumps my shoulder, then does the same to Leigh. "Let's order a round of margaritas to take the edge off."

Leigh and I nod, but my stomach rolls. Everything is falling into place, but I can only hope it will be enough.

Luca and I spent the five hours between the team meeting and the game making phone calls to every owner we could get a hold of. We shared with them my relationship with Bishop and asked for their support.

Many of them shrugged us off, remarking they wouldn't go on the record saying they approved but agreed they wouldn't fight any ruling made by the commissioner. A few vehemently disagreed and will no doubt be vocal against us. Only three congratulated me.

When it came to telling them about Vaughn, they were hesitant to believe us. After Luca shared the contents of his meeting and the recording with them, they unanimously agreed if I didn't fire him they would make sure the commissioner did. If there's one thing the league takes seriously, it's cheating. I find it funny because they all cheat in small ways every day—pitchers with tar hidden on their gloves or forearms, base coaches watching the pitchers grip and giving the batter a tip—they just don't get caught. It's a catch twenty-two, but it's a small win and I'll take it.

I'm back in my seat, still waiting on that margarita, when my phone buzzes.

> **LUCA:** Clubhouse. Now. Vaughn is heading down with the commissioner.

"Shit."

"What?" Leigh looks up questioningly, but I'm already out of my seat.

"Vaughn's heading to the clubhouse with the Commissioner," I say, already on my way to the door.

I tear through the executive concourse and down to the clubhouse with Indie and Leigh hot on my heels. When I get there, Luca and Carson are waiting outside Graham's office.

Luca's eyes land on Leigh before he begrudgingly pulls them to greet me. "They're inside already."

Hands shaking, I wipe my sweat-covered palms against my skirt. "Here goes nothing."

I swing open the door and find Graham, a statue behind his desk, with

Commissioner Falco and Vaughn flanking him. Bishop sits in one of the plush seats in front of them, his hands fisted on his thighs.

They all swivel their heads to where I stand in the door, and my heart stutters when Bishop's hands relax and his mouth hitches at the corner.

"What's going on here?" I ask, flicking my gaze between them before landing a hard glare in Vaughn's direction.

"Player business. Nothing that concerns you," Vaughn sneers, cracking his knuckles like he's ready for a schoolyard brawl.

Bring it, asshole.

The commissioner straightens his spine. "Vaughn insisted we get ahead of the fight in the sixth and come up with a course of action to share with the press after the game."

"I just bet he did," I mutter.

"What's that supposed to mean?" Vaughn scoffs.

"Only that you've been gunning for Bishop since the draft."

Vaughn rolls his eyes, but he can't help the upward twitch of his lips. "He should have thought of that before he punched Travers in the face."

Bishop slams his hands on the desk and growls. "I told you what he said. I wasn't going to let him imply our owner could suck George off to soften the blow of the scandal."

My eyes go wide, and I whip my gaze to Bishop. "He said what?"

"Here nor there, Mr. Lawson," the commissioner says with a sigh, like they've already had this discussion. "Fighting is a punishable offense in this league and needs to be dealt with. As I was saying before Ms. York joined us, the league standard is a five-game suspension and a seventy-thousand dollar fine. The same will be handed out to Mr. Whitmore for intentionally hitting Julio Travers with a pitch with the adjustment of three games and only a twenty-five thousand dollar fine."

"Worth it," Carson quips behind me.

Bishop out for five games and Carson for three is going to hurt the team, but at least they will be served during spring training. Both of them can afford the fines, exorbitant as they are.

Vaughn steps forward and leans against Graham's desk, twisting toward the commissioner. "He made a mockery of our team before the season started and has held up that standard today. I stand by my request for Lawson to be traded."

"What your club does with your players is between you and your staff."

The commissioner is not wrong to stay out of it, but I had hoped he'd stand his ground and point out that teams fight all the time when tensions are high in a game. That's not exactly grounds for trading a player away. Then again, Bishop isn't a typical player, and this isn't a normal situation.

Vaughn's lips twist into a maniacal grin. "It's funny you should mention that, George."

He reaches into his suit pocket and produces a stack identical to the one he handed me this morning.

My brow raises, challenging his move. "Are you sure you want to do that, Vaughn?"

I shouldn't be giving him the chance to think this through. Either way, he's done, but I'd rather tell the commissioner about Bishop and me on my terms.

"Absolutely," he sneers, stretching his hand out further.

Commissioner Falco takes the photos and fingers through them, a gasp falling from his lips. He looks up at Bishop and then at me. "Are these real?"

"Yes, they are," I confirm. "Bishop and I met over a year ago at a charity function. We shared a night together then. Neither of us expected our romance to rekindle, but we found our way back to each other during spring training as we helped each other heal from the grief of the crash. I love him, and he loves me."

"Is this true?" He turns to Bishop.

A smile spreads across Bishop's face, and he stands to his full height. "With all my heart, sir."

"You both know about the fraternization policy."

"Uh, if I may, Commissioner." Luca steps from behind me and situates himself between the commissioner and me. "Willow hasn't been involved directly in Bishop's contracts. She's voiced that she doesn't want to see him traded, but beyond that, this is an area she's been hands-off. Strictly speaking, if there are checks and balances put into place, there is no reason this relationship couldn't be completely aboveboard. There's an owner in the NHL that fell in love with a player on her team. We could look at how they've structured and see if something similar could be used here. We've also spoken to many of the other owners across the league, and they've shared they won't put up a fight if you rule in the favor of these two."

"You what?" Vaughn shouts, veins bulging along his receding salt and pepper hairline. "This is preposterous. You can't possibly be considering letting these two carry on this affair. It will set a precedent for not only this team but the league."

"Again, I can only speak for the league," the commissioner says, "but I'm inclined to look at the checks and balances Mr. Donati has proposed, and assuming they don't interfere with our policies, whatever these two do behind closed doors is their business."

"You've got to be kidding me." Vaughn throws his stubby hands up before turning his ire on me. "Your father would be ashamed of what you've done with this team."

I smirk. He just doesn't know when to shut up. "That's a pot calling the kettle black, don't you think?"

"Nail him, Willow," Carson mutters.

Vaughn swallows hard but still wears the mask of a man who believes he's gotten away with murder. "I'm not sure I know what you're talking about."

"While we're airing grievances, I'd like to formally announce the removal of Vaughn Logan as my President of Baseball Operations."

"You can't fire me!" Vaughn bellows, his face turning a bright cherry red. "I'll sue you for wrongful termination."

The commissioner's eyes go wide, and for a moment, he gapes at the mouth before schooling his features. "You're well within your rights, Ms. York, but if I may ask, on what grounds are you releasing him from his duties?"

A smile stretches across my face. "He's the one who orchestrated the cheating with the umpires, not my father."

"HA!" Vaughn rolls his eyes. "You really think I would do that? I'm the one who has kept this team together from the day he took over the team. Why would I ruin everything I've built?"

Vaughn's voice fills the space, but his lips don't move.

I couldn't have planned it better myself.

Carson steps forward, his phone in his hand playing the recording he took of Vaughn admitting everything to me.

"That's not me," Vaughn scoffs, trying to backpedal. "They probably had that doctored up to get rid of me."

"Would you like me to pull the footage from the executive corridor this morning?"

"There aren't any cameras up there." His eyes dart from Graham to the Commissioner to Luca, looking for anyone to back up his claim.

None of them do.

"Are you sure?" I press. There absolutely aren't any cameras, but with the way sweat pours off Vaughn's forehead, it's clear he doesn't know that for sure.

"Is this true, Vaughn?" Commissioner Falco asks, cold betrayal written across his face.

Vaughn doesn't reply. Instead, he turns to me, the chords of his neck pulsing and desperate fear in his eyes. "Come on, Willow. You know I wouldn't put this team in jeopardy."

"You're right. Not this team." I look up at Bishop and over to Carson. "This team is stronger than the sum of its parts, which doesn't include you. The team that came before them, on the other hand, has your sticky fingers all over it, and I plan to wipe them clean."

Vaughn's voice shakes as he bellows, "This was supposed to be my team, not yours!"

I give him a smug smile and shrug. "My father didn't see it that way."

"Rethink this, Willow." His voice softens as he tries to rewrite history as if it will save him. "I have helped you every step of the way since you've taken over. You've been nothing without me."

"That's where you're wrong, Vaughn. I wanted your help navigating a world I thought I knew nothing about. I gave you too much rope. It turns out it's just what you needed to hang yourself. All along you've seen me as my mother's daughter, a pampered princess, but you forgot one crucial thing. While I might have been Adriana York's plaything, I am also Richard York's protégé. It took me far too long to realize he raised me to love this game—this team—and it was never about his legacy. He strived to instill in me the importance of the family within these hallowed halls. For the Yorks—the ones that matter anyway—it's never been about the money."

"You'll run this team into the ground," Vaughn snarls and starts around the desk toward me.

Bishop steps in front of me at the same time as Graham jumps to his feet and jerks Vaughn back, pressing him against the back wall with a forearm to his throat.

I place a hand on Bishop's bicep and look up at him, nodding my thanks as I step around him and address my former President of Baseball Operations. "We might not succeed, but we'll go down with smiles on our faces knowing we did it together."

"That's right baby, Renegades for life," Bishop says. He presses a kiss to my temple and whispers only for me. "I'm so fucking proud of you."

"So, Bishop and Willow are staying?"

I turn around to see who asked and find the entire team staring back at me, each of them holding their breath, waiting to hear the verdict. The game must have ended, and they've wedged themselves in the doorway behind Indie, Leigh, Carson, and Luca. My family. Not by blood, but by the trials and tragedies that have brought us together.

The commissioner shakes his head, but the hitch in his lips tells us what we want to know before he says it. "Pending an official investigation, they're staying."

The entire team goes feral with cheers, and my heart skips a beat.

This is what I dreamed of. This is the start of my legacy.

I look up at Bishop and find the mischief I saw that first night we met, freezing on a balcony, mixed with a hint of what looks like forever etched in his eyes.

"Who are we?" he asks.

"Renegades, baby."

491

EPILOGUE
Willow

Opening Day

It's a perfect day for baseball in New York. Rain came through last night and pushed out the gloom, leaving a perfect crisp spring day with fluffy clouds and sunshine.

As much as I loved my time in Fort Myers, I'm happy to be back in the city that never sleeps and ready to get this season started. It feels like a brand-new start—for me, for Bishop, and for our team.

But there was one stop Bishop needed to make before he could move forward.

Compared to the sea of headstones tarnished by weather and time, Tommy's is pristine. A simple oval top with shoulders on either side. It reads:

THOMAS JERAMIAH WOODS

1994 - 2023

Loving Son, Brother, and Teammate

We stand, hands intertwined before his grave, the weight of loss heavy upon us.

Bishop looks down at me, tears rimming his deep brown eyes. "Give me a minute."

"Of course."

I let go of his hand and step back, praying he can still feel my love as he crouches down like he would behind the plate and softly speaks to one of his best friends.

My heart aches for him, but it's accompanied by a swell of pride. This man has endured more loss than one person should in a lifetime, and he still managed to claw his way back and learned to persevere.

That doesn't mean there still aren't hard days. Sometimes he'll stare out at the field he loves and get a far-off look in his eyes, and I know he's not seeing his current teammates, but the ones he lost. I hold him a little tighter on those nights and always on the ones that come after a session with Jolene. She's good for him. She pushes him to think outside the box and make it make sense. Just like he does for me. In that aspect, we make a good team.

I'm not sure how much time has passed when Bishop falls to his knees and his shoulders shake with heavy sobs.

In an instant, I'm there, wrapping him up in my arms.

Bishop clings to my coat and buries his face in the crook of my shoulder as he releases the emotions he's pushed down for so long. Silent tears run down my face as I run my hand up and down his back to remind him, and myself, we're not alone.

After he's let every tear fall, Bishop pulls back and wipes his eyes. "You know I haven't been here since the memorial when this was nothing more than a pile of dirt. Seeing it and not hearing him anymore, it's like it's finally sinking in that he's really gone."

I cock my head to the side. "Hearing him?"

Bishop chuckles. "After the crash, I heard him, Jackson and Norah in my head a lot. Norah filtered out early on. And when Jackson woke up, his voice disappeared too. But Tommy—Tommy was with me until the day of the fight."

I gasp. "When you accepted the new team."

"Yeah," he says, a strangled laugh bubbling from his throat. "You know he would have loved you. I can imagine the two of you would have had a blast ganging up on me. Even for a rookie with a fuckboy mentality, he had his head on straight. He was a good kid."

"He always will be."

He nods. "Jolene said something the other day that's resonating with me right now."

"What's that?"

"Healing isn't linear." Bishop's lips twitch upward, and he tips his head toward me. "You said something similar to me that day in the equipment room. But sitting here, in front of Tommy's grave, I feel like I'm being tugged back to those moments after the crash. Guilt and anger are slamming me from all sides, settling in my stomach like an endless pit. But at the same time, it's different." He laces the fingers of his left hand through my right. "I have you. I have the team. I have my family. And unlike before, I'm open to those things bringing me back to life—bringing me joy. I want to live. I didn't back then. But fuck, if I don't still feel the weight of it all."

Tears burn at the corner of my eyes. I run my free hand through his wind tousled-hair and cup his stubbled chin. "You're allowed to feel all those things. Feel them, acknowledge them, give space to them, but as long as you continue to remember who you are and how far you've come, then grief and joy can coexist. And that's what makes life beautiful."

Bishop stares at me with hope in his eyes. "I love you."

"I love you too."

He leans in and presses a kiss to my lips. "I'm so damn lucky to have you."

I shrug playfully. "I like to think so."

We spend the next half hour sitting there enjoying the sunshine, and I listen as Bishop tells me stories about Tommy and the rest of his teammates.

The peace in his voice gives me hope for his future.

"You missed the turn," I say, whipping around as the street that leads to my father's penthouse fades from view.

Bishop's eyes don't veer from the road. "That's because I have plans for us before the game."

I raise a brow. "What plans?"

There's a part of me that wants to argue. The gala went off without a hitch. Birthdaypalooza might have been a bust, but that one night was the best birthday present I could have asked for. We raised well over a million dollars for Renegade Hearts, and it was the first time Bishop and I got to step out as a couple. The media went nuts, labeling us a love story for the ages. Of course, there are those who love to troll the internet and say we are going to ruin the franchise, but for every one of those assholes, there are a thousand more people there to cheer us on.

Between that excitement and all the meetings for the league investigation into Vaughn's cheating scandal and the board's involvement,

Bishop and I have had next to no downtime to just be a couple. I was looking forward to the few hours before Bishop and I have to be at the field for today's game.

Then again, given the hint of mischief glinting in his eyes, I'm curious what these plans are.

Bishop reaches out and places his hand on my thigh, digging his fingertips into the denim of my jeans. "If I told you, it wouldn't be a surprise."

For a planner like me, they are the worst. I like to know what's coming. I want to plan for any and all possibilities.

I roll my eyes. "I hate surprises."

He looks over, gaze narrowed above a wicked smile. "I know."

A few moments later, he pulls his truck into the player parking lot at Manila Stadium. It's empty except for a few members of the ground crew who are here to prepare the field for the game.

After helping me out of the truck, he silently leads me with a hand at the small of my back through the player entrance to the newly renovated clubhouse.

"I like my decorating better," he says offhandedly under his breath.

I scoff and roll my eyes. "Maybe if the guys wanted splinters in their asses every time they sat down."

Bishop laughs and wraps his hand around mine. He leads me to his locker and sits me down on the plush high-back rolling chair.

"I have a belated birthday gift for you."

Reaching up, I finger the dainty silver gargoyle pendant at my throat that he gave me the night of the gala—my actual birthday. "You didn't need to get me anything."

"This was always the plan. It just took me a little bit to get everything from Nikki."

I raise a skeptical brow as he turns and pulls out a worn orange binder from his locker and hands it to me. The leather is soft except for where a black gargoyle is embroidered on the front. I run my hands over it and flip it open.

My heart swells, and I let out a tiny gasp. There, nestled in plastic protectors, are signed playing cards of every member of the Renegades current lineup, starting with the man standing before me.

"You—" I look up at him, tears streaming down my face. "You did all this for me?"

"I'd do anything for you, Kitten." Love drips from every word. "I know this was something you shared with your dad every year on your birthday, but I didn't think one should pass, especially this one, and you not have a reminder of him."

"This is perfect." I flip through the pages, running my fingers over every card and commit to memory the team that brought us together.

"I'm glad you like it."

"I love it." I smile and set the book down on Carson's chair to the left of Bishop's locker. Cupping his face with both hands, I melt into him, desperate to feel his arms around me. "Thank you."

Bishop's gaze heats as he sweeps me into his arms and brushes his lips against mine. "You're welcome."

He kisses me again and I let myself get lost in him. This man holds my heart with renewed reverence and gives me presents worthy of a book boyfriend. And he's all mine.

Bishop lets out a low and gravelly moan, and I shiver, making it my personal mission to hear it again before he steps out on that field.

"Fuck, Kitten," he curses softly, breaking away. "I can't wait to take you up against this locker so, every time I dress for a game, I remember this moment."

I shudder an exhale and grin. "Yes, please."

He takes a step back. "But first, we need supplies."

"You brought the toy bag?" I ask incredulously.

Bishop chuckles, his joy infectious. "Not this time."

He twists around and grabs something from his locker, bringing it between us.

I slowly blink, checking to make sure I'm seeing correctly. "Is that a jar of dirt?"

"Only the best from Manila Stadium," Bishop says proudly. "And a four-leaf clover."

My mouth drops open, and I tip my head back and laugh as I remember the words I typed in an attempt to make him smile. "Oh my gosh, you thought I was serious?"

"Baby, you never mess with a baseball player when it comes to superstition. Today we fuck for luck."

"I don't even know what that means." My side hurts from laughing, and I can barely breathe. "I made it up."

"Too bad." Bishop shrugs, pulling my hips against his already lengthening cock. "I have plans that include taking this team all the way to the playoffs. That means we start today with luck in abundance."

I can't hold back my smile, even as I roll my eyes. "How did you even get a four-leaf clover?"

"I had one sent from Ireland. I wasn't sure if it had to be sourced from the motherland."

"I made it up!" I cry, unable to believe the lengths this man has gone for a chance at luck.

"You gave it life. Now it needs to happen." He reaches up and runs his thumb over my lower lip. "Think of the team, Willow."

I clench my thighs together, heat coiling in my lower belly. "I'd rather not if I'm about to fuck you covered in dirt and a four-leaf clover."

His eyes shine with curiosity, and I realize he's not going to let this go. I'm about to get fucked in this state of the art club house with dirt smeared all over my body. What does it say about me that I'm not turned off by it?

I take a step back. Bishop sucks his lower lip between his teeth as I peel off my coat and pull my shirt over my head.

This all started locked on a balcony with him giving me the strength I needed to face the future. Now here we are, survivors of tragedy, building a life neither of us could have imagined. We don't need luck on our side. We made this all on our own and will continue to do so every day for the rest of our lives.

But if this is what he needs—dirt and a four-leaf clover—I'm more than willing to give it to him.

I reach up and unclasp my bra, letting it fall to the floor.

"Pop the top off that dirt."

THE END

Thank you so much for reading RENEGADE RUIN!! I really hope you loved Bishop and Willow's journey as much as I did when writing them.

Need more of this incredible team? Keep an eye out on my socials or join my NEWSLETTER to stay up to date! The next installment of The Draft Series is slotted to release this fall!!

I appreciate each and every one of you for taking this journey with me. As an Indie Author, I would love your help spreading the word about RENEGADE RUIN. If you enjoyed the story, please consider leaving a review on Amazon, Goodreads, or even referring it to a friend. Even a sentence or two makes a huge difference.
Thank you for taking this journey with me.

xoxo

Hayden

ALSO BY HAYDEN LOCKE

The Draft Series

MIDNIGHT RENEGADE (Prequel Novella)

RENEGADE RUINS (Bishop and Willow)

RENEGADE RIOT (Coming Fall 2024)

Love in Aspen

FINALLY HOME (Weston and Cami)

ALSO BY HAYDEN LOCKE
WRITING AS K.M. RIVES

As many authors do, I also write paranormal / fantasy romance under the

pen name K.M. Rives.

If you love vampires, wolves and fae I invite you to check out August and

Emery's story in **THE CULLING OF BLOOD AND MAGIC** series.

THE REPLACEMENT

THE INTENDED

HYBRID MOON RISING

THE UNITED

ACKNOWLEDGEMENTS

Oh my! What a freaking rollercoaster ride.

This story came from a minute-long TikTok video explaining the disaster draft protocol for all major league sports. From the start I knew this was Willow and Bishop's story. Ask any writer and they will tell you sometimes the characters demand more of you. And these two definitely did. They broke my heart and put it back together over and over again. They were a healing journey I didn't know I needed. And now they are my gift to you.

This story would have never come to life if it wasn't for a few very special individuals.

To my husband—my rock, my home. Thank you from the bottom of my heart. You allow me to dream big and make them a reality. You never stop cheering me on—helping me plot through any holes that pop up and bringing me tacos and beer when I need sustenance. Your fresh perspective and knowledge of the male orgasm is forever and always appreciated!

To my daughters—Thank you for always reminding me everyone needs a break for cuddles. You guys are my world. #betheromance

To the book community—

Holy hell, I must say I am blown away by the kindness and support of authors, bookstagrammers and readers who have taken a chance on this story. I was so nervous that it was too heavy, and emotional for a sports romance, but you all have given me the confidence to believe in my intuition. Every single time I am tagged in a gorgeous photo or video, I get a giddy smile on my face. You seriously make my day and inspire me to keep telling emotionally charged stories of boys in tight pants.

To Tehia—my penguin with a parachute—I'm so glad I got you in the divorce. This book would not have happened without you. From the moment we met you believed in me with the force of a damn hurricane and you made sure I never forgot what a beautiful badass I am. You loved my characters like they were your own, and always had a handy what if question for me when I felt lost in the plot. Thank you for being my sounding board, my cheerleader but most of all thank you for being my friend. Love you boo.

To Rachel—my fearless editor and friend. I am admittedly shit with commas but you'd never know it looking at this book. You made this story shine in every way possible! Not only that, you never stopped cheering me on and loving this story. Even with all the angst. Thank you for believing in me, listening to every hair brain idea and for loving em dashes as much as I do.

To Silver: I am in complete awe of you and your ability to create incredible art from my ramblings. I am forever grateful that you took me on as a client and gave life to this story through art.

To Steph—I love doing life with you. Thank you for always hearing my intricate story ideas and reining them in and calling me out when I inevitably have a moment of plot crisis at seventy-five percent. Also thank you for reminding me it's rein not reign.

To Cass—the way you love gives me life. Thank you for always checking in on me and sending me all the Star Wars videos that make me cry at 7am. This story took a part of my soul and you made sure to refill my well. I can never thank you enough for your friendship and guidance.

Alex—you are the cheerleader I never knew I needed. Thank you for all the weekend writing sprints and for talking through my endless plot ideas.

Danielle—thank you for reading this story and giving me life at the end of this process. It was such a joy to read through your comments and see my book through your eyes.

To my alpha and beta readers—I would be dead in the water without you. Every step of the way you fiercely loved these characters, cheering for their healing and love. Thank you for sticking with me .

And finally thank you to my readers.

Every. Single. One of you.

I wouldn't be here without you.

I am so grateful I get to do this job. Thank you for every sentence you read, every review you leave, every post you make. I see you. Thank you for taking a chance on me and my stories. You guys are magic.

xoxo
Hayden

ABOUT THE AUTHOR

Hayden is a California girl living in a North Carolina world…for now. After all, home is where the Army sends her husband next. When she isn't writing with music on way too loud, you can find her soccer momming it up, wrangling her two daughters into a game of hide and seek, or enjoying the finer things in life like supporting her favorites sports teams with an ice-cold beer in hand.

Stalk Hayden on her social media to find out what's coming up!

514